D0345541

WITHDRAWN

ABSENCE
OF
MERCY

ABSENCE OF MERCY

A LIGHTNER AND LAW MYSTERY

S. M. Goodwin

CROOKED
LANE

NEW YORK

This is a work of fiction. All of the names, characters, organizations, places and events portrayed in this novel are either products of the author's imagination or are used fictitiously. Any resemblance to real or actual events, locales, or persons, living or dead, is entirely coincidental.

Copyright © 2020 by Shantal LaViolette

All rights reserved.

Published in the United States by Crooked Lane Books, an imprint of The Quick Brown Fox & Company LLC.

Crooked Lane Books and its logo are trademarks of The Quick Brown Fox & Company LLC.

Library of Congress Catalog-in-Publication data available upon request.

ISBN (hardcover): 978-1-64385-521-9
ISBN (ebook): 978-1-64385-522-6

Cover illustration by Karen Chandler

Printed in the United States.

www.crookedlanebooks.com

Crooked Lane Books
34 West 27th St., 10th Floor
New York, NY 10001

First Edition: November 2020

10 9 8 7 6 5 4 3 2 1

This book is dedicated to my agent Pam Hopkins and my editor Faith Black Ross.
Pam, thanks for believing in my work.
Faith, thanks for loving Jasper and making his story even better.

PROLOGUE

New York City
April 1857

Felix Dunbarton was drunk.

And why not? he thought as he staggered down Broadway; this new deal had the money *pouring* in. Oh, there was no denying the risk was high—life-threateningly high—but Felix stood to make millions in the years ahead. Soon he could replace all the money he'd borrowed, with nobody the wiser.

Bawdy offers came at him fast and thick from the women festooning every lamppost and lounging in every doorway. From dawn till dusk this section of Broadway was the most stylish street in the city—hell, in the entire country. But after the sun went down?

It was a whole new world.

A heavy mist softened the harsh light from the streetlamps, giving the night a dreamlike quality. The air on these few blocks was like a fog all its own, a miasma of cloying perfumes warring for attention: gardenia, rose, lilac, and a dozen other scents his olfactory organ couldn't identify. Beneath it all was a far less pleasant odor.

Felix passed two identical women and snickered to himself. They'd draped their bodies close enough to the gaslit shop window that he could see their nipples, which they'd rouged and accommodatingly displayed above matching blood-red satin corsets.

"Good evening, Mr. Dunbarton," the Harris sisters chimed in their lilting Dublin accents, their red hair far too bright to be the product of nature.

Felix tipped his hat but kept walking. After peddling their wares for three years, the two sisters were most likely riddled with syphilis or gonorrhea.

He'd first encountered the twins just after they stepped off the boat from Ireland and into Madam Solange's whorehouse. Back then her brothel was in the dangerous Five Points area and the French-woman's girls had been much cheaper than they were now. But the wily madam knew how to attract a higher class of customer and had speedily parlayed her avarice, lack of conscience, and business acumen into a far tonier house on Mercer Street.

Everything Madam offered was first-rate: the finest liquor, the softest sheets, and the youngest girls. Every savvy gentleman knew that the younger the whore, the smaller the chance of disease. The age of consent in New York City was ten years old—at least until the bloody-minded reformers had their way and ruined everything.

Felix hadn't needed to call on Madam's services for almost five months now—not since he'd been clever enough to secure his own entertainment at a fraction of the cost, not to mention how much more convenient his little arrangement had been.

Until tonight.

Felix ground his teeth at what he'd encountered when he showed up at the usual Saturday rendezvous place an hour ago: nothing. Not a damned person in sight—including the jackass they had paid a bloody fortune to have the girls ready and waiting.

Fueled by frustrated lust and fury, Felix had ransacked the entire building looking for someone—anyone—to vent his wrath on. But all he'd managed to find was something so goddamned sticky it almost yanked off his shoe with every step.

As if on cue, he stutter-stepped again.

"Dammit!" Felix stopped and fished his flask from his breast pocket; thank God Cates had refilled it before he'd left the house tonight. He took two deep pulls and returned the flask to his pocket before teetering on one leg to examine the bottom of his shoe. He couldn't see anything in the near darkness between the streetlights, but when he put his foot down, it stuck.

"Christ," he muttered. Well, Solange's was just around—

"Good evening, sir."

Felix yelped and spun around. It took a moment before he spotted the source of the voice—just inside the garbage alley, her face obscured by fog and shadows.

"Who is it?" Felix slurred, mortified that he'd shrieked like a woman.

"My name's Amy, sir."

Felix frowned. "Do I know you?"

"No, sir."

He peered into shadows. All he could see was the filthy hem of her skirts and her shoes—small brown ankle boots, hardly the footwear of an experienced trull, more that of a girl.

It's just a girl.

Emboldened, he threw out his chest and strode toward her—his bloody shoe sticking with every step. He stopped at the alley entrance, looking for other, larger shapes in the darkness. A wealthy man couldn't be too careful; pimps often lurked in the background, waiting to cosh and rob a man while he was dipping his wick.

"Why don't you come out into the light, sweetie?"

"I'm not s'posed to be workin' this area. If the others see me, they'll give me a thrashin'."

"We're all alone." That wasn't quite true—there were at least five whores lounging within spitting distance, but they were hidden by the fog.

The girl shook her head.

Felix stared at the outline of her young, girlish figure and felt a pleasurable stirring; perhaps he might get what he needed tonight *without* paying Madam Solange's extortionate rates. He grinned and shuffled unsteadily toward her, not stopping until they both stood in shadow. She was staring down, her hair a thick blond curtain covering her face.

"Look at me, girl." Her head swung up, and he stared down into a face that was wide-eyed, girlish, and tear-streaked.

"Why are you crying, sweetie?"

She swallowed hard enough for him to hear it. "I'm scared." She caught her plump lower lip with white, even teeth and gazed up at him.

She was a beauty. Felix's breath hitched, his heart sped up, and blood roared in his ears; he began to harden.

Why not have a bit of fun? He slowly stripped off his right glove, finger by finger, taking his time and savoring her rapt expression. When his hand was bare, he began to open his trousers.

"There's no need to be scared," he said in a voice rough with need. "I'll make sure—" The girl's eyes darted over his shoulder and Felix swung around, alarm bells screaming in his head.

But it was just a woman—another whore, judging by her clothing. His hand froze on his half-open fly. "Who the hell are you?"

The woman wore a fringed shawl wrapped around her head, and it obscured all but her eyes—eyes that were so heavily made up it was impossible to discern shape or color.

He took a step toward her. "I *said*, who are you?"

Amy's voice came from behind him. "She don't speak good English, but she's helpin' me—it's safer together on the street."

Felix stopped a few feet away from her and chuckled. "You want to watch, do you?"

"Yes." Her hoarse, gravelly whisper was that of an old, old woman, and she barely reached his shoulder; she was no danger to him.

"Perhaps I should charge *you* for the pleasure," he taunted, and then snorted at her widening eyes. He pivoted unsteadily on one foot and had to catch himself against the rim of the rubbish bin to keep from falling on his ass. The world tilted and spun and his stomach surged up his throat. He gritted his teeth against the nausea, forcing it down. "*Wha*—" He rubbed his eyes to clear his watery gaze before glaring down at the girl, his vision still wavering. "What the hell are you waiting for? Get over here." She took a few tentative steps toward him. "That's right," he said in a soothing voice. "Now, on your knees. Good girl," he praised when she complied. Felix caught his lower lip between his teeth as he stared down at her kneeling form, his groin heavy. "Undo my trousers." She made short work of the remaining buttons and then pushed down his drawers.

"Yes, yes, that's a good gir—"

Something snapped around his neck and jerked his head back. Felix staggered, his mouth wide open but no breath going in and no sound coming out. He scrabbled at the cord or rope—*a garrote*, his stunned brain shrieked—trying to wedge his fingers beneath it. But it was too tight, and only getting tighter.

Something hard rammed into his lower back and drove him forward. The girl was still kneeling and Felix stumbled over her, his hand fumbling to break his fall while he slammed into the brick wall headfirst.

There was the sound of an egg cracking and then pain—stabbing, agonizing, explosive pain.

He slid to the rough cobbles, and the rope around his neck tightened like a tourniquet. Darkness spread from the edges of his vision. Felix whimpered, but the sounds were only in his head. *Oh God! God! Please—*

Lips kissed his temple. "Good-bye, Felix."

His eyes flew open at the voice, shock lifting him from his agonizing stupor.

And then cold metal sliced through layers of wool and linen, not stopping until the blade bit deep in his side.

Intense nausea accompanied fiery pain, and his stomach contracted, attempting to void itself. The ring of pain around his neck lessened and he made one last push to scream. But all that came out was a gurgle so soft only Felix heard it.

CHAPTER 1

London
April 1857

Detective Inspector Jasper Lightner stared at the dead couple tangled in the bloody bedding. According to Detective Sergeant Murphy, they were—ironically—named Joseph and Mary Bickle.

Mr. Bickle had a neat slit across his throat that stretched from ear to ear. A bloody cleaver lay beside him, and he cradled his wife in his arms. From a certain angle, he looked to be asleep.

The same could not be said of Mrs. Bickle, who'd been struck so hard in the forehead with the cleaver that her head was almost in two pieces. The unseasonable spate of freezing weather had left the small room so cold that frost glinted on Mrs. Bickle's exposed brain matter.

"What do you reckon as to the cause of death, sir?" Sergeant Murphy, a half foot shorter than Jasper, grinned up at him.

Jasper's lips twitched, but he ignored his waggish subordinate's levity. Instead he crouched down and peeled back the bloody, frozen-stiff blanket to expose the bodies. The woman wore a soiled, threadbare chemise and the man filthy flannel drawers sans shirt. Mrs. Bickle's right arm and shoulder bore several bruises, and four long scratches ran down Mr. Bickle's left bicep. "Estimated time of d-death?"

Murphy chewed his lip as he stared at the bodies, then shook his head. "It's too damned cold, so checking for rigor won't give an accurate result?"

Jasper nodded.

"But I'd say it's been a good thirty-six hours."

"And why is that?"

"Well, right here." Murphy pointed to Mrs. Bickle's feet. "The rats have been chewin', and this looks like it was frozen when they were workin' on it. This cold snap has been brutal, but to freeze 'em like this? I reckon it took a while."

This was not a murder that required a great deal of intellect or experience to unravel, but Jasper spent the next three-quarters of an hour inspecting the victims and the room with Murphy because that's why the Detective Department of the Metropolitan Police employed him: to instruct on criminal investigation techniques.

When he and Murphy finished making sketches and taking notes, Jasper turned to the two silent men hovering just inside the doorway. They were staring with blatant fascination at Jasper's famous walking stick. Today he carried the bronze eagle, which he'd propped against the wall.

"You may t-take them now," he said.

The men jolted at the sound of his voice and went into action.

"Did the neighbors hear or see anything, Sergeant?" Jasper savored a tiny surge of pleasure at completing a sentence without a stammer.

Murphy flipped open the notebook Jasper required all men he trained to keep—and *utilize*. "There was only one neighbor here when I arrived—an older woman from 'cross the hall. She heard the couple arguin' four nights ago—but nothing since."

Yes, Jasper thought, eyeing the frozen bodies, this looked like an argument that had been over for some time.

"None of their n-neighbors thought to check on them?" Jasper tightened his lips, as if that could pull the slip back into his mouth.

Murphy—inured to Jasper's speech impediment—paused in his page flicking to cut his superior a look of amusement. "It's not that kinda ken, sir."

Jasper now knew that *ken* was a street word for dwelling. It was one of the many words he hadn't known when he began this job. While Jasper had been teaching investigative methods to the sergeants, they'd educated him about a previously unknown version of London.

He glanced at the dismal room around him, which reeked of stale gin, boiled cabbage, and unwashed bodies. The Bickles lived in a dark room, meaning it was in the middle of a subdivided building and had no windows. The house would once have been a single-family dwelling—and, judging by the ornate cornices still in evidence, a very nice one. Now it housed at least twenty families.

Jasper was no longer as shocked by the squalor as he'd been when he started at the Met, but he was still horrified that people could tolerate such a hardscrabble existence.

The men from the deadhouse were having a difficult time detaching the frozen bodies from the blood-soaked ticking. They'd split the seams, and damp straw was escaping from the mattress.

Jasper turned away from the gruesome operation. "How long have they l-lived here?"

"They took lodgings 'ere"—Murphy cleared his throat—"*here* three weeks ago."

Jasper smiled; they were a fine pair of bookends. While Murphy's heavy cockney brogue wasn't the same thing as a stammer, it wasn't likely to help his assent within the Met. He was impressed that Murphy was trying to improve himself, or at least improve his chances for advancement.

Jasper had stopped trying to fix his stammer years ago. He'd also stopped trying to hide it. Most importantly, he'd stopped *not* speaking just to avoid butchering words. He no longer allowed others to shame him into shutting up. He supposed that, in itself, represented a certain sort of achievement.

Murphy flipped a few pages and said, "Mr. Bickle was a butcher over at a place in Smithfield."

Which would explain the cleaver.

"And Mrs. Bickle was a workin' woman."

Ah. So, had Bickle killed his wife because she was a poor earner?

Or perhaps it had been *her* idea to sell her body and he'd learned of it after the fact and killed her in a fit of jealousy? Or maybe he'd merely reached the end of his endurance for a life so grim and devoid of hope?

What does any of this matter? a bored voice in his head asked. *There's no mystery here: gin, desperation, and poverty. It's clear how they died and equally clear nobody except you cares.*

People like the Bickles left no record of their lives, no imprint on this world, but Jasper could make sure their deaths did not go unnoticed.

Ah, so you are a file clerk for the dead?

Jasper ignored the taunting question, wondering—not for the first time—if everyone had to tolerate voices in their heads, or only those who carried a chunk of metal in their skulls.

The men had lifted the Bickles onto the pallet, mattress and all. They rammed their burden through the narrow doorway and clattered into the dark, narrow hall before disappearing.

A uniformed peeler appeared in the open doorway. "Lord Jasper Lightner?"

"Yes, I'm *Detective* Inspector Lightner."

"Commissioner Mayne sent me, my lord," the bobby said, missing Jasper's pointed response. "It's the 'ome secretary that wants to see you."

Beside him, Murphy stiffened, no doubt impressed by a summons from both the head of the Met *and* the Home Office.

Jasper's reaction was a bit more visceral. A summons from Sir George Grey could mean only one thing: Jasper's father. And anything having to do with his father was never good.

He nodded at the messenger. "We're almost f-finished here, and then—"

"Commissioner Mayne asked that you go directly, my lord."

Which meant right this instant.

Murphy piped up. "I can finish up 'ere, my lord, er"—he grimaced—"that is, Detective Inspector."

Jasper sighed. He'd only just trained Murphy to leave off *my lord*ing him, and now he'd need to break him of the annoying habit all over again.

Outside on the street he inhaled deeply, replacing the stench of the room he'd just left with coal smoke, horse manure, and the harsh bite of lye from a nearby renderer.

He hailed a hackney. "Four Whitehall Place."

Alone in the carriage, his thoughts grew less controlled. It had been almost two years since his father last interfered in his life: when he'd forbidden Jasper from accepting a position with the Detective Department.

They'd hardly spoken since, but every time Jasper's name appeared in the newspaper, he expected an angry visit from the older man.

He stared out the filthy carriage window and recalled the last conversation he'd had with his elder brother.

"Father is an old man, Jaz," Crispin said when Jasper confessed he'd not be going to Kersey Park for Easter this year. "His heart has been giving him trouble lately. You should make your peace with him."

His brother, a year his senior, had never understood Jasper's antagonistic relationship with their father. Crispin was their father's pride and joy, and for good reason, as far as Jasper was concerned. He loved his brother fiercely and didn't envy him either their father's affection or his position as heir. Crispin was universally beloved and would make a far better caretaker for all the people who lived on their family estates than their father ever had.

It wasn't that their father had gambled away the family fortune or dragged their name through the mud—the latter something he'd accused Jasper of doing. It was that he was a cold, rigid man who had the fear and respect of his dependents, but never their love.

"We're 'ere, gov," the driver said through the narrow vent, interrupting his thoughts.

Jasper glanced out the window and saw that they'd stopped while he was gathering wool. He climbed out and paid the driver, staring unseeingly at the battered carriage as it rumbled off down the street. Whatever Sir George had called him here to say, Jasper doubted he'd like it.

He was tempted to ignore the summons and go back to the station. What was the worst that could happen? He couldn't believe the department would discharge him. It wasn't only his practical skills that they valued; there was also the fact that Jasper could gain access to places every other member of the force—Commissioner Mayne included—could only dream about. He was their special weapon: a policeman with connections to most of the ruling families in England.

Another hackney slowed beside him. "Need a ride, sir?" the driver asked.

Jasper shook his head and turned away. Whatever was waiting for him, he might as well face it.

★   ★   ★

Jasper didn't recognize the young man seated at the desk outside the home secretary's office, but it was clear the man knew who Jasper was.

He leapt to his feet, twin spots of color on cheeks that looked too young to require a razor. "Major Lord Lightner—" His color deepened even more. "Er, Detective Inspector, that is, sir—what an honor." Admiration shone like a beacon from the youngster's eyes.

Jasper had become resigned to such responses since his return from the war, but that did not mean he enjoyed them. Exaggerated tales of his brigade's heroism and their disastrous charge had been waiting for him when he was invalided back home from the Crimea in early '55. Rather than fading into obscurity, the suicidal engagement had gained mythic stature, thanks to that bloody Tennyson poem.

"Th-Thank you," Jasper said. "And you are?"

"Oh yes—sorry, sir. Hedley Selwood." He bowed deeply. "I believe you knew my brother at Eton."

Jasper skimmed the surface of his memory, careful to avoid the cracks and fissures that led to a boundless void.

Selwood, Selwood, Selwood . . .

Astonishingly, a fat, shiny-cheeked face materialized in his mind's eye: Richard Selwood, the Earl of Ingleton's heir.

"Dickie Selwood," Jasper said. His pleasure at remembering the man was overpowered by a sharp pang that his memory didn't work as well when it came to recalling far more important matters. But his mind had a will of its own, and sometimes it yielded up the most trivial things without any effort. Things like Dickie Selwood.

"How is Dickie these d-days?" Jasper asked out of courtesy rather than interest.

"He is Ingleton now, sir."

"Ah. I'd not heard of your father's d-death. I'm sorry for your l-l-loss."

"Thank you, sir. It has been almost three years now, and Dickie is a regular old man these days—married and with children already."

"Give him my regards."

"Absolutely, sir." Selwood kept nodding, clearly loath to end the conversation. Jasper knew he was working himself up to broaching Balaclava.

"I understood the home s-secretary wished to see me r-rather urgently."

The boy snapped to. "Oh yes, yes, of course, sir. Right this way." He led Jasper to the massive doors to Sir George's cavernous office and flung one open. "Detective Inspector Lightner to see you," he bellowed, with enough pomp to please a royal duke.

The home secretary was on his feet and smiling. "Ah, Jasper, welcome. How good of you to come so quickly."

As if Jasper had had any say in the matter.

"A p-p-pleasure to see you again, Sir George."

"Come in, come in—do have a seat." He cut Selwood a brief glance. "See that we are not disturbed."

"Yes, Home Secretary." The door closed behind the young man without a sound.

"I hope I've not pulled you off anything important, Jasper."

"Nothing that can't wait, sir." No, the Bickles were not in any hurry.

Sir George's eyes slid from Jasper to one of the hooded dome chairs that faced his desk. "You see who's come for a visit?"

Jasper was not surprised when the Duke of Kersey's face emerged from the shadows of the chair's deep hood.

He met His Grace's cold, pale-blue eyes and gave a soft, unamused snort of laughter.

"Hallo, F-Father. What a p-p-pleasure."

CHAPTER 2

Jasper left the warm comfort of the pub, his head muzzy from too much whiskey. He generally avoided hard spirits, as they exacerbated his head injury and often brought on debilitating migraines. He preferred opium to alcohol and morphine to either of those, but those seductive substances came with headaches all their own—a costly lesson he'd learned from personal experience.

Besides, a decent dram of Irish whiskey was far easier to come by, and some days it was worth the headache. Today was one of those days.

It was full dark, and the weather had turned nasty while he'd been in the pub. He considered hailing a hackney but decided the heavy, freezing rain matched his foul mood to perfection. He pulled his coat collar up around his ears and hunched against the bone-chilling wind. A long walk would help to clear his head, which he should do before allowing Paisley to see him in this condition.

Sometimes Jasper thought employing a valet was more work than having a wife—especially a servant as observant, intelligent, and opinionated as Paisley. The man would've worried himself into a state by now, envisioning Jasper wandering around the city lost or in a daze—even though he hadn't suffered such an incident in well over a year.

Jasper didn't like distressing Paisley, but tonight it couldn't be helped. After the half hour he'd spent with his father and the home secretary and then his wretched conversations with the Bickles' neighbors, Jasper hadn't been fit company for man nor beast.

As difficult as it was to credit, his visit to the Bickles' cramped, dirty, and desperate lodgings had been even worse than his time with the duke.

Jasper had expected to learn nothing of any significance about the Bickles from their neighbors, but what he *hadn't* expected was the utter eradication of the couple's existence. Not only had all physical trace of them been cleared away, but a family of four had already been installed in their dismal room, looking as if they'd lived there for ages. The image of them eating their grim evening meal had burned itself into his mind.

Don't worry, Jasper, you'll forget about them—just like you've forgotten everything else in your life.

This snide observation had a ring of truth but was not, strictly speaking, accurate.

His prior life was not entirely lost to him; he retained skills like riding a horse and loading a pistol and even a good deal of his medical training. But his memory of people and events preceding October 25, 1854—both big and small—was often fragmented or nonexistent.

The duke had accused him of possessing a convenient memory rather than suffering any ill effects from the shrapnel that had pierced his skull. Perhaps His Grace was correct—at least to some degree—because Jasper remembered some things very clearly indeed.

Like the day he learned he'd never again have to stand in front of his father's massive desk, enduring the duke's cold, scathing stare and justifying his very existence to collect his meager allowance.

Yes, Jasper could remember the day he'd learned of his Aunt Sarah's bequest, but he had no memory of the woman whose generosity meant he'd never again be dependent on his father.

Forgetting specific events didn't bother him as much as forgetting people. And the person he most regretted forgetting was himself and the kind of man he'd been before his brain was scrambled. Although he doubted that he was materially different when it came to his tastes and characteristics, he couldn't help wondering if he'd once had some sort of plan for his life.

He must have possessed drive or ambition to have studied medicine. Or perhaps that was wrong—perhaps he'd merely done so to spite and embarrass his father?

What had happened—if anything—to cause him to leave England and spend his last two years of schooling in Paris? And why had he abandoned his medical training a mere six months before completion to join the army?

Jasper had never kept a journal, nor had he confided his reasons to his friends—not even his brother. It was probable that the memories were lost forever and he'd never know the answers.

He stopped at a busy street, keeping well away from the splashing wheels and muck-filled road as he waited for a chance to cross. His mind drifted back—as it had done all evening—to the meeting in the home secretary's office.

"I b-beg your pardon, sir, but you w-wish me to do *what*?"

"New York City has created a new police department modeled on ours and has asked for our assistance. You're the perfect person to aid them."

"But I know n-nothing about structuring p-police departments."

"They don't want you to help with the creation of the force. They want your expertise training their investigators—the same as you are doing here. They haven't asked for just anybody, Jasper—they want *you*."

Jasper had been tempted to yell *bollocks* but had tried a more measured response first. "If I m-may be so bold, Sir George, how would they even have h-heard of me?"

"Come now, I think we both know your methods, as well as your zeal, are rather distinctive."

As distinctive as the odor of horseshit in this room.

The secretary continued. "The board is very impressed, just as we were, with the time you spent with the former chief of Sûreté nationale, Eugène Vidocq, both before and after the war. They view you—quite rightly—as his natural successor in the new science of criminal investigation."

"I'm honored to be p-put on the level of Mr. Vidocq, but I'm afraid s-s-somebody has overestimated my abilities, sir."

The duke gave a loud, scornful snort, his first contribution to the conversation. "Vidocq is a thief, forger, and worse."

Jasper could not argue with his father; the founder of the Sûreté had spent almost as much time running from the law as he had enforcing it.

"True, Your G-Grace, but he also happens to be one of the finest m-minds on the subject of criminal b-behavior."

"Because he *is* a bloody criminal."

Again, that was undoubtedly true. But Eugene Vidocq was so much more.

Jasper had first met the man when he was a student in Paris. He still recalled his first meeting with Eugène, when the older man had come to the college of medicine with the body of a convict.

Thanks to Jasper's head injury, the case itself was lost to him, but he remembered the clever and charismatic Frenchman.

After the war he'd gone back to Paris, half-obsessed to reconnect with a man who claimed to retain every memory he'd ever made. Did Vidocq employ some system or technique to store and retrieve memories? If he did, perhaps he could teach it to others. Perhaps Jasper could use it to recover his own memories?

While the old policeman hadn't possessed any magical memory tricks—just a phenomenal memory—he *had* taught Jasper more about criminal investigation in six months than many policemen learned in decades.

Of course, consulting with Vidocq about his memory hadn't been the only reason for his trip to France. Unbeknownst to anyone aside from the home secretary and a few others, his trip to Paris in mid-'55 had been Jasper's first detective assignment.

The duke pounded his fist on the arm of his chair. "Is your cracked brain wandering again?"

Jasper met his father's furious gaze. "Why are you here, Your G-Grace?"

Sir George replied before the duke could open his mouth. "Your father is on the Police Service Committee, and they've—"

"There is a position for you—assistant superintendent commissioner," the duke said. "And you will bloody well take it."

"I don't believe I'm f-familiar with that position, Your G-Grace."

"You know damned well you'll be the first." He looked away from Jasper as if the sight pained him, which it probably did.

"Why d-do I think this is a titular p-position?"

The duke's head whipped around. "Because it *is*, you fool." His eyes narrowed, frustration joining fury. "If you *refuse* to take a seat in Commons, and if you *refuse* to use your utterly undeserved windfall to benefit your family's estates, and if you *refuse* to take an acceptable wife and see to the breeding of her—something your brother shows no signs of doing—then the *least* you can do is not shame your family on a weekly basis." He took a folded rectangle of newsprint from his lap and hurled it at Jasper. "Here you are *yet again* with one of your goddamned sticks."

It was a front-page article about a theft ring the police had recently broken. As the lead detective, Jasper had been present at the arrest—an arrest that had involved a good deal of violence. The newspaper had delighted in laying out details of the fight, complete with a creditable drawing of him wielding one of his rather famous—or infamous, depending on whom you asked—walking sticks.

Jasper gave the duke a cool look. "What of it?"

The duke's eyes bulged, but before he could answer, the home secretary again stepped into the breach.

"It's true the new position is largely symbolic . . . *now*—but that could change over time. More importantly, it would remove you from the dangerous and unsavory elements you're exposed to in your current duties."

Jasper didn't bother reminding Sir George that he'd used those very same dangerous and unsavory elements to lure Jasper into working for him in the first place.

"Either I take this p-position or go to N-N-New York?"

Sir George hesitated, cut a glance at the duke, and then nodded.

"Would you t-tell me more about the p-position in New York, sir?"

His father made a noise like an enraged gander. "Are you bloody *mad*?"

Jasper thought that was probably a rhetorical question.

"I *cannot* believe for an instant that you'd consider such idiocy," the duke said, his voice choked with rage.

Jasper almost smiled. So, his father had overplayed his hand. He'd believed the situation he'd engineered for his embarrassing son left him with only two choices: quit the force or take the tedious sinecure he'd created.

"*Jasper!*" his father yelled, when Jasper failed to answer. His voice was so loud it rattled the crystal decanters on a nearby console table.

"Please, Sir George," Jasper said with quiet firmness, "I would like to hear m-more about New Y-York."

After a long, tension-filled silence, the home secretary said, "This will be much in the same vein as the conferring that took place between our department and Vidocq back in the thirties when we sent men to Paris to—"

"Even *you* cannot be so foolish as to consider this, Jasper," the duke said. "There is nothing but Irishmen and savages in charge of the entire damned country. Ha! I say in charge—it's bloody chaos over there. They'd like nothing more than to get a naïve Englishman with your connections in their clutches. These men will eat somebody like you alive. You'll come crawling—"

"How long a stay d-did they have in m-mind, Sir G-George?"

The duke stormed out after that, leaving Jasper to ascertain the details without his father's histrionics.

The home secretary made Jasper's choices clear: he could take the new position or he could go to America. What he could *not* do was continue to embarrass his family in his current position. Whatever hold the duke had over Sir George, it must be powerful, because the man was adamant.

"What h-happens after a year?" Jasper asked, when Sir George told him the length of the assignment.

The older man had not been able to look him in the eyes. "Let's leave that discussion until you return."

So, Jasper was left with a simple decision: submit to his father's will and take a position that would be no better than a figurehead, or abandon the life he'd made for himself here—such as it was—and travel thousands of miles into the unknown.

He tried to view the subject objectively. Why did he cling so desperately to this job? Merely to have something to occupy his time?

He pondered that question as he moved through the frozen rain that was now beating hard on his hat, the patter an insistent tattoo that sped his thoughts as well as his steps.

He could always reject both choices and do nothing; he was a wealthy man, after all.

But he recalled all too well what he'd done in the months *before* Sir George approached him. Yes, his memory of *that* time was crystal clear.

Jasper stopped at yet another cross street. When he glanced up, he saw where his feet had carried him; he'd walked over two miles. He frowned at the elegant Georgian facade of his townhouse, looking past the soft glow of gaslights to the distinctive spider-web muntin above the front door. There were welcoming lights in the windows, and Paisley would have a hot meal waiting for him—no matter the time.

Jasper tucked his stick under his arm and flexed his fingers. Even with fur-lined gloves, they were numb. He was wet, tired, and more than a little bosky, yet he was loath to go home. He took out his watch: it was after ten o'clock.

There would be no sleep for him tonight, at least not without assistance. And there were only two things that helped him sleep. So, it was just a question of what type of assistance he needed—or wanted.

He pocketed his watch and tipped the water from the brim of his high-crowned hat before stepping closer to the curb and raising a hand. When a hackney rolled to a stop beside him, Jasper was genuinely curious as to which of the two addresses he would give the driver.

"Seven Curzon Street," he said, and then climbed into the clammy darkness of the carriage.

He tossed his hat onto the scarred leather bench across from him, pulled a handkerchief from the inner pocket of his coat, and put aside the decisions he'd have to make soon. But not today.

His body, tense and tight only moments earlier, was now humming with anticipation of the night ahead.

And if his current mistress—a lush, libidinous widow who shared Jasper's appetites and never asked bothersome personal questions—was not at her snug townhouse on Curzon?

Well, then he'd give the driver the second address—the one to an establishment in Limehouse that catered to his other vice and was never closed.

CHAPTER 3

London
Late May 1857

Jasper had hoped to leave London without encountering his parents at the going-away bash his brother insisted on hosting. It wasn't an unreasonable hope, as the duke usually spent the Easter break at the family seat in Somerset.

Usually. But not this year.

The first people he saw upon entering the large salon at Kersey House were the duke and duchess.

Crispin was engaged in a conversation across the room but caught Jasper's eye. He grimaced and shrugged as if to say, *Well, what did you expect?*

Jasper shot him a menacing look that was only partly feigned. The bastard had *known* their parents would be here—he'd probably invited them—and he'd withheld the information, fearing Jasper wouldn't come. And he'd been right.

"Darling!" the duchess cooed, a suffocating cloud of expensive perfume surrounding him when he leaned down to kiss her pale, smooth cheek.

"Mother, you are looking w-well," he said, not untruthfully. The Duchess of Kersey had always been an exceedingly lovely woman, but Jasper knew her youthful beauty came at a high cost. He could smell the faint odor of garlic beneath the cloying perfume, and the slight sheen of perspiration on her milky-white skin was not healthy.

He could have told her the arsenic she took to maintain her flawless complexion would eventually kill her. But he knew the duchess well; she'd never listened to him in the past and was unlikely to begin now.

"You are looking well too, Jasper." She scrutinized his person more closely than the most exacting accountant studied a ledger, her brain totting up the cost of his clothing quicker than an abacus.

It irked his mother that economizing measures had become necessary in the duke's household; it irked her even more that Jasper had no need to stint himself anything.

He studied her while she studied him. He'd hated his resemblance to his mother when he was younger. They shared the same thick, wavy chestnut hair, fine-boned good looks, and dark eyes fringed with long lashes—all well and good for a beautiful woman but mortifying for a boy.

Like him, the duchess was taller than average, and her slender form was well proportioned. He'd shot to six feet before he reached thirteen, his arms and legs so skinny, fragile, and pale that they'd earned him the nickname Birch at Eton.

His brother, on the other hand, was the spit and image of their father: short, stocky, and blue eyed, with thinning blond hair.

"Gieves and Hawkes?"

Jasper looked up. "Hmm?"

"I asked if your suit is Gieves and Hawkes," she said, naming the duke's tailor.

"P-Poole." Jasper knew his mother would think his tailor not only a pushing upstart but also too modern with his design.

Her arched eyebrows told him he'd guessed her thoughts correctly.

His father came to stand on his other side, rather than beside his duchess, reminding Jasper that he was the duke's second least favorite person.

"Hallo again, Father."

The duke eyed him with open dislike, and Jasper knew they were both recalling the last time they'd spoken, two weeks before, after his father had learned that Jasper had accepted the New York posting rather than remaining in London and becoming his cipher.

His Grace had arrived at Jasper's house unannounced and pushed past the butler, marching into the library, his face a dangerous shade of red. They'd both proceeded to give vent to opinions and accusations that had simmered between them for decades and had been better left unsaid.

Jasper's memory, as faulty as it was, latched on to his father's final salvo: *I shall see you back here in six weeks with your tail between your legs.*

"Your brother told me you are leaving two days hence," the duke said now. "Which ship are you taking?"

"The *P-P-Persia*."

The duke's mouth twisted with disgust; Jasper knew that his stammer upset the older man—even after all these years. Although he no longer cared what his father thought about him, Jasper's stutter always became worse in the duke's company.

Still, he thought with amusement, the home secretary had done his fair share of stammering at that meeting too. So perhaps Jasper wasn't the only person the duke affected that way.

A hand landed on his shoulder and squeezed. "Jaz! It's great to see you." Crispin stepped into the wide gap between Jasper and their father. "I was beginning to think you'd not come."

"I could hardly m-miss my own p-p-party, could I?"

"It's a good thing, or Tish would have hopped on a packet and hunted you down in New York." He glanced over Jasper's shoulder, and his smile became dazzling. "Ah, there she is," he said. "I was just telling Jaz it was a good thing he showed his face."

Jasper forced himself to turn and greet the woman who'd once been his fiancée. Not that he could recall much of their time together or why it had ended.

"Hallo, L-L-Leticia." His perfect sister-in-law was the only person who made him feel embarrassed by his stammer—not that she did so intentionally. No, Leticia was as kind as she was beautiful. Or at least he thought she was.

He gestured to the cavernous room around them, which held a good seventy-five people. "Thank you f-for all this."

She took his hand, squeezing it with both hers. "Don't be daft— of course we couldn't let you go to the Wild West without a proper send-off."

Crispin laughed. "New York City is hardly the Wild West, darling."

She turned her extraordinary blue-violet eyes on her short, balding husband. "Crispin is going to miss you terribly, Jaz."

He flinched at her use of his pet name, but Leticia's smile didn't falter.

Before Jasper could answer, the duchess said, "Are you certain of your decision, darling? I understand New York City is *quite* dangerous."

Jasper was stunned by her unprecedented display of maternal concern.

But then she continued, "Those American girls and their rapacious, title-hunting mamas are positively savage. They're infesting even the best houses in London. You'll need to take care you don't fall victim to some dreadfully vulgar mushroom."

So, his mother wasn't concerned for his life, merely his bank account and the family name. "It's fortunate I don't possess a title, M-Mother."

"You'll be quite the most eligible bachelor in New York. You'll have every American debutante on the run." Leticia smiled up at him.

"It's more likely to be the other way round," his brother quipped. "How are you at sprinting, Jaz?" Crispin chortled at his jest, and Leticia laid a slender hand on his shoulder.

"You're going to think me terribly scatterbrained, darling, but I can't recall which case of champagne you wanted me to take next." She cut Jasper an apologetic smile. "Would the three of you mind terribly if I borrowed Crispin for a moment?"

Jasper knew the answer to that question was a resounding *yes*, but of course nobody admitted it.

Leticia and Crispin took all conversation with them, leaving the three of them standing like wooden totems.

"Ah," the duke said, the first to seize an opportunity to escape. "There is Hilliars; I must have a word with him."

The duchess gave an equally vague excuse a moment later—but went in the opposite direction. His parents spoke to each other even more rarely than they spoke to him.

The tension they'd brought with them drained away, and Jasper relaxed. He'd not seen his father and brother together for some time and was stunned by how much Crispin had come to resemble the duke.

Jasper had been eight when he discovered that he would never look like their father.

Like so many valuable pieces of information he'd acquired over the course of his life, the knowledge had come from a servant. His old nurse, Nanny Brown, had been chatting with some other domestic whose name he no longer recalled.

"The young marquess is the very image of His Grace," said Nanny's companion.

"Aye," Nanny agreed. "But what he lacks in looks, he'll make up for in disposition—he's a sweet lad."

"And what about Master Jasper?" the forgotten servant asked in a hushed voice. "Now *he'll* be a handsome one. He doesn't look a bit like the duke; he's Her Grace all over again, with his lovely hair and those romantic eyes."

Nanny had not responded immediately, and even at eight, Jasper knew the silence was significant.

When she did speak, her voice was gruff. "Aye, the poor little lad. It's a shame His Grace takes out his anger at the duchess on the boy. He had nothing to do with who his father is."

The ground shifted beneath him at her words.

Up until then Jasper had assumed it was his stammer the duke despised. He'd believed that if he could fix himself, his father would love him as he did Crispin. That day he'd learned it was his very *existence* the duke loathed.

As for his mother? Well, she didn't hate him and had never been cruel—at least not intentionally. She hardly acknowledged his existence at all. She simply had no interest to spare for anyone but herself, not even her sons. Jasper couldn't remember if she'd been different—more affectionate or caring—before his sister died, but he somehow doubted it.

He could hardly recall the four-year-old girl who'd died when he was fifteen, but the portrait of her that hung at Kersey Hall was evidence that she too was some other man's child, perhaps even Jasper's full sibling.

He'd never asked the duchess who his real father was; he didn't care. He wondered now at his disinterest. Surely such a lack of curiosity could not be a good characteristic in a detective?

Crispin returned. "So, have you sold off that fine bay you rode at Everton's hunt last season? Or are you giving him to your favorite brother as an extremely early birthday gift?"

The two of them drank Crispin's fine brandy, insulted each other's equestrian skills, and generally enjoyed themselves as more people packed into the huge room.

All too soon they were interrupted as others drifted over to pay their respects to the guest of honor. It was challenging to meet so many people whom one was expected to know and remember, and it wasn't long before his head began to ache. Jasper had avoided large functions since his return from the war, and today was baptism by fire.

Sometimes he recognized faces he couldn't put with names; sometimes he knew their name but had no recollection of who they were or how he knew them; and then—worst of all—sometimes there were people he knew nothing about.

Thankfully, nobody appeared to notice anything amiss, and he navigated dozens of transactions without awkwardness. Either he was very good at hiding his defective memory or they were very good at hiding their surprised reactions.

There was a third possibility, one he didn't like to face: perhaps these people—supposedly his closest friends and family—had never known him well enough to notice that he was different now.

They laughed, drank, made the same comments, and asked him the same questions: *What a lark this will be; I should tag along with you! You'd better watch out, or you'll come back with an American wife just like poor O'Toole did. You're staying* how *long?* And Jasper's personal favorite: *But how can you bear to go somewhere you won't* know *anyone?*

He was chatting with yet another schoolmate he didn't know and reminiscing about antics he couldn't remember when an image of Joseph and Mary Bickle flashed through his mind. Jasper hadn't thought about the dead couple since the day their bodies were found—not surprising, given what else had happened between then and now. But now they came back in a rush, flooding his mind with images, sensations, and even smells.

Jasper recalled the almost vertiginous surprise he'd experienced when he realized that two people had been discovered dead that morning and that less than twelve hours later all traces of them were gone—forgotten.

He threw back the contents of his glass, the fiery liquid burning its way down his throat, and looked around at the people who were nearest and dearest to him.

It was morbid, but he couldn't help wondering: if he were found dead by his own hand tomorrow, would any of these people be able to help a detective determine why he'd done it—or, at the least, who he'd been?

He knew, with chilling certainty, that the answer to that question was no. How could it be otherwise? How could anyone know who Jasper was when he didn't even know himself?

CHAPTER 4

Mid-June 1857
On board the *Persia*, New York Harbor

Jasper enjoyed a cigar as he watched the ship's gradual arrival into New York Harbor. He was viewing the city from the stern, which did not provide the spectacular view he would have had from the bow but was considerably less crowded.

Paisley came to stand beside him, emanating disapproval just as he'd been doing since the day Jasper told him they were moving. Although his valet was not happy about their relocation, he'd never said a word. But, like an old married couple, they no longer needed words to convey their displeasure.

Jasper was accustomed to living in a city, but he'd never seen anything as vast as the one spread out before him. Eagerness to explore such a metropolis mingled with skepticism that he'd really been sent here to instruct New York policemen in investigatory techniques.

One thing the duke had said that day had stuck with him: the police force was overwhelmingly Irish or of Irish extraction. The last thing a sane human would do was send an Englishman—not to mention an English *lord*—to instruct Irishmen.

If Jasper were a paranoid man, he might wonder if his father had actually *planned* this posting as a tidy way to put a period to his existence. After all, if the duke could not force Jasper to pour his money into the family coffers, then surely the next best option was to get rid of him. Or better yet, have *somebody else* get rid of him. How convenient for the duke if American hooligans—of either the criminal or the law enforcement variety—took care of his ungovernable and screamingly wealthy offspring.

Jasper exhaled a plume of smoke as he considered the seemingly improbable possibility.

He knew his father believed that a dead Jasper would mean a great deal of money for the dukedom. After all, he had no wife or children and wasn't close to any other family members; who else could Jasper possibly leave his wealth to but Crispin?

Jasper smiled. It was a shame he'd never be able to witness the duke's expression when he eventually learned the truth. Still, he was in no hurry to die merely to serve his father an unpleasant surprise. Not yet, at least.

"My lord?"

Jasper looked up at the sound of Paisley's voice. "Hmm?"

"The captain sent a steward to say he will ensure we disembark first."

He smiled at his servant, whose narrow-eyed expression told him that he already knew exactly what his obstreperous employer would say.

"We are in the b-birthplace of democracy, Paisley." He flicked the stub of his cigar over the side and watched its long arc to the churning waters below. "We should disembark in a d-democratic fashion."

★　★　★

An hour later, Jasper was deeply regretting his decision. It wasn't only the democratic press of humanity that was overwhelming—in smell, composition, and sheer numbers—it was the man who'd been sent to bear-lead him from the harbor into the city.

Alderman Cornelius "call me Corny" Dell had not stopped talking from the moment they'd been introduced. Jasper was not clear on Dell's relationship to the new Metropolitan Police or its superintendent—Frederick Tallmadge. One moment Dell intimated that the commissioners had personally chosen him to welcome Jasper; in the next breath he mentioned his friendship with Mayor Wood.

Jasper had asked Dell twice to address him as Detective—not *my lord*, *Your Lordship*, or—heaven forfend—*Your Grace*.

But what Mr. Dell lacked in auditory ability, he made up for in vocal skills.

"Superintendent Tallmadge wanted to greet you personally, my lord, but he was called up to Albany at the last minute. The commissioners have put you up at the Astor House." He cut Jasper a quick, uneasy look. "Tho' money has been tight for the new department, with the procurement office in such a tangle—" He grimaced. "Anyhow, I think they ain't planning to foot the bill more than a week."

Jasper hazarded a guess at what *footing the bill* meant.

Dell cleared his throat. "Do you have any plans in that direction? Er, housing, that is?"

"My man will secure l-l-lodgings for me."

Dell's eyes widened, and Jasper believed he was taking note of his stammer for the first time. That was not difficult to believe, considering he'd not allowed Jasper to get more than three words out before now.

Dell stared at him the way a child gaped at a circus acrobat, waiting for the next trick.

So Jasper opened his mouth and obliged him. "If I d-do require more than a week, please assure the b-board I fully expect to pay my own shot."

The other man's expression was one of barely suppressed glee. At first Jasper thought it was because he couldn't believe an English aristocrat could do something as common as stammer.

But then Dell said, "It just so happens I've got my finger in quite a few pies and would be glad to show your servant some fine properties I believe would suit Your Lordship."

Jasper tried to erase the mental image of Dell putting his grubby fingers in pies or anything else. He looked to where Paisley was supervising the loading of trunks onto a ragged wagon. His valet's ramrod-straight spine was even stiffer than usual, and he was positively vibrating with indignation at the sight of Jasper's expensive Cave luggage being forced to suffer a ride on such a conveyance.

When Jasper failed to accept Dell's offer, the American cleared his throat and tried again. "What I meant to say is, if he requires acquaintin' with the better parts of the city, I'd be glad to show him around."

Jasper's lips twitched at the thought of his crushingly snobbish servant spending even an hour with a loquacious mushroom like Dell and not killing him.

"Thank you for your g-generous offer, Mr. Dell. I'm afraid Paisley is most p-particular in his requirements, and to indicate he required help would be insulting." He gave Dell a conspiratorial look. "I'm sure you know how sensitive one's s-servants can be to perceived criticism, particularly old family r-retainers."

Dell cocked his head, breathing in and out through his mouth.

"Besides," Jasper continued, "P-Paisley was with me in the Crimea—surely the streets of New York City p-pale in comparison to a war zone?"

Mention of his time in the army had its intended effect and distracted Dell from persisting with his tiresome offer of assistance. But the diversionary tactic was not without cost, and Jasper spent the following minutes fielding asinine questions from the war-obsessed but geographically ignorant Dell.

He was trying, without success, to describe the position of Sevastopol when Paisley approached.

"I shall ride with your luggage, my lord." The day was stiflingly hot, but Paisley's words came out with ice crystals on them.

Dell bristled. "It ain't as if you have to worry about thievery—you're with *me*. And I'm known and respected all over these parts," he added, as if they might have missed that information the first half dozen times he mentioned it.

Paisley cut Dell a look filled with venom, bestowed the slightest of bows on Jasper to communicate his opinion of their current predicament, and strode back to the wagon.

Dell's voice appeared to have seized.

"You must excuse P-Paisley, Alderman. I'm afraid he tends to be oversedulous when it comes to the care of my p-possessions. I'm sure he didn't mean to cast aspersions of any sort," Jasper lied.

Dell's cheeks were bright red. "Humph." He turned away from the departing wagon and gestured to the waiting carriage. "After you, my lord."

One good consequence of traveling with such a garrulous companion was that Jasper was free to give his attention to the scene passing outside the carriage window.

It was not so different from London, and the journey from the docks was like a trip up the social ladder. The poorest of the poor clung to the waterfront like barnacles, feeding off the money that came in with the ships, pilfering inadequately guarded cargo, meeting the demand for manual labor that ebbed and flowed with the tide itself, and catering to the merchant sailors who flooded the docks, their pockets stuffed with money they were eager to spend.

Even at noon, there were already dozens of prostitutes lolling about half-naked in their quest to net an oysterman, whaler, or gentleman traveler coming over on a ferry to conduct business.

"Commissioner Matsell didn't want you here, my lord, and when he and the mayor heard it was a done deal, he wanted to start you in Five Points. 'Course Matsell was recently discharged and the new commissioners want you at White Street—"

"Wh-White Street?" Jasper asked.

"White Street is the temporary headquarters of the Metropolitan Police—the *real* police in the city." He gave Jasper a reassuring smile that exposed less than a full complement of yellow teeth. "You've got people lookin' out for you, my lord."

So, they would not throw him directly into the festering urban wound known as Five Points, at least not right away. "S-So I will be stationed out of White S-Street?"

"Er, no." Dell gave him an odd smile.

"But you s-said—"

"Superintendent Tallmadge *didn't* want you at White Street."

Jasper was beginning to get a headache.

"You'll be goin' to the Eighth Precinct, one of our nicer stations. I'll bring you by once we've stopped by the Astor and—"

"I should like to stop by the station f-first, Mr. Dell." Jasper forbore adding that he'd like to do so *without* a wittering sycophant attached to his hip, since he doubted he could dislodge the man even with a hammer and chisel.

"But I thought you'd want refreshment first?" When Jasper failed to respond, Dell leaned forward, as if confiding a secret. "I'm not sure how much of the current situation you've been apprised of, but there's a bit of a, er, well, stand-off between Mayor Wood and Superintendent Tallmadge. I just want you to know that you can put your trust in me, since I'm a neutral third party." Dell had the decency to blush at what was obviously a lie, but that didn't stop his mouth from moving. "Anyhow, the matter of the new force is under adjudication—as we say here."

"I see." And Jasper *did* see: he'd walked into the middle of a political quagmire. Sir George had been confident that contentions between the outgoing Municipal Police and the newly legislated Metropolitan Police would have been resolved by the time Jasper arrived. It appeared that wasn't the case.

"I think it would be just as well if you avoided the station until you speak with Superintendent Tallmadge. He'll be back by tonight and come by the hotel." Dell gave Jasper an ingratiating grin. "We can wait in comfort; the Rotunda bar and restaurant is known for its fine food, drink, *and* the best company."

"I'm most eager to meet the superintendent and sample what the Astor House has to offer, Alderman. P-perhaps after I meet my new captain—what is h-his name?"

"Er, Captain Owen Davies."

"I'd l-like to meet Captain Davies and p-pay my respects."

Dell must have seen something in Jasper's expression that made his shoulders slump. "Well, if you're certain—"

"Quite."

The man was a politician and nothing if not adaptable. "Actually, that's an excellent idea—I should have thought of it myself. It'll help you to get the lay of the land."

"How many officers work at the Eighth Precinct?"

Dell scratched his head. "I don't rightly know. See, some of the wards are—well, let's just say they're not firmly under Mayor Wood's control, so there are more men who support the new police than you might think still out in the various precincts. Davies is one of the precinct captains who stayed, but—" Dell stopped and gave Jasper a nervous grin, all the while turning his sweat-stained hat with sausage-like fingers, his ragged nails encrusted with dirt—or worse. "Anyway, Davies might chafe at the bit, but he'll assist you in every way possible and pull aside the best patrolmen for your training."

The tremor in Dell's hands was marked, and his bulbous green eyes, which seemed to be in constant motion, landed on Jasper's own hands, which were gloved in black leather and resting motionlessly on the head of his walking stick. Dell frowned and shoved his hands into the sagging pockets of a worn and dirty frock coat that looked as if it had once been ochre.

Jasper moved the stick, laying it across his lap, the motion breaking Dell's rapt gaze.

"I understand there is already a c-core of detectives in each of the p-precincts."

"Er, yes, my lord, that's true—and some fine ones, I'm sure. But the commissioners are interested in scientific methods and were most impressed with the time you spent with the Frenchie, er, Medoc? Modic?"

"Vidocq," Jasper supplied.

"Yeah, him. Anyhow, there was some article you wrote on—"

Jasper did not help him out; he was curious to see what the inventive man would come up with.

But Dell gave up. "Well, on criminal matters, anyway." He gave Jasper an ingratiating smile. "The Detective Department of the London Met is the best in the world. Even better than Paris, although that Veddick gent certainly got results, didn't he?" Dell didn't require an answer to carry on a conversation. "Yes, all the civilized—"

The carriage shuddered to an abrupt stop, and a staccato rapping made Dell squawk with surprise. A head popped up outside the window.

Dell glared at the figure and said some very vulgar words. "I beg your pardon, my lord," he said to Jasper, then yanked down the window and demanded testily, "Who the hell are you?"

"Er, Patrolman O'Malley, sir. I'm from the Eighth." He wore a dark-blue uniform very similar to a bobby's.

"What is it?"

The young man's eyes slid from Dell to Jasper and then back. "Sergeant Billings sent me, sir."

Dell turned to Jasper. "Billings is a good man," he said in a voice meant to be a whisper but so loud it could be heard over the noise of the street. He turned back to the patrolmen. "Yes?"

"Er, there's been a murder, sir, behind Solange's, and Detective Featherstone is at the scene."

Dell turned to Jasper again. "Featherstone is *not* one of ours." Dell's head swiveled back to the boy. "Investigating crimes is Featherstone's *job*, isn't it?" He made as if to close the window, but the boy's next words stopped him.

"The sarge said you were fetchin', er"—his eyes swiveled to Jasper and then back to Dell—"the, uh, English detective today."

"Yes, that's correct; this is Lord Lightner you're currently delaying." Dell spat the inaccurate honorific at the quailing patrolman.

"Er, Billings said you might want to bring in the new detective. And the mayor sent a man who said—"

"The mayor?" Dell shrieked. "How the hell did he get into this? Lord Lightner isn't under his direction."

"Er, the mayor—"

"I don't give a good goddamn what the mayor says," Dell said, apparently forgetting he'd just been claiming friendship with said mayor a few moments earlier.

"Sergeant Billings said you'd say that, sir. He said to mention the dead man is Mr. Alard Janssen."

Dell recoiled as if he'd been jabbed in the forehead. "Good God— Janssen's been *murdered*?"

"Yes, sir."

Dell's brain whirred so loudly that Jasper could hear the cogs clacking.

He gave an abrupt nod. "Go on, then—we'll be along behind you." He turned to Jasper. "This is . . . er, well, it ain't good."

"What is n-not good?"

He cut Jasper an uncomfortable look. "Beggin' your pardon, my lord, but Solange's is a whorehouse. As nice as it is, I reckon it ain't the kinda place Your Lordship is used to."

Jasper was amused. "You n-needn't apologize, Mr. Dell. We have brothels in L-London."

Dell was not a man to appreciate irony. "If what that young mut-tonhead said about the dead man being Janssen is right, then you might be the best person to handle this."

"And why is that?"

"Janssen and Governor King were the main voices for trainin' up a scientific police department. It wouldn't be no lie to say Janssen was one of the men who had you brought here. He and King were real close. I doubt the governor would want a man like Featherstone investigatin'." Once again he gave Jasper an ingratiating smile. "You could say that you bein' on this investigation would be a way to thank Janssen for his part in bringin' you here."

Jasper wanted to laugh at the irony. Instead, he gave the profusely sweating politician a grave smile. "Well then, Alderman, when you p-put it that way, I'll be honored to offer my assistance."

CHAPTER 5

Jasper felt like a performing bear as he knelt beside the dead body to conduct a cursory examination. There were at least a dozen people standing about: perhaps six patrolmen, several passing pedestrians who'd stopped to watch, and—if he was not mistaken—three working women.

They were in the rubbish alley behind Madam Solange's, and all eyes had been fastened on Jasper since the moment he'd arrived.

In addition to O'Malley—a pale, skinny young man with protruding ears and a faint Irish accent—there were four other patrolmen in a clutch, muttering to one another while O'Malley eyed them with open hostility.

Their detective was a man named Featherstone, an English surname, but the detective was clearly a product of America. There was a palpable sense of dislike between all the patrolmen—regardless of national origin—and the detective. If body posture was anything to go by—and Jasper believed it was—Featherstone might be more despised than the interloping son of an English duke. At least for the moment.

Alard Janssen lay on his back in the rubbish. His expression was one of openmouthed shock, but his eyes were closed. Jasper assumed that somebody other than Janssen had closed them. He was dressed in expensive evening garments, which were hacked and bloody on one side. Jasper didn't see a hat, gloves, or cane.

Janssen was a man who'd enjoyed rich food and too little exertion, and his paunch was significant. Jasper figured him for sixteen or seventeen stone. In addition to his weight, the blood vessels on his nose and cheeks exhibited the sort of bloom associated with heavy, sustained alcohol consumption.

His necktie had been stretched out and his shirt collar was half torn off, revealing ligature marks and abrasions that looked to have been made by rough rope. Jasper took out his handkerchief and plucked a few fibers from the swollen wound, tucking the folded handkerchief back into his pocket. There was a large swelling over the larynx, which had been crushed.

There were fingertip-size bruises and shallow scratches around the neck wound, meaning either the killer or the victim had grabbed the area. Flesh beneath Janssen's nails indicated that he must have struggled.

Jasper bent low to sniff Janssen's mouth. The odor of death was strong, but—

He frowned and took another deep breath, then another. There was a subtle sweetness, a smell so slight that he might have missed it had it not been an odor that sped his heart rate.

"Why's he doin' that?" one of the prostitutes—who couldn't have been more than thirteen or fourteen—asked O'Malley, who stood beside her looking not much older himself.

His peach-fuzzed cheeks turned a brilliant red. "You hush up, Annie Holiday," he hissed.

Jasper checked Janssen's eyelids, neck, and jaw before taking the dead man's arm and continuing his exam. Next he removed one shoe, then began at the knee and worked down to Janssen's toes. When he'd finished, he turned to the young patrolman.

"Please m-move everyone *all* the way out of the alley." There was grumbling and foot-dragging, but soon there was just Dell, Featherstone, and the uniformed policemen.

Jasper unbuttoned Janssen's trousers.

"Good God!" Dell gasped. "What the hell are—"

"If you are squ-squ-squeamish, I recommend you g-go with the others," Jasper said sharply.

The alderman gaped but remained where he was.

Jasper pulled up Janssen's shirt and loosened the tape on his drawers before pulling them down far enough to examine the dead man's stomach.

"Wh-what are you looking for?" Dell asked.

Jasper smiled slightly at the other man's stammer. "Signs of p-putrefaction, which are first v-visible in the lower right abdominal area." Blood had pooled beneath the skin on the front of Janssen's body, which indicated that he'd either died on his front or been put in that position soon after.

Once Jasper finished examining the rest of Janssen's chest, he turned to Featherstone. "Help me t-turn the body." The detective blanched but moved quickly enough. Once Janssen was facedown, Jasper lifted his shirt and coats and examined his back.

"What are you looking for now?" Dell had inched closer but wrinkled his nose and stepped back when he noticed that Janssen had soiled his trousers.

"Marks that would indicate h-how he was killed, in what p-position, perhaps ab-brasions." There was bruising on the mid-back that was likely from the killer's knees, perhaps as he pulled on the garrote. Judging by the height of the bruise and Janssen's own height—approximately six feet—the killer would have to be at least five foot seven, and likely taller, if he'd made the marks while standing. Then again, the marks might have come from the murderer kneeling on Janssen once he'd brought the man to the ground.

Janssen's head was covered in thick brown hair; there was no swelling or blood.

The last thing Jasper examined was Janssen's side. The shirt had been so badly shredded that strips of fabric were buried in the wound, some of the blood dry and hard. It took several minutes to carefully pull the cloth away. When he peeled back the last piece of jagged material, his eyes widened: in addition to one, two, three, four stab wounds, it looked as if a chunk of flesh had been removed.

He rocked back on his heels, a memory from the war—before Balaclava—slamming into him. It was just after the Battle of Alma and Jasper had caught a soldier cutting off the ears of a dead enemy soldier.

"It's a souvenir, sir," the man had said, apparently insensible to the horror of his actions.

The murderer took a souvenir from Janssen.

He tucked that thought away for later examination.

"Good God!" Dell said, staring at the section of large intestine that bulged out of the wound. "Is he *missing* flesh?"

Jasper ignored the question and visualized the scene. The killer would have come at him from behind and dropped the rope around his neck, throttling him into unconsciousness or near enough before releasing hold of the garrote and then stabbing him. Two weapons were used: did that mean two assailants or a very dexterous killer?

He looked up from the body. "When was he f-found?"

Featherstone glanced at Dell as if for guidance.

"Don't look at *me*, you idiot." Dell was green around the gills and keeping his gaze assiduously turned away from the dead body. "This is exactly why Lord Lightner was brought here—to instruct. You should listen, learn, and obey his orders. In fact, just consider him your superior from now on."

Featherstone's mouth pulled down into a mutinous frown as he turned to Jasper. "Uh, about an hour ago, my Lordship."

"You *fool*! It's *my* lord or *Your* Lordship. Don't you know—"

"Inspector Lightner will be sufficient," Jasper said, pushing to his feet and wincing slightly as he straightened his gammy leg. He glanced up and down the alley; it was narrow and ran the length of the block, rubbish bins near each door. "This seems a very b-busy area—how is it that a body could go unnoticed d-during daylight hours in such a p-p-public place?"

Featherstone appeared stunned—either by the question or by his stammer—and then his lip began to curl; ah, so it was the stammer.

Jasper was accustomed to this expression from some men. Indeed, he'd had to fight half the boys at school before the torment ceased. Bullies didn't disappear with age, and even as an adult, he'd encountered outright laughter and derision.

If he needed to establish authority among brutish men, he was prepared to mete out the necessary discipline. He suspected, from the jeering expression on Featherstone's face, that the detective would likely require such discipline if they continued working together.

"Detective Featherstone?" he repeated when the other man failed to respond.

Featherstone looked from Jasper to Dell, and Jasper could see he'd forgotten the question.

"Well, answer him, you fool—he asked why the body was only discovered an hour ago."

"It was hidden under those." Featherstone pointed to a pile of pallets lying haphazardly near the building.

Jasper went for a closer look. There was a great deal of dried blood on the filthy cobbles, certainly enough to assume Janssen had been killed there. There was also a smear of blood where somebody had dragged the body. He glanced at the detective and pointed to a door with the number fifteen carved into the wood. "Is this th-the brothel's door?"

"Er, no, sir. This is a dressmaker's. That's Solange's." He pointed to the door closest to the street, number fourteen.

"Who found him?"

"Er—"

"Me! 'Twas me that found 'im, Your Lordship." The speaker was one of the smallest adults Jasper had ever seen. Dark eyes peered out beneath eyelids as wrinkled and papery as onion skins. The man spoke with the distinctive accent of a Londoner—somebody from the rookeries, by the sound of him. Despite the heat, he was wrapped in layer upon layer of mismatched clothing, his scrawny neck poking out of a collar twice as large.

"What's your n-name?"

The diminutive Londoner threw out his chest and straightened to his full height, which did not add much. "Jemmy Hart, my lord."

"Am I correct in b-believing we are countrymen, Mr. Hart?"

Jemmy grinned, and it was a dreadful sight, his teeth blackened and tilted like headstones in a very old graveyard. "Aye, my lord. Lonnon born an' bred." He blinked around him, as if confused how he'd ended up in this alley.

"You f-found this g-gentleman?" Jasper asked.

"Aye, covered up 'e was. The pallets is usually stacked, so I fought mebbe somfing was 'idden beneef 'em."

"Who t-turned him over?"

"'Ow do you know someone turned 'im?" Mr. Hart asked.

Featherstone half raised one hand. "I did."

"And are you the person who moved the b-body over here?"

"Yes, Your Lordship."

"Why?"

Featherstone blinked. "I beg your pardon?"

"Why did you m-move him?"

"Er"—he shrugged—"I dunno, my lord."

Barely audible snickers turned the detective's cheeks a brick red, and he glared around at the assembled men, daring the culprits to do it again.

Jasper took pity on him. "In the f-future, leave the body where you find it until the scene can b-be thoroughly examined."

"'E looks like that ovver bloke," the rag-and-bone man piped up.

"What?" Jasper and Dell spoke at the same time.

Jemmy looked from Jasper to Dell and hunched his shoulders under the latter's glare.

"What other m-man, Mr. Hart?" Jasper asked.

The alderman answered before Hart. "He's an old drunk who doesn't know what he's sayin', my lord. They already got the killer in those cases."

"What c-cases?" Jasper asked Dell.

"There were two murders a few months back—two wealthy gentlemen, Wilbur Sealy and Felix Dunbarton. Both were killed by a crazy whore."

"How were they m-m-murdered?"

"They *caught* the killer, my lord." Dell took a step toward Hart. "Tell him, you old fool. Tell him you don't know what you're—"

"Mr. D-Dell?" Jasper spoke softly.

Dell stopped mid-rant. "Er, yes?"

"I suspect my valet will be concerned when we d-do not arrive at the hotel in g-good time," he lied. "P-perhaps you might check in on him at the Astor? I c-c-could meet you there for a drink—after I've finished here."

Even in the dimness of the alley, Jasper could see the man's pupils flare at the mention of alcohol. Dell paused as if he were giving the matter some thought, but Jasper knew he'd already made up his mind. Between his desire to spread the grisly news of Janssen's murder and his need for a drink, he was already halfway to the Astor House in his head.

His tongue darted out like a lizard's and moistened his lips. "I wouldn't want to leave you here without—"

Jasper motioned to the clutch of policemen, whose eyes were bouncing back and forth between them as if they were watching a game of racquets. "One of these g-gentlemen can see I return to the hotel s-safely. Can they not, Detective?"

"What?" Featherstone blurted, looking unhappy at being dragged back into the discussion.

"Yes, of course they can, my lord," Dell answered for the other man, already sold on the notion of a drink in a comfortable bar rather than standing about in a filthy alley with a corpse.

Jasper looked at the detective. "P-Perhaps you might notify the c-coroner?"

Featherstone bristled. "I sent word immediately."

"Ah, good. Well, then you can stop b-by the station and explain the situation to Captain Davies. Tell him I'll c-come by with a pre-liminary report when I'm f-f-finished here."

Once again Dell answered for Featherstone. "Yes, yes, that's an excellent idea, my lord. Come along, Detective, His Lordship has things well in hand here."

Jasper waited until the obstacles to his questioning moved off down the alley before turning to the remaining patrolmen, all of whom were staring at Jasper's Russian-silver Venus de Milo–topped walking stick.

"Patrolman O'Malley."

The young man startled. "Er, yes, my lord?"

Jasper gestured to the growing crowd at the mouth of the alley. Half of them were craning their necks to get a glimpse of the body while the other half were gawking at Jasper. "There are some p-potential witnesses who require interviewing."

"Er, witnesses?"

"Put two p-patrolmen to guard the entrance to the alley and instruct them to k-keep away onlookers. Dispatch the remaining patrolmen to c-canvass the nearby establishments. We w-want to know whether anyone in these businesses was acquainted with the deceased or noted his p-presence over the last twenty-four—n-no, make that forty-eight—hours. If so, at what t-time, who was he with, and so forth."

Jasper could see O'Malley was busy translating his sentence and made a mental note to avoid words like *dispatch* and *canvass* in the future.

He clarified. "F-First, ask if anyone saw Janssen last night."

"Er, today's Sunday, sir; most places won't be open."

Ah, he'd forgotten. "Well, knock on doors and speak t-to who-ever answers."

"Er, yes, sir."

Once the patrolmen were gone, Jasper turned to the toothless lit-tle Londoner. "What didn't you wish to say in f-f-front of Mr. Dell?"

Hart cupped a hand to his ear, his rheumy old eyes glinting. "What's that, milord?"

Jasper sighed and extracted the handful of silver that Paisley had put in his pocket that morning—mainly Spanish, Dutch, and English coins. Foreign coins, he'd been told, were more welcome than paper money in most places in America. He handed Hart a worn Spanish one-quarter real.

Hart's toothless grin assured him he'd chosen correctly, and the man squirreled the coin away in the recesses of his ragged coat.

"Have d-done with your theatrics and tell me what you know."

"There was two other rich gents kilt with a knife."

"And b-both killed by st-st-stabbing and garroting?" Surely the city would be in an uproar if wealthy businessmen were being slain in the streets?

"I dunno anyfing about the first bloke. I found the second before they brung him down to the Points."

Jasper held up a hand. "Wait. Who is *they*?"

"Dunno, do I? I was just foraging like and I found 'im."

"Who was this m-man?"

"A bloke named Dunbarton."

"And you say somebody m-moved Mr. D-Dunbarton?"

"I sawr him, din't I? Big as loif be'ind the dress shop, mebbe 'arf a block from this narsty French cow's ploice."

Jasper blinked. "You mean you f-found the body near *here*?"

"Aye, just down there." He jabbed a finger toward the door Featherstone had said belonged to the brothel.

"Show me." He followed Hart down the alley.

★   ★   ★

"It was roight 'ere." Hart pointed to the pile of detritus stacked up almost as high as the bin.

Jasper called over the two patrolmen guarding the alley entrance. "P-Please move all debris to there." He pointed to the other side of the alley.

"What did the p-police say when you told them the b-body had been m-moved?" he asked Hart while the patrolmen worked.

"I din't tell 'em, did I?"

Jasper sighed; of course he hadn't. "Describe what you saw."

"'E were lyin' tucked in beside the bin, and rubbish was built up loik and blocking the body from the street."

"Now wh-when was this, exactly?"

Hart scratched his head. "I don't remember just now."

Jasper could check actual dates in the police files. "G-Go on."

"The best places to get prime goods is these few alleys." He pointed at one of the battered doors past the brothel. "Roight there is where the Kemp sisters do their evil work."

"Evil work?"

"Aye, they be baby killers." Hart's twisted expression was one of loathing. "They charges premium prices, and only the better sort can afford 'em. They throws out some of the best rubbish. When I passed by Kemps', they'd not brung out anyfing, so I went on and did be'ind all the swells' shops." He made a zigzagging motion with one hand to show the path of his labors. "*Nuffink!*" he said. "So I was jess comin' out be'ind one o' the toff shops." He cut Jasper a quick glance when he recalled he was speaking to a toff. "Any'ow, I sawr 'im, as bold as you please."

Jasper took another coin out of his pocket. "D-Describe every detail."

Hart's eyes were riveted to the coin. "'E were facedown, not faceup, loik the swell today." He pointed to the spot the patrolmen had just cleared. "'E were lyin' between the bin and the brick wall. At first I saw only 'is feet stickin' out. Then the rest o' 'im—'is bloody, cut-up shirt."

"He h-had no vest or coat?"

"Nah, 'e did, but they was roight slashed to bits. Blood all over 'im—too much to bovver wiff takin' most of 'is kit. I was troiyin' to get 'is shoes off when a couple o' coppers came along." He paused and shook his head. "A roight shame it was, leavin' them shoes."

"*Policemen* f-found the body—*here*?"

"Aye, two coppers."

"B-But you said the body was d-discovered in Five P-Points?"

Hart shrugged. "'Swot I read."

Jasper studied his diminutive witness, who was squirming and anxious. He'd have to come back to that later.

"What time d-did you find him?"

"Mebbe free or four o'clock."

"What did he look l-like?"

Hart's brow furrowed. "'E looked dead."

Jasper almost laughed. "But what did his *b-body* look like—the injuries?"

"Oh. Lots o' blood. So much I couldn't see much o' 'is back." He shifted until his back was to Jasper and reached a hand to his side. "'E'd been cut about 'ere." He drew a horizontal line just below the ribs. "There was innards pokin' out."

"You said you r-ran off without t-taking anything?"

Hart's expression was so innocent that Jasper knew he was guilty—of *something*.

Jasper eyed the little Londoner hard.

"What, gov?" Even beneath the dirt, his face turned red.

"T-Tell me the truth."

Jemmy swallowed noisily.

"Mr. Hart, d-do you realize how it l-looks? You discovering not one, but *two* d-dead bodies?"

Hart's jaw sagged low enough to graze the cobbles. "You ain't sayin' I *kilt* these blokes?" He flung up his hands. "Whoiy the bleedin' 'ell would I tell you about it if I 'ad?"

"Then t-tell me what you took."

"Awright, awright! I took his 'at and 'is wallet."

Jasper had to admit he'd not been expecting that. He'd suspected Hart had taken the shoes and coat—but the rest? Why hadn't the killer robbed him?

Because it was murder, not a robbery.

"What was in the w-wallet?"

"A couple dollars."

Jasper decided to leave that particular lie be. "What else d-did you take?"

Hart gave him a look that would have done a martyr proud. "I took 'is coat—'e wouldn't be needin' it, would 'e? Besides, it was all bloody and cut; I barely got anyfing for it."

"Anything else? What about his w-watch—jewelry?"

His eyes slid back to Jasper and then quickly away.

"Mr. Hart?"

"Foin." He gave a defeated huff. "I prigged a ring wiff a red stone. Just a small one." He held up a thumb and forefinger to demonstrate. "An' 'is watch. But I 'ardly got any money out o' the watch 'cause the face were all bunged up."

"Bunged up?"

"Loik mebbe 'e squarshed it when 'e fell."

"You t-took his hat, w-wallet, coat, ring, and watch. Anything else?" Not that Jasper imagined the man had much else of value on him.

"No! I swears on me honor."

"W-Was his body still warm?"

Jemmy gave him a look of pure horror. "Crikey! 'At's a bit gruesome, ain't it?"

"Mr. Hart."

"Awright." He held up both hands. "Naw, 'e was cold."

"Was it easy to t-take the ring from his f-finger?"

"Yeah, 'e weren't stiff-loik."

"And you say the b-body was later discovered in Five P-Points?"

"Aye, in Murderer's Alley."

Jasper frowned at the improbable street name.

"Why you lookin' at me loik that? I din't name it."

"How long after *you* f-found the body here was it discovered in this M-M-Murderer's Alley?"

"Er, not for another day."

"You mean that m-morning?"

"No. I mean the day after."

"You're t-telling me somebody kept the body for a f-full *day*?" He didn't bother to keep the skepticism from his tone.

"I ain't sayin' nuffink but what happened."

"And you d-don't recall the date?"

Hart scowled. "It so 'appens I *do*. It was the noight Bill Morissey fought Nate McDaniel. April somefing," he added, scratching his head.

Jasper extracted a coin from his pocket and held it up. "If I w-want to see you again, where will I f-find you?"

"I ain't got no reglear 'ome, but most nights I go to O'Reilly's saloon."

Jasper handed Hart the coin and waited until the old man had scarpered before turning back to the alley.

Based on the bloodstain, Dunbarton had not come very far in before he was murdered—just a few steps from the brothel's back door. Jasper walked the length of the alley; there were six doors and multiple rubbish bins, meaning the alley was utilized by several businesses. Assuming the old man wasn't completely off his nut, had one of these business owners paid to move Dunbarton's body? If so, why not move this one too?

He noticed O'Malley hovering a few feet away and motioned him closer.

"How g-goes the questioning?"

"Nobody answered anywhere but the house on the end. The maid got the owner, a Mrs. Kemp, and she said nobody came to the house last night. I talked to a few of Solange's girls, and they said none of them was with him." O'Malley hesitated. "But there's hardly any girls there right now."

"B–Because of the Sunday closure laws?"

"Er, well, those don't exactly matter here." He chewed his lip and shrugged.

Right, those laws wouldn't be enforced at the better establishments. For all Jasper knew, the mayor himself might be lounging about in the brothel as they spoke.

"I'd l–like to speak with the owner."

"The girls said Solange has been up in Boston and isn't due back till tomorrow."

Is *that* why the body hadn't been moved?

"I w–want you to go back inside and t–talk to *everyone*. Find out who knew J–Janssen and the l–last time he was here, whom he s–saw, that sort of thing. D–Do you know some of these other officers w–well?"

"Aye, sir."

"Ch–Ch–Choose one you trust to accompany you and be thorough. Can I t–trust you to d–do that, Mr. O'Malley?"

The boy bristled with pride. "Yes, sir."

"Tell me what you know about the m–murders you mentioned b–before."

"Er, murders?"

Jasper guessed this annoying habit of repeating everything he said was O'Malley's way of gaining himself a little more time to consider a question. Or perhaps he was just stupid.

Either way, one must work with the tools one is given, Jasper.

Not only sound advice, but critical for his current position, where he knew nobody and nothing. Jasper forced himself to wait patiently.

"Uh, yes?" O'Malley said after a long pause.

"Is that a question, P–Patrolman?"

O'Malley flushed to the roots of his sandy blond hair. "No, my lord. Er, that'd be Wilbur Sealy and Felix Dunbarton. Both those cases were in the Sixth, 'cause they were murdered inside the Points. They got the killer, but she hung herself before she could swing—a whore." His downy cheeks reddened. "Beggin' your pardon, my lord."

Where on earth had these men gotten the idea that aristocrats would be embarrassed by the mention of brothels and whores?

"I d–don't suppose you know who the d–detective was?"

"Uh. Well, it happens I do, my lord. It was Hieronymus Law."

Jasper took a moment to absorb the rather remarkable name.

"The thing is, my lord—"

"Yes?" Jasper prodded.

"Law ain't on the force no more. Er, rumor is he got caught in some trouble over that case, and when McElhenny caught him, Law punched him in the face."

"McElhenny is his w–watch commander?"

"Aye—his captain."

"D–Do you know the source of the disagr–gr–greement?" Jasper frowned; dammit but he was bloody tongue-tied today!

O'Malley—his brow deeply furrowed—was too taken with his own thoughts to have noticed. "I heard Law was takin' money to hide evidence and Captain found him out. I couldn't say myself—'cept I know he's a prickly bastard who keeps to himself—Law that is, not the cap'n," he hastily amended.

"Was this recently?"

"Not long after the whore hung herself. My cousin is at the Sixth, and he said nobody's seen Law since he was put in the Tombs."

The Tombs. Even in Britain people knew of the infamous New York jail that swallowed live men and spit out corpses. And now it seemed Jasper might have to visit the place if he wanted to speak to the improbably named Hieronymus Law.

But a trip to the prison could come later, if necessary, after he'd read the police files.

Before he did anything more on this case, he needed to visit the Eighth Precinct and pay his respects to Captain Davies, his new superior.

CHAPTER 6

"You must be Lord Lightner," the officer manning the Eighth Precinct front desk stated, unknowingly increasing Jasper's rank by an order of magnitude.

"Inspector Lightner will s–suffice."

"I'm Sergeant Billings, the one who keeps things runnin' round here," he said, a slight smile on his grizzled face.

So, here was the man loyal to the Metropolitan Police but working under a captain whose allegiance was not so clear. Jasper was impressed that he was still smiling.

"Captain Davies is expecting you, Inspector. You can go on up to the top floor."

"Which office?"

"Just follow the yellin'."

When Jasper reached the third-floor landing, he followed the sound of ranting, which led him to an enormous office at the southwest corner of the building. A short, stout man was pacing while shouting. His back was toward the corridor, so he missed Jasper's entrance.

The recipient of his anger, Detective Featherstone, met Jasper's eyes briefly through the office window, his cheeks flaming.

The ranter spun on his heel, spied Jasper, and snapped something at the detective, who shot to his feet and darted out of the room quicker than a sewer rat up a drain.

"Cap'n wants to see you," Featherstone said as he hurried past.

"Thank you, Detective," Jasper called after him. He glanced around the small anteroom for someplace to leave his hat and cane, but there was none.

Captain Davies was standing with his fists on his hips, staring out the window, when Jasper entered his office.

He turned and gave Jasper a look of thinly veiled dislike. "I'm sorry I wasn't at the harbor to greet you when you arrived."

Davies did not sound sorry. In fact, he sounded extremely hostile. He also sounded like a Welshman, although his accent was faint.

"Alderman D-Dell g-greeted me and was quite helpful."

Davies snorted and gestured to one of the chairs across from his desk before dropping into his own. "I'll just bet he was. I wouldn't hang your hopes on him being a trustworthy ally; the man is as slippery as an eel. So, Billings tells me that he decided to rope you into an investigation ten minutes after entering our fair city."

Jasper balanced his hat in his lap and propped his stick against the arm of his chair. "It was longer than t-ten minutes, sir—almost fifteen."

Davies ignored his attempt at humor and picked up a piece of paper lying on his desk. "This is an *order* from White Street assigning you here." He crumpled it into a wad and then threw it on the floor. "The only reason you're sitting here right now is because the mayor happens to agree about putting you under my supervision." He lifted another piece of paper and crumpled that one too. "This might be the first and only time Tallmadge and Wood will ever agree on anything, *my lord*. As much as I'd like to tell them both to go to hell, I'm going to knuckle under, but I don't have to *like* it. Do you get my meaning?"

Jasper thought his meaning was perfectly clear. "Yes, sir."

"Let's get one thing straight right now, *my lord*."

Jasper lifted his eyebrows.

"I don't want you here."

"I've d-deduced as much, Captain."

Rather than pacify Davies, his mild words appeared to provoke him. "I know you answer to your home secretary and get your pay directly from Albany." He raked Jasper's person with narrow, hate-filled eyes, his gaze lingering on his silver-handled walking stick. "Not that I expect you need the pitiful salary an honest working man earns." His mouth twisted into an ugly sneer. "So that means I can't fire you or send you packing."

It didn't seem like a question so Jasper didn't reply.

"I'm not stupid—I'm fully aware you wouldn't be sitting here in all your splendor, plaguing me, if there weren't some powerful forces at work to get you here. Although whether you'll *stay* here is another matter. Janssen was the governor's mouthpiece when it came to training a new, *improved*, scientific detective department. But now he's gone. Seems like someone decided to kill off one of your most ardent supporters." Davies's smirk said he wouldn't lose much sleep over the matter.

"That is a trifle . . . c-concerning," Jasper said.

"I couldn't have said it better myself. Luckily we've got *you* here to solve our problems."

"Thank you, sir."

The humor drained from the captain's face. "While you are under *my* roof—which hopefully won't be long—there's one thing you'd better understand, *my lord*."

"Yes, Captain?"

"*I* am in charge here. Not the council, not the board of bloody aldermen, not Tallmadge and his bloody police commissioners, not your powerful friends in Albany, and definitely not *you*."

"Understood, sir."

Davies's scowl deepened. "You might be the son of a bloody duke in England, but over here we got rid of the monarchy, and nobody is interested in having it back. If you think you can go throwing your aristocratic weight around like your father does in Ceredigion—" Davies gave an ugly cackle at the look on Jasper's face—no doubt shock—at the mention of the Duke of Kersey's Welsh estate.

Davies nodded although Jasper hadn't said a word. "Yes, it's a small world, isn't it?—at least in Britain where men like your father own a big chunk of it. And that's where I lived before I made my escape, my lord—bowing and scraping from the time I could walk and living under the thumb of the bloody Duke of Kersey."

Jasper could have told Davies that was something they had in common, but he doubted the angry Welshman would be sympathetic.

"So, you listen to me, my—" Davies uttered an incomprehensible jumble of consonants that Jasper assumed was both Welsh and very insulting. "There is only one boss in this station house"—he jabbed himself in the chest with a thick finger—"and it's *me*." He was red-faced and shaking, a vein pulsing insistently in his temple. "Now, Featherstone tells me Janssen's death is like two cases handled by the Sixth. It's our custom here to transfer cases that might be part of another precinct's investigation."

"Understood, sir. I'll write up my p-preliminary notes and observations and t-turn—"

"No." The captain punctuated the word by slamming his open palm down on his desk, his jaw working from side to side as if he were gnawing a particularly tough chunk of gristle. "No," he said again, shaking his head, a sly smile curving his lips. "If this is some new lunatic out killing, then the case is ours. If it's the same lunatic who killed Sealy and Dunbarton? Well, then this case seems to have been tailor-made for *you*, my lord. It will be the perfect opportunity to demonstrate your *superior* English detecting abilities."

Davies was no fool; this case would make the person handling it profoundly unpopular within the entire force, not just the Sixth Precinct, which might very well have arrested an innocent woman and driven her to suicide.

Yes, this was the perfect case to give to somebody you despised and hoped to get rid of. If Jasper failed this little test, he'd be on a boat back to England before you could say Jack Robinson. With his tail tucked between his legs.

Then don't fail, Jasper.

He smiled at the furious man across from him. "I'm flattered by your t-trust in me, Captain. From what I know thus far—which is v-very little—there are s-s-several similarities between Janssen's murder and the t-two other gentlemen you mentioned."

"Is that so, my lord?" David asked with poorly concealed mockery. "Why, you *are* a fast learner; here only a few hours and you've already determined that. I suppose that means you'll have to pay a visit to my colleague in the Sixth—Captain McElhenny—as he had the pleasure of supervising those cases. You might want to have a care about how you broach the subject; I'm sure he won't be happy with any imputations that he bungled things, arrested the wrong person, and drove her to suicide." Davies gave an ugly laugh. "Don't let anything he says offend you; I'm afraid he lacks my civility and polish." He laced his fingers together and rested them on his rounded stomach, smiling like a man who'd consumed far too much at the dinner table but couldn't resist one last bite. "You'll want to be careful wandering around Five Points, my lord. It would be easy for a man like you to lose his way. I'd hate to have to tell your esteemed father you'd been hurt. Or worse."

Jasper wondered what Davies would say if he knew the duke would not only welcome such an eventuality but probably offer generous compensation to the person who brought it about.

The captain's smile grew larger—and more unpleasant—when Jasper failed to comment.

"I'm sure neither our savage streets nor our pitiful criminals will pose much of a problem for a man with *your* formidable skills and illustrious background."

"That's very k-kind of you to say, sir. And thank you for the opportunity to w-work on such an interesting—and challenging—case. Mr. Dell indicated you would have a list of c-candidates for me?"

Even from several feet away, Jasper could see the other man's pupils shrink to black specks. His expression—almost gleeful a moment earlier—was instantly truculent. "*Alderman* Dell has no right promising you a damned thing. I already *have* detectives who know what they're about. I won't have you bothering them or hindering their work. If you want somebody to tag along on your expensive bloody coattails, you can take one of the patrolmen. Hell, take two—and take the goddamned street sweeper while you're at it. Take anyone you want—just not one of my detectives. Perhaps you might ask *McElhenny* to loan you one of his detectives, since the man probably—*rightfully*—believes this should be his case." Davies sat back in his chair with a watchful, expectant air: he'd thrown down his gauntlet, and now it was Jasper's turn.

"Is there a d-desk I might use?"

Davies looked almost comically disappointed by Jasper's refusal to rise to the bait. He waved a hand dismissively. "Ask Billings; he manages such things."

Jasper stood.

"Oh, and *my lord*?"

"Yes, Captain?"

"You'd better go and inform Janssen's widow of his untimely demise." He smirked. "Shouldn't be terribly difficult for you—she's *your* sort of people, after all."

"Thank you, sir."

"Now get out," Davies muttered, his attention back on his desk.

Jasper shut the door behind him and smiled as he pulled on his gloves. He almost felt sorry for the man he'd just left. The captain had been hoping to humiliate or goad Jasper into quitting and leaving, but what the Welshman failed to understand was that the Duke of Kersey's servants and tenants weren't the only people he'd treated like serfs. Indeed, His Grace had saved the lion's share of his malice for his own son.

Surviving childhood with the duke had been very much like protecting a castle from invaders. Over the years Jasper had become an expert at repelling attacks, repairing breaches, and strengthening defenses while he awaited his father's next offensive. Now, in his thirties, his castle walls were impregnable. Thanks to the duke, nothing—and nobody—could ever get close enough to hurt him.

Davies had been insulting, combative, and rude—three behaviors Jasper abhorred. They were also three behaviors guaranteed to bring out his contrarianism. If Davies had wanted to be rid of him, he'd gone about it the wrong way.

He had no intention of allowing Davies, or anyone else, to send him back to England with his "tail between his legs."

CHAPTER 7

A man dressed in the clothing of an upper servant opened the door to the Janssen house, anxiety pouring off him in waves even though his expression was blander than gruel.

"I'm Detective Inspector Lightner with the M-Metropolitan Police." Jasper handed over one of his private calling cards. "I need to speak to Mrs. Janssen."

The servant's eyes widened as he took in the name on the card. "This is about Mr. Janssen?"

Jasper must have shown his surprise, because the man waved him into the foyer, where he picked up a single sheet of paper, a "special edition" from one of the penny newspapers that seemed to litter the city—both literally and figuratively.

MILLIONAIRE ALARD JANSSEN BRUTALLY MURDERED!

New York City had industrious newspapermen; it was barely three hours since he'd been called to examine the body.

"Butters, who is it?"

Jasper glanced up to find a tiny woman descending the curving marble staircase. She looked as if she'd just stepped out of an eighteenth-century portrait depicting Puritans. Her plain white bonnet covered her hair entirely, and her high-necked, long-sleeved black crepe gown had a full skirt, but the crinoline beneath it was practical rather than fashionable. A capacious white apron ran from her neck to the hem of her gown. The only hint of color was her eyes, which were a startling blue.

The yards of black crepe rustled like the surf as she came floating toward them, her glare directed at Jasper. "If you are from the newspapers, you'd better—"

"Oh, no, madam, please—" Butters said in a tone of mortification, brandishing Jasper's card. "This is the new English policeman—Lord Jasper Lightner."

She snatched the card from his hand and stared at it. When she looked up, her smile was unpleasant. "The duke's son, come to the colonies to solve all our problems. If you're here to share the ill tidings, you're too late. I'm here to offer my assistance to Zuza, who has no idea of the frenzy this will create. I'm Mrs. Dunbarton."

Jasper frowned, not sure he'd heard her correctly. "You're—"

"You heard correctly; Felix Dunbarton was my husband."

He opened his mouth to speak, but she wasn't finished.

"Suzanne Janssen is a close friend of mine." She thrust her small, bare hand toward him as if she were lobbing an explosive device. She squeezed his fingers hard enough to grind the bones together and then pumped his hand up and down.

"A pleasure to m-m-meet you, ma'am."

Her eyes might be a celestial blue, but the expression in them was pragmatic. They raked over Jasper's person with cool calculation. "My, my, my. I'd heard you were pretty, but the rumors didn't do you justice, Lord Jasper."

He recoiled at her cold mockery but smiled rather than rising to the bait.

Her own lips curled into something that should have resembled a smile but didn't. "Handsome, wealthy, *and* good-natured. What a blessing for American women that you stammer—otherwise you'd be far too perfect. Don't worry; I daresay such a small flaw shan't deter my countrywomen from shamelessly flinging themselves at your feet."

Jasper was reminded of Captain Davies. But at least the Welshman had good reason to hate him; why the devil did *this* woman loathe him so vehemently?

"I f-feel like there is a compliment hidden in your words s-somewhere, Mrs. Dunbarton, so I shall say *thank you*."

She snorted and turned to the butler, who was hovering nearby with an anxious frown. "Put your two biggest servants outside and make sure nobody *else* is admitted. Follow me, my lord." She strode toward the stairs.

Jasper easily kept pace with her far shorter stride, despite her brisk pace. "H-How long have you b-been here?"

"A newspaperman appeared at my front door just after two o'clock to ask my opinion on the recent murder. I daresay he was hoping to catch me unawares."

Jasper had difficulty imagining the small woman in front of him ever being caught unaware.

"I knew poor Zuza would be like a babe in the woods."

"Zuza?"

"Mrs. Janssen."

"She has n-no family here to support her?"

She gave a short bark of laughter. "You mean nobody other than me?"

Well, yes, actually.

Jasper couldn't imagine this harsh, combative woman being much of a comfort to anyone, but it was hardly his place to say so.

When he didn't answer, she said, "No. Her mother and father are on a tour of the Continent, and her only brother died last year. I've sent word to an aunt, but she lives in Boston."

Once they reached the landing, she led him down a long, brightly lighted corridor: no tomfoolery with shrouded mirrors, stopped clocks, and covered windows when Mrs. Dunbarton was in charge.

"I daresay the lack of gloom makes you believe there is a lack of grieving," Mrs. Dunbarton tossed over her shoulder.

Jasper found her ability to know what he was thinking—if not interpret it correctly—rather unnerving.

She stopped in front of a door and glared up at him. She was tiny, her head not reaching his shoulder, yet she gave the impression of being far larger—huge, even.

Jasper prepared for more insults.

"Alard told everyone *all* about you. He was quite proud of his part in bringing you here. Zuza was going to give a dinner for you next week."

"That is v-very kind of her."

"Kindness has nothing to do with it. Zuza prides herself on having the newest frippery before anyone else."

Being referred to as *frippery* was hardly complimentary, but he found himself smiling. She'd already brought up his stammer—which nobody *ever* mentioned in polite society—and impugned his utility as anything other than an attractive ornament in less than ten minutes. What would she say next?

Her eyes narrowed at his lack of reaction, and Jasper saw a hint of an emotion other than hostility in her startlingly blue eyes.

Even without a scowl, she was not a pretty woman. Her narrow, high-bridged nose was too big for her small, round face, and she had thin, tightly compressed lips with perpetually turned-down corners. Yet looking at her was no hardship. Jasper decided it was her *vitality*, for lack of a better word, that drew a person's eye.

Of course, he'd once seen a cobra in North Africa, and that had drawn his eye too.

She turned the chatelaine that hung from a thick gold chain while she stared at him; it was her only jewelry, and fiddling with it was the first sign of nervousness she'd exhibited.

"I hope you'll be the only one coming to question her, Detective Inspector."

Ah, so she did know his proper title.

"I d-don't anticipate anyone else will need to speak with her," he temporized, having no earthly idea what the higher-ups might do. "I c-can request my captain put p-p-patrolmen by the front door to dissuade newspapermen." He could imagine Davies's reaction to *that* request.

"Uniforms would only add to the circus atmosphere. I employ several large footmen who have experience with newspapermen. If Zuza needs them, I'll send them over." She pursed her lips, opened her mouth, and then closed it in an unprecedented gesture of uncertainty. Jasper had known this woman only a few minutes, but he did not imagine she exhibited indecision often.

When she didn't speak, he asked, "Have you heard the c-circumstances of Mr. J-Janssen's death?"

"Yes, the journalist took some relish in relating that news. Obviously, you think this killing is related to Felix's and Wilbur Sealy's deaths." Before Jasper could either confirm or deny her supposition, she snorted and glanced at the watch pinned to the bodice of her gown. "I don't have time for this. If you want to speak to me about Felix, you may call on me."

The invitation surprised him. "Is there a c-convenient time?"

"I don't sit about my house waiting for afternoon callers. If you want to speak to me, you can come to the New Beginnings School for Young Ladies. I am there most days between two and six o'clock."

His mouth twitched at both the whimsical name and her abrupt command.

"You find it amusing that a woman of my class would engage in worthwhile employment, *my lord*?"

"Not at all. It is just that the n-name s-sounds rather utopian."

"Trust a man—an *aristocratic* man—to think a new beginning for young women utopian rather than a basic human right." She turned her scornful gaze away and yanked open the door. "The police have sent their emissary, Zuza. It seems you will be the first to host the matrimonial prize of the year, after all."

The only occupant of the small sitting room was perched on a gold-silk Empire settee.

"Hetty," she chided softly.

Mrs. Janssen was painfully thin and possessed the sort of fragility that elicited the usual masculine urge to protect a delicate female. It crossed his mind that Mrs. Dunbarton had not elicited this chivalric response even though she was far smaller and slighter than her friend.

"Good morning, Lord Jasper." Her hazel eyes were red and swollen, but her smile was brave. "What a welcome to New York you are getting."

"M-My deepest condolences, ma'am. Thank you f-f-for seeing me today."

"Of course. Please." She motioned to the chair across from her.

"I suspect you don't wish for my presence," Mrs. Dunbarton said, again reading Jasper's mind and this time interpreting it correctly. "Ring for me when you've had enough of Lord Jasper, Zuza, and I will show him the door. I will send up tea." She shot Jasper another glare. "See that she eats something."

The door shut with a decisive snap, and Mrs. Janssen smiled wryly. "You mustn't mind Hetty, my lord; she tends to be—"

"Direct?" *Grating, rude, insulting, judgmental, and abrasive?*

Mrs. Janssen's pale cheeks tinted a delicate pink. "Was she terrible to you?"

"N-Not at all," Jasper lied.

"She is a *very* good friend to me." She caught her lower lip and worried it. "I know this will bring up Felix's death all over again—the newspapers, the prying, the whispers. Yet she came; she knows how this feels better than anyone. Well, anyone other than Emma, of course. That's Emmaline Sealy," she added at his look of confusion.

"Y-You are acquainted with Mrs. Sealy?" Jasper wasn't entirely successful in keeping the surprise out of his voice: three dead men whose wives not only knew one another but were friends?

"Oh, not close associates, but we all move in the same circles. I would call Emma more of an acquaintance; she's not like Hetty."

Jasper didn't imagine many people were.

"They are close f-friends?"

"No." Her brow wrinkled, and a flush spread across her pale cheeks. "Actually, I don't know. You'd have to ask Hetty. All I know is that Emma used to volunteer at several of Hetty's charities. But then, so do many others."

"Used to?"

"I haven't seen Emma in some time—not since before her husband's—" She gave a jerky shrug and smoothed her already smooth skirt. Her hands were trembling; she laced them together.

Jasper took out his notebook. "Do you feel you c-could answer a few q-questions about your husband?"

"Of course."

"When did you see him l-last?"

"Not since Friday morning."

"He d-didn't come home last night?"

"I didn't see him." She paused, looked away, and swallowed. "He often spent his Saturday nights . . . elsewhere."

"Do you h-have any idea where?"

She met his gaze squarely. "No."

"H-Had you heard from him at all s-since Friday?"

"Yes, he was to go to a dinner, but he sent a message."

"What d-did the message say?"

"Just that he'd be unable to attend."

"When did you receive this?"

"Yesterday after six."

"D-Do you know why he changed his m-mind?"

"His message didn't say."

"Was that unusual?"

"Not really. He *did* try to be courteous, but he'd lose track of time when something captured his interest."

"On S-Saturdays?"

She frowned. "It might happen on *any* day."

"D-Did he keep an office?"

"No, he used his study for that sort of thing."

"What sort of thing?"

"Oh. I assumed you meant business."

"What sort of b-business?"

"I don't know."

"Can you think of anybody who might have known wh-where he was yesterday evening? F-Friends? His valet?"

"He was between valets, since his last man—who'd been with him for years—finally retired. He'd been using footmen or Butters until he engaged another. As for friends, I don't know many of his acquaintances. Alard and I kept quite different schedules. If we saw each other, it was usually at dinner or some function."

"I d-dislike prying, ma'am, but I have to ask if you were h-having d-difficulties."

She gave a soft, bitter laugh. "We didn't spend enough time together to have difficulties." Her cheeks flushed, and she amended, "We were not close. We just—well, we had our own interests."

Her story was nothing unusual. The upper classes could afford to ignore each other once their marriages began to pall. People like the Bickles had to face each other day in and day out.

"How long were you m-married?"

"Not yet five years."

"D-Do you have children?"

A bolt of pain spasmed across her face. "No."

"Where were you last n-night?"

"I was at a dinner at the Hamilton Fish residence."

"What t-time did you g-get home?"

"There was dancing after dinner, and I believe I finally left around one thirty."

"D-Did you go out again?"

The door opened, and Mrs. Dunbarton stood in the doorway, a girl with a tray beside her. "Put it on the table, Mary."

The room was silent while the maid deposited the tea tray. Mrs. Janssen stared at her hands, and Mrs. Dunbarton stared at Jasper.

She yanked her accusing eyes off him long enough to ask her friend, "Is aught amiss, Zuza? Do you want me to—"

"I'm fine, Hetty," Mrs. Janssen said sharply, and then she tried to smile, but the result was ghastly. "I'm *fine*," she said more calmly.

The two women locked eyes for a long moment, until Mrs. Dunbarton nodded and closed the door.

"You asked if I went out again," she said, not looking up from the tea she was preparing. "The answer is no. I had a dreadful headache. My maid undressed me and brought up warm milk. I went to bed sometime around two thirty." She cut him a quick look. "How do you take your tea?"

"Strong and b-black, please. By the by, I am under st-st-strict orders to m-make sure you eat," he reminded her.

She sighed and placed a single biscuit on her plate.

"May I take a l-look at your h-husband's-study?" he asked as she prepared the cups.

"I'll tell Butters to escort you." She hesitated, then asked, "Do you believe this was a personal killing or a robbery gone bad?"

"D-Did you know of anyone who would w-wish to kill him?"

Instead of replying *no, of course not*, as many people would, she paused. "I want Alard's killer to be apprehended. At the same time, I don't wish to cast aspersions."

"Understood."

"An angry man showed up here not long ago and shoved past poor Butters to gain entrance. He managed to get up *here* before two footmen were summoned to haul him away."

"When w-was this?"

"Perhaps two or three weeks ago. Butters will know."

"Was your h-husband here?"

"No, it was just me."

"Did you s-speak to the man?"

"He had a message for Alard. He said to tell him that the shipment had been promised and paid for and that he would not be held responsible if they did not deliver the goods—I distinctly recall he said 'deliver the goods.' "

"Any idea what h-he meant?"

"No."

"D-Did you tell Mr. Janssen?"

"He said he'd never heard of the man and chided Butters for failing to keep him out."

"I d–don't suppose this man gave his name?"

"Oh, I'm sorry—what a ninny I am. Yes, he certainly did. In fact, he was most emphatic about it—Amos Baker."

Jasper wrote down the name. "Was that all h–he said—'deliver the g–goods'?"

"He was furious—shouting. I was too scared at the time to listen closely, but I do recall one thing he said: 'Tell your husband that his life won't be worth a brass farthing if he tries to worm out of the arrangement.' "

CHAPTER 8

The Tombs

Hieronymus Law's bare feet touched the opposite wall of his cell—although calling it a cell was exaggerating a bit. It was more like a broom closet in a very tiny house. It was barely big enough to hold him, a pile of damp, lice-infested straw, and an overflowing bucket of waste.

Oh, and it also accommodated the three hallucinations who'd recently joined him. At least Hy thought they were hallucinations, not that he was a good judge of such things after living in a pitch-black hole for . . .

Well, he had no idea how long he'd been there. Even if he'd been able to make marks on the rough stone to keep track, he wouldn't be able to *see* them.

The Tombs was the darkest place he'd ever been. Hell could not be any darker than his cell.

The only light that penetrated the dank five-by-five room came once a day along with the guard who took away his empty water can and pushed in a full one. At least that happened most days, but Hy hadn't received a new can of water in a while. Or he didn't think he had.

The Tombs wasn't just dark, it was also damp and bloody cold. It had been built over the old prison, which had been built over the Collect Pond. Because it was a jail, nobody had taken much care draining the pond before building on it. As a result, the stone blocks beneath his ass and back had shifted, twisted, and buckled.

The crippling chill from the old pond seeped up between the gaps and turned the stones to ice. The manacles that held him chained to the wall were like cold fire around his raw, bleeding wrists. His skin was cold, his muscles were cold, and even his bones were cold. He ached with cold—or at least he had until a day ago, maybe two, when he'd begun to feel warm. And then warmer still, until finally he was feverishly hot, but with a cold sweat.

His change in body temperature had coincided with the arrival of his three companions.

The stench, the darkness, the chill, and being cramped and restrained were bad—miserable, in fact—but they were *nothing* to the thirst. He was so thirsty he was beginning to suspect a lack of water was making him hallucinate. Unless the people crowding his cell were real?

Dora McCurdy had been the first to arrive. Hy hadn't thought about her for years—fifteen, at least. He must have been nine or ten when he first saw her. She'd been the first girl he noticed *that way*: gold-red curls, skin like cream, lips pink like the inside of a seashell. She was wearing a pretty yellow dress and seemed unconcerned by the pungent, overflowing bucket of shit and piss that was less than a foot away from where she was standing.

She looked at him with eyes as blue as the sky. "What happened to your clothes, Hy?"

Her question made him remember he was wearing only his flannel drawers—the same pair he'd been wearing for weeks. Heat flooded his neck and face, and he tried to cross his arms over his chest, but they were chained to the wall.

"A modest, godly girl would lower her eyes," Father Thomas chided, taking up at least a quarter of the room with his surplice-shrouded bulk.

Even in the darkness, Hy could feel the weight of the priest's disapproval.

"I always knew you'd end up here, Hieronymus," Father Thomas said, shaking his great shaggy white head sadly.

"Oh, hush up, you!" Only Großmutti Law—who'd died when Hy was seven—would dare speak to a man of God like that. She was a strict Calvinist and had no time for the Catholic Church or its henchmen. It wouldn't have been her choice to send Hy to the orphanage.

"Send you to those papist handmaidens to indoctrinate?" his grandmother demanded, as if Hy had spoken out loud. "I'd sooner you'd been raised by wolves."

The priest bristled at his grandmother's slur and they commenced to brangle, which they did often. As the two of them bickered, Hy couldn't help marveling that even his hallucinations were beyond his control.

He drifted into a shallow, uneasy doze, lulled by the sound of their voices.

"Shhh," Dora hissed, jolting him awake. "Somebody's coming." She was glaring at the others, a dainty finger over her lips.

Hy reckoned that Dora had broken up the argument just in time, as his grandmother looked on the verge of hitting the priest with the dense loaf of German rye she held cradled in her lap.

The next noise he heard was the distinctive rattle of keys and the turning of a heavy tumbler; Dora had good hearing.

The thick wooden door creaked open, and a fireball of pain slammed into his forehead. The light didn't just stab the front of his eyes; it stabbed from behind, the sides, and below, squeezing his head with jagged pincers. He ducked low to cover his face with his forearm but couldn't block all the light or stop the pain.

"P–Put that lantern aside, Mr. Schumer. You're bl–blinding him." The voice was clipped and hard like diamonds, underlaid with confident command. Even discounting the stammer, Hy had never heard an accent quite like it.

His jailer responded to the voice's authority instantly and the light eased, casting the figure in the doorway into relief, the soft glow illuminating his face and person.

If the accent had been one of a kind, the man who owned it was even more unusual. He had a face to match his voice: a defined jaw and chin; high, angular cheekbones with a narrow nose. Below it were thin lips pursed in a frown. He had dark, deep-set eyes that glittered with an emotion Hy wasn't currently equipped to decipher.

He was tall—although still shorter than Hy, who at six and a half feet looked down on most men.

And then there were the man's clothes, which were so blindingly clean and obviously expensive that they appeared obscene in the confines of Hy's filthy, cramped, miserable cell.

He was the most immaculately gloved, hatted, and clothed man Hy had ever seen. And yet he didn't appear girly. No, he was what money would look like if it sprouted arms and legs and wielded a walking stick.

"Go fetch some water," he told the guard, his dark eyes flickering dispassionately over Hy's half-naked body. "And locate a blanket and some c-c-clothing. It's bloody freezing."

"Um, but Lord Lightner, the warden said—"

"My authority comes d-directly from the mayor *and* the commissioners, Mr. Schumer. This p-prisoner's condition is a disgrace, and I daresay heads would r-r-roll—beginning with your *own*—if it were to c-come to anyone's attention that you were st-st-starving him to death."

"But, my lord, I wasn—"

"You may l-leave the lamp."

"But, it's *dark* in here, sir. I might—"

"I d-dislike repeating myself, Mr. Schumer. Are you going to m-make me do something I do not l-like?" He'd not raised his voice. If anything, it had become softer. His profile, which was limned by the light behind him, was like something from an ancient coin: hard and unyielding.

"All right, all right, Yer Lordship—I'm goin'. But it'll take a while," Schumer grumbled, his voice fading along with the slow shuffle of his feet.

"Good afternoon, Mr. L-Law. I'm Detective Inspector Lightner. I wonder if I could have a few m-moments of your time?"

Hy could only stare in slack-jawed wonder.

The tall, broad-shouldered shadow leaned toward him. "Are you c-conscious, Mr. Law?"

Hy looked at his three companions, hoping for guidance. But, for once, they were silent.

"Are—" Hy cleared his dry, raw throat, wincing at the pain and swallowing the metallic tang of blood. "Are you real?"

The man—Lightner—dropped to his haunches, his quick movements stirring the sour, reeking air of the cell. Hy caught the faint smell of perfume.

Dora giggled. "Not perfume, silly—*cologne*."

"Yes, Mr. Law," Lightner said. "I'm r-real." A hand—gloved in cool, butter-soft leather—landed on his shoulder and gave a light, reassuring squeeze before disappearing.

Hy hadn't realized until that moment just how alone he'd been—for how long? Weeks? Months?

"How—" Hy started, but his throat was too dry and the words became stuck.

"You shouldn't speak, Mr. Law. W-Wait until the guard brings water." He stood up, making a small sound of discomfort when his knees cracked. He surveyed the cell, the nostrils of his aquiline nose flaring before he fixed his thoughtful gaze on Hy. "I d-daresay you are wondering how l-l-long you've been in here." His thin lips twisted into a smile that lacked humor. "The record of your entry has been l-lost—like so many things concerning you," he added cryptically. "But as far as I've been able to d-discern, you've been in the Tombs almost eight w-weeks—since the day you, er, struck your c-captain. According to the g-guard, you've been m-m-moved several times since then and have been in *this* cell for less than t-two weeks. Mr. Schumer claims you w-were transferred here because you were b-b-belligerent and a danger to yourself and other inmates. He s-said you were pu-put on a diet of water to"—Lightner tapped his chin with one finger—"what was his phrase? I b-b-believe it was 'to calm you d-down.' " Lightner frowned. "I must s-say it appears to have worked—almost too well, in f-f-fact. I suspect Mr. Schumer would have been summoning an undert-t-taker if you became *too* much calmer."

Hy closed his eyes and let his head fall back against the wall, Lightner's words spinning inside his addled brain. Eight weeks.

You deserve worse, Hieronymus Law, you incompetent bastard. This voice did not belong to his three companions, but to his conscience, which—unlike the rest of him—hadn't been diminished by incarceration or starvation.

"I'd hoped to speak to you t-today," the clipped voice continued. "But I had n-no idea you would be in this c-condition. I think our conversation will have to w-wait until tomorrow, after you've had some food and water." There was a long pause, during which the three apparitions in the corner had a heated conversation, the outcome of which was an unprecedented point of agreement: Hy needed to keep the man here—at *all* costs.

"Talk about what?" Hy asked. The words were no louder than the skitter of dry leaves across cobbles.

The Englishman stared at him for a long moment before he spoke. "Have you ever heard of a b-b-businessman named Alard Janssen?"

Hy blinked at the unexpected question. "Er—" His throat caught and he coughed.

"Just nod if you have."

Hy nodded; he'd *heard* of Janssen—every copper in the Muni knew Janssen had been one of the wealthy reformers behind the new police department.

"Mr. J-Janssen has been garroted and st-st-stabbed to death."

Lightner's words were like a kick in the gut, and Hy's stomach cramped and heaved. But there was nothing to bring up.

"Steady on, old m-man," Lightner said after Hy stopped, compassion coloring his voice.

Hy's mind circled back to what the man had said: Janssen was dead—another millionaire strangled and stabbed. That could only mean—

"I've been told Janssen's m-murder is very s-similar to those of Sealy and Dunbarton."

Hy's jaws clenched at the sound of names he wished he'd never heard.

"I can see by your face you know w-w-what that means. I'm afraid somebody is either aping the k-killer's methods or—" He had the mercy not to finish.

Oh God.

"Takin' the Lord's name in vain won't help your eternal soul, lad."

Hy ignored the priest and tried to focus on Lightner, who'd resumed speaking.

"—and so I went r-round to the Sixth Precinct station, wanting to have a l-look at the files on Sealy and Dunbarton."

Hy knew what he was going to say before he said it.

"Your Captain McElhenny told me b-both f-f-files had gone missing. He c-claims you d-destroyed them."

Hy was grateful his throat was too sore for him to speak, or he'd have been yelling.

"He is *n-not* very happy that this case is in the h-hands of the Eighth P-Precinct. I get the distinct feeling he will n-not b-be cooperative."

Hy's mind boggled at the thought of *this* man talking to the coarse, not-too-smart captain of the Sixth.

"I'm afraid Captain McElhenny is not your gr-gr-greatest admirer—but I'm sure you were aware of that. In addition to d-describing your assault in detail, he s-said you'd taken b-bribes to hinder the investigation."

Lightner's words were like a knife in his chest. Raw denial pulsed in his veins, but he kept his mouth shut; nobody had cared about the truth then, they'd care even less now—especially this stranger.

The Englishman idly spun the handle of his cane, making it twirl like a top. The handle appeared to be a silver woman—naked, Hy suspected, although the lighting wasn't good enough to confirm that.

Lightner's teeth flashed a startling white in the gloom. "I believe my captain—D-D-Davies—dislikes me almost as much as McElhenny does y-you. I d-daresay he'd put me in a cell right beside you if he c-could." His smile grew into a full-fledged grin. "So we have that in c-c-common."

Hy reckoned that was *all* he shared with the refined creature standing across from him.

"But that's not all we have in common," Lightner said, as though Hy had spoken out loud. Which he very well might have.

The man cocked his head and fixed Hy with his dark gaze. "I'm sure that b-being in here all these weeks—with only your c-conscience for company—has g-given you time to reflect. Making one bad d-decision does not mean you are a bad man, Mr. Law. I would imagine absol-lution is something you've thought about a g-great deal."

Hy doubted the man would want to hear what he was *really* thinking: that if he ever got out of this fucking cell, he'd run so fast and so far nobody would ever find him. He also considered, very briefly, telling Lightner what a liar McElhenney was.

He did neither. Instead, he nodded.

"Excellent. So that l-leads me to my last p-p-point. Captain Davies despises me so much he gave me this case—no doubt be-believing I would fail sp-sp-spectacularly, shame myself, and be sent scurrying b-back to England."

Hy suspected Davies was correct. Again, he kept that to himself.

"You're probably w-wondering where you c-come into all of this."

Actually, Hy was wondering if Schumer had gone to fetch a higher authority rather than clothing and water. He was bloody terrified the man might return with the warden and take Lightner away before Hy could find some way to convince the man to help him.

Still, he could hardly admit as much, so he nodded again, and Lightner's smile told him it was the correct response.

"I thought you m–might be. You see, rather than d–d–dissuading me, Captain Davies has fired my curiosity to find this k–k–killer. I'm n–not sure if this r–recent killing was like the others, and it appears you are the b–best source of inf–information about the first two victims. I will make sure any assistance you offer is cr–credited to you and advocate for your f–f–freedom."

"I have notes," Hy wheezed.

Lightner's lips curved into a genuine smile. "I was *hoping* that was the c–case. I'll talk to somebody about g–getting you out of this cell in ex–ch–ch–change for your notes."

Hy stared up into the other man's smiling face and shook his head *no*.

Lightner's smile drained away, the expression replaced by one that made hairs all over Hy's body stand up.

"You want m–money?"

The tone he used made Hy's ears burn with shame. But, in for a penny . . . "Out," Hy coughed. "Want out."

"I just s–said I w–would—"

"*Now.*"

Lightner's dark eyes glinted as he stared down at him; Hy was not making a friend.

"You don't need friends, Hieronymus," Großmutti reminded him. "Tell the man whatever you need to tell him to make him get you out."

"Two notebooks. One each—case," Hy rasped. "Out now. Only deal." The effort of forcing out the words sent him into a fit of coughing, and for a moment he believed he'd die from sheer pain; death would be a bloody relief.

He recovered from his paroxysm as weak as a kitten. The atmosphere in the cell had become even more unpleasant. Father Thomas and Großmutti were arguing violently about Hy telling lies; Dora was crying about him leaving; and the English detective was studying him the way a man might look at a stray dog he'd just tried to feed—and which had bitten him. Hy closed his eyes. He'd done plenty in his short life he wasn't proud of, but he usually drew the line at barefaced lies.

He listened for the sound of the Englishman taking his leave, unwilling to open his eyes and watch as freedom—and, yes, maybe even a chance at absolution—walked out the door.

But the cell remained quiet; even his companions were silent. The torturous silence stretched and stretched—

"I'll g-get you out."

Hy's eyelids snapped open. Had he said . . . *out?*

Father Thomas slapped his sizable thigh and laughed. "You see, Hieronymus, they're sending you home!"

"Home?" Dora put a dainty, perfect hand on each rosy cheek. "Oh, Hy." Her blue eyes shimmered. "You're not *leaving* us, are you?"

"Mr. Law?" a distant voice said. "*Mr. Law?*"

"The two of you just let him be," Großmutti snapped in German, ignoring the girl's crying and the priest's glare. She gave Hy a loving smile. "See what I told you, Hieronymus? God will understand a little untruth if you—"

"*Mr. Law?*"

Hy's head snapped up at the sharp voice.

Lightner's cold, aristocratic features were creased with worry. "C-Can you hear me, or have they damaged something in your h-head?"

Hy stared.

"Are you in internal p-pain?" When Hy hesitated, Lightner frowned. "You must tell me—did they beat you, Mr. L-L-Law?"

Hy shivered at the chill in his voice. Lightner was one of those men who didn't bluster. Instead, he'd mastered that rare knack of sounding more menacing the quieter he became.

Hy shook his head, terrified that the Englishman might decide to take the matter up with the guard—that Hy might be stuck here. And that he might never get out.

"I'm fine," he whispered, his voice a dry husk. And he *was* fine, certainly fine enough to get up and walk—if not run—out of this hellhole if given the chance.

Lightner propped his weight on his fancy cane while looking down at him—assessing him in silence.

They *had* beat him, as a matter of fact. So badly his ribs still ached, even all these weeks—*eight!*—later. But he didn't care about that right now because his brain had become stuck on a single word that wiped all the beatings and suffering from his mind.

"Out?" Hy was afraid the whisper might be smothered by Großmutti and Father Thomas, who'd resumed their strident bickering.

But Lightner heard him—somehow—and nodded. "Yes. I'll g-get you out of this cell in exchange f-for your case notes."

Hy squeezed his eyes shut, as if that would somehow stop the cacophony of cheering in his skull. Over the racket, one phrase rang over and over again like a church bell: *out of this cell.*

He worked his mouth to find the moisture necessary to force out one word. "How." As questions went, it was vague, but the other man knew what he meant.

"Captain Davies—rather un-w-w-wittingly, I believe—gave me the authority I'll need to free you. He told me I c-could have anyone in New York City to assist me with my p-p-politically unpopular, extremely high-profile, impossible-to-solve mu-murder investigation." Lightner chuckled with what sounded like genuine amusement. "At l-least until he is able to send me packing. Until then, I c-can have anyone; anyone aside from one of his p-police detectives, that is."

"You want *me* to work for you?" The knowledge that this man wanted his assistance was . . . flattering.

"No."

The word clanged in the tiny stone cell, and the shame that came with it surprised him. Even now—even here in the depths of hell— he could still feel ashamed.

"I don't need your help, Mr. L-Law"—nor did he want it, Lightner's tone said. "But that is a fiction I m-m-must promote if I am to g-get you out. All I w-want is your notes. Once you give me those, you will be f-f-free to do whatever you choose. I r-recommend you get as far away from N-New York City as you are physically able. I don't think C-Captain McElhenny will take your liberation well." He paused, fixing Hy with a look that bored into him. "I asked your captain if you were c-coming back to w-w-work once you were released from jail." He shook his head. "After seeing you t-today, I realize that what I *should* have asked him was if he ever p-p-planned on releasing you."

Hy could have told Lightner that he already knew what future McElhenny had planned for him. After all, he'd heard the man say it more than once when he'd come to the Tombs to direct Hy's punishment—back in the early weeks, before he'd broken Hy and lost interest in him.

But he kept his trap shut; he was already humiliated by the look in Lightner's eyes—pity mingled with disgust.

The barely audible sound of boots on stone came from the corridor.

"J-Just to be sure we are clear: your notes for your freedom. Do we have a d-deal?" the Englishman asked as the footsteps grew nearer.

Hy met Lightner's cool stare and made one more black mark on his soul. "Deal."

CHAPTER 9

I t was nine thirty by the time Jasper walked into the foyer of the Astor House.

"Lord Jasper?"

He turned to find a hotel functionary hurrying toward him.

"Good evening, my lord. Superintendent Tallmadge and Mr. Dell are waiting for you in one of our private dining rooms."

Jasper was momentarily nonplussed; so, Dell really *had* waited for him.

"Sir? This is for your room." The concierge handed Jasper a key, hesitated, and then said, "Your servant—er, Mr. Paisley—had you moved to a suite rather than what the commission paid for."

Jasper bit back a smile. "P-Please see that the bill comes to me rather than the c-commission."

"Yes, my lord." The other man sagged with relief.

Jasper followed him through a magnificent set of double doors into the Astor House's Rotunda restaurant. An enormous circular mahogany bar dominated the center of the room, and most of the bar-stools were occupied. Along both sides were curved counters, which seated yet more men in evening garb. The concierge escorted Jasper toward a series of ornate wooden doors. He opened the second door, which held a small, elegant dining room where two men sat eating.

A tall, bone-thin man with gray hair stood and approached Jasper, his hand extended.

"I'm Frederick Tallmadge. Thank you so much for joining us, my lord."

"My p-pleasure, sir."

Tallmadge looked at the concierge. "Set another place for Lord Jasper."

"Thank y-you, Superintendent, but I've already eaten," Jasper lied. He was dead on his feet, and his head had begun to throb some time ago.

"Perhaps a drink?"

"Whiskey, please."

Tallmadge gestured to Dell, a flicker of distaste on his patrician features. "I know you're already acquainted with this gentleman."

Dell's eyes were red rimmed, his suit even more wrinkled and stained than earlier. "His Lordship and I are old friends," Dell said with a shaky grin. "So you reckon Janssen was murdered by the same riffraff him and his reformer friends were always trying to help?" Dell asked, either unaware of or unconcerned about the grim look Tallmadge was giving him.

What an odd couple they were.

Tallmadge took charge of the conversation. "Please, have a seat, my lord. I understand you've already spoken with Captain Davies."

"Yes, sir."

"I've also received a message from City Hall." Tallmadge's expression of wonderment told Jasper this was not a usual occurrence. "It appears Mayor Wood and I have found a subject on which we can agree: you being in charge of this case."

Jasper wondered who would tell McElhenny that. "I'm flattered b-by your faith."

"I feel I owe you an apology for bringing you into this mess. When the Metropolitan Police Bill passed back in April, we knew there would be trouble, but we had no idea just how much. Several of us—Alard Janssen included—had hoped to begin our new force with a science-based detective department like yours in London. But matters have . . . well, they've dragged on. And now you've landed in the middle of it."

Tallmadge sat back and swirled his wine in his glass. "The commission is one hundred percent behind you." He gave a sharp laugh. "That isn't saying much, seeing how we're holed up on White Street like fugitives. I think putting you in the Eighth isn't a bad idea at all."

So, Jasper would be Tallmadge's man in the enemy's camp.

"C-Captain Davies has been m-most helpful," Jasper lied.

Tallmadge cocked an eyebrow, and the glint of weary amusement in his eyes spoke of intelligence. Jasper thought he had the look of a man committed to his duty rather than crusading. He knew from reading the papers that Tallmadge had been at least the third or fourth choice for the position, only after several others had rejected the contentious job offer.

"I'm sure the mayor is eager to resolve this case in a way that doesn't expose the incompetence—not to mention corruption—that is rife throughout his department. If Davies's support doesn't prove sufficient, you may always approach the commission."

"Was he killed like Sealy and Dunbarton?" Dell persisted.

Tallmadge opened his mouth as if to chide the other man, then seemed to think better of it. "You can speak the truth here, my lord."

Jasper had no intention of saying anything more than what he'd already seen in the special edition of the *Herald.* "Mr. Janssen was garroted and stabbed—"

"So it *was* like the others. You think the Sixth arrested the wrong woman?" Dell's expression was avid.

"It's best not to go throwing such accusations around, Mr. Dell," Tallmadge said sharply, only to ask Jasper, "Do you believe it could be the same killer?"

"I d–don't know very much about the earlier m–murders."

"You must talk to Captain McElhenny." Tallmadge grimaced. "One of the mayor's staunchest men; he's probably going to be less than cooperative."

"I've seen him."

"Already?" Tallmadge sounded pleased by Jasper's industry.

"He told me the case f–files have disappeared."

Both men gaped.

"Do you believe him?" Tallmadge asked.

"Shouldn't I?"

Tallmadge opened his mouth, appeared to think better of what he was going to say, and closed it again.

"It sounds the same as the other killings to me," Dell said. "Maybe the woman the Sixth arrested was part of a group of robbers?"

Tallmadge cut Dell a look of intense dislike and stood. "It's been a long day and you must be exhausted, my lord. I'm sure you must know this case is a priority. While it would be a great tragedy if the

Sixth's arrest was responsible for the death of an innocent woman, don't let fear of a police scandal keep you from finding the truth."

In other words, Tallmadge would be thrilled to see such a cock-up attributed to Mayor Wood's Munis.

Jasper took his leave of both men, his feet dragging with weariness. When he reached his room, he inserted the key, but before he could turn it, the door swung inward.

"Good evening, my lord."

Jasper sensed, by Paisley's frosty greeting, that the hotel was not to his liking.

"Good evening, Paisley." He handed over his hat, gloves, and cane before unbuttoning his overcoat.

Paisley sniffed. And then sniffed again.

"Yes, I know; I stink. You'd better run me a bath."

Paisley lifted the coat from his shoulders and then stared at the hem; Jasper saw that he'd gotten blood on it during his examination.

"Er, blood," Jasper admitted sheepishly.

Paisley's frown went all the way to his core. "It may never come out."

Jasper didn't argue; he knew he'd lose. Instead he strode to the bedroom, loosening his stock. "How was your first d-d-day in New York City, P-Paisley?"

Paisley made a noise that conveyed volumes. "I procured several newspapers for you, my lord. Unfortunately, the most respected, the *New-York Daily Times*, does not have a Sunday issue."

Jasper didn't tell his servant that he'd had enough of New York's news for the day. Instead he said, "Did you g-go out and about, or merely entertain yourself by t-terrorizing the hotel staff?"

Paisley ignored both questions. "I found a house that might be acceptable, my lord." He helped Jasper out of his closely tailored morning coat.

"You found a p-place after only one day? Your industry is c-commendable." A frigid silence met his teasing. "I take it your urgency is your way of saying you do not c-care for this hotel?"

His valet acknowledged Jasper's words with the slightest of sniffs. So, a *yes*, in other words.

"If you l-like the house, then I like it," Jasper soothed. He unbuttoned his waistcoat, gave it a subtle sniff, and recoiled. Paisley took it between two fingers and laid it over a nearby clotheshorse, glaring at it as if it were a dead corpse, which is what it smelled like. Jasper hadn't realized the stench of the Tombs would cling to him quite so persistently.

Paisley knelt to remove Jasper's ankle boots while Jasper worked on his collar and cuffs.

"Do you wish to know where the house is, my lord?"

"No, b–but you want to tell me. So, where is it?"

"It is called a brownstone and is located on Union Square—East Sixteenth and Fourth Avenue, to be more precise." He paused and then added, "There is a little green that boasts a new statute of the American rebel George Washington."

Jasper laughed. "*General* Washington isn't considered a rebel here." He shrugged out of his shirt while Paisley pulled off his stockings.

"It was built only a decade ago," Paisley added. Judging by his ambivalent tone, he hadn't yet decided whether *new* was a good or bad thing.

"Excellent, a n–n–new house—we've not lived in one of those b–before, have we? It shall be an adventure."

An ominous silence followed his attempt at raillery. Although the man did not *want* to live in this foreign city, by God he would do his best to find Jasper the perfect situation.

"Shall I schedule an appointment for you to view it, my lord?"

"That won't be n–necessary, Paisley—lease it, or r–rent it, or whatever one does. I trust you implicitly."

If Paisley had been the sort of man who was given to smiling, he would have smiled at that.

"How was your day, my lord?"

Jasper opened his mouth to tell him about the current chaos surrounding his new position, then paused. How could he say anything when he didn't know himself?

Paisley's expression didn't change, but his bearing became more alert, like that of a hunting dog scenting game.

"It was . . . interesting."

His valet did not ask him what he meant but bent to pick up his discarded trousers and drawers, which he took to the dressing room before returning with a dark-blue yukata.

Jasper slipped his arms into the sleeves and tied the sash. "I take it you've read the p–paper and seen the stories about the c–current police muddle?" Paisley nodded. "Let's just say things are rather unsettled at the m–moment."

"I see, my lord. If we do not stay here, shall we be returning home?"

Home. How was it possible for a person to imbue one word with so much yearning? And why didn't Jasper feel that yearning? After all, it was *his* home that he'd left packed in mothballs and draped beneath Holland covers. Why didn't he feel any desire to return to London?

With your tail between your legs?

"I haven't g-given that eventuality any thought," he lied.

Paisley inclined his head and left—probably to go out and procure fireworks to celebrate their possible departure. Jasper knew the man was thrilled, although he would never demonstrate his feelings by so much as a twitch.

He took one of his cigars from a box Paisley had set on his dressing table. They were special, not like the ones in all the other boxes his valet would have distributed throughout the hotel suite for Jasper's convenience. *These* cigars were composed of powdered opium and tobacco, a substance the Chinese called madak.

Madak had been fashionable in China until it was banned for recreational use some hundred years earlier. Now it was allowed only for medicinal purposes. Jasper had discovered madak in London at a Chinese herbalist shop. It was the same place where he'd undergone acupuncture for his migraine headaches. If he remained in New York, he would need to find an acupuncturist, as it was the only treatment that worked once a headache set in.

Madak was a suitable palliative for minor head pain—like the sort of pain he was experiencing this evening, a dull throbbing likely born of tension and a lack of food rather than a full-blown migraine. As usual, the ache originated from the site of his cranioplasty. When he'd returned to London, a doctor had advised reopening his skull and using a new bone-graft procedure to replace the metal plate. Jasper supposed he might do so if the pain ever became intolerable. But for now, he had madak. He tried to use the cigars judiciously, because relying on opiates, even diluted ones, was a double-edged sword.

He lit the cigar, inhaled deeply, and held the smoke in his lungs for a long moment before releasing it. The jolt of euphoria rendered him slightly boneless, so he propped himself against the frame of the big sash window, staring out over the flickering lights of the city. The ache in his temples lessened a bit more each time he filled his lungs. Even better, the drug also stopped his racing thoughts.

When he was pleasantly dulled, he went to his bath chamber.

"Shall I lay out your evening wear, my lord?" Paisley asked.

Jasper took one last draw on his cigar before handing it to his valet, who carefully tamped out the burning end without destroying the other half of the cigar, which Jasper would smoke before bed if his headache persisted.

"I d-don't think so." He yawned and shrugged out of his robe, tossing it to Paisley before sliding into the steaming water with a groan of pleasure. Jasper closed his eyes; he'd be fortunate if he could stay awake long enough to get out of the tub.

"You have some mail, my lord."

"Anything important?" he asked without opening his eyes. Paisley opened all Jasper's correspondence unless it was marked confidential.

"Several invitations, sir."

"Why the d-devil is anyone still in t-town at this time of year?" In the summer months, London was deserted as *ton* families fled the heat for their country estates.

"I'm given to understand the recent financial and political instabilities have kept some men of business—and their families—in the city, my lord."

That made—unfortunately—too much sense. After the *Dred Scot* decision in March, Jasper's man of business had urged him to pull out of several railroad investments in the American West. Many people were predicting that civil disaster loomed on the horizon for the young nation.

Jasper flexed his damaged knee, which felt quite good after such a long, active day. He stretched out in the long tub, lulled by the sounds of Paisley moving about the apartment. He'd almost drifted off to sleep when his valet's voice startled him.

"There are two dinner invitations you might wish to look at, my lord."

Jasper yawned but didn't open his eyes. He could feel Paisley's gaze burning into him; the man wouldn't leave him in peace until Jasper did what he wanted. He sighed and glared up at him. "Go on then, f-fetch whatever you believe I *need* to look at. You can read them to me while I bathe. And while you're at it, order me s-something to—"

"I took the liberty of ordering your supper. It will be up shortly, my lord." Paisley's smug words were punctuated by the sound of knocking. He frowned and marched out of the bathroom.

Jasper grinned as he soaped one of his feet, feeling a twinge of pity for the staff at the Astor House, who were about to learn the meaning of true tyranny. If Paisley specified a time for the meal to be delivered, he meant that time *exactly*. Not early; not late.

Jasper forced himself to give the matter of New York society some thought. In London he'd avoided society affairs for years, even before the war. Since taking the job at the Met, he'd developed a "society" of his own. True, it was a rather limited society that consisted of working long hours alongside men who would never accept him, engaging in strenuous physical exercise for mental peace and general fitness, reading copiously for work and pleasure, and spending the occasional evening with one of his two vices.

That's not society, Jasper; that's pitiful. And it's certainly not living.

Jasper grimaced at the annoying thought. Perhaps it *was* pitiful. As for not living? He lived just fine, thank you very much.

However, a solitary existence had been possible because he'd not needed to exert himself to learn how London worked. New York, on the other hand, was a puzzle that would require a good deal of effort to comprehend.

"This just came for you, my lord." Paisley held up an envelope.

"Open it for m-me." Jasper stood, taking the towel Paisley brought from the warmer.

"It is from a Mr. H. Law, my lord."

"Well, that was certainly qu-quick." Jasper wrapped the towel around his waist, tucked in the ends, and wiped his hands before reaching for the letter.

Detective Inspector Lightner:

I'm sorry, sir, but there are no notebooks.

"Bloody hell," he muttered.

I lied to get out of The Tombs, but you said something that stuck with me, sir—about finding absolution. I don't have notes, but I know the details of those cases like the back of my hand.

If you want to report me for failing to fulfill my part in the bargain, I'll be at Number 6, Spivey Lane.

I apologize for my lie and would like to help.

H. Law

Jasper barked out a laugh. "That sly b-bastard."

"Is something wrong, my lord?"

"This isn't what I w-was expecting," Jasper said, tossing the note into the small bin beside the sink.

"Perhaps the person who sent it made a mistake?"

"He m-made a mistake, all right," Jasper said grimly. He'd been a gullible fool, and Law had used him as handily as a skeleton key to get out of his cell. If the man had possessed an ounce of sense, he'd have been on a fast boat crossing the river right now. Captain McElhenny wouldn't be the only angry man Law would have to dodge if he stayed in the city.

CHAPTER 10

A headless man thundered past on a wide-eyed bay.

Jasper thought it was Somerset Sackville, although it was difficult to say without a head. Still, he recognized Sacky's fine gelding, Dancer, whom the man had loved more than his wife.

Sacky's boots were in the stirrups, and his gauntlet-clad hand still held firm to the lance tucked under his right arm. His body was listing a bit as Dancer tore past and was quickly swallowed up by the thick, low-hanging smoke that obscured the way ahead.

The crack of a gun and pain in his shoulder were simultaneous, the impact causing his body to jerk. Beneath him Horus swerved and then corrected his footing without Jasper's help, barely avoiding slamming into a horse passing on the right.

You're getting left behind, the cool voice in his head advised.

Turn around! Run! Run! another voice shrieked, drowning out the first.

Jasper urged Horus on with slight pressure from his calves, and the horse shot forward.

Blood from his shoulder wound flowed down his arm, warming at least part of his freezing body. It also soaked his glove, causing the slick leather reins to slide like eels between his quickly numbing fingers. Artillery fire from the Fedioukine Heights struck the man on his left, turning horse and rider into a haze of pink mist.

Jasper's vision blurred red, but he couldn't spare a hand to clear his eyes.

The earth shook beneath Horus's feet as the Russian artillery pounded away, the sulfur and blood and terror in the air thick enough to coat his tongue: it tasted like death.

The world was cloaked in smoke and echoed with explosions and the screams of horses and men. Jasper lost sight of the men from the Seventeenth who'd once flanked him.

"*Close in! Close in!*" It was Jasper yelling, although he hardly recognized his own voice, which was drowned beneath the wailing of the wounded and the hysterical laughing and shouting of those still fortunate enough to be alive.

A shadow burst from the haze and slammed into Horus; boots and stirrups caught, briefly tangling before Jasper could wrench his leg free. The agony from his twisted knee was even sharper than the wound in his shoulder; his vision doubled and then tripled with pain. Jasper blinked to clear his watering eyes. When he could see, the soldier beside him was gone, his riderless horse shearing off into the smoke.

Just ahead, two soldiers exploded and sent ragged chunks of man and horse raining down in all directions. Horus slowed but didn't falter as he navigated mangled corpses.

The shots had missed Jasper by mere seconds.

Fear at what he'd just avoided mingled with blood and pulverized bone and made his gorge rise. He retched until his chest burned, but the cholera had left nothing inside him to bring up.

The barrels of the Russian guns emerged from the haze without warning. Horus reared and gave an equine scream of terror. The world became a babble of languages, the explosion of guns, and steel clashing against steel, cast iron, and bone.

Jasper's arm moved without orders from his brain. Although his attack was sluggish and uncontrolled, his saber struck a fleeing Russian soldier in the back of the head. The blade hit just below his helm and sank deep. The man staggered to the side and would have yanked Jasper out of his saddle if he'd not released the pommel.

Saberless, he reached for the knife he kept strapped just below his knee, but his left arm no longer responded to his commands. Instead, he held tight to Horus with his legs and awkwardly groped for his side arm with his right hand.

He'd just taken aim at a Russian soldier when a horse and rider soared over the gun on Jasper's left and slammed into Horus's flank, sending his shot wide. Jasper clung to his saddle with burning thighs as Horus was forced into a too-narrow gap between abandoned guns. Jasper's right leg—his only fully functioning limb—got mashed between his horse and the cannon. Cold fire blazed up his right side, and his pistol slid from his fingers. Horus reared and screamed at a charging Cossack, one of his hooves kicking the bayonet out of the man's hand before coming down on his head.

A deafening shot exploded somewhere close, and Jasper's head filled with blinding light and a thousand needles of pain.

Squinting through his agony, he urged Horus on, but the big gelding staggered a few steps and then collapsed, crushing Jasper against unforgiving cast iron. He couldn't breathe. He was choking, dying—

"My lord—*my lord!*"

A face loomed above him as Jasper's yell filled the darkness.

Strong hands grabbed his shoulders and held him pinned. "You are dreaming, my lord. You are here now—it is a dream. It is *only a dream.*"

Jasper's eyes darted, expecting to see the filthy walls and bloody floors of the hospital in Scutari. Instead, he felt a soft bed beneath him, with sweat-soaked sheets coiled like serpents around his naked, shivering torso.

He blinked up through the dimness.

"Paisley?" His voice was hoarse from screaming.

"You are safe, my lord."

Relief surged through his body, sucking the air from his lungs. He struggled to breathe, in and out, in and out. *I'm safe now*, he told himself, not quite believing it.

★　★　★

Jasper was never able to sleep after he'd had The Dream, so he pulled on a pair of drawers and commenced the exercise program he'd been following for as long as he could remember—which, granted, wasn't saying much. He had no bags to work, so he did an extra one hundred sit-ups and push-ups. By the time he finished, his body was limber, loose, and slick with sweat.

Awake and invigorated, he toweled himself dry, slipped on his robe, and drank coffee, reading the newspaper while Paisley set out his shaving equipment.

Neither of them spoke about the dream he'd just had: they didn't have to; they'd both been at Balaclava that day. Although Paisley hadn't been in the battle itself, Jasper knew his servant had suffered a hell of his own when Horus's body was found—but not Jasper's.

For almost a day, Paisley believed him dead or captured.

By the time a young corporal brought Jasper back, barely conscious and draped over his saddle, his normally stoic valet was frantic. It was the only time in almost two decades that he'd seen Paisley lose his temper. It was also the last time Paisley gave in to his emotions, even counting the nightmarish weeks in the hospital, where vermin, disease, and filth were more dangerous than the exhausted surgeons who dug shrapnel out of his skull and shoulder.

A knock on the door pulled Jasper away from his memories, and he looked up to see Paisley carrying a breakfast tray.

Jasper grimaced; he despised eating so early in the morning. "I'm n–not hungry."

The shift in Paisley's expression was so slight that the average person would not see it without the aid of a magnifying glass.

But Jasper was not the average person.

He heaved an exaggerated sigh. "Very well, you t–tyrant. Put it over here and pour me another c–cup of coffee."

Paisley managed to gloat without changing expression.

"You will be gone all day, my lord?" he asked as he handed Jasper the steaming cup and arranged the various plates on the side table the same way Jasper's nurse had done to tempt his appetite when he was little.

"Yes, most likely." Jasper couldn't help noticing that Janssen's murder was on the front page of all four newspapers Paisley had ordered delivered.

"I thought your Trickers might do, my lord."

Jasper looked up. "Hmm?"

"I know it is unconventional, but you will have to wear your rust trousers with the black Gieves and Hawkes. Your Lobbs will never be the same after the treatment they received yesterday."

He knew Paisley was displeased with him when he referred to every item of Jasper's clothing by proper names. He had no earthly idea which of his shoes was a Tricker but supposed it must be a sturdier brogue than the pair of soft leather ankle boots he'd worn yesterday. He had to admit he'd not expected quite the level of filth he'd encountered during his brief investigations.

"I'll wear buckskins and Wellies if you w-wish," Jasper said mildly, biting into a piece of toast to hide his smile.

"We shall not be reduced to such straits as that, my lord. Not yet." Jasper turned back to the paper.

Alard Janssen: Philanthropist, reformer, devoted husband, and pillar of the community found murdered in a rubbish alley.

Jasper was displeased—but not surprised—to see that details of Janssen's murder, such as the stabbing and garroting, had also made it into the article, along with speculations that this killing might be related to the earlier two. Wherever the newspapermen had acquired their information, they'd not yet learned about the missing flesh.

Jasper was just about to turn the page when an abbreviated report of an assault caught his eye. He read it, laughed out loud, and then said, "Listen to this, Paisley:

Assaulted by his Wife—James Finn and his wife Johanna got into an altercation about eleven o'clock at their residence on No. 109 Wash- ington-Street. Johanna was drunk at the time and struck her husband in the head with a hatchet, inflicting a deep and dangerous wound. The wounded man was taken to the hospital, and Mrs. Finn to the First Ward Station, but she was yesterday dismissed, it being decided that she gave her husband no more than he deserved.

"Very droll, my lord."

"Tsk, tsk. You have no s-sense of the absurd."

"If that is the sort of justice the American police mete out, then the situation is worse than absurd: it is criminal."

"What? You don't believe some crimes are justified?"

"The law is the law." He punctuated his proclamation with a long, rasping hiss of the razor on the strop.

"There is no place f-for anything else? What if this man had been b-beating his wife?"

Paisley grunted, refusing to be drawn, so Jasper turned back to the *New-York Daily Times* and an extended discussion of the recent meet- ing of the board of councilmen, which had devolved into a brawl—or perhaps it was more accurate to say the brawl had been punctuated by brief moments of discussion. The substance of the dispute was, naturally, the current disarray of the city's police force. The minutes read more like a pub scrap than a meeting of government leaders.

Jasper flipped through the rest of the paper: a proposal for improving the machinery for laying telegraph cable, the daily shipping news—Jasper saw his own name listed among yesterday's arrivals—various amusements, public notices, and houses for let.

"There is a section for properties to let." He held up the paper.

"Thank you, my lord. I have the matter well in hand."

Which was Paisley's way of telling Jasper to mind his own business.

"Shall I send your acceptance to the Loman dinner party tomorrow night, sir?"

"No, I have too much to do."

"What about the Bergin dinner next week?"

"You won't stop hounding m-me until I agree to go, will you?"

"I believe there is to be dancing, my lord."

"Well, that s-s-settles it, then. Send the d-damned acceptance and polish up my dancing slippers."

"Very good, my lord."

Jasper tossed the paper aside and stood. "Have a look for a c-club while you're out and about today."

That wiped the smug expression off Paisley's face. Jasper hadn't belonged to a club of any kind since university. But here in New York he was a social neophyte, and the quickest way to get up to speed on who was who was to socialize.

"An athletic club, my lord?"

Jasper took the seat in front of the mirror, where Paisley was waiting.

"And social—p-perhaps I'll join one of each." He watched his servant's face in the mirror for a reaction while Paisley soaped him.

He was not disappointed. Paisley raised his eyebrows the merest fraction of an inch—the equivalent of a full-blown eye roll in any other man. "Of course, my lord."

Jasper grinned.

Paisley picked up the freshly stropped razor. "I cannot be responsible for your nose if you pull faces while I am shaving you, my lord."

CHAPTER 11

Jasper was walking through the lobby when somebody called his name.

He turned to find Hieronymus Law and barked out a laugh. "Mr. Law. I m-must admit you are the l-l-last man I expected to see this morning. You l-look as though a strong wind would knock you over. You should be at home in b-b-bed." *Or on a packet to some foreign land.*

As Law came closer, Jasper saw that the man looked even worse than he'd initially thought; it was a bloody miracle he was upright. Not only was he gaunt, but one of his eyes was partially swollen shut, and his skin was an unhealthy shade of yellow. He was nicked and cut all over, as if he'd shaved with a scythe. Jasper had seen more prepossessing cadavers.

At a hair over six feet, Jasper did not find himself looking up often, but Law was a veritable giant. Cleaned up and shaved, he was younger than Jasper had first thought—closer to twenty-five than thirty. Hands the size of serving platters tightened on the rim of his battered brown hat. "I wanted to apologize." Law met Jasper's gaze as well as he could with only one eye. He had the startling green eyes and ginger hair of an Irishman, but his accent was American. "I shouldn't have lied. It was just—"

Jasper had no interest in watching the man grovel. "You d-did what you had to; don't let the m-matter concern you."

"I'd like to help."

"What you *should* be d-doing is f-fleeing the city." And Jasper should probably be fleeing with him. "McElhenny will send men for you the m-moment he knows you're at liberty."

"But he couldn't arrest me if I was helpin' you, right?"

"I have my p-pick of officers who haven't been s-s-sacked for reasons of m-moral turpitude to help me find my way."

Law's bruised jaw tightened. "I can run from New York, sir, but I couldn't run from myself."

Jasper gave the man a hard look; to his credit, Law didn't squirm.

"I can tell you all about Sealy and Dunbarton; I remember it like it was yesterday. Donahue—the man I partnered with—left the force about a week before they arrested Caitlyn Grady." He stumbled slightly over the name. When Jasper merely stared, Law worried his cracked and peeling lower lip. "I ain't gonna say I've never done nothin' wrong, but I ain't the sort who'd sit by while an innocent woman went to the hangman."

Jasper thought back to the brief exchange he'd had with Captain McElhenny yesterday. He had to admit McElhenny's ranting hadn't made sense. The excitable, ill-humored Irishman had vacillated between saying Law took money from the woman and making it sound like the detective had sacrificed the prostitute to further his career aspirations. Jasper had smelled the lies on McElhenny when he claimed that it had been Law who destroyed the case files.

To own the truth, Jasper was impressed that Law hadn't run off; he'd come here to offer his help.

Maybe he has nothing to run off to—or no money to run off with? Perhaps he will use this opportunity—and authority—to extort money, the way many dirty coppers do?

"I'm n-not sure whether *you* will want to w-work with *me*. I have n-no tolerance for lying or c-corrupt practices. I know p-protection-money rackets and bribery are pervasive, but I will n-not countenance such behavior."

"I know you've no reason to believe me, sir, but all the stories McElhenny told about me ain't true." Law hesitated, opened his mouth, seemed to rethink himself, and then pressed his lips together.

This is a mistake, Jasper. Go back upstairs, have Paisley pack, and leave. Who cares if the duke laughs when you return scant weeks after setting off?

Only the thought of returning to London and no employment kept Jasper standing where he was. Besides, wasn't it his Christian duty to give the man a second chance—to practice forgiveness?

The voice in his head laughed.

"I'll take you on," Jasper said, getting the words out before he changed his mind. "But if I f-find you've c-c-crossed the line even a little, I will see you in p-prison myself. Don't lie to me again, D-Detective, not even by omission."

"Understood, sir."

Jasper gestured to the hotel doors. "I'm off to check on the g-good d-doctor Feehan and then to Solange's."

"Feehan's a drunk, sir. Whoever sent Janssen to him shoulda known better. He ain't done a decent postmortem in years." Law frowned and then added, "Unfortunately, he's the one who did the work on Dunbarton."

"Ah. W-Well, perhaps he made a copy of the p-postmortem for his own records, as the p-police copy was l-lost with the file."

Law made a noise that did not sound promising.

Outside the hotel, the doorman had the carriage Jasper had called down for.

Law took the rear-facing seat, his hat perched on his lap, his eyes on Jasper's stick. He was carrying the amber today, and he offered it to the other man, who gave him a startled glance before taking the smooth ebony wood cane. His giant, rough hands were surprisingly deft as he examined the handle, lifting the lump of amber to study it closer.

"Is that a—?"

"A scorpion. It's called an inc-c-clusion."

Law held it up to the brownish light coming through the dirty carriage window. "It don't seem right to say a bug is beautiful, but it's somethin' else. Old, is it?"

"It could be fifty m-million years old."

Law's lips parted in amazement. "I was feelin' old this mornin', but that makes me feel a mere lad."

Jasper smiled and took the proffered stick.

"I hope you don't mind, sir, but I stopped by the Eighth on my way over."

"You're a very b-brave man, Detective."

"I wanted to speak to Captain Davies myself—as a gesture of respect—and thank him for the opportunity."

Lord, Jasper was sorry he'd missed *that* conversation.

"And how did Captain D-Davies receive you?"

"Er, well, he wanted to know what the hell I was doin' there, but I reminded him of what you told me yesterday."

Jasper laughed. "Did you, now?" He was beginning to like this man.

Law's freckled skin darkened. "He told me he didn't want to see my face around his station."

"Ah well, you have c-company in that, Detective."

"I ain't got no right to be called that, sir."

"The title is yours for as l-long as you work with m-me."

Law's smile was small and fleeting. "Thank you, sir. You said yesterday that Janssen was killed the same way as Sealy and Dunbarton?"

"I'm t-told the manner was s-similar, but without postmortem reports, I have no r-real idea. Why don't you t-tell me about the others."

"A garrotin' with cuts to the midsection, on the right side?"

"Janssen's cuts w-were on the left."

Law asked, "Er, this might sound odd, sir, but what kind of cuts?"

"F-Four stab wounds—all delivered with some force, in my opinion." Jasper mimed holding a knife in his fist. "I b-believe they were delivered in punches, slightly tearing the w-wound on removal. The direction of the tears indicates the k-killer was behind him. The knife had a p-prominent guard with quillons that left indentations in the flesh." Jasper flipped open his notebook, in which he'd sketched the impressions of the guard, and handed it to Law. "And of c-course the missing chunk of flesh." He cocked his head. "S-Sound familiar?"

"Aye, sir. Er, all except them quillon things. I'm afraid I never noticed. As to the chunks of flesh—yeah, both men were missin' a bit. McElhenny said to keep that part just between us—he said heads would roll if people heard of desecration of a corpse and that the heads were likely to be ours. So it was just me, Donahue, and McElhenny." He paused, then added, "And I 'spose Doc Feehan."

Law swallowed, and Jasper knew they were thinking the same thing. "I guess that narrows things d-down a bit."

"You don't think—"

"That it was one of you f-four?" Jasper smiled faintly. "You've g-got an excellent alibi, D-Detective."

Law gave a sickly laugh.

"I d-daresay more people learned of the m-mutilation than you think. Still, it seems w-we are either looking for the same k-killer or somebody with *some* connection to those two murders. Or another Shakespeare enthusiast."

"I'm sorry, sir?"

"*The pound of flesh which I d-demand of him is deerely bought, 'tis mine, and I will have it.* It is Sh-Shylock's famous line from *The M-Merchant of Venice.* Tell me, Detective, what did you m-make of that missing flesh?"

"I didn't know *what* to make of it—and I didn't connect it to no Shakespeare *pound of flesh.*"

"You say Feehan did D-Dunbarton's postmortem—somebody else did Mr. Sealy's?"

"Er, well, sir, that's a problem. We didn't get one for Sealy." Jasper frowned, and the other man nodded. "I know, I know—it's right shoddy policin'. Somebody—probably his family—bribed one of the coroner's doctors to write up a certificate. The undertaker took the cert to the city inspector's office for a burial permit. The inspector shoulda *refused* the permit, but money likely changed hands." Law shook his head with disgust. "So when Dunbarton died, I went with the body myself, but there wasn't nobody except Feehan to do the job. I thought he did all right, but then I don't have medical know-how. Feehan said Dunbarton died from the stab wounds rather than strangulation."

Jasper took out the handkerchief he'd preserved from yesterday and opened it for Law to look at the fibers. "I took that from Janssen's neck."

"It looks like hemp—same thing that was used on the other two. The paper said Janssen was found in an alley between Broadway and Mercer—near Solange's?" Law asked.

"Yes."

"Sealy and Dunbarton were found near a different brothel, Molly O'Reilly's. Not exactly behind it, but close enough. Donovan Street, where their bodies were found, is a place no sane man would venture into at night—dark, cramped, with some of the worst buildings in the city. Folks call it Murderer's Alley. Lots o' people live above *and* below street level on that alley, but you'd think every one of them was blind and deaf. If you were wantin' to commit murder, a person couldn't pick a better place."

"I don't b-believe Dunbarton was k-killed in M-Murderer's Alley."

"I beg pardon, sir?"

"I talked to a m-man yesterday who said he saw Dunbarton's body not l-long after he was murdered—before the b-body was moved to Murderer's Alley."

Law's battered face was a mask of disbelief. "Moved? From where?"

"About th-thirty feet from where J-Janssen was murdered."

"Are you sayin' somebody took the body *all* the way down to the Points?"

"According to this m-man."

"Who told you this?"

"A rag p-picker showed me the p-place. I d-don't believe he has any reason to lie. Besides, there is evidence of a g-great deal of b-blood on the cobbles."

"How do you know this rag picker ain't the killer?"

"Mr. Hart certainly seems to have h-had opportunity—"

"Jemmy Hart?" Law asked.

"You know him?"

"Aye, he's been a picker since I was a lad. Old Jemmy ain't the killin' sort. I can't see why he'd lie about such a thing either." Law sat back in his seat hard enough to rock the carriage. "You've been here less than one day and found this out."

"I assure you, that w-was a m-matter of luck." Jasper considered passing along Hart's bizarre claim that the body had been held for an entire day before it was discovered but decided to leave it be. After all, he wasn't sure whether Hart had the best memory for dates. He could check the postmortem for Dunbarton before bringing anything up. However, he felt duty bound to mention what Hart had said about the coppers. "I have reason to b-believe that p-police officers were the ones who m-moved the body."

Law didn't look as surprised as he should have. "Hart said he saw coppers from the Eighth?"

"He just saw policemen."

Law cut Jasper a questioning look. "You reckon they were involved in the murder?"

"Hart m-made it sound as though they j-just encountered the body—after he'd stripped it of its v-valuables. Is m-moving bodies a lucrative b-business?"

Law grimaced. "Sometimes."

"P-Paid by shopkeepers?"

"Aye." Law didn't look too eager to share.

"Tell me m-more about Sealy and D-Dunbarton."

"Anythin' in particular?"

"Whatever s-struck you."

Law gave the question a bit of thought and then said, "Did you find somethin' sticky on Janssen's shoe?"

Jasper blinked. "S-Sticky?"

"Pine resin—both victims had it stuck to their shoes."

"To be honest, I d-didn't think to look. Is that a c-common occurrence in New York? Do you have p-pine resin on *your* shoe, Detective?"

Law's split lip twitched up at the corner. "I can't recall that ever happening. I didn't think much of it when I noticed it on Sealy—really I only noticed 'cause I helped to lift him and got some on my hand. It's a pain in the arse to get off. When the same thing happened with Dunbarton?" He shrugged. "I thought it was, well"—he stopped, his expression sheepish—"some sort of symbol, you know?"

"A killer's c-alling c-card?" Now there was a sentence for a man who stammered.

"Sometimes gangs do it—leave signs. Although around here it's usually animal parts and the like."

"Did you f-f-find anything to suggest these were g-gang killings?"

"Nothin'. 'Course that don't mean somebody didn't pay thugs to kill both of 'em. Not that those men were the sort to hang about with Roach Guards or Dead Rabbits."

Jasper had heard of both gangs. "Is g-garroting and mutilation a popular m-method of murder among g-gangs?"

"Naw, a brick to the head, a bullet, or a knife for that lot. Anyhow, we looked into places you'd find pine resin, thinkin' that might give some clue where they'd been earlier, although I reckon, the way that shi—er, stuff—sticks to things, they could have stepped in it a week earlier."

"D-Did the two men employ v-valets?"

"Er, I dunno, sir. Why?"

"No v-valet worth his salt would allow his m-master to go out with sticky shoes. S-So at least you could n-narrow down the time when each m-man encountered the r-resin."

Law's massive shoulders slumped. "Ah, I didn't think of that, sir. You'll be thinkin' we were a real pair of meatheads."

The unexpected word surprised a laugh out of him. "W-Well, it isn't something a p-person would think unless they knew about p-personal servants. Tell me about the uses f-for resin."

"It's used for a *lot* of things: shipbuildin', carriage manufacturin', expensive furniture makin', train cars, and on and on. 'Course we looked for businesses within walkin' distance of Murderer's Alley." He scowled and left the obvious unstated.

"The idea is a g-good one. We must check places around Solange's. Were the two m-men involved in the s-same business endeavors?"

"Their people weren't forthcomin', if you know what I mean."

Jasper knew what he meant: the wealthy would hardly be eager to lay out their financial records for a policeman.

"I scrounged up a little, but just things that were generally known. Dunbarton's pa left him money—nobody knows exactly how the old man made it, 'cept it wasn't no place legal. Dunbarton Junior wasn't as sharp as his pa, and he apparently pissed most of it away. He had a job—president at Ohio Life Insurance and Trust. The gossip is that Dunbarton's wife—Hesperis van Rensselaer—" He winced. "Who the hell would name a girl *that*?" He held up a hand before Jasper could answer. "You don't need to say it, sir. I shouldn't be one to talk about names."

Jasper smiled, but he had to agree. *Hesperis* was less than flattering—Longfellow's "The Wreck of the Hesperus" came to mind.

"Dunbarton married Miss van Rensselaer about three years ago. She rescued him from dire financial straits, and he rescued her from spinsterhood." Law frowned. "I saw her once, when I went to collect her written statement from her father. He didn't want coppers anywhere near his daughter, but she shoved her way in anyhow. The woman is a plain little squab with a tongue like a razor."

Jasper thought the description cruelly apt.

"She's known for bein' blunt, offendin' people, and workin' at her various charities." He scratched his bruised jaw, winced, and dropped his hand. "I guess she's rich enough to get away with it."

"Is she related to S-Stephen v-van Rensselaer the Fourth?"

"Aye—her uncle—they're *all* related to each other, no matter the surname. That sort stick to their own kind," he added in some disgust.

Jasper didn't tell the detective the same was true in England. Nor did he tell him that he'd received an invitation to a dinner being given by a van Resselaer—probably not Hesperis, as she was in mourning. Not to mention the fact that she seemed like the last woman on earth to host entertainments—unless said entertainment involved men like Jasper, a pillory, and public ridicule.

"The marriage was a business deal, by all accounts." Law gave Jasper a quizzical look, as if to say the son of a duke probably knew all about bartering sons and daughters for empire-building unions.

Jasper could have told him he was more familiar with the *evasion* of such unions.

"Anyways," Law continued, "his money problems seemed to go away."

"Children?"

"No."

"And Sealy?"

"Sealy made his money out in California in '47—he was early to the 'rush—before statehood. The gossip is that he came to his claim in an underhanded way. He got outa minin', moved back east, and built some factories that manufacture pots and pans. Sealy also married above himself. Well, at least socially," Law amended, his democratic notions kicking in. "New York blue blood, Emmaline Visser. The Vissers are old patroon, but not so well-heeled as the van Rensselaers. I don't think Sealy needed bailin' out financially—mighta been the other way round, actually. Again, I'm just guessin', since I wasn't allowed to *talk* to either Mrs. Dunbarton or Mrs. Sealy." When Jasper didn't say anything, he added, "You don't look surprised, sir."

"I'm f-fully aware the wealthy insulate themselves from unpleasantries—particularly when it c-comes to protecting their females. But I'm s-s-surprised neither woman wanted to speak to you." He was especially surprised that Mrs. Dunbarton hadn't sought *Law* out. He smiled faintly. "Unless they didn't want the k-k-killer to be found, of course."

Law snorted. "As far as alibis go, both wives had good ones. Mrs. Dunbarton wasn't in the state when her husband was murdered, and Sealy's missus was in the middle of a charity dinner with hundreds of New York's finest. It seems to me"—he cut Jasper an uncomfortable look—"not that I'm any expert, mind, but it seems to me the Dunbartons and Sealys each lived separate lives. The wives spent their time raisin' money for poor women and orphans while their husbands were whorin' it up. I reckon Mrs. Dunbarton and Mrs.

Sealy didn't have nothing to add to the investigation because they didn't *know* their husbands."

Jasper thought about the duke and duchess. They avoided each other like the plague, but they made it their business to know plenty about each other—plenty of *bad* things. Jasper suspected that was true for these couples as well—not that he'd gotten much from Mrs. Janssen the day before.

"If y-you weren't allowed to speak to the w-wives, who did you s-speak to?"

"The women's fathers—*a little*—but that wasn't helpful, since neither man lived in the city. Neither of 'em seemed all that interested in findin' the killer. All they cared about was protectin' their daughters from *us* and avoidin' newspapermen. Being found dead in such a nasty part of town didn't look good for either man, and I think both families were afraid of where an investigation might lead."

Jasper could certainly understand *that*.

The carriage had come to yet another standstill, and Jasper glanced out the window.

It was a stark contrast from the Astor House's marble, crystal, and carpeted splendor to a street that was ankle-deep in filth. Shoeless children played, listless chickens scratched, and tiny ramshackle shops carried out their business. They would have made better time walking. Although that did not look like a pleasant endeavor, as the odor of human and animal sewage was strong, even inside the carriage.

Law continued, "Since the wives had alibis, I turned to business associates. As the sayin' goes, follow the money when you're looking for mischief. I thought it made more sense than an angry whore attackin' and killing two healthy men. I found out Dunbarton met Mayor Wood at City Hall the week before he was killed, and two weeks before that too." Law's face darkened slightly, and he said, "I learned that by sneakin' a look at Dunbarton's calendar when his secretary stepped out for a minute." He gave Jasper a challenging look. "I know that's probably not something you approve of, sir, but the man left it open on his desk. Sometimes that's the only way a man like *me* can learn things. Besides, Dunbarton's secretary was about the most uppity bastard I'd ever met. You'd have thought I'd committed murder just askin' the usual questions and lookin' around a bit. He reported me to McElhenny for being *insubordinate*." He snorted. "How could I be insubordinate when I wasn't his subordinate?"

Jasper smiled at his logic. "You m-must have told this t-to your captain—Dunbarton's meeting with the mayor?"

"He just about came apart at the seams when I suggested lookin' into those meetings. He said what he always said when somebody rich or powerful was involved: 'Heads will roll, and they'll be ours.'" Law sighed. "He pointed out—rightly so—that the mayor ain't the only person with an office in the building. Hundreds of people work there. He also said that even if it *was* the mayor Dunbarton was goin' to see, they were likely political meetin's."

Jasper realized the carriage had ground to a halt, but they'd been too busy talking to notice. Now they both looked out the window. A carter had lost one side of his wagon, strewing barrels of what looked to be ale all over the street. Children, dogs, and several adults danced in the beer puddles that had formed.

"I think we should g-get out and walk," Jasper said.

"Aye, this looks like it will take a bit. Especially because of that—" Law gestured to a small collection of uniformed men on the side of the street. One of the men raised a baton just as another struck him in the midriff; within seconds, there was a full-fledged brawl as Metropolitan fought Municipal.

"G-Good Lord."

Law shook his head in disgust. "It's like the world went mad while I was inside." He opened the door of the cab and then hopped out into the street, his boots squelching audibly in the mud.

Jasper glanced down at his shoes—his Trickers—which were clean enough to eat off. He sighed as he imagined Paisley's expression when he brought them home encrusted with mud, shit, and worse.

CHAPTER 12

Hy navigated a steaming pile of animal manure as he crossed White Street. Walking beside the son of a duke, he couldn't help wondering what the other man thought as he looked around him. Strangely, Hy felt . . . embarrassed on behalf of his native city.

They paused to let a young, shoeless girl drive a gaggle of deafening, honking geese across the muck-filled street.

"You got places like this in England, sir?" Hy asked when he could bear it no longer.

Lightner kept walking, face forward, his lips curving into an odd smile—a smile that said he had an active inner life, one he didn't often share. Hy supposed a crippling stammer might not lend itself to conversation.

"The entire East End of London c-comes to mind."

"Bad, is it?"

"Bad enough."

Why the knowledge that people half a world away were suffering from poverty made Hy feel better, he had no idea.

Something about seeing the area—one he'd seen every day as a policeman—with a stranger, and such a stranger as *this*, made him see with new eyes. He'd always noticed the filth, of course—you'd need to be blind not to, and even then your nose would let you know what was around you—but he'd never before noticed the grinding desperation. The Englishman nodded politely as he passed two women standing in the doorway of a bawdhouse. Both whores opened their shawls and flashed their naked tits, calling to him in wheedling voices, using words so vulgar Hy would never have thought to speak them in a woman's presence. They were bone thin, with raw, scrofulous skin and fine red webbing on their noses and cheeks. He was no stranger to prostitutes—to poor ones, at that—but he couldn't recall seeing any quite as grim.

If the bawds were skinny and unhealthy, the clusters of children on every corner gutted him. There was a deadness in their young eyes that was well beyond despair.

It all made him tired; it made him wish he'd taken the Englishman's advice and just run off—far away from this city.

"T-Tell me, Detective, what else did you happen to s-see in that book?"

It took Hy a minute to remember what book he was talking about. "I only had time to check back five or six weeks before Sealy's death, to see if the two men had any dealings with each other—nothin'—and then ahead a couple weeks, just to see what he'd be missing. It seemed like all Dunbarton did was go to meetin's with other insurance companies and banks. But there *were* two things that stuck out: Dunbarton had been going to a man named Benjamin Hoyle's house every week for five weeks."

"Benjamin Hoyle," Lightner mused. "I know that name."

"He makes guns—lots of 'em. Second biggest manufacturer next to Colt."

"Perhaps it was insurance related?"

"Hoyle don't use Dunbarton's company."

"Interesting. So Sealy's name never showed up in D–Dunbarton's calendar?"

"Actually, sir, none of the names were in the book—just addresses. For example, it just said 'City Hall 10' on two Wednesdays, and then Hoyle's address on Fifth and Thirty-Sixth every Thursday at the same time. I went to both places for two weeks, figuring maybe I'd find out what went on. I didn't get much from goin' to City Hall. You wouldn't believe how many people the mayor sees every day. The coppers who guard the doors said there were too many people to remember.

"Anyhow, I went by Hoyle's." He frowned. "The man must scare the livin' daylights out of his servants, 'cause none of them would talk about who visited the house on *any* night—not even for money. Both times I stuck around for a couple hours. There were two private carriages, but they went round back with their passengers." He glanced at Jasper. "Is that strange—goin' round back?"

"It sounds as if they w–wished to hide their visit."

"That's what I figured. One of the carriages came both times. It was somethin' else: big, glossy, black with windows all around—and *gold* splash guards, if you believe it. More gold trim on the doors, and the fanciest gold lamps I've ever seen. Oh, and two *huge* footmen ridin' on the back. Still, I did get—"

"I'm sorry—but you said two large footmen?"

Hy nodded.

"How did you know they were footmen?"

"They're the ones who have to wear all the fancy clothes—what's it called?"

"Livery."

"Yeah, livery. Is that footmen?"

"Usually. Do you recall what c–color their livery was?"

"Black with gold."

Lightner nodded. "I interrupted you. P–Please go on."

"I never did see the big gold carriage leave—I reckon it musta gone out the back way, which was guarded better than a bank. But I did follow one of Hoyle's visitors who came in a hackney—a man named Amos Baker."

The Englishman chuckled. "Well, well, well."

"What is it, sir?"

"I heard that n–name yesterday from Mrs. J–Janssen. She claims Mr. B–Baker threatened her husband—that he said something to the effect that Janssen's life wouldn't be worth a *farthing* if he tried to worm out of the arrangement and failed to deliver the goods."

Hy whistled. "Well, there's one helluva connection."

"What do you know about B–Baker?"

"He's got a couple ships, and he started out as a captain. He still makes runs from time to time." He gave Jasper a grim look. "He works with slave-takers."

"Slave-takers?"

"Men who capture escaped slaves for money. Baker gets a boat full of runaways and takes 'em down to the Southern ports—supposedly to return them to their owners but really to sell."

Lightner's brow creased. "I thought s–slavery was illegal in N–New York?"

"It is, but the Fugitive Slave Law makes helpin' a fugitive slave—or even not *stoppin'* one—punishable by jail time and hefty fines. Police are supposed to apprehend any slaves and turn them over, but—" He shrugged.

"States don't l-like being t-told what to do by the federal g-government?" Jasper guessed.

"Aye, a lot of coppers won't knuckle under, but there's some that do, mainly for the rewards—money and even promotions."

"This is how Baker earns his m-money—reselling escaped slaves?"

"At least some of it. McElhenny threatened me if I tried to speak to either man. But that didn't mean I couldn't check on their alibis. Hoyle was out of town when Sealy was murdered—in New Orleans. He was here and had no alibi that I could tell for Dunbarton's death. Baker was on one of his boats the night of Dunbarton's death, but not Sealy's."

"And the m-mayor?"

Hy laughed. "You're jokin', right?"

"You s-said Dunbarton met with him at least twice."

"Jaysus. You're a dangerous man, sir. Er, beggin' your pardon."

"No apology n-necessary."

"Does it make me a terrible copper that I didn't check to see if Mayor Wood had an alibi?" Hy figured going after the mayor might have landed him in a worse place than the Tombs.

Lightner just smiled at the question. "Tell m-me about their p-politics—Sealy's and Dunbarton's. Were they r-reformers like J-Janssen?"

"It seemed to me their politics changed with their company, if you know what I mean. Both men were on the boards of a half dozen charities. Dunbarton gave money to both Wood and the candidate runnin' against him in the last election."

"So, not an ardent r-reformer, then."

"I didn't get that impression, no." Hy stopped. "This is it, sir."

They both looked up at the two-story clapboard house, which was leaning distinctly to the left. Hy climbed the splintered wooden steps and knocked, then waited.

He'd raised his knuckles to knock again when the Englishman said, "I'll g-go look around back."

Hy's first impulse was to ask him to wait and not go on his own, but he knew the man wouldn't appreciate a slight to his masculinity.

Besides, just because he dressed and spoke like a dandy didn't mean he couldn't handle himself.

"You lookin' for Doc?"

Hy turned to find a boy of about ten, his clothing cleaner than that of most of the children he'd seen on his way there but not by much.

"I am."

"I can tell you and the flash gent where he is." The boy's bright blue eyes, the only bright thing on his person, squinted up at him, his lips pursed in a smile that said he knew one of them would pay.

He was right.

Hy might not be flush, but he could afford this sort of dun. He'd been bloody lucky his cousin Ian hadn't sold all his things while he was in the Tombs—even if he'd rented out Hy's room. Hy kept his money hidden in a hollowed-out Bible, knowing that was the last place Ian would look.

The boy stared at the coins in his hand, his small body taut and focused, like a cat about to pounce.

Hy held up a three-cent coin. "What's yer name, lad?"

"Davy, sir."

"Do ye hang about the doc's house?" he asked, allowing his speech—which he'd been trying to clean up for the aristocrat—to fall back into familiar patterns.

The boy shrugged, and Hy made as if to put the coin back in his pocket.

"I live next door," Davy said hastily. "I'm yer fella," he added with a bit of a wheedle.

"This is for five answers."

"One."

"Three."

"Done."

"Where's the doc?"

"Over at O'Reilly's."

"Was anyone else here today?"

"No." The boy grinned.

Hy sighed. "Was anyone here *last night*?"

"Aye, sir—two coppers with a dead 'un." He paused and frowned. "I wanted to watch what they did, but Ma dragged me in. So," he said, holding out a grubby fist. "I reckon that's three."

Hy flipped him the coin.

Davy caught it and spun on his bare feet. "Doc didn't come home last night," he called over his shoulder, sprinting as if Hy would go after him and take back the coin. "That answer's free 'cause I tricked ye before."

Lightner came around the corner just then, his gaze inquiring as he watched the boy run off.

"Doc is at Molly O'Reilly's—or that's where he was headed last night. The boy said some coppers dropped off a body and that Doc ain't been home."

They looked at each other for a long moment.

"I want you t-to see the b-body before it turns putrid. Although in this h-heat—" Lightner let the thought hang in the humid air between them.

It took only moments to pry off the lock and hasp and open the door that led to a tiny surgery. The smell of death in the cramped room was eye watering.

A sheet-covered body lay on a trestle table and dominated the center of the room; the Englishman pulled back the sheet and snorted. "His shoes and socks are g-gone."

Janssen's feet were bare and swollen, his skin stretched like a gruesome sausage casing.

"It happens," Hy admitted, ashamed for the men he worked with—men who'd strip a dead body they'd been entrusted to deliver.

"It h-happens in London too." Lightner lifted the corner of the shirt to expose the knife cuts. "Take a l-look."

Hy leaned closer to examine the gory wound. "This is pretty swollen, but it looks the same—other than bein' on the left side." He glanced up. "You think maybe there's two killers? One who does the stabbin' and one who does the chokin'?"

"P-Perhaps. I c-can't imagine somebody making w-wounds like this using a nondominant hand." Lightner picked up his cane and turned the amber knob halfway round until it made a soft *snick*. Then he pulled on it and handed Hy the short, thin-bladed dagger.

"That's handy," Hy said, turning the blade to examine it.

"It's sharp," Lightner warned.

Hy held the dagger as if he were going to stab something. "I'm right-handed and can stab with my left hand," he demonstrated. "I can get a lot of force behind it, but it's not the hand I'd use if I was strangling *and* tryin' to stab a big bloke like Dunbarton or Janssen." Hy handed Lightner the knife, which the Englishman took with his left hand. "You're a lefty?"

"Yes, and I'm far less d-dexterous with my right." He gave a slight smile. "For all that my various t-tutors tried to b-beat left-handedness out of me."

The man was smiling, but Hy could see he was serious. For some reason, he'd not expected that a duke's son would be subjected to beatings.

Lightner gestured to a blur of bruising at the front of the throat. "Do you see this?"

"What's it from?"

"I'm thinking a knot in the r-rope would explain the crushed l-l-larynx. It was a method of g-garroting popular in India some t-twenty years ago. Have you s-seen such cases before?"

"Never heard of it." Hy shook his head. "Why do that *and* all this?" He gestured to the bloody mess that was Janssen's side. "Doesn't that seem, er, I dunno—*cruel*?"

"It seems a gruesome—not to mention awkward—way to k-kill somebody." The Englishman frowned, then said in a musing tone, "It almost seems as if the k-killer is sending a m-m-message."

Hy blinked. It did? Before he could ask what kind of message, Lightner glanced around the room. "I d-don't see any instruments, no place for p-paperwork. It doesn't look as if m-much work gets done here."

"Feehan is as useless as tits on a boar, sir. I've got another fellow I trust for this sorta thing. We can use him next time—" Hy broke off. "I don't mean that I think there will *be* a next time."

"I think it p-probable."

"Based on what?"

"If this is the s-same killer, then they've n-not only gotten away with murder twice, but they allowed another person to pay for their crimes. They could have gotten away undetected, yet here they are, killing again using the s-same m-method. Why would somebody d-do that?"

"So you think it ain't the same man?"

"That, D-Detective, is what I intend to f-find out."

★   ★   ★

Jasper had thought the detective's description of Murderer's Alley was an exaggeration. In truth, Jasper didn't feel safe visiting the location even in broad daylight with a hulking police officer beside him.

They held handkerchiefs over their mouths, as raw sewage filled the streets and was enough to make a man ill.

"Right here." Law pointed to a stretch of filth-covered cobbles between two sets of rickety stairs that led down into rooms Jasper didn't even want to think about. Overhead were dozens of glassless windows that had been made by removing sections of clapboard. People hung out of half of them, and others were covered in rags shifting listlessly in the heavy air. Jasper could tell by the sheer volume of waste clogging the street that there would be hundreds, if not thousands, of souls packed into the grim buildings.

The temperature in the closed-in alley was excruciating.

Jasper's lightweight coat was not nearly light enough.

Paisley would run screaming back to England if Jasper knelt to examine the cobbles for signs of the earlier murders. Besides, there was so much filth—excrement, both animal and human—that it would be impossible to tell.

He tilted his head back to look up at the windows, and the dozen or so people who'd been looking out all disappeared, like so many gophers down holes.

"I'm finished," he told Law, who heaved a sigh of relief, sweat running in rivulets down his reddened face.

They walked down the alley to Baxter Street, the buildings looming over them as if hurrying them on their way. Less than half a block away was Molly O'Reilly's, whose door was propped open, music from an out-of-tune piano pouring out even though it wasn't yet ten in the morning.

As they entered the saloon, Law leaned down and whispered, "That's Lorena Paxton, sir—over by the bartender."

"And she is?"

"She runs the place."

"What of M-Molly?"

"Before my time."

Madam Lorena looked up and saw them, her carmine-tinted lips curving into a carnivorous smile. She was a striking auburn-haired woman wearing a revealing gold-and-red gown that clashed violently with her hair. She looked younger than Jasper would have expected—surely not much more than thirty—but then he didn't have extensive experience with madams and brothels. At least none that he remembered. He found them sordid, and even the most sophisticated decor could never dispel the feeling.

Not that Molly O'Reilly's was sophisticated. Indeed, a thick patina of grit overlay every surface, including the customers—of which there were quite a few for such an early hour.

"Well, hello, Hy, you look like you've been to hell and back. I didn't expect to see you." The madam gave a raucous laugh. "Ever again, in fact." Madam Lorena slid her arms up the big man's chest and around his thick neck and yanked his head down, planting a loud, smacking kiss on his mouth.

"Good God, Lorie," Law muttered, wiping red paint off his mouth, his battered face much the same hue.

The madam turned her sparkling brown eyes on Jasper. "Well, look at *you.*" She subjected Jasper to an inspection that left him feeling naked. "I *know* I've never met you before. But I can guess who you are: the English duke's son—Lord somethin'-or-other—who rolled off the boat only yesterday?"

"That is p-p-precisely who I am—D-Detective Inspector Something-or-Other."

She laughed, and Jasper appreciated the result, which was surely her intention in wearing a gown that was cut so dangerously low.

"Handsome *and* witty." She cut Law a saucy look. "You drink on the house for bringin' him to me first, Hy."

Law tried to demur, but Jasper said, "Thank you; a drink would be l-lovely."

"What's your fancy, *my lord?*"

Jasper suspected she wasn't talking about alcohol. "I'll l-l-leave the choice to you, ma'am."

"Oh, no *ma'am*-ing here—call me Lorie. I, on the other hand, will only call you *my lord.*" She leaned close, her full breasts pressing against his arm. "And I hope to be calling you *often.*" Her milky-white arm snaked around his shoulder, and she played with the hair at the nape of his neck as she whispered, "You can have *anything* you want, my lord."

"That's very g-generous, Lorie." Jasper carefully disentangled himself on the pretext of taking a seat on one of the rickety stools.

"As it s-s-so happens, what I'd like is to t-talk to D–Dr. Feehan, if he is still here."

"Talk?" She pouted at Jasper and then turned away, gesturing for the barkeep. "Three of my finest, Jimmy. I need somethin' to loosen up my lordship here."

The bartender took a bottle from beneath the bar rather than behind it.

Miss Lorena turned back to Jasper. "Now you *know* that talkin' wasn't what I meant, honey." Her look was teasing, but Jasper saw steel in her pretty eyes. "I'd like to welcome you to the Points all right and proper. If you don't want *me*, that's just fine. Trust me, sugar, it's *orl korrect* if you don't swing toward the ladies—"

Law groaned. "Lorie, dammit—"

The madam raised a dismissive hand at Law's mortification. "I don't make it widely known, but I've got some fine young gents I can provide for your pleasure, or one of each, if that's your fancy. All on the house for a man like yourself." She hesitated and added, "Provided you agree to sit here at the bar for an hour before *an'* after."

Jasper blinked. "You wish me to sit at your b-bar? May I ask *why*?"

"Honey, your voice *alone* is reason enough for me to fuck you. As for the rest of you?" She gave him another incinerating inspection. "Well, I could just eat you up with a spoon."

Jasper had absolutely no response to that.

"You've got class. And class is good for business."

Jasper considered telling her that a floor one's feet didn't stick to or more frequent bathing by both clientele and employees might also increase her business, not to mention her establishment's prestige. Instead he said, "If I c-could speak to Dr. Feehan, I promise to c-come back and m-make myself . . . *seen*."

She studied him with eyes as cold as a glacier. "But not right now."

"Not right n-now," he agreed. "I'm on d-duty, you see."

She cast Law a look from beneath lowered lids. "You want to give old Hy here a good example to follow."

Jasper smiled. "Exactly."

She laughed as she turned to a woman lounging beside the piano player. "Go pour some coffee into Doc, Sally, and tell him he's got a guest. He ain't in the best condition, my lord," she said once the girl left. "You'll have to make do with me until he's able to talk."

"It j-just so happens I was h-hoping to ask you about Mr. Alard Janssen. Are you f-familiar with him?"

"Oh, lover, what whore in this city ain't? That man would fuck a knothole in a fence. Well, he *would* have," she insisted at Law's agonized groan. "God have mercy on his soul." She crossed herself.

"When was the last t-t-t-time you s-s-saw him?" Jasper ground his teeth, hating his wretched tongue in that moment.

Miss Lorena Paxton gave him a knowing smile, as if she were accustomed to making men stammer.

"Funny you should ask—he was here Friday. But he wasn't here to fuck."

"Lorie!"

Jasper looked at his associate, whose face had continued red since they'd walked in the door. Who would have known his rough-and-tumble-looking detective was so prudish? Jasper had half a mind to send him on some errand—perhaps to a nunnery—where he'd not have his sensibilities outraged every ten seconds by harmless innuendo and vulgar language. He caught the man's eyes and frowned. Law, impossibly, turned one shade darker. But he clamped his jaws shut and gave an abrupt nod.

The madam watched this exchange and then laughed, once again pressing her chest against Jasper's arm, her hand sliding all the way up his thigh. "My, my, my," she said with a husky chuckle, "you're just *fine* all over, aren't you?"

Jasper shifted his body slightly before he embarrassed himself.

The madam grinned and removed her hand. "Hy wasn't always such a prude, my lord." She winked at him. "You come in by yourself if you want to have a chat about the kinda things we used to get up to."

"You know each other w-well?"

"You could say I know Hy *intimately*."

Law gritted his teeth. "We grew up together, sir."

"Ah."

"My lord don't care about that, Hy. He wants to know about Janssen—isn't that right, sugar?"

"What was Janssen h-here to do, if not to eng-engage in intercourse?"

"What do men *always* do if they ain't drinkin', fightin', or fuckin'?"

"Why do I f-feel the answer to your question is not r-reading scripture?"

She threw her head back and laughed, her action attracting the eyes of every male in that part of the bar. Once she'd collected herself, she said, "He was talkin', darlin'."

"To whom?"

She turned. "Jimmy—did you talk to Janssen the other night?"

The lanky bartender ambled over, rag in hand. "He was in here for a bit."

"Lord Jasper wants to know if he had anything interestin' to say."

"Interesting? No. He said he was looking for somebody."

"Who?"

Jimmy shrugged. "He didn't say, and he drank up and left, so I'm guessin' whoever it was wasn't here."

"D-Did he say anything else?"

Jimmy's narrow brown eyes slid to the madam, who shrugged. "Oh, go on—tell him whatever you heard."

"He wanted to know why Lorie only hired, er, well, old crones. His words, not mine, Lorie," he added hastily.

"What d-did he mean?" Jasper asked the madam.

"His sort wanted virgins—or at least what they were *told* were virgins—but he'd take a real woman if he had to." She grimaced with disgust. "I take it he was headed over to Solange's?"

Jimmy nodded. "That's what he said. He said he'd much rather pay an American whore than a French one, but—" Again he shrugged.

"Was his predilection w-widely known?"

"I'm guessin' madams and pimps knew what he wanted." She snorted. "And probably any of his cronies who shared the same tastes."

So, a reformer with a penchant for virgins. Jasper wondered if Mrs. Janssen knew about her dead husband's particular vice.

"D-Did Janssen come to your saloon often?"

"He'd been here more often these past few months." She frowned. "And he came in with some other man just last week. You remember him, Jimmy?"

"Yeah, he didn't stay long, and I didn't get his name, Lorie."

"I didn't know who the other man was—well, I *didn't*, Hy," she insisted in response to Law's snort of disbelief. "I haven't fucked *every* man in this city, Hieronymus Law, no matter what you might think—you big prig." She turned to Jasper. "I can check the book to see if either of them took one of my girls."

"Thank y-you; I'd appreciate that."

"Is that so, sugar? Well, I look forward to you *showin'* your appreciation. Now, anythin' else?"

"Did D–Dunbarton and Sealy ever come in here?"

Her eyes widened, and not with pleasure this time. "Oh no. We ain't back to that again." She turned on Law, her expression vicious. "You bastards already killed one of my girls—a girl who was obviously innocent, since it turns out the lunatic is back to killin'. Haven't you done enough, Hy? Don't tell me you're back here trawling for another whore to hang."

"Calm down, Lor—"

She was fast, remarkably so. If she'd been holding a blade, Law would have been squirming in agony on the floor. Or dead. As it was, he wore a hand-shaped print on his cheek.

"You sanctimonious son of a bitch! Don't you *dare* come into my business and tell me how to think or speak or what to do—not after what you did to Caitlyn."

You could have heard the proverbial pin drop, and the air shimmered with incipient violence. Jasper had never participated in a pub brawl before; he wondered if that was where they were headed. He didn't fancy Law's chances against the fiery madam.

"We're n-not here to arrest anyone," Jasper assured her. "We're here to ask a f-f-few questions."

She pulled her eyes off Law as grudgingly as a drunk relinquishing a bottle.

"Yeah, Sealy and Dunbarton came in here. Like I told Hy *back then*, neither of them did their fuckin' here. They came to play cards—they liked my tables 'cause I run an honest shop."

"They c-came in together—they were f-friends?"

She shrugged. "I don't know if they were friends, but they were friendly."

Jasper thought she made an interesting distinction. "Do you remember if either of those t-two men ever met J-Janssen in here?"

"No, I can't remember—why should I even try?"

"What about if I p-promised to sit for *t-t-two* hours at your bar?" he offered.

Her lips twitched as she fought a smile. "Look at *you*, my lord. A bit of a whore yourself, eh?"

Beside him, Law's body jolted at the accusation, but his mouth—thankfully—remained shut.

Jasper grinned. "I've been c-called worse."

She gave another of her low, sultry laughs, and some of the tension eased out of the room. "I can't remember ten minutes ago, sugar, but every businesswoman worth her salt keeps a book, and I may have made note of it. How's that?"

"That would be l-lovely."

Law gazed at the madam's back as she ascended the stairs, the mark on his face a stark stain on his cheek.

Jasper was considering what—if anything—to say when a loud voice came from their right.

"You must be the *stupidest* fucking squarehead alive, Law."

The big detective jolted and turned toward the doorway, where Jasper saw the outline of three men: two men in uniform and one in plain clothes.

The barroom, which hadn't yet recovered from Lorena's outburst, again simmered with tension. For his part, Jasper needed to run the new man's phrase through his head several times before he could translate it, as the newcomer spoke with the broadest Irish accent he'd ever heard.

All three men came to a halt a few feet away; they were looking at Jasper rather than Law.

"You must be the limey," the man dressed in plain clothes said, his nasty grin exposing several blackened teeth.

Jasper inclined his head. "I'm afraid you have me at a d-d-disadvantage, as I d-don't know your n-name."

All three men's jaws sagged in a way that made Jasper smile. It was a common reaction: shock, disbelief, humor, and then derision. He watched the familiar parade of emotions move across their faces and waited.

It was the leader who recovered first. "Well, I'll be d-d-d-damned!"

His associates laughed uproariously, and even a few of the bar patrons chuckled.

Jasper sighed. It was, he supposed, time to make an impression.

CHAPTER 13

Hy was a fool; he should have known stepping foot into Molly's was like hiring a damned town crier, but he could hardly help with an investigation if he were ducking and dodging McElhenny's goons every step of the way.

Hy faced the man who'd been his first partner at the Sixth back when he'd walked a beat—a man who still hated Hy's guts because he'd reported Ryan's brutality with a robbery suspect, a level of violence that left the suspect a drooling vegetable. Ryan's reprimand—a two-month delay in getting his detective badge—had been too minor, in Hy's opinion, but Ryan had never forgiven him for it.

"What do you want, Ryan?"

Officer Terrence "Terror" Ryan pulled his eyes off the Englishman with obvious regret, his smile slipping when he looked at Hy. "Cap'n wants to see your ugly mug—couldn't imagine *why*."

Coming from a man as ugly as Ryan, it wasn't much of an insult. "I was going to see him today."

Ryan crossed his arms in a mocking stance. "Oh, *were* you now." When Ryan said the words, it sounded more like *ahh, waer yeh neow*. Although Ryan had gotten off the boat from Ireland when he was a lad, his accent was stronger than that of any man in Dublin. In Hy's opinion, he was the sort of Irishman who gave the Irish a bad name: vulgar, rash, and brutal.

"If that's the case, you can come with us now," Ryan said, when Hy didn't rise to his taunt.

Before Hy could answer, Lightner spoke. "Detective L-Law is working for m-me."

Ryan gave the Englishman a look of exaggerated interest. "I'm glad you mentioned that, me l-l-l-lord. The cap'n says you can forget about Janssen's case—we'll take care of that." He grinned. "We've just been by Feehan's to collect the body and send it to Doc Kirby." Ryan fanned the air in front of his nose. "Mighty ripe, he is." His men laughed. "So you"—he pointed a finger at Lightner—"can fuck off and find somethin' else to investigate. And you—" He turned to Hy.

Hy had excellent reflexes honed by years of boxing when he was younger. But eight weeks of abuse in the Tombs had taken their toll, and he never even saw Ryan's baton coming.

Lightner, on the other hand, had not only anticipated the detective's attack—he blocked it and disarmed the man.

The pretty walking stick he'd been holding all morning became a blur of amber and ebony. The Englishman himself hardly seemed to move as his cane cracked Ryan's wrist and sent the black baton flying. Nobody was more surprised than Ryan, who gave a startled yelp and clutched his arm.

By the time Hy thought to stop the copper nearest him—a huge block of a man named Seamus Houlihan—Lightner had already smacked the other uniformed copper, Brandon O'Connor, in the throat with the flat of his hand. The movement appeared light and quick—more like a love tap—but it was enough to drive the bulky plug of a copper gasping to his knees.

When Law looked up from the writhing patrolman, it was to see the tip of the walking stick resting lightly in the vulnerable hollow of Ryan's throat. Ryan was still as a statue, aware of how little effort the Englishman would need to expend to cause him a great deal of pain.

"Detective L-Law is working for the Eighth P-Precinct now," the Englishman said, using the same polite tone he always employed. He flashed his teeth, but Hy wouldn't have called it a smile. "As for the J-Janssen murder case? Please refer Captain McElhenny to Mayor Wood or Superintendent T-Tallmadge."

When Lightner lowered the stick, Ryan seemed to recall where he was—in the middle of a saloon full of loose-lipped Irishmen in the Points; his humiliation would be known in far County Cork before the day was over. Hy didn't bother to hide his grin.

"Come on, lads." Ryan smacked the back of O'Connor's head, as the big man was still on his knees. Ryan's gaze was riveted to

Lightner, and his hatred was a pulsing, tangible thing. The English-man had earned himself an enemy today. And all because of Hy.

"You might think the mayor or some bloody committee runs the Points, but you'd be wrong—*dead* wrong." Ryan's hand uncon-sciously massaged his wrist, and he wrenched his eyes off Lightner just long enough to shoot Hy a murderous glare. "We're not done yet, Law." He made his exit to the sound of loud whispers and choked laughter. Ryan wasn't quite out the door when loud clapping came from overhead.

Hy turned to find Lorie standing up on the landing, wearing a smile that stretched from ear to ear.

"Oh, Lord Jasper!" She clutched her bosom with one hand, staring at Lightner, who was once again lounging gracefully on his barstool, his patrician features as unreadable as ever. "I think I just fell in love."

★   ★   ★

Once the excitement over the kerfuffle was over, Lorena Paxton led them upstairs.

"I checked my book back to the beginnin' of the year while you were playin' with Ryan," she said over her shoulder as she led them down the hall to the door at the end. "Janssen sat at my tables, but he must have had some other arrangement, because he didn't take a girl here until May." She stopped and turned to Jasper. "Before you ask, there wasn't nobody special; he tried 'em all. As for whether he knew Sealy or Dunbarton, they all three played cards here, and they all had the same taste for *girls*. That's all I know." She opened the door and motioned them inside.

The three of them looked down on an alarmingly yellow man, who lay on a narrow bed.

"What's wrong with him?" Law asked.

Lorena Paxton shrugged. "He's been gettin' this way more and more often. I pay him to check the girls, and then he just seems to lose his senses. Nellie—the girl he had last night—said he went through an entire bottle of whiskey. He's down for the count." Her mouth pursed. "He sold all his equipment for cuttin' people up to pay some gambling debt." While she spoke, the doctor never twitched. "I'll keep him here till he's dried out and probably after, too."

"Oh?" Jasper said.

"His house went the way of his equipment."

"Ah."

"He's the only doctor I know who'll come into a place like mine. Nobody else cares about a bunch of whores." She fixed them both with a hard look. "If I don't take care of my girls, nobody else will."

★ ★ ★

They opted to walk over to Centre Street to hail a hackney, since an omnibus had lost a wheel and traffic was locked in both directions up and down Baxter.

Hy studied the other man from the corner of his eye; Lightner looked just as pleasant as ever, and yet he'd stopped two men—not small or weak men, either—cold in less than thirty seconds. Hy didn't think he'd ever met anyone who was so hard to read; except for a moment of annoyance at the Tombs, he hadn't seen the Englishman show any emotion at all. It was like there wasn't a real person behind the courteous manner and inside the well-dressed body.

Hy had felt an unexpected surge of anger—and a bit of embarrassment—when Ryan mocked the Englishman's stutter. As if it weren't bad enough with all the nasty shit people said about the Irish—how they were all drunks and criminals—men like Ryan made it worse for the rest of them by acting like a thug. Yet Lightner's expression hadn't flickered. Was he so accustomed to mockery that it just slid off him? If so, Hy envied him that ability—an ability *he* didn't possess. He also envied him the ability to put two men down so quickly.

"Can I ask you something, sir?"

"You m-may ask me anything, Detective."

"That thing you did back there—with your hand?"

"It is *savate*, although I've p-put my own stamp on it. Savate is a French street fighting t-technique that d-developed in the port city of Marseilles. I've incorporated elements of *la c-c-canne* as well." He lifted his walking stick. "The skill is a p-product of my m-misspent youth." He wore a faint smile.

"You barely seemed to tap O'Connor, er, the big fellow, with your hand, and he went down."

"The p-point of contact is the heel of the h-hand, although it might appear to be a s-slap or push." He glanced up at Hy. "It's a h-handy form of c-combat when a man doesn't l-look as formidable as you."

Hy gave an embarrassed laugh. "I wasn't very formidable back there, sir. Thanks for stoppin' Ryan. If you hadn't, I'd probably be facedown on Lorie's barroom floor right now."

Lightner accepted his gratitude with a nod. "T-Tell me, what did Detective Ryan mean?"

"You mean about who runs the Points?"

Lightner nodded.

"Just that Wood isn't a Tammany man—people figure because he's a democrat, he's in with the rest of 'em, but he ain't. At least he ain't right *now*, not after he ran for a second term without first gettin' Tammany's approval."

"Tammany Hall is the d-democrat organization?"

"Aye." Hy cut Lightner a look. "You *do* need to understand their power here, sir. It's—well, let's just say Tammany is less a political organization and more a gang. You don't want to get sideways with them."

"I shall t-take that into consideration. So, we have a J-Janssen-Dunbarton-Sealy connection in that the three m-men played cards together." He paused and then added, "I'll have to ask Mrs. D-Dunbarton about that."

"You're goin' to see her?"

"Did I n-neglect to mention she was at Mrs. J-Janssen's house yesterday?"

"Er, yes, sir, you *did* forget to mention that." So, working with the son of duke meant entry *anywhere*.

"We spoke briefly." Lightner's lips twisted into an odd smile.

"What did you think of her, sir?"

"V-Very intelligent, but, er, c-combative."

Hy laughed at his careful description. "She sure gave her pa a piece of her mind that day. And then started in on me—tellin' me about police incompetence."

"Yes, I received a piece of her mind yesterday; I d-daresay Mrs. Dunbarton hands out p-pieces quite liberally."

For once, Hy didn't envy the man his ability to go places Hy himself would never be welcomed.

CHAPTER 14

Solange Dupuy was an extraordinarily lovely woman—one of the most beautiful Jasper had ever seen. She wore a thin red silk dressing gown that did more to enhance than conceal the curves of her lush body. As beautiful as she was, he was not drawn to her. Indeed, there was something repellent about Mrs. Dupuy.

"M-My men will need to question all your employees," Jasper said, as he and the Frenchwoman sat in what looked to be her private sitting room.

"Again? They were here yesterday."

Her accent should have been charming, but the acquisitive glint in her eyes was difficult to overlook.

"Most of y-your employees were elsewhere yesterday." He gave her a polite smile. "I'm sure you wish to c-cooperate."

She heaved an exaggerated sigh. "I'll send down the girls who are alone and see the other customers on their way—will that be enough for you?"

Jasper ignored her question. "Tell me about Mr. J-Janssen."

She shrugged, her voluptuous body rippling beneath the blood-red silk. "There's not much to tell. He was a good customer until about six or seven months ago, and then he stopped coming—at least for girls. When I asked him where he was getting—" She stopped and gave Jasper an assessing look. "I'll put it this way: Mr. Janssen had expensive tastes that not many will supply."

"P-Please don't be coy," Jasper said pleasantly, struggling to mask his revulsion. "We c-can just as easily have this c-conversation in a cell in the T-Tombs."

Her nostrils flared, but she said, "He liked young girls."

"How young?"

"Everything here is legal, and all the girls want to be here."

"How *young*?"

She shrugged, her expression bored. "Always the legal age, but they must be *la vierge*. You understand?"

Jasper decided that the searching of her establishment would be very, very, very thorough. Indeed, it would likely require the closure of her business for several days, perhaps longer.

"You say he'd been going elsewhere for some t-time. Did he tell you where he was having his n-n-needs met?"

"No, he refused. He'd just smirk whenever I asked him where he was going." He could almost hear her teeth grinding. "First it was Sealy, then Dunbarton and finally Janssen—three of my best customers, all lured elsewhere."

Jasper pressed so hard that the nib of his pencil snapped and tore through the paper.

"I beg your pardon, what w-was that?" he asked, realizing he'd missed the last thing she'd said.

"I *said* those three paid top dollar, and for months somebody else got all their money. Well, until these past few months."

"What happened these p-past few months?"

She looked at him as if he were an idiot. "They're dead."

"*B-Before* they died."

"Oh. Well, Janssen came back."

"But not Dunbarton and Sealy?"

"No, they just came here sometimes to drink and meet their cronies."

"Dunbarton had meetings here? With whom?"

"Well, Janssen—those two were as thick as thieves."

"Anyone else? S-Sealy?"

She gave an irritable shrug. "I don't recall."

"P-Perhaps you might check your b-book?"

She frowned. "How do you know I keep a book?" Jasper cocked his head, and she scowled. "Fine. I'll check."

"Was Janssen here Saturday night?"

"No," she said sharply, and then muttered something indecipherable and angry sounding in French. "He was supposed to be here, because he made a special arrangement the last time he was here—a very *expensive* arrangement."

"But you d-don't know if he was here or n-not Saturday night, since you were—where was it again?"

"Boston—but I *know* he wasn't here."

"How?"

"I just do."

"Do you have w-witnesses that you were in B-Boston?"

Jasper knew he was bad to enjoy her horrified expression.

"You can't think *I* had anything to do with his murder?"

Jasper smiled.

"Yes, I have *several witnesses*," she huffed. "Several *respectable* witnesses."

"Good. You can g-give their names and addresses when we take your statement. When was the last t-time *you* saw Janssen?"

"Last month," she said without hesitation. "A week or so before his usual night—"

"Usual n-night?"

"Yes, he always came on the second or third Saturday of the month—well, that is what he used to do."

"You're saying he c-came here for a prostitute last month?"

"Yes, and he was very pleased after his last visit, so he made an arrangement for this past Saturday." She stopped and grimaced. "But he didn't come, and now I'm stuck with—" She glanced at Jasper and changed tack. "Who knows if I'll make my money back from someone else?" She looked to him for sympathy and found none.

"What w-would you say if I told you that M-Mr. Dunbarton had been murdered near your alley d-door—and then m-moved?"

Solange flinched slightly but then laughed. "I'd say you were lying." The Frenchwoman was an excellent liar herself, but Jasper had seen the flash of worry in her eyes.

"I'd like to s-see that book you m-mentioned. The one with all the names and d-dates."

She gave a rough, bawdy laugh that did not match her delicate features. "And why would I do that?"

"I should hate to have to sh-shut down your p-place of business," Jasper lied.

Her eyes narrowed. "I have powerful friends, Detective. I *should hate* to have to ask them for help." Jasper smiled, and she recoiled. When he didn't respond to her threat, she said, "I keep my book in French. You wouldn't be able to read it."

"Let me w-worry about that."

Jasper could hear the gears grinding in her clever mind. "You promise not to take action about anything you read?"

Jasper laughed.

"Then why should I give it to you?"

"To stop me from tearing your p-place apart brick by b-brick to find it."

Her eyes sparked with intense dislike; Jasper seemed to be making enemies without even trying: Featherstone, Davies, Mrs. Dunbarton, Ryan, and now this woman. He'd been here less than two days; who knew what the rest of the week would bring?

★ ★ ★

Mrs. Dunbarton's school for young ladies was just behind Canal on Lispenard Street.

Jasper would have walked, but he wanted a few minutes to look at the book Solange had grudgingly given him. And so here he was, in another hackney. As ever, the street traffic was a snarl of carts, pedestrians, and the ubiquitous omnibuses.

He could see immediately that it was a daily journal that recorded business rather than private musings. Judging by the dates, this one began at the first of the year. It was in French—a language in which he was fluent—and had neat columns of women's names on each page. Beside each name were other names—male—and dollar amounts.

Some of the women's names appeared only once, and the amounts next to those names was staggering; these had to be the young girls.

Jasper flipped through the pages, feeling sicker with each name. In addition to Janssen's name last month, he saw several men listed whom he'd heard of—a prominent banker and a politician. He worked his way back from today, counting the female names that appeared only once; he counted fifty-nine names. Fifty-nine. The number was horrifying; where were all these girls coming from?

The cab rolled to a stop, shaking Jasper from his grim musing. The hackney deposited him in front of a neat, tidy building sandwiched between two ramshackle tenements. A prim, simple sign reading *The New Beginnings School for Young Ladies* hung above the front door.

Jasper let himself into a smallish foyer that looked freshly painted and smelled of beeswax. The dark-wood wainscoting was glowing.

"How may I help you, sir?"

The question came from a young woman seated behind an imposing mahogany desk in front of double doors; the arrangement put him in mind of a gatehouse protecting a castle.

"I'm Detective Inspector J-Jasper Lightner with the M-Metropolitan Police." He handed her a card. "I'm here to speak to Mrs. D-Dunbarton."

The girl's eyes widened when she saw the honorific on the card, and she sprang to her feet, exposing a modestly designed blue stuff gown with a long white pinafore like Mrs. Dunbarton's. "One moment, er, my lord; I'll go find her."

"Thank you," Jasper said, but she'd already yanked open the door and fled.

He examined the foyer walls, which had a series of framed prints extolling the virtues of diligence, education, and cleanliness.

"Ah, Lord Jasper."

He turned, his lips curving into a smile at the sound of the acerbic voice. "Mrs. D-Dunbarton, thank you for seeing me. I apologize f-for not coming yesterday."

She strode toward him and shoved her hand at him. Today he knew what to do with it. She was dressed identically to yesterday, and Jasper suspected Mrs. Dunbarton favored black even when she was not in mourning.

"I imagine you were quite busy yesterday," she said, her head cocked as she looked up at him with her appraising stare.

"D-Do you have a few moments?"

"A very few." She gestured to the door behind the desk. "I'll be in the teacher's sitting room, Miss Kitchner."

The girl nodded, big eyes on Jasper.

Behind the door was a long corridor with more doors. Mrs. Dunbarton marched to the left, the susurration of her crepe gown loud in the narrow hallway. "I'm pleased all my teachers are in class right now, or there would be another six women all gazing worshipfully at you."

Jasper glanced down at the woman marching beside him, but her hideous bonnet hid her face from his view.

She stopped in front of the door at the end of the hall and turned to look up at him. "I'm sorry. That was cattish and uncalled for. I'm not sure what it is about you that makes me behave like such a targe."

Jasper didn't know either. He opened the door and inclined his head.

She preceded him and gestured to the small sitting area. "Please have a seat."

Jasper sat, propping his stick against the arm of the chair and setting his hat on his lap.

She glanced at the watch pinned to her bodice. "I can spare fifteen minutes."

Jasper opened his notebook to the questions he'd jotted down. "Will you t-tell me about your m-marriage?"

"Our marriage was a business arrangement right from the start."

"That is n-not so unusual."

"It is in that *I* approached *Felix* and suggested marriage. I can see that surprises you."

"I'm beginning to think n-nothing you do could surprise me, Mrs. D-Dunbarton."

"I will take that as a compliment," she said, echoing his words from yesterday. "I'm no beauty, and the young men were not exactly queuing up to offer me marriage." Her eyes held a rare glint of humor. "It's likely I would've remained a spinster all my life, and that wouldn't have suited me. My father had already torn out most of his hair trying to force me to conform or convince various cronies to take me off his hands, but there were no takers."

Jasper tried to imagine himself married to her and had to admit the notion held no appeal. Although, he thought with some amusement, it would be diverting to watch her and Paisley jockey for power in his household.

"You say y-you approached Mr. Dunbarton?" Jasper prodded.

"We met at Zuza and Alard's wedding—he was an acquaintance of Alard's, although not a close one. Felix would never admit to it, but I think he probably paid for an invitation so he might be thrown in the path of wealthy, eligible females. Felix was fifteen years older and had never married. I daresay he would have remained a bachelor, but he'd made a series of dreadful investments in the late forties and was almost insolvent. I know this because I demanded full disclosure of his debts before I agreed to marry him."

Jasper's testicles contracted slightly; he had to admire Dunbarton's fearlessness, if nothing else about the man. "W-Would it surprise you to know your husband p-played cards with both Mr. Sealy and Mr. J-Janssen?"

"It wouldn't *surprise* me, but I didn't know about it."

"You were close with b-both the J-Janssens?"

"I knew Alard well—he is of our set—but I wouldn't say we were close. But Zuza is a dear friend."

"Did they have a h-happy marriage?"

"You'd have to ask Zuza."

"Surely a w-woman with your forthright opinions has an impression?"

She laughed. "Touché. But please tell me you won't arrest anyone based on my *impression*? I have the feeling that is what happened to the unfortunate woman they arrested for Wilbur's and Felix's murders—it was somebody's *impression* that she was guilty."

"You d-don't believe Caitlyn Grady was guilty?"

"I thought it was preposterous. Perhaps a woman might get angry enough to kill her *own* husband—but why kill another woman's?"

A laugh slipped out before Jasper could catch it. He could see by the glint in her eyes that she appreciated his response.

"Not to mention the girl was hardly larger than me. You saw Alard Janssen, Inspector? Well, Felix was even larger." She hesitated and then said, "Did you know I met her?"

"Who?" Jasper asked.

"Miss Caitlyn Grady."

"No, I *didn't* know that." Why the hell hadn't Law told him about this? "When was this?"

"Not long after she confessed. I received a letter from her, asking to see me—to apologize for what she'd done. The captain at the Sixth Precinct tried to dissuade me, but I wanted to hear what she had to say."

"What did she say?"

"That she was sorry. It wasn't a long conversation—no more than a few minutes."

"And she admitted to killing them?"

Mrs. Dunbarton frowned. "Well, not in so many words, but she apologized. Still—"

"Yes?"

"I don't believe she was the murderer."

"Then why confess?"

She gave an unladylike snort. "I'm sure you or I would sign confessions if enough pressure was applied."

Jasper studied the dry-eyed woman across from him, not quite sure what to make of a widow who could calmly discuss visiting her husband's confessed murderer.

"Coldhearted."

"I beg your pardon?"

"You were wondering what is wrong with me that I can talk about Felix's murder like this."

"That is q-quite a skill you have, Mrs. Dunbarton—reading m-men's minds." And Jasper had to admit he didn't like it.

"Not really. Men are simple creatures. They are easily understood and managed if one is firm and consistent."

"You make us s-sound like p-puppies with a p-propensity to soil the carpet."

That amused her. "That's because you *are* a lot like puppies—although not when it comes to your wants."

"Oh? And what d-do we want?"

"Money, power, and sex—not necessarily in that order."

Jasper's eyebrows shot up his forehead.

"I suppose you find my plain speaking vulgar."

"Are we really s-so simple?"

She ignored his question. "I think Zuza and Alard had a marriage that suited their needs."

He could see that was all she'd say on the matter. "You t-told me how you came to be married—but you didn't tell me if your m-marriage was happy."

She gave him a look of exaggerated shock. "Why, my lord, do you think *I* might have killed Felix in a fit of pique? And then developed a taste for it and killed my friends' husbands too?" Her eyes narrowed in a mock-sinister stare. "Shouldn't *you* be nervous in this room with me? Alone?"

He couldn't help smiling. "I once h-heard a wise l-lady say that a woman might kill *her own* husband but not another's."

She laughed, the sound surprisingly girlish. "You are a rare man indeed, Detective Inspector, one who listens to what a woman says. What would your compatriots think if word of that got out? Don't worry—I shan't tell anyone. But to answer your question, my marriage to Felix was much the same the day he died as it was the day we married. We rarely spent any time together, knew very little about one another, and had no expectations of each other—well, other than the obvious ones of avoiding disgracing the family or driving us into bankruptcy. I saw Felix no more than a few times a week. He had his ventures, and I have mine."

"Yet I understand your h-husband was on the board of at least one of your charities, so you must have had some common interest."

"That also was a business arrangement. Alard found several of my buildings for me—including this one—and Felix was president of Ohio Life Insurance and Trust and financed the sale. The contract called for an executive on the board, so Felix took that position."

"Was Alard on the b-board?"

"No, although both he and Zuza donated a good deal of money to several of my charitable enterprises."

"Was Sealy also active in the school?"

Her lips curved. "Why, Inspector, are you trying to say there is some connection between my *school* and these murders?"

Jasper returned her smile. "I am a d-detective, Mrs. Dunbarton; that is what I d-do: ask questions."

"First off, let me tell you this, my lord: I've set up seventeen charities."

"That is a g-great number."

"It is. So, keep in mind there are, on average, a dozen board members for each venture, and then there are all the donors. While it seems coincidental that some of the men who were involved in the charities were murdered, you must be aware that there are only a few hundred wealthy New Yorkers who can afford to offer such support." Her gaze turned serious. "I heartily endorse your zeal for apprehending a murderer, but donors are skittish, and they won't want to be associated with causes if they are tainted with rumors. I won't suffer, but the women and children we help will. I'd just as soon not have scandalous innuendos inadvertently make their way into the newspaper."

"I understand." He not only understood, he respected her concern.

"To answer your question, one of Wilbur Sealy's construction companies managed the repairs and remodeling of this building. The board engaged him because he and Felix were acquainted—don't ask me *how*, because I don't know."

"Have you ever heard of a m-man named Amos B-Baker?"

Her smooth forehead wrinkled; after a moment she shook her head. "I don't think so."

"How about B-Benjamin Hoyle?"

"I know *who* he is, but we are not acquainted."

"Is he a d-donor?"

"I don't believe so."

"Do you k-keep a list of your donors?"

She sighed. "I shall let you look at it, but I keep it in my study at home, not here." She gave him an appraising look. "I understand you're considering taking the lease for number sixteen on Union Square." Jasper stared, and she chuckled. "Why do you look so shocked? You know how servants are; they probably knew you'd be leasing it even before *you* did. We will be next-door neighbors." A slow, almost playful smile stretched her lips. "So now *you* have a connection to me as well. Perhaps somebody should investigate *you*, my lord."

Jasper smiled. "I'll confess the connection to my d-detective. So, if you d-don't think Miss Grady killed the two men, who d-d-do you believe did?"

"I haven't a clue. And, to be honest, I don't really care." She smirked at his look of surprise. "Come, come, Inspector—I think we both know what kind of man my husband was. If you don't know, you're not much of a detective. If I didn't know, I wouldn't be much of a wife. I know where my husband spent many of his nights— places like this Solange's, where Alard's body was found. I daresay it is no coincidence that both Felix and Wilbur were also found near a brothel."

Did she know exactly *what* sort of sexual partner her husband had favored?

Before he could come up with a subtle way of asking, she continued.

"The people of my class raise their daughters to believe in rosy futures in which people wear lovely clothes and live happy lives. The men we marry—our knights in shining armor—are supposed to protect and shelter us from life's hard realities. From a young age I rebelled against the shackles of ignorance." She gave a humorless laugh. "I learned firsthand that a rosy future was a mirage. My own father has a second family with his mistress—which my mother pretended to know nothing about. But I was under no illusions. I told Felix I would never interfere with his activities so long as he did not interfere with mine. Our relationship was harmonious, but I did not like my husband, and I refuse to feign sorrow at his demise. Felix engaged in repellent pastimes, and it finally caught up with him."

Jasper wondered if she *wanted* to be a suspect in her husband's murder.

"D-Do Mrs. Sealy and Mrs. J-Janssen know?"

"About *Felix*'s philanderings—or their husbands'?"

"The l-latter."

"I should think they do. Do I know for certain? No. Believe it or not, my lord, one's husband's infidelities are not a subject a woman wishes to discuss with her friends. Now, as to whether it bothered them if they did? I doubt Zuza minded. As for Emma Sealy, I don't know her well enough to say. Well, that's not exactly true—I *did* get to know her better after Felix was murdered. I'm sure you can imagine how that brought us together. As to her marriage? I saw them often enough at various social gatherings; Wilbur made no effort to hide his disinterest in his wife. I believe Emma is a beautiful person on the inside, but I could not honestly call her pretty. Wilbur Sealy, on the other hand, was a very attractive man—at least on the outside." Her eyes flickered over Jasper, and her lips curved slightly. "Women will make fools of themselves for such men."

Jasper ignored the dig. "You s-say he was attractive on the outside; d-did you not care for him?"

"I actively *despised* the little I knew of him. He married Emma only for her connections; her father shoved Emma into the marriage because *he'd* fiddled away all the family's money. It was a similar arrangement to my marriage, but Wilbur made no secret of his disdain for poor Emma. At least Felix always treated me with respect in public."

"Mrs. Janssen said you might know where Mrs. Sealy is now."

She stared at him for a long moment, weighing something. "Don't make me regret telling you this, my lord. Emma is in a facility here in the city."

"A f-facility?"

"Yes, a sanatorium. I'm afraid Emma is not well."

"What ails her?"

"You'd need to ask her that."

There were only a few ailments that people did not speak of publicly: insanity, opium or laudanum addiction, and sexual diseases.

"Is she still helping you with your ch-charitable ventures?"

"She still donates, but she hasn't been able to help as much—even before Wilbur's death. I tried to convince her that she needn't hide herself away." She gave an uncharacteristically helpless shrug. "But she refused my assistance."

Jasper hadn't believed Mrs. Dunbarton was the sort of woman to take no for an answer.

"She's fragile, my lord. I do hope you'll exhibit a little mercy when it comes to your dealings with her."

Jasper thought it was an odd word to choose—*mercy*.

"You'll find her at the Acton Institute." Her lips curved into a bitter smile. "It is straight up Broadway, not even a mile away but a different world."

★   ★   ★

A different world turned out to be the perfect phrase for it.

"If you'll wait here, my lord, I'll see if Mrs. Sealy is available."

Jasper took a seat in a waiting room decorated in muted shades of brown and gray, with touches of green here and there. He had to admit it was a soothing environment and didn't feel at all like a hospital or asylum. At least not the sort he'd seen in Paris, the Crimea, or London.

The door opened, and a tall, well-dressed man entered, gripping Jasper's card. "Lord Jasper?" he asked, grinning like a man who'd just received excellent news. "I'm Dr. Acton." Jasper endured the obligatory, bone-crushing handshake. "I understand you're here to see Mrs. Sealy?"

"If she is available."

Acton rubbed his hands together in an eager handwashing gesture. "Well, it depends."

"On?" Jasper prodded when the man seemed to have stalled.

"What this is pertaining to."

Jasper frowned. "Is she b-being kept here against her w-w-will?"

The doctor's lips parted, and he stared at Jasper, arrested. "That's quite a stammer you have, my lord."

Jasper sighed, resignation rather than irritation flaring as he realized he couldn't deal with *this* particular situation with his cane and fists. Still, he'd be damned if he'd listen to whatever quackery Acton was hoping to peddle before getting what he wanted.

"It just so happens stammering is one of the afflictions we treat at the Acton Institute."

"I'm n–not intere—"

"It's a revolutionary treatment," Acton continued, warming to his topic. "What we do is—"

"Have the s–subject stuff their m–mouth with pebbles?" Jasper asked.

Acton frowned. "No. Actually—"

"Make a h–horizontal cut at the base of the t–tongue and remove a triangular-shaped p–p–piece of flesh?"

Acton recoiled. "Goodness, no. We advocate—"

"Declaiming poetry while running up hills? Placing a c–c–cork between teeth and cheek? Sp–Sp–Speaking only while lifting dumb-bells? Trunc-cating the uvula? A d–diet of unleavened bread and ewe's m–m–milk? Removing m–molars? Ins–serting a golden f–f–fork under the tongue? F–F–Fasting? Public humiliation?" Jasper smiled at Acton, who was wide-eyed and openmouthed. "I th–thank you for your offer, but I d–don't wish to be cured, Doctor; I'm happy as I am. Aristotle and N–Newton stammered; that is g–good enough company for me. Now, may I sp–speak to Mrs. Sealy?"

Acton nodded, his cheeks scarlet. "Of course, sir. I never intended to deny you access to Mrs. Sealy. I only came to warn you that she's been quite ill these past few months and she tires easily. Also, she doesn't have access to a mirror." His expression turned grim. "Please remember to moderate your expression when you meet her."

CHAPTER 15

One of the memories he'd been unfortunate enough to retain from his time in Paris was that of patients with gummatous syphilis. Comparatively speaking, Mrs. Sealy was not badly off. Yet.

She offered him a white-gloved hand when he entered her private sitting room, and Jasper bowed over it.

"Th-Thank you f-for seeing me."

Her misshapen cheeks pinkened. "Oh, it's a pleasure, Lord Jasper. Besides, I was expecting you—Hetty said you would likely visit."

"But I just—"

"She told me yesterday when she came to inform me about poor Alard." She smiled, the expression very sweet for all that her features were disfigured by a half dozen gummas, one of which had begun to weep.

"Ah, I see."

"I was just about to have my tea. Would you join me?"

He looked into her soft brown eyes, which held the eager expression of a person who didn't get many visitors. "That would be l-lovely."

"Put the tray on the table, Martha," she said to a hovering maid. Once the girl left, she turned to Jasper. "You're surprised that Hetty anticipated your visit."

"I shouldn't b-be. She is a clever lady."

"Yes, one of the smartest people I know. And also one of the kindest."

Kind wasn't the word Jasper would have used, but he thought he understood what she meant.

She began to prepare the tea, and Jasper noticed she didn't remove her gloves. There were spots of blood showing through the white cotton, especially on her left hand, which appeared to be dominant. He suspected there were other gummas and that even this minor activity caused her pain.

"Hetty said you asked Zuza about Alard's business dealings?"

"Yes, that's correct."

"I'm afraid I don't know anything about Wilbur's business." Her eyes teared as she spoke her dead husband's name, and she pulled a handkerchief from her right sleeve. "I need to apologize in advance for being so emotional, but I'm afraid I feel his loss most keenly." One tear broke away and trickled down her cheek, stopped by the shilling-sized gumma beside her mouth. She dabbed it carefully with her handkerchief and gave him a tremulous smile. "Hetty said you were curious about a man named Amos Baker?"

Jasper had a brief urge to muzzle Hetty. "Have you heard of him?"

"I'm afraid not. Wilbur believed a woman had no place in business. He didn't approve of Hetty and wasn't one of her admirers."

Jasper could understand not liking the woman, but he couldn't see not *admiring* her.

"Mrs. D-Dunbarton is a woman of b-business?"

"Oh, well, you know—all her interests. Even though the schools, libraries, and other charities don't earn a profit, they require a great deal of management, which Wilbur viewed as a masculine pursuit."

"D-Did your husband know Mr. Dunbarton?"

"They were acquainted, but I shouldn't think they knew each other well. I didn't really become close to dear Hetty until after Wilbur was—" She broke off and dabbed at her eyes.

"C-Can you think of anyone who didn't like your h-husband or b-bore him a grudge?"

"Oh, no! Wilbur was just lovely—everyone liked him. He was very warm—very gregarious. He came from New Orleans, and he always said the hotter climate burnt away a person's reservations."

Jasper was trying to come up with an inoffensive way to ask her about the disease her husband must have given her when she solved the problem for him.

"Wilbur had been married before." Her eyes lost their luster and became as hard as stone. "It was his first wife who gave him this."

She gestured to her face. "She was not a woman of virtue. But she came from a wealthy family, and they threatened Wilbur if he sought a divorce for her infidelity. He had no idea that he was sick when we married." She cut him a quick, almost nervous glance—as if daring him to disagree. "He was devastated when he learned he'd been the one to pass this curse along to me."

"When d-did you find out?"

"It's been almost three years now." Again she gestured to the gummas. "These had been forming for some time, but only recently—" Her face spasmed. "Only in the past six months or so did this happen." By *this* she meant that the gummas had begun to suppurate. "I looked fine for *ages* after the first, er, well . . ."

That was the nature of syphilis. For some people there were no initial symptoms; for others there were sores and lesions. For the fortunate, the tertiary stage would never manifest, but a person would live in fear, wondering.

Jasper studied her ruined face, wondering how she could credit her husband's cock-and-bull story. Sealy mightn't have known he had syphilis when he married her, but he would have known after her symptoms manifested, and yet—according to Solange, his procurer—until about six months ago he'd gone on having sexual relations with *children*. How many girls had he raped and infected?

He deserved to die, Jasper.

Jasper recoiled from the vicious thought, stunned that it could originate in his head.

For once, he engaged the voice: *It's not my role to judge; it's for the courts to determine guilt or innocence.*

How very noble of you, Jasper. I'm sure all Sealy's victims would appreciate your nobility.

As Jasper looked across at one of Sealy's victims, he lost the strength to argue.

★　★　★

Hy was beginning to think fondly of the Tombs.

"She belongs to *me*!" the Frenchwoman screamed again, clawing and fighting like a wild animal as Hy led the little girl away.

Hy had found her when he'd requested the key to search a locked room. The employees claimed that only Solange had the keys.

Wherever Solange had gone—likely to complain to whoever took care of police difficulties for her—she'd taken three hours to return. And then Hy had argued with her for another half hour to get the bloody key, until finally he'd told her he'd kick down the door.

And then he'd found *this*.

"Gimme your coat, O'Malley." The girl wore only a chemise.

"My coat? But—"

"Goddammit, just give it to me! She can't go out like this," Hy yelled at the gaping young patrolman.

"She can't go *anywhere*!" Solange hollered right back.

With only one patrolman to hold her while O'Malley shrugged out of his coat, the Frenchwoman broke free, got her hand around a vase full of flowers, and hurled it.

Hy stepped in front of the girl and ended up covered in water and flowers. "That's it!" He grabbed the madam by her shoulders, not bothering to be gentle about it. "You're goin' to spend some time calmin' down." He turned to O'Malley, who'd finally given the scantily clad girl his coat. "Take her down to the station and lock her up until she quits screamin'."

"Er, what for?"

"Detention on suspicion," Hy snapped.

Solange was yelling in French so loudly that Hy didn't hear the door open.

"You!" Solange shrieked at the new arrival, almost breaking free of O'Malley and Markham in her fury to get to Lightner.

Hy was so grateful to see the Englishman that he wanted to hug him.

Lightner took in the scene and then cocked one of his eyebrows. "Is aught amiss, D-Detective?"

A bubble of hysterical laughter tickled his throat. "Er, you could say that, sir." They both winced at a particularly piercing shriek as the two patrolmen hauled Solange out of the room.

Lightner gestured to the girl.

"I found her *chained*." He jabbed a finger toward a bed that was visible in the next room. He lifted her skinny arm to show the raw wounds made by the manacle. "That witch had her *locked* in here." He glanced down at the girl, who'd followed him around as docilely as a lamb. "I think she's drugged."

Other than a slight tick in his jaw, Lightner gave no sign of what he was thinking.

Hy began to feel a bit frantic. "I ain't leavin' her here, sir. Solange claims she *owns* her, but I—"

"No," Lightner agreed, as mildly as ever. "We c-couldn't do that." He turned to the girl. "What's your name, Miss?"

"She don't speak English." Hy's head was getting hotter as he realized how hysterical he sounded.

The Englishman said something to the girl in several languages and shook his head when he got no response. "She's not French, Prussian, Italian, or Russian."

"You speak *all* those languages?"

Lightner crouched down at eye level with the girl. He gently tilted her face to the light. "I think they've g-given her laudanum."

"I reckon she's no older than twelve and maybe as young as nine."

The girl reached for the silver handle on the Englishman's cane, which Hy saw was studded with small—likely precious—blue stones.

"You like that?" Lightner asked, his smile the most genuine one Hy had yet seen. "Why d-don't you keep it safe f-for me?" He handed her the cane, and she took it in both hands while he stood slowly before meeting Hy's gaze. "What are your p-plans for Madam Solange?"

"I thought a few days in lockup might calm her some."

Hy saw amusement in his eyes. "Assaulting a p-police officer?"

"Aye, sounds about right."

"It will also give us some t-time to deal with the g-girl. How goes the s-search of the building—anything?"

"Nothin' here but her." The girl was turning the cane around so that the stones caught the gaslight from the wall sconce. "We talked to everyone who was here the other night, and it seems Solange told the truth—at least about Janssen not making it here."

Lightner looked down at the girl. "Do you have a p-place to take her?"

"I don't think she should stay in the city, or Solange'll find her."

The Englishman nodded. "Are you f-finished here?"

"Aye, mostly."

"I'd like you to find Mr. B-Baker."

Hy grinned. "I'd like that too, sir."

"Send word if you get him. If I don't see you again t-tonight, then meet me at my hotel in the morning." Lightner extended his hand to the girl, who took it without hesitation, a trusting action that felt like a boot in Hy's gut because he suspected she'd been just as trusting with Solange.

"Where you takin' her, sir?"

"Somewhere safe. It's my g-guess that when M-Madam Solange stops shouting, she'll c-claim we've abducted her young r-relative. I w-wouldn't be surprised if w-we were ordered to return her."

Hy thought the same thing. Whatever the nasty bitch had paid for the pretty little girl, she doubtless wanted it back.

"I think it's b-better if you don't know where I'm t-taking her," Lightner added. "That way M-M-Madam and her powerful friends can't have you thrown in jail if you refuse to t-tell."

"But what if they throw *you* in jail?"

Lightner's smile made Hy shiver. "Oh, D-Detective, I certainly hope they t-t-try."

CHAPTER 16

It was just past six o'clock when Jasper's hackney rolled to a stop in front of Mrs. Dunbarton's house. He looked from the stone mansion to the girl, who'd fallen asleep on the bench seat across from him. Jasper wasn't surprised she didn't wake; she was in the arms of Morpheus, a state Jasper knew all too well.

He climbed from the carriage and closed the door quietly. "Stay here," he told the driver, narrowing his eyes. "Do not m-move an inch."

"Aye, sir. I ain't goin' nowhere."

It was likely that Mrs. Dunbarton was doing what socialites all over the city were doing—preparing for an evening out—but she was his best hope.

The man who opened the door was dressed in the clothing of a butler, but his demeanor was more like a soldier's as he gave Jasper a cool foot-to-head inspection.

"May I help you?"

Ah, a fellow Englishman. Jasper gave him a card, and the man's expression did not so much as flicker.

"I need to speak to Mrs. Dunbarton r-rather urgently."

He'd expected resistance—given the odd hour—but the butler took a step back and motioned Jasper into a large, cool foyer.

Jasper glanced back toward the street at the driver, who was sitting on the box seat and staring into space. "I've l-left somebody in the cab—a child—c-could you have a servant go wait b-beside it, just in case she wakes?"

The butler exhibited not even a twitch at such an odd request. He turned and snapped his fingers. The footman who answered the abrupt summons was a monster of a man—likely one of the two Mrs. Dunbarton had mentioned yesterday. Jasper couldn't help noticing that the man's livery was gray and navy blue.

The butler led Jasper to a sitting room. "Please have a seat."

The room was almost aggressively free of knickknacks and clutter. That didn't surprise him; Jasper had a difficult time imagining Mrs. Dunbarton collecting thimbles or dolls.

He'd just gone to look at the prospect out the east-facing window when the door opened and Mrs. Dunbarton strode in. The woman must have been roosting somewhere in the foyer to have gotten there so quickly.

"I thought Cates must have been mistaken when he told me Lord Jasper Lightner was in my sitting room." She was dressed in the same clothing she'd worn earlier. "You've come for the list?"

Jasper frowned. "I b-beg your pardon?"

"The list of donors?"

"Oh. N-No, not exactly."

She cocked her head, her expression curious.

"This is c-certainly the m-m-most unusual c-call I've ever made on a lady." Lord, how he wished he wouldn't have a fit of the stutters in front of *this* woman.

"I feel honored."

"I h-hope you will continue to d-do so. I've brought you a y-y-young girl." He grimaced. "That is n-not how it sounds."

"Please, do go on."

She put Jasper in mind of a small bird—the sort you might dismiss at first glance but would later realize was quite taking. Perhaps a coal tit, or some equally bright-eyed little creature.

"I t-took her from a b-brothel. She was to be s-s-s—"

"I understand." One moment she was a sweet little bird; the next she was one of the Erinyes. "And you brought her to me." Her tone was flat, almost detached.

"She n-needs to get out of the city. Quickly. You're the only p-person I could think of who might be able to help. If you c-cannot, perhaps you might steer m-me toward somebody who can?"

She studied him in a way that brought back a long-buried memory of one of the tutors his father had employed to break Jasper of his stammer. Mr. Devlin had been ancient—or so he'd seemed to a seven- or eight-year-old Jasper—and when he'd looked at him, Jasper had felt as though the old man were looking *into* him.

That was the way Mrs. Dunbarton was staring, as if she could see his inner workings. He felt . . . exposed.

Who knew you could be such a fanciful idiot, Jasper?

He opened his mouth to apologize for intruding on her evening when she did something he'd not yet seen her do: she smiled.

"You've brought her to exactly the right place, my lord."

★   ★   ★

Mrs. Dunbarton was able to discern the girl's name using a series of gestures.

She was called Agota, she was twelve years old, and she came from Budapest. The gestures were not accurate enough to determine how long she'd been in New York, but Jasper and Mrs. Dunbarton did learn she'd come with her mother. Her crying indicated that something bad had happened and that they'd been separated or her parent was dead. The girl shivered when the name *Solange* was uttered. There were finger-shaped bruises on her arms, and Jasper assumed she'd fought her captors and that was when she'd been drugged.

Mrs. Dunbarton herself took the little girl up to bed, after instructing her butler, Cates, to escort Jasper to the dining room. When he'd tried to protest, she'd mocked him.

"Why, Lord Jasper, do you mistake me for a debutante? Are you concerned with despoiling my reputation? Or are you just stodgy? I'm a widow, sir, and have earned my right to dine with whomever I please in my own house." Her thin lips had twisted into her standard smirk. "Or perhaps you don't *wish* to dine with me? Perhaps you have other, more pleasurable plans?"

Well. What could a man say to *that*?

"In the interest of n-not appearing *st-stodgy*, I accept your kind invitation."

The dining room, like the other parts of the house he'd seen, was uncluttered and tasteful, the furniture chosen for comfort rather than fashion. There were decanters on the sideboard, and Jasper enjoyed a whiskey while inspecting the large painting over the dormant hearth. It was a seascape—a Turner, he believed, although he was no art critic—that depicted the ocean either during or right after a storm.

Like the woman who owned it, it was not the sort of image that soothed. As he studied the tempestuous sky, he wondered what he was doing there.

Dining alone with widows is nothing new for you, old chap.

That was true; Jasper disported himself exclusively with widows. Though somehow he doubted Mrs. Dunbarton was interested in the sort of *disporting* he generally got up to. Jasper couldn't help smiling at the ridiculous thought; he couldn't recall the last time a woman had taken a dislike to him the way Mrs. Dunbarton had. Although she appeared to be thawing toward him—somewhat—since he'd brought the girl.

Even so, he couldn't picture this evening ending the way his dinners with widows usually ended: naked, sweaty, and satiated.

Jasper wasn't sure if that thought disappointed him or not.

Sometimes I think you lost more in the Crimea than mere blood and bone, Jasper.

Perhaps he had, or perhaps those few moments in what Tennyson had aptly called "the valley of Death" had simply put life into its proper perspective. Jasper knew—and was bloody thankful—that he'd never feel so alive again. He'd felt every nerve in his body that day. Sometimes he thought he'd used up a lifetime of emotion on that seven-minute journey through hell.

The door opened behind him, and he turned.

"She fell asleep almost as soon as her head hit the pillow."

He lifted his glass. "Would you like a d-drink?"

"Yes, please—the one in the tall decanter."

Jasper poured her a glass of what looked to be sherry.

"Do you think Agota will suffer negative effects without any opiate in her system?"

"Tomorrow you m-m-might put just a few d-drops of laudanum in some water if she exhibits agitation, nausea, or nervousness."

"You sound as if you speak from experience."

Jasper had to laugh. "Is there anything you *w-wouldn't* ask a person?"

"Very little," she admitted. "That is why I'm dining alone with *you* this evening."

"Well. I h-hope that is a lesson to you."

It was her turn to laugh.

The door opened again, and servants bearing trays streamed into the room.

"I hope you don't mind eating unfashionably early, but I'm afraid I can't abide dining at midnight."

"I'm f-famished," he said, not untruthfully.

"This will be a humble repast compared to what you're probably accustomed to," she said, as the first course—a mere nine or ten serving dishes—was arranged on the table. "And I don't like to be bothered by hovering servants, so you shall have to serve yourself. I hope that is not a problem?"

Jasper smiled. "If I b-become confused, I'm sure you c-can instruct me."

"I cannot imagine a situation in which you require my instruction, my lord." She motioned for the footman to move a dish nearer Jasper. "You must try some of the larded oysters; they are my cook's specialty."

The door shut behind the last servant. "Go on, my lord, I know you want to talk about your case." She put a sizable dollop of creamed parsnips on her plate while Jasper helped himself to oysters.

"I n-never discuss work over a meal," he lied. "Tell me about *your* work."

"Let us leave work behind us," she countered, adding a poached fillet to her plate. "You already know a good deal about me: I was a failure as a debutante, I asked a man to marry me, and I'm a callous widow who doesn't abide by the norms of mourning. What about you, my lord? I understand you are a wealthy man, and yet you work? And how is it that you've managed to escape the matrimonial noose? How old are you?"

He swallowed his mouthful of oyster. "This is d-delicious," he prevaricated, taking a sip of wine.

"Cook won't tell anyone what spices she uses, but I've determined that it is sheep lard that gives the dish its distinctive character. Did you really want to know? Or are you simply avoiding my impertinent questions?"

"Yes, with g-great care, and thirty-four."

"I'm not sure you will be so successful at remaining a bachelor if you remain in New York. You must be aware of the American obsession with the English aristocracy."

"An obsession you've m-managed to avoid."

"Well, not entirely."

Jasper's eyebrows shot up.

"Here I am, dining with you, after all." She smiled, looking like a mischievous little girl bent on tormenting some unfortunate little boy. "I must admit I'm looking forward to all the heartache this meal will cause when word gets out. In fact, I may put an advert in the *New-York Daily Times*. I can almost hear Caroline Astor's howls when she learns I've gotten the jump on her." She laughed. "Just think, my lord! A simple dinner might spark another spate of murders—*my* life might be in danger. Would you investigate?"

"I w-would insist on it," he said, smiling.

"Tell me," she said, raising another loaded fork to her mouth. "How is it that you came to be a policeman?"

"I went to school in P-Paris and became acquainted with the g-gentleman credited with forming the S-Sûreté. When I returned from the Crimea, Sir Richard Mayne heard of the c-c-connection and invited me to join the Detective D-Department of the Metropolitan P-Police in an instructional capacity." As usual, he left out the part about the home secretary and his initial, sensitive investigation in Paris.

"What did you study?"

"Medicine."

"You are a doctor?" For once, she didn't look mocking.

"I l-left school before my studies were c-complete."

"Even so, that must be useful in your work?"

"It c-can be."

"Tell, me," she said, hopping to another topic. "Did you happen to meet Miss Nightingale during the war?"

It was a question he got often. "W-We did not meet in Scutari, but my father and W. E. N. have always h-hunted together, although their p-politics could not be more d-different. As a child I went to Embley P-Park several times. Florence and Parthenope are a few years my senior and viewed me and my b-brother as pests. Are y-you an admirer?"

"I admire her industry but find much of her writing harsh when it comes to the feminine sex. How many siblings do you have?"

Jasper hesitated, as he always did when it came to this question. "J-Just my elder brother."

"You don't sound sure."

Jasper laughed.

"I'm sorry—I'm terribly rude, I know."

Jasper didn't think she *sounded* sorry. "I had a sister—f-far younger—but she died when I was f-fifteen."

Her mocking expression disappeared. "I'm sorry."

Jasper was too, even though he'd hardly known Amelia. Not only had she been over a decade younger, but he'd been away at school for most of her short life.

"Are you close to your brother? Or do you envy him his position as heir?"

"We are close, and n–n–no, I've never wanted what my b–brother has." Leticia's face flickered through his mind, her image as insubstantial as mist.

Mrs. Dunbarton picked up her wineglass, which Jasper noticed was—surprisingly—empty. He stood and fetched the bottle, lifting it questioningly.

"Please." Her eyes roamed his body in a bold fashion that made him wonder if she really *needed* more alcohol. But she was no child, so he filled her glass.

"D–Do you have siblings?" he asked once he was seated.

"No, much to my father's displeasure. I am his only child by marriage, but he has seven sons and daughters with his mistress."

The same thing happened in England, but gently bred females didn't mention it at the dinner table. Jasper looked up from his thoughts to see her take a sip from her glass; she had an anticipatory glint in her eyes, and he realized that she enjoyed baiting him and he'd risen to it every time.

Bested by a mere girl.

He could not deny it; she was a force of nature.

Nor could he deny that he found her company increasingly enjoyable.

CHAPTER 17

Hy shifted from foot to foot in the foyer, nervously examining his surroundings.

First off, the hotel room had its very own foyer. Who needed a foyer in their hotel room? He'd stayed in two hotels—inns, really—on his only two journeys out of New York City. Neither one had had a foyer.

In fact, he couldn't recall having ever *seen* a foyer before. He wasn't sure if he'd even known the word existed before Lightner's servant told him to "wait in the foyer."

He *knew* he'd never seen a servant who carried himself with so much dignity. More starched up than Lightner, that was for sure. And prouder looking than the president of the United States. Hy knew that for a fact, since he'd seen the last president—Mr. Pierce—several years ago when he'd come through New York; the man had looked like a bootblack compared to Lightner's servant.

Hy pulled out his watch; it was a quarter past four—he'd been standing in the foyer ten minutes and had left the scene almost half an hour ago. He hoped to God that O'Malley had kept prying eyes at bay. He'd have taken the body to Bellevue, but he knew Lightner would want to see the scene, with the body as it was found.

"Detective."

Hy about jumped out of his skin at the sound of the crisp voice.

"His Lordship will be ready to leave in a quarter of an hour." The servant was dressed now, looking twice as intimidating as he had wearing his robe and sleeping cap—which should have diminished his dignity but hadn't.

His cold, pale-gray eyes flickered over Hy and left him feeling six inches high. "I'm Paisley, His Lordship's valet. He suggested you would like tea."

Hy tried to read Paisley's expression. Did he want Hy to accept this offer or stand there and wait? He honestly couldn't tell from the man's face, which was as expressive as a stone carving.

"His Lordship has instructed me to make tea," Paisley repeated, his gaze, impossibly, frostier. He motioned toward another room; it was a gesture that, from anyone else, would have looked welcoming. Mr. Paisley made it look like an invitation to a firing squad.

Hy preceded him into a room that looked like a parlor—but five or six times bigger than any parlor he'd ever seen.

"Have a seat."

Hy chose a big wingback chair that looked like it might bear his weight, and Paisley disappeared through a door, closing it with a snap and leaving Hy free to gawk.

A massive fireplace—dormant—took up most of one wall. Beneath his scuffed old boots was highly polished wood covered with carpets that looked to be worth more than he'd earn in a lifetime. Rich, supple leather chairs sat cheek by jowl with end tables boasting marble tops. He lifted the lid of a carved box and saw slim, almost black cigars inside; they smelled delicious.

Life with the nuns had been spotlessly clean, but it was spartan. As for before then—the months he'd lived on the streets after Gro mutti Law died and before he went to the nuns—Hy remembered only fear, freezing cold, and constant, gnawing hunger. What must it be like to come from this world of plenty? Why on earth would a man like Lightner *work* if he didn't have to?

Everything in the room made Hy feel battered, crude, and unworthy, a reaction that bothered him. The room was like a too-rich dessert that left him queasy, and his eyes ached from the glare of so much opulence. And this was just a *hotel* room. What must a duke's house be like? Lightner must have grown up in a world so completely—

Another door opened and the man in question came out, shaved, shod, and looking fresh as a daisy. It wasn't until he got closer that Hy saw the strain around his dark eyes. Just as on the prior two days, he wore clothing that managed to look finer than that worn by any other uptown gents Hy had ever seen; not that there was anything flash about his black coat, charcoal pants, and gleaming black leather shoes. The only color in his outfit was his vest, which was a dull black silk with indigo embroidery. Hy was glad he'd thought to have his landlady brush and press his only suit after work the night before.

"Good morning, Detective," Lightner said.

The door the valet had gone through opened, and the servant entered carrying a tea tray piled high with a stunning assortment of biscuits and cakes.

"Er, good morning, sir." Hy stared at the beautiful food, his stomach making a demanding grumble that caused his face to heat. "Sorry to wake you so early."

"Well, m-murderers don't sleep, it appears."

Paisley gestured to a cup and gave Hy an inquiring look.

"Er, milk and three sugars."

"You'd best eat while you have the t-time," Lightner said, taking a cup of black, unsweetened tea from his servant.

Hy restrained himself, placing only two items on his plate—a white frosted cake and something that looked like a custard-and-fruit tart. He had to keep swallowing, since his mouth was watering so badly that he was afraid of opening it. If he drooled in front of a man like Paisley, he just might have to crawl under the table.

"I'm sorry this was all I could procure at such short notice, my lord." The valet handed Lightner a plate he'd heaped with delicacies, but his master shook his head, a faint frown of distaste on his thin lips. Undaunted, the valet didn't move until Lightner sighed, snatched a biscuit—the smallest—and gave his servant a perfunctory smile.

"Who, where, how?" Lightner asked, setting the biscuit down in his saucer, untouched.

"Stephen Finch, a wealthy society gentleman. The body was found behind Lizzy Horgan's brothel. That's not in the Eighth, but between the Sixth and Fourteenth." He saw Lightner's grimace. "When I left, it was only O'Malley and two boys from the Fourteenth. Captain Norris at the Fourteenth is McElhenny's brother-in-law, but he hates his guts, so his sergeant called us instead of the Sixth."

Lightner snorted. "I *suppose* we should be g-grateful for that."

Hy grinned at his wry tone. "It's lucky for us Billings pulled the night shift, 'cause he sent word to me an' O'Malley." Hy had been amazed—and heartened—at the duty sergeant's actions. His last sergeant, at the Sixth, would have galloped from his post directly to the scene to be the first to rifle the pockets of such a wealthy victim.

"S-So," Lightner said, "Another b-brothel and another alley. Who f-found him?" He paused and then added, "Please t-tell me it wasn't Jemmy Hart."

"No, sir. It was a group of young lads who'd just been bounced from Lizzy's for bein' rowdy. They'd gone round the building hopin' to sneak in the back entrance."

"Method?"

"Garrotin', stabbed in the side—*left* side—and a piece o' flesh missin'."

Lightner took a drink of tea, set down the cup and saucer, and stared at his servant, who was fussing with items on the tray, clearly hoping to force more food on him.

"Fetch my things, Paisley," he said in a clipped tone that sent the man off to do his bidding, but not without a narrow-eyed look at his employer's untouched biscuit.

Lightner gestured to the many delicacies left on the tray. "Please t-take some with you, Detective. Paisley has as m-much of a sweet t-tooth as I do, so whatever you d-don't eat will likely get th-th-thrown away."

Hy was horrified by the thought of such waste. He took out his handkerchief—a clean one, thankfully—and put a flaky pastry in it. He hesitated, then added another before wrapping them up. Once he'd tucked that in his pocket, he took a white-frosted cake that had a rose made from chocolate on top. It would never survive a journey in his coat, so he commenced eating. He was barely able to stop from groaning in ecstasy.

The Englishman chuckled. "Paisley will enjoy having somebody to f-feed."

Hy was pretty sure the haughty servant didn't care whether Hy ate or starved.

Lightner was coated, hatted, gloved, and in possession of a cane—this one bearing a handle that was a black panther—just as Hy finished his delicacy.

The valet must have magically arranged for a cab—or the hotel kept them hanging about at all hours—because one was waiting for them. Although summer didn't officially start for another week or so, spring had fled early this year. Hy didn't know how the other man could bear wearing an overcoat in such weather, but he appeared cool and impervious as he settled onto the seat across from him.

"Oh, by the by," Hy said, "I went down to the docks to poke around and met Baker's shoresman. His employees don't like Baker much, say he's tightfisted and an arrogant ass."

"Unhappy employees c-can be excellent sources of information," Lightner agreed with a slight smile.

"It turns out that people aren't the only thing Baker has been shippin'." Hy allowed himself a dramatic pause. "He also had a whole pile o' guns in his last shipment."

"Ah, enter Mr. H-Hoyle. Did your source know the destination?"

"The ship made stops all the way down to Cuba. There she filled up with rum, sugar, and cigars. The man wouldn't tell me who bought the guns, but he was quick enough to say Baker keeps a house over by the railroad depot, at Fourth Avenue and East Twenty-Ninth. I went over there to see if he was in town, but Baker's servant—who also sounded like he hated him—said he was probably in a whorehouse. I popped by Mr. Hoyle's mansion, just 'cause I was in the area. His servants clammed up, like before, but I *did* get out of them that Hoyle's been out of the city for the past week and doesn't return until Friday."

Lightner nodded. "We'll track B-Baker down today, after *this*. D-Did you have an opportunity to examine the scene?"

"The boy who took the rubbish out said there was no body when he was out at twelve thirty. The young drunkards stumbled on Finch around two forty-five or so, and Lizzy Horgan sent for the coppers not long after. I looked at the body, but I couldn't tell if he'd been killed there or not."

"S-So, our killer was there between half midnight and threeish. Either he—or they—killed the v-victim then, or they d-dropped off his corpse. Is it a busy area?"

"It's quiet—but never completely empty."

The carriage slowed, and Hy breathed a sigh of relief when he saw there was still only O'Malley, one other patrolman, and a few onlookers, mostly working women, blocking the entrance to the alley. He said a quick prayer that they could examine the scene and deal with the body before they drew the attention of newspapermen. Or worse, coppers from the Sixth.

CHAPTER 18

Unlike Alard Janssen, Stephen Finch was a well-preserved man in his late thirties or early forties.

Jasper stripped off his gloves, threw them into his hat, and handed both to O'Malley. He turned back to the corpse and was just about to crouch down when Paisley's horrified face rose up before him. He sighed and unbuttoned his coat. After he'd shrugged out of it, he handed that to O'Malley too, who received it as if Jasper had just handed him the crown jewels; Paisley would approve.

He moved the lantern closer to the body. "You say he was in this p-position when you arrived?" Jasper asked the patrolman who'd arrived first.

"Er, no, sir; I turned him over."

"Never touch a dead body unless it is to ascertain that the p-person is indeed d-dead."

The boy's jaw dropped, his witless expression causing Jasper to realize what a prize he had in O'Malley.

The marks around Finch's neck were visible, as his shirt had been badly torn.

"Are his c-collar and stock lying about?" Jasper asked, the question sending the patrolmen scurrying.

While they searched the alley, Jasper lifted Finch's shirttails, which were already untucked.

He and Law examined the wound in his side in silence.

The big detective looked at him. "Are you thinkin' what I'm thinkin', sir?"

"A d–different knife?"

Law nodded.

Not only did it look like a different knife, but the chunk of flesh was much smaller, more like a large nick, not deep enough to expose Finch's organs.

Law pointed to the cuts. "I count six of them."

"The hand's p-pressure on the knife—upon removal—will leave these marks." Jasper pointed to the bottom of the vertical slashes. His eyes met Law's. "These cuts were made from the f-f-front, not the back."

Law nodded his agreement.

"Will you ch-check his shoes, detective?"

Law ran his hand over the soles of both shoes. "Nothin'—at least no stickier than usual."

Jasper searched Finch's pockets: no watch, no wallet, and no ring on his hands. The man wasn't wearing an overcoat, and there was no hat or gloves.

Jasper looked up at O'Malley, who straightened and said, "Er, we didn't find no collar or tie, sir."

"He'd already been stripped of his valuables when I got here, sir," Law said in a quiet voice. "It could have been the killer, the drunk boys who found him, or—"

They both looked up at the patrolman standing beside O'Malley. His face reddened when he found himself under scrutiny, but he didn't look guilty so much as alarmed.

"Did somebody check his pockets?" Law asked.

Now the lad looked terrified. "No, sir! I didn't! I—"

"We are n-not accusing you, Patrolman."

The boy swallowed, then nodded.

"Mr. F-Finch looks to be somewhere b-between twelve to thirteen st-stone," Jasper said.

"Er, stone, sir?" Law asked.

"Ah, yes—it's pounds here," Jasper said. "That's fourteen pounds per stone, so . . . one sixty-eight to one eighty-two."

Law nodded. "Sounds about right."

"Approximately s-seven percent of the human body is blood; g-given the severity of the wounds, there should be a great deal more b-blood."

"So, he was moved like Dunbarton?"

"We'll have a l-look around." The corpse was warm, but then so was the morning—stiflingly so. Finch's skin didn't blanch when Jasper squeezed his flesh, so it seemed likely he'd been dead at least a few hours. But rigor had barely set in, so probably no more than six hours.

Jasper turned to Law. "Help me turn him."

On his back were several large, dark bruises, as if a heavy killer had knelt on him. "These are more p-pronounced than Janssen's bruises." He glanced at Law.

"Er, sorry, sir; I don't remember if there was bruising on Sealy and Dunbarton."

The skin on both of Finch's palms was scraped, and one fingernail was almost ripped away. There were multiple fingertip-shaped bruises at the back of the neck but none on the front, where Finch would have grabbed.

"Think it was the same rope?" Law asked.

"Same fiber, but maybe th-thinner. The ligature marks are shallow, and neither the larynx or hyoid is damaged, so the cause of death was not strangulation."

"Was Janssen's?"

Jasper considered the question. "My first thought was n-no. But it could have b-been a combination of his crushed larynx inducing hypoxia and the stab wou-wounds that killed him." He noticed there was a smear of blood on Finch's guinea-gold head and parted the hair; there was a large lump, which looked to have swollen and split.

"That's quite a goose egg," Law said.

Bodies could often appear to become bruised after death, but he'd felt the difference in the past—antemortem contusions were firmer, in his experience. Jasper pressed the lump.

"I th-think he was struck while he w-was still alive. To leave a swelling this size, the blow would have b-been hard enough to stun him, if not p-put him out."

"So"—Law held up a big hand—"this one seems different than the others, at least Janssen. Smaller rope and not as severe garrotin'." He folded down one finger. "Stabbin' from the front and six instead of four cuts." Another finger. "Less flesh cut out." A third. "A knock on the head." A fourth. "Pine sap/no pine sap." He folded down his thumb and started on his other hand. "Am I missin' anything? Oh— Finch was moved, Janssen wasn't."

Jasper nodded.

"So, two killers workin' together, and a different one did the stabbin' this time?"

"Or this is a d-different killer from Janssen's."

"But why would somebody try to copy the same method?"

"P-Perhaps they were hoping to g-get away with murder and b-blame it on somebody else."

Law groaned. "This is giving me a sore head, sir."

Jasper agreed.

Law stared at the body. "So, either one person killed all four but changed it up—but not *too* much—to make it confusing? Or one person killed Dunbarton, Sealy, and Janssen and another killed Finch. Or one person killed Dunbarton and Sealy, and one killed Janssen, and another killed Finch? So we could have one, two, or even three killers."

"Now y-you're hurting *my* head." But that didn't make the other man's assessment any less accurate. Jasper sighed and took out his watch: it was just after five. "Shall we g-go speak to these ladies first"—he gestured to the working women who'd congregated at the end of the alley—"and then Mrs., er, what was it?"

"Horgan, sir."

O'Malley was arguing with an extraordinarily beautiful young woman when they approached. His face was red and sweaty and his eyes were wild; he regarded Jasper as if he were the Second Coming. "Ah, Lord Jasper. Er, could I—"

Jasper smiled at the girl. "Please excuse us a m-moment," he said, taking O'Malley by the arm and leading him a few feet away.

"You appear distressed, P-Patrolman."

"I think she's crazy, sir."

Jasper laughed. "Oh?"

"None of the rest of 'em saw Finch—except her. But she won't tell me anything more." He hesitated and then added, "She said she wanted to talk to the English lord."

"I suppose that would be m-me."

O'Malley blinked. "Er . . ."

Jasper looked over at the lovely young woman; she was currently rubbing herself against Detective Law, who was staring skyward as if seeking divine assistance.

"She said all kinds of things, sir—the other girls said she's a liar."

"I see," Jasper said. "But we question her j-just like any other w-witness. Sometimes a lie c-can tell us as much as the truth."

O'Malley nodded but looked unconvinced.

They went back to where the other two waited.

"I'm Velma, *my lord.*"

Jasper looked down into a heart-shaped face with plump, bow-shaped lips and wide blue eyes glinting with excitement and a horrifying lack of intelligence. He took her hand and bowed over it, the action earning him a transcendent smile.

O'Malley cleared his throat. "Er, she said—"

"I can talk for myself," she snapped, and then turned her smile on Jasper, her finger playing suggestively with what looked to be an expensive earring. "You'll be wantin' to know about Mr. Finch, I reckon?"

Law frowned at the girl. "Tell us what you know. *If* you know anything."

She cut Jasper a wounded look, as if to say, *Aren't you going to rescue me from this barbarian?*

Jasper merely smiled.

The next fifteen minutes would have been amusing had they not been standing twenty feet from a murdered corpse. Jasper and Law took turns, alternately placating and threatening.

Yes, she'd seen Finch. No, she'd not talked to him. No, she didn't know what time it was. Yes, he'd been with somebody—Mary. No, she didn't know how long they'd been together, but they'd been fighting.

She was complaining about how unfair the madam was to her when another patrolman trotted into the alley. "Lord Lightner?"

Jasper sighed at the inaccurate honorific but left it alone. "What is it?"

"Sar Billings sent this for you—it's the dead man's address, sir. Mr. Finch was married."

Jasper took the piece of paper. "Thank you." He turned to Law, who was watching O'Malley bicker with their witness. Jasper wouldn't be surprised if the two young people started pulling each other's hair soon.

He beckoned Law. "Let's leave this to P-Patrolman O'Malley to finish. I want to speak to the woman who owns the p-place. And then I get the p-pleasure of informing yet another woman that her husband has been m-murdered."

CHAPTER 19

Lizzy Horgan's business was more impressive from the front than from the rubbish alley behind it, but—unlike Solange's—it was undeniably a brothel for men of more moderate means.

The double set of battered doors was locked, so Law banged on the wood with the heel of his fist. "You believe what—er, Velma—said, sir?" Law asked as they waited.

"She seems a b-bit . . . odd."

Law snorted at the understatement.

"Have you b-been here before?" Jasper asked, unsurprised when the other man blushed at the question—it seemed to be a national characteristic: blushing when a brothel was mentioned. Perhaps some residual reaction from the Puritan era, even though Law appeared as Catholic as the pope.

"Er, a time or two, sir."

The door swung open, and a statuesque black woman stood in the opening. She had the most arresting hazel eyes Jasper had ever seen. They were also red rimmed and bloodshot. "Why, gentlemen," she said, her remarkable eyes meeting Jasper's. "I'm afraid we're closed. Although"—she tapped one long finger against her lower lip, her speculative gaze blazing a trail across Jasper's body—"for *you*, I could make an—"

"We're here to speak to Lizzy, *Mister* Haslem," Law said.

Jasper blinked, and the woman's—or man's—features seemed to shift. Now that the suggestion had been planted, he saw that the brow was a bit too pronounced, the slender hands were broad and ropy across the back, and an Adam's apple peeked out above the high-necked dressing gown.

Haslem gave Law a dismissive sniff and tossed long, loose coils of jet-black hair before turning her—or his—attention back to Jasper. "I'm *Mary* Haslem. And you are?"

"D-Detective Inspector Lightner." Jasper took the proffered hand and bowed low over it. "The p-p-pleasure is mine."

When he stood, both Haslem and Law were gawking at him, Law in shock and Haslem with open appreciation. "Why don't *you* come on in and make yourself at home." She cut Law a cursory look. "I s'pose *you* want to come in too, Mr. *High*-Rony-Mus Law?"

Jasper had believed his detective's face was red before. Now it was like a glowing coal.

"You t-two know each other?" Jasper asked.

"Not like that," Law hastened to assure him.

Haslem snorted. "It surely *ain't*. I have standards."

"I didn't know you were out," Law said, as prickly as a hedgehog.

"Well, it seems you don't know *everythin'*, now, do you? *I* heard you spent a little time in the Tombs your own self." She didn't wait for a reply but waved an arm to the cavernous saloon. "I'll go get Lizzy. She got home late after dealin' with her *troubles*, so she's tryin' to get a little rest."

"T-Troubles?" Jasper asked.

"You'll have to ask her about that, honey," Mary said with a sultry smile, then turned and sashayed toward the big bar at the opposite end of the room, her ample bottom moving from side to side in seductive invitation.

Law leaned down and said in a low voice, "Er, sir?"

"Yes, D-Detective."

"That's a man, sir."

"S-So you've said. Have y-you ever heard the proverb *you can catch more f-flies with honey than vinegar?*"

Law's bushy ginger eyebrows descended. "Aye?"

Well, *that*—as you c-call Haslem—is a witness, a witness who c-calls herself Mary. Right now, *she* is a cooperative w-witness. If she wishes us to c-call her Queen V-Victoria, we will d-do so."

Deep grooves formed around Law's compressed lips. "Aye." The word sounded as if it had been physically squeezed from his lungs.

★　★　★

After Mary returned from alerting her employer, she settled them before the dormant fireplace and brought over a bottle and three glasses. When Jasper hesitated, she propped a hand on one of her hips. "I don't trust a man who won't drink with me."

Jasper took the glass, entertaining visions of showing up on Mrs. Finch's doorstep slobbering drunk. "Thank you," he murmured, doing no more than wetting his lips on the rim. Haslem was too busy arranging her person on the chaise longue in the most seductive pose to notice.

"I *know* what y'all wanna know: and no, Mr. Finch wasn't here last night." Her eyes had begun to water, and she rubbed them. "And if anyone would know the answer to that, it'd be *me*. I was his favorite here." Law snorted, and Haslem narrowed her eyes at him. Her gaze shifted to Jasper. "Stephen was real kind to me."

"When w-was the last time you saw him?"

"Sunday."

"Was he here since?"

"You mean did he see *another* women here?"

Jasper nodded.

Haslem's eyelids dropped to half-mast. The expression was meant to be seductive, but it wasn't convincing with her red-rimmed eyes. "I kept him satisfied, if you know what I mean."

Law muttered something Jasper couldn't hear, and Mary scowled. "Does *he* have to be here?"

Jasper cut the detective a resigned look. "M-might Detective Law speak to some of the other g-girls while you and I chat?"

Law gave Jasper a look of disbelief.

Haslem grinned. "You go on up and knock on Velma's door, High-Rony-Mus. She's about right for you."

Law stood, his clenched fists hanging like giant hams at his sides.

"Why don't you take the statements of the w-women we *didn't* m-meet outside, Detective."

"Yes, sir," Law said, six and a half feet of truculence.

"You'll have to kick some boys outa those beds," Mary called after him with a laugh.

Once he'd stomped off, Mary took Jasper's hand, her skin smooth and cool. "There now, I just *knew* you wanted to have me all to yourself."

Jasper laid a hand over hers, gave it a gentle squeeze, and then lifted it.

She made a moue of disappointment, took a sip of whiskey, fiddled with the neckline of her dressing gown, and finally heaved a put-upon sigh. "Fine. Let's talk." Mary gave a careless shrug, but Jasper was not fooled—the expression in her eyes was one of pain.

"You liked Mr. F-Finch a great d-deal."

Her eyes flashed. "I'm just an ex-slave *whore*, Detective. It ain't for me to *like* anyone a *great deal*. Especially not no rich white man." She made a defeated noise and slumped back onto her chaise, her arms crossed protectively around her body, a tear rolling down her cheek. She gave Jasper a challenging look. "You know what they called me in the papers when I was arrested—*wrongfully*?"

"No."

She gave a watery, slightly hysterical laugh. "*They* called me a monster—an abomination, but the things I've seen men do—" She bit her lower lip, the tears falling faster. "I'll tell you this much—of all those *men* who come to me? Only Stephen didn't sneak and hide who he was seein' here." Her smile was grim. "Believe me when I tell you I get *plenty* of business."

Jasper did believe her. There were numerous molly-houses in London to attest to the fact that a great many men preferred their own gender. But in England, the punishment for homosexual acts was death, and you'd never find somebody like Mary Haslem behaving so openly.

"It's true I liked him," Haslem said, tears now streaming. "And now—" She dropped her head into her hands, giving herself up to grief.

Jasper offered his handkerchief, and she took it without speaking.

Her carefully curated feminine facade dropped away, and Mary Haslem's body shook with the low, moaning sobs of a man in anguish.

Jasper did not consider homosexual acts—or the men who engaged in them—beyond the pale. Indeed, both at public school and in the army, two places where feminine company was in short supply, it was not unheard of to give one's mate *a hand* and offer one in return. Of course, one did not speak of such things.

But he *was* a stranger to homosexual *love*, just as he was to *any* kind of romantic love—at least any that he could remember.

That is a sad, sad admission, Jasper.

He couldn't argue with that.

His sister-in-law's face flickered through his mind, but Jasper didn't chase Leticia's image. If there was one memory he didn't regret losing, it was his past with the woman who was now married to his brother.

However, while Jasper might not be familiar with love, he *did* recognize passion when he saw it. And passion, next to money, was one of the most common motivations for murder.

As the sobs died to sniffles, Mary returned. The transformation was subtle, her movements as she daubed at her eyes increasingly feminine. She offered the handkerchief back.

"P-Please, keep it, Miss Haslem." Jasper hoped she wouldn't need it again but wasn't optimistic. "How d-did Mr. Finch seem the last t-time you saw him?" He paused. "Now when was that again?"

"Like I already said, it was *Sunday*. And he was the same as ever."

Mary, Jasper decided, was not the best liar in the world.

"I understand the t-two of you had an argument?"

She scowled. "I know that'll be Velma who told you that. I saw how she was hangin' around like a vulture when y'all were lookin' over poor Stephen's body. That little bitch is *always* listenin' in on other people's business. It wasn't no *argument*." She paused and then added, "We had a disagreement about all the whorin' he did. Sometimes I get jealous—that's natural, ain't it?"

"He'd b-been seeing somebody else?"

"He *said* he hadn't, but I'd barely seen him lately. Stephen Finch was *not* the sort of man to go without."

"D-Did that make you angry?"

"Of course it did! I—" Her eyes widened. "I mean *no*, I wasn't *mad*, I was just—just—dammit, I don't know! You're makin' me all nervous and stupid. It's *true* I was yellin'—just a little."

"Could you t-tell me where you w-were last night?"

"I was *here* all night long."

"Working?"

"Er, no. I had a headache and went to bed real early."

"Is there somebody who can c-confirm that?"

"You're not thinkin' I'd hurt Stephen? Why, I *loved*—"

"Mary?"

They both turned at the sharp voice, Jasper getting to his feet.

"Oh, Lizzy." Mary's voice pulsed with relief. "This is the policeman that's come to solve Stephen's murder—Detective Lightner."

Once again the woman before him did not adhere to his idea of a madam. She was tall and slender—perhaps five foot eight or nine—and her bearing was ramrod straight. Her dark hair was restrained in a tidy chignon, and her pale, even-featured face looked free of cosmetics. She was the opposite of Miss Paxton, her expression serious and unsmiling, her blue gown simple and modestly cut. And, unlike the other woman, she didn't appear pleased to have a duke's son sitting in her saloon.

"I'm Elizabeth Horgan, Detective." There was nothing of the coquette about her; had Jasper met her on the street, he would have taken her for a schoolmistress. A very attractive schoolmistress.

Horgan and her employee exchanged a look Jasper couldn't decipher.

"He was just wantin' to know where I was last night," Mary said breathlessly.

"Mary was with me." Miss Horgan was a better liar than Haslem, but not by much. Jasper wondered if she was aware of the danger she was courting with her untruths. "We were entertaining a gentleman. Together."

Jasper had to admit the vision that flitted through his brain at her words was titillating. He could see by her miniscule smile that this was what she'd intended. So, not a schoolmistress after all.

"Um—" Mary's eyes darted between Jasper and her employer, and he knew she was wondering—hoping madly—that he didn't recall her earlier statement.

"What t-time was that?" he asked the madam before Mary could speak.

"Hmm." She brushed past him, her body barely touching his. He caught a whiff of perfume—something earthy and spicy, with just the faintest hint of sweetness beneath it . . .

Blood roared in his ears, and he locked eyes with Miss Horgan as she lowered herself into the chair beside him. Her pupils were small—mere pinpricks—the iris a crystalline blue.

Jasper looked away, his gaze dropping to the white knuckles of his hands. He unclenched his fingers and resumed his seat.

Mary cleared her throat, her eyes bouncing nervously back and forth between them. "Um, Lizzy—"

"What time were you t-together?" Jasper repeated.

"All night."

"Uh, Lizzy?"

"What *is* it, Mary?" Mrs. Horgan snapped, not looking away from Jasper.

"I told the detective you were out last night, er, late. And that I was alone."

The madam's eyes widened as she turned toward her cringing employee.

"I'm sorry, Lizzy—I just—" Mary shrugged.

"Shall w-we start again?" Jasper suggested gently.

"You'd better tell him the truth," Horgan said.

Mary heaved a sigh. "I wasn't here—I was at my mama's. It was my weekly night off."

"Why did you lie?"

"You know why."

He did; a mother's alibi was not the most convincing.

"Where d-does your mother live?"

"Way up north—in Seneca Village. Or what's left of it."

"And w-will your mother be able to confirm this?"

"Yeah, I was there all night."

"Where were you S-Saturday night?"

Both women frowned.

It was the madam who answered. "We were both here that night, Detective. I have a half dozen employees to vouch for us."

Mary's eyes, he noticed, had watered. "That was my last night with Stephen."

So, her mother for an alibi one night, a dead man for the other.

"And y-you, Mrs. Horgan?"

"It's Miss Horgan. And me *what*?"

"Where w-were *you* last night?"

"I was with someone, but not here."

"I don't suppose you'd be w-willing to tell me this *somebody's* name?"

"A talkative whore would soon be out of business, Detective."

"I'm afraid a p-police investigation takes precedence over c-commerce."

The look she gave him was one he suspected she reserved for cus-tomers who tried to evade payment. "All right, Detective—you want to know who I was with? I had a visitor early yesterday evening: a government official. He was here to let me know my business would be closed as of this morning. He only shared that information with me after drinking the better half of a bottle of my most expensive whiskey and helping himself to one of my girls—and then not pay-ing. *That's* why I was out last night; I was running around the city, calling in favors." She gave a bitter laugh. "Let's just say there wasn't much *talking*. I could give you names of some *fine* gentlemen—*four* of them—but I don't want to draw any further attention to myself than I already have. So, if you want to arrest me, you'd better get on with it."

"Why c-can they close you?"

"The real reason? Because I'm the only business on this stretch of Broome Street who refuses to sell my building. The reason listed on the order? That I'm in violation of several laws involving licenses and bonds." She snorted. "Basically, if the city actually enforced the regu-lations they're claiming I'm violating, they'd put ninety-five percent of liquor-serving establishments out of business."

"You have no recourse?"

She gave him a self-mocking smile. "Let's just say my efforts last night were less than persuasive. I'll probably sell. And now that I'm closed, I'll sell cheaply, more cheaply with each day that passes. What else did you want to ask, my lord?"

"Have you ever heard of W-Wilbur Sealy, Felix Dunbarton, or Alard Janssen?"

"Who hasn't?"

"Were they c-customers here?"

"No." She had a beautiful mouth; her long upper lip was thin-ner than the lower one, which gave her a kittenish look in contrast to an overall serious mien. When she smiled—even bitterly, as she was doing now—the expression was far more enticing than Lorena Paxton's sensual grin or Solange Dupuy's stunning beauty. "I don't cater to men looking for virgins, Detective. It's why I'm down here in the Bowery and not uptown—like Solange Dupuy. That woman would sell her own daughter if the price was right."

Jasper had to agree with her assessment. "So those men purchased v-virgins?"

"Not here they didn't. All I know is all three, at separate times over the past few years, approached me to ask for virgins—very *young* virgins."

"Excuse m-my ignorance, ma'am, but can such girls be easy to p-procure?"

"They're a commodity, like anything else men buy and sell. Two years ago they used to be more expensive, but they're getting cheaper as more and more step off ships every day."

Still wish to find the person who killed those men, Jasper?

The thought was no less shocking than the first time it entered his mind, but it *had* become more difficult to dismiss.

"What of M-Mr. Finch? Was he another such m-man? Would I f-find him at Solange's?"

Mary made an affronted noise. "He would nev—"

Elizabeth Horgan glared at her employee, and Mary's mouth closed with a snap.

The madam gave Jasper a cool look and lifted a shoulder in an elegant shrug; everything about this woman, aside from her profession, was elegant.

Not to mention her very elegant pastime, Jasper.

The pulse at the base of his throat throbbed at the mere memory of the distinctive, sickly sweet odor of opium he'd smelled a few moments earlier.

Pathetic.

Jasper had to agree. He swallowed his hunger and forced himself to pay attention to what Miss Horgan was saying.

"Mr. Finch was a man of broad tastes but not, to my knowledge, a pedophile. Nor was he indulging *any* of his tastes *here* last night. I can *personally* attest that he wasn't here before nine, which is when I left. The last time I *personally* saw him was on Sunday."

"Your employee V-Velma said she saw Mr. Finch here last night."

Miss Horgan laughed. "She'd need damned good vision to have seen him." At Jasper's questioning look, she said, "Velma was at a private party along with three other girls up on Twenty-First and Fourth."

"Ah." Jasper had a brief urge to throttle the beautiful young liar. "I shall n-need the names of these other w-women in your statement."

"Gladly."

"Is it p-possible Mr. Finch could have b-been here without your knowledge last night?"

"Anything is possible, Detective. But it's unlikely—I know what my girls are doing; watching over my employees is my job, and I'm good at it."

Jasper could believe it. Still, you couldn't watch everyone all the time.

"Did Mr. Finch ever c-come in here to m-meet business associates or gamble?"

"Not that I recall." For once, her answer sounded honest. She glanced at Mary, who shook her head. "He wasn't much for cards, and I never saw him with no other men."

Again, Jasper thought that had the ring of truth to it. "Do you know Amos Baker or B-Benjamin Hoyle?"

It was Mary who answered this time. "Every freedman and woman in New York knows about Baker," she said grimly, "but I don't know a Hoyle.

"Baker would have known he wouldn't be welcome here," Miss Horgan said, with a glance at Mary. "As for Hoyle—he makes guns, doesn't he?"

"Why d-do you think Mr. Finch was f-found behind your business?"

"I'd like to know the answer to that myself, Detective."

"Could you p-provide me with a list of employees or other c-customers Mr. F-Finch might have seen here?"

Miss Horgan inhaled deeply, then exhaled with deliberate slowness before answering. "I don't keep records of who my customers talk to, but I can get you a list of the girls he saw." She glanced again at Mary. "It's not a long list."

"It w-w-would make things easier."

"For whom?"

"For you, Miss Horgan," he said gently. This time it was Jasper who let his gaze wander to her fidgeting employee, who'd last been seen arguing with the deceased and possessed the world's worst alibi: the word of a mother.

"I'll get you a list," she said, and then scowled—managing to make the expression charming. "It's not as if I have a business to run anymore."

CHAPTER 20

"Peter Haslem has been in prison before, sir—at least twice," Law told him the instant they stepped out of the building.

Jasper hailed a hackney. "Eighth P-Precinct," he told the driver. "Oh? What was she in j-jail for?"

"Grand larceny—five years at Sing Sing."

Sing Sing, Jasper knew, was the state prison some thirty miles north of the city.

"His lay was to lure rich men into alleys and steal their wallets while, er, well, you know—" Law's heavy jaw tightened. "He worked with somebody who was never caught. Most of his victims were too ashamed to come forward, but five eventually did. Three said they felt a hand in their pocket and when they tried to turn, somebody knocked 'em unconscious. When they woke, they'd been robbed. A few times even stripped of their clothing. The other two said—"

"Sometimes they were allowed to f-f-finish their business and then an irate s-s-spouse or family member appeared and demanded p-payment?"

Law looked away from Jasper's intent stare. "I know what you're sayin', sir—the diddle is a common one."

"V-Very. Besides, Haslem has an alibi—she was apparently with her mother all night."

Law snorted, and Jasper didn't know whether he did so because of his choice of pronoun for Haslem or because of the flimsy alibi.

"What about Saturday night?" Law asked.

"She was with F-Finch."

This time Law laughed. "You d-don't really think she's—goddammit—*he's* tellin' the truth?"

"We're g-going to take her w-word for it until we learn otherwise." Jasper could see the other man didn't like his answer. "Did you question Haslem about Sealy and Dunbarton?"

"Haslem only got out of jail a month ago."

"Was this the ch-charge you mentioned?"

"Naw; this was just two months on a disturbance-of-the-peace charge."

"What w-was she doing?"

"Haslem and several others had an antislavery meetin'."

"That's illegal?"

"No, but it turned into a brawl when some Dead Rabbits showed up. But look, sir, Haslem not bein' here for Sealy and Dunbarton doesn't mean anything. We *know* whoever killed Finch probably wasn't the same person. Velma claims she saw Finch last night. Horgan would lie for Haslem—she's got a weakness for strays and freaks."

Jasper flinched slightly at the word *freaks*, a name he'd been called often enough by teachers, schoolmates, and his father.

"B-Being a f-freak is not evidence of guilt, Detective." Jasper spoke as quietly as ever, but the way Law's eyes widened told him he'd not been entirely successful at hiding his annoyance. "There are at least th-three witnesses to attest that V-Velma wasn't even at the brothel last n-night. Rest assured, D-Detective, we're n-not done with Haslem, b-but I would prefer to have evidence before we st-start arresting people."

Jasper suspected Law couldn't be rational about Haslem. His reaction was more normal than Jasper's own acceptance of behavior that was widely considered sexually aberrant—not to mention criminal in Britain. But then Jasper indulged in some rather aberrant behaviors himself, so he wasn't one to point fingers.

"I t-told Miss Horgan you'd take down her written statement this afternoon. We can compare it with my n-notes. Make sure to ask about her whereabouts on Saturday." They hopped out of the hackney at the station.

Law's eyebrows rose. "You suspect Lizzy?"

"I suspect everyone."

Law found that amusing.

Jasper opened the door to the station and almost collided with O'Malley.

"J-Just the man I wanted to see," Jasper said.

O'Malley gave him an uncertain smile, two bright spots of red on his pale, hairless cheeks. "I went along with Mr. Finch's body—just like you said, sir—and was just comin' to tell you that you got a message from the mayor." He shoved a slip of paper at Jasper.

Please come to City Hall at your earliest convenience.

It was signed *Fernando Wood.*

"Oh," O'Malley said, when Jasper looked up. "Sergeant Billings said, well, er, no office for you yet, sir. There's another desk in the bullpen." He jerked his head toward the big glass-fronted office off to the left.

Jasper had never heard the term *bullpen.* Featherstone and several other plainclothes policemen were lounging in the room, glaring in his direction. He had no intention of sharing the details of his investigation with Featherstone and his cronies, nor of leaving anything important lying about where it could be pinched or destroyed.

"C-Come with me." Jasper led them back outside and around the corner of the station.

"Mr. O'Malley, I want you to go b-back to Miss Horgan's and search every inch of the b-building. The d-detective will join you after running an errand."

"Should I bring more men?" O'Malley asked.

"No. I just want the t-t-two of you—I don't t-t-trust anyone else." O'Malley gave a startled gasp at such antipolice heresy.

"Are we lookin' for the murder weapon, sir?" O'Malley asked.

Jasper's lips twitched at the naïve question. "That would b-be ideal, but barring a bl-bloody knife or signed confession, I w-want you to check the m-mattresses, look under dresser d-drawers, check b-baseboards for hiding p-places, look for bloodstains—anything out of the ord-ordinary. And g-get the women t-talking as much as p-possible. Sound good?"

O'Malley looked nervous, but he nodded. "Yes, sir."

"Excellent. Would you please s-s-summon a hackney for me?"

When the boy left, Jasper turned to Law and gave him the piece of paper with Haslem's mother's address. "First thing: go get her statement."

Law glanced at the name on the paper and nodded.

"Once you're done with that, help O'Malley. What I r-really want to do is search Haslem's room, but I d-don't want to single her out."

"Yes, sir." Law hesitated. "What about payin' Baker a visit?"

Jasper cursed softly. "He'll have to wait until I come back after whatever *this* is." He gestured to the mayor's note.

Law cleared his throat. "Are you going to ask Mayor Wood about Dunbarton?"

"I intend to."

Law grinned, but the expression quickly melted away. "Look, sir, I know you're wantin' to be careful about this thing with Haslem, but I need to tell you that word that we're searchin' Horgan's word will get out—no matter how careful we are—and people will jump to conclusions. Peter Haslem isn't exactly unknown. People will put two and two—"

"And that is f-fine, D-D-Detective, as long as *we* don't help any of those people with their addition." He smiled at the younger man. "D-Don't let your m-mind become too attached to any one theory j-just yet. With the p-prior cases so cold, we n-need to be creative."

"Creative?"

"A great deal of d-detection is an art f-form." Jasper chuckled at Law's flat stare and climbed into the waiting carriage. "I l-look forward to seeing what you c-come up with. Right now, I n-need to go do some c-creative work of my own."

★   ★   ★

City Hall was fronted with grand Doric columns of the sort Jasper was already beginning to associate with government buildings in this country. The mayor's seat of business had the look of French Renaissance Revival and occupied a sort of park. It was also rather down-at-heel, and he'd seen mention in the paper of demolishing it and building a new hall. Perhaps if the city just waited, the feuding police or gangs would take care of the demolition free of charge.

Uniformed officers were stationed outside, and there appeared to be a great number of them, as if they'd been posted to subdue an unruly crowd. Jasper would have to ask Law if that was normal activity for a June morning.

Two uniformed officers detached themselves and approached as Jasper ascended the steps; he couldn't help noticing that both men wore side arms.

"I'm here to s-see the mayor." Jasper handed one of them the note.

"This way."

The mayor's office occupied pride of place in the rather ramshackle building. There was no functionary outside, so the officers knocked, and an older man answered the door.

"Ah, Lord Jasper, thank you so much for coming. I'm Mayor Wood."

Jasper experienced an odd sense of déjà vu at the situation, especially when a man with a shock of snow-white hair in an ornate ladder-backed chair turned toward him. Sitting next to him was none other than Cornelius Dell.

Dell grinned, but the lines of strain around his eyes told Jasper he wasn't feeling too sprightly. "'Mornin', my lord."

The mayor's eyes slid from his guests to Jasper. "Er, you already know Mr. Dell. This is Mr. Randolph Symington—Mr. Stephen Finch's father-in-law. He wished to be here as a representative of the family."

Jasper was nonplussed—what next? A representative from the *New-York Daily Times*?

"Mr. Symington saw this." The mayor held up a copy of the *Herald*, which shrieked: *THE POUND OF FLESH KILLER STRIKES AGAIN!*

Jasper was impressed by both the speed and the ingenuity of the New York newsmen.

He bowed to the white-haired man. "Please accept my c-condolences, Mr. Symington."

"Excuse me for not getting up." Symington waved to his chair, which Jasper realized was wheeled.

"Have a seat, my lord." Wood motioned to the chair beside Symington, studiously avoiding looking at Dell.

Just what the hell was going on? Who *was* Dell, and why did powerful men like Tallmadge and Wood tolerate his presence when it was clear that they despised him?

"I'm afraid you've come to our great city during a troubled time," Wood said, his expression theatrically solemn. "We're in the middle of a constitutional crisis, if you'd not already—"

"It's a goddamned mess," Symington cut in, his gravelly voice suiting his leonine looks. "This foolishness is nothing more than an invitation to criminals to openly pursue vice." He shot Dell and Wood a look that should have left burn marks. "It's gone on long enough." The warning was clear.

Wood looked unhappy at the older man's words but didn't contradict him.

"But that's not why I asked you here, er, Lord Jasper." It was easy to see that the honorific sat uneasily on Symington's Democratic tongue. Usually Jasper would have invited the older man to call him Inspector, but something about Symington—indeed, about this entire situation—had already worked its way under his skin, and he was in no hurry to put the man at ease.

Wood spoke next. "I should confess I was opposed to bringing you here—to New York, that is—not because of *you*, but because of the current situation. I hope there are no hard feelings?" Wood's angular features shifted into a scarecrow-like grin.

"Of c-course not."

"Good, that's good. Now that you *are* here, we're honored to have your expertise. I must admit I'm surprised that I've not had to deal with opposition from White Street." He paused, as if to allow Jasper to contribute information on the matter.

Jasper looked at Dell to see his reaction, but the alderman's eyes were closed, his mouth had fallen open, and his breathing was stertorous.

When Jasper failed to volunteer any information about White Street, the mayor's jaw tightened, a flash of displeasure in his eyes as he propped one bony hip against the edge of his desk and crossed his arms, his pose that of a man hunkering down for a serious conversation. "This killing is a tragedy, and—"

"Oh, for God's sake." Symington turned to Jasper. "Bunglers!" he shouted, causing Dell to startle but not wake. "Nothing but a clutch of goddamned bunglers."

"Er"—Wood cut a quick glance at Jasper—"what Mr. Symington is saying is that because the murder method is similar to that in the Sealy and Dunbarton cases—er, is that true?"

"I couldn't say, Mr. M-Mayor."

"What the hell do you mean, you can't say?" Symington demanded. "Wood ordered you put on the case." He glared at the mayor from beneath brows like snowdrifts. "Goddammit! Did Davies not—"

"Captain D-Davies was most helpful," Jasper lied. "But the case f-files for Sealy and Dunbarton were with the Sixth P-Precinct, and they are m-missing."

"Missing?" both Wood and Symington said at the same time, wearing equally stupefied expressions.

"What do you mean, *missing*?" Symington demanded.

Jasper tried to think of a word clearer than *missing*. "The f-files are gone."

Wood's expression shifted from surprise to horror. "This is *exactly* what those bastards are looking for." He cut Jasper a frantic look. "Have you told anyone about this? Newspapermen?"

Jasper frowned. "No."

The mayor's pasty cheeks darkened at Jasper's expression. "Uh, of course you haven't. I beg your pardon. Did you speak to McElhenny?"

"He's the one who told me they were missing."

Symington's gruff voice filled the awkward silence. "What the hell do you need those for? Everyone in the city knows they were strangled and stabbed—just like Finch—weren't they?"

Before Jasper could answer, the mayor spoke. "It is our concern— mine and Mr. Symington's—that this murder will be used by those opposing us as a weapon, proof of the Municipal Police Department's ineptitude."

Jasper thought that a fair assessment.

"None of that matters." Symington glared at the mayor. "What *matters* is the mess this will cause."

"M-Mess?"

"I'm sure even in England you've heard of the Burdell case?" Symington said *England* the way another man might say *sewer*.

Jasper blinked at the sudden change of subject. "The woman acquitted of m-murdering her husband. I'm afraid I don't understand—was Mr. Burdell strangled and s-stabbed?"

"No, no, *no*," Symington said. "I'm talking about the fact that the damned case was on the front page of every newspaper for weeks, every minor detail fodder for the public's insatiable hunger for scandalous drivel. The same was shaping up before those fools at the Sixth found Sealy and Dunbarton's killer. I have to admire the woman for having the decency to do away with herself and spare the public the expense of a trial, not to mention a ridiculous spectacle." Symington leveled a gnarled finger at Jasper. "Understand this: I will *not* have my daughter subjected to such a circus."

Mr. Symington was, Jasper suspected, a man whose will had not been thwarted in a long, long time. He reminded Jasper of the duke.

"What Mr. Symington is saying is that this case needs to be handled with, er, discretion—and speed." His eyes slid nervously to Dell at this last part. Dell remained sleeping.

Symington snorted. "What I'm *saying* is that I don't want to read my family's personal details on the front page of the paper every goddamned day for the next six months."

Jasper glanced at the two-inch headline on the *Herald* and almost felt pity for the man. "I'm afraid there is v-very little I can d-do about that."

"I know that. I meant the *speed* at which you progress. No dillydallying. Get this done in a timely fashion."

Jasper had the urge to laugh but wisely restrained himself. "Even if I *were* to arrest a suspect tomorrow—which is highly unlikely—an inquest and t-trial would take time, and those aren't my p-purview but that of your c-coroner and district attorney." And a case like this would be fodder for newspaper sales indeed. "I h-have no suspects, nor enough evidence to j-j-justify an arrest." Jasper hoped they understood his meaning: he would *not* be arresting somebody just to please them.

"You let me worry about Edward Connery and Oakey Hall," Symington said, his eyes narrowing spitefully at the coroner and district attorney's names. "Just keep this investigation the hell away from me and my affairs. And my daughter," he added, as if it were an afterthought. "Do you understand me, my lord?"

Oh yes, Jasper understood. Could he prevent such a *circus* from occurring? Unlikely. Did he have any desire to prevent such an eventuality? Not particularly.

He smiled. "Of c-course, Mr. Symington."

Symington's face looked as if it might be trying to smile back. The attempt was ultimately unsuccessful. He settled for a nod and a self-satisfied *harrumph*. "I knew the son of a duke would understand my desire to avoid sensationalized newspaper stories."

Jasper was tempted to point out to the older man that he was currently cooling his heels in a foreign country for exactly the opposite reason, but he suspected Symington would take his true measure quickly enough and come to dislike him sooner rather than later. Why hasten such a disagreeable eventuality?

"It's fortunate my daughter and grandson aren't here, so at least they're being spared the worst of this mess," Symington added.

"Oh? Where is Mrs. F-Finch?" Jasper asked.

"She's at my country house outside Albany—she was in the straw in February and didn't come to the city this year."

Well, that was interesting.

"When was the last t-time Mr. Finch visited his w-wife?"

Symington's jaw worked at Jasper's question, the noisy clacking of his dentures like castanets in the quiet room.

"About a month ago, to my knowledge."

"I would like t-to speak to Mr. F-Finch's servants."

As Symington considered Jasper, Jasper considered him. The railroad magnate—so wealthy his name was famous even in Britain—was a self-made man, if Jasper had ever seen one, not that he had extensive experience with such creatures.

As the harbinger of a new era, Symington doubtless viewed Jasper as a useless appurtenance of a decaying society. Even so, he would recognize that the peerage still held much of the power—if no longer all the wealth—in Britain. And the one thing a man like Symington would respect aside from money was power. So Jasper wasn't surprised when Symington capitulated to his impertinent request with relative grace.

"Very well. I'll write the address on the back of my card—that will get you in the house."

"Thank you, sir," Jasper murmured.

"Well then," Wood said, rubbing his hands as if he'd just completed a dirty task. "I suppose that is that."

Jasper couldn't help smiling at the other man's evident relief that a problem—this investigation, as well as Jasper himself—had been so quickly and tidily solved. "I told Davies to offer you every assistance," Wood said. "Please feel free to pull his best detectives off whatever they are working on. After all"—Wood's smile was so oily it was likely to catch fire if he got too close to an open flame—"you're here to instruct our fine Municipal Police in the art of detection."

Jasper wished Davies had been here to hear this.

"Thank you for your support, Mayor—also for putting the city's b-b-best detectives at my disposal." He would remind the man of that promise if necessary.

Jasper began to push himself to his feet. "Well, if—"

Symington's voice arrested him. "I understand you're something of a businessman yourself, Lord Jasper."

Jasper's eyebrows arched. "Sir?"

Symington chuckled, but his attempt at laughter sounded as merry as a barrel of nails being rolled over rocks. "I know you're an investor in Cyrus Field's Atlantic Telegraph Company. I've put a bit of my own money into the effort."

Symington's words surprised a laugh out of him. "P-P-Perhaps it is *you* who should be instructing on the subject of d-detection."

Wood laughed, and Symington once again attempted a smile, but his heart was clearly not in it. He was a man with a mission. "I'm in the process of gathering men of like minds for a new venture."

Beside him, Dell's eyelids rolled up like Roman shades.

Jasper smiled. "I'm afraid I'm n-not—"

Symington held up a hand. "Now, now, don't be hasty." He glanced at Wood and nodded.

The mayor leaned toward him, an eager glint in his eyes. "I've got one word for you, my lord: rubber."

Jasper nodded cautiously. "Rubber," he repeated.

"The man who can successfully link the rubber-producing areas of inland South America to an Atlantic port will be able to print his own money."

"Ah. Then I should have to arrest that m-man," Jasper said with a smile.

All three men stared in perplexity, and it was Dell who understood the jest first and gave an overly hearty laugh. "You've a sharp wit, my lord." He grinned proudly at Wood, like a battered old tomcat that had just brought in a choice rat. "Didn't I tell you he was clever?"

Wood ignored the question.

Symington, only a step behind Dell, was not amused. "This is not a time for caviling, my lord. What do you know about railroads?"

"I know how to p–purchase a ticket to r–ride on one."

Symington's nostrils flared. He continued speaking, but it was through tight jaws. "We are even now engaged in conversations with an engineer—a man endorsed by the U.S. government—who's surveyed the Madeira and Mamoré Rivers: the area is perfect for a railroad. This venture will bring undreamed of returns to shrewd investors." Symington spoke with the fervor of a medieval martyr, his eyes burning as he warmed to the subject of money. He'd not looked a fraction so feverish about his dead son-in-law or bereaved daughter.

"Was Mr. Finch an investor in this v–venture?"

Symington blinked at the change in subject, and Wood stepped into the conversational breech. "Mr. Finch was—"

"What difference does it make what my son–in–law invested in?" For the first time since Jasper had met him, the older man wore an expression other than scorn or irritation—he looked affronted.

"You m–mentioned shrewd investors, and I wondered if he was one of them."

"Are you asking me questions in your capacity as a policeman, my lord?" Symington glared at Jasper like a man who'd suddenly realized that what he'd believed to be a harmless insect was really a creature with a propensity for stinging.

"If I'm to find his k–killer, it would be helpful to know who Mr. F–Finch was, who his associates were, his interests, so forth. And as you were s–s–somebody who knew him well, your insight would be helpful."

Symington glared as he absorbed that, and Jasper waited for the cantankerous millionaire to explode.

But the old man surprised him. "I'll speak to you about my son-in-law now, and never again—do you understand me?"

"Yes, I understand." Which didn't mean he wouldn't ask more questions whenever he chose.

"Stephen wasn't the man I wanted my daughter to marry. He was—and there's no other word for it—a namby-pamby reformer sort."

That was four words, or at least three, but Jasper wouldn't quibble.

"His family once owned a good chunk of Manhattan but had long since lost it. He couldn't see the larger picture. I'll give you an example. Shortly after he married my daughter, I told him about an opportunity to purchase land where the new park will be. A *lot* of land. But he was too *nice* to engage in business based on information from a friend in the city government. Nor did he have the stomach for throwing a few *freedmen* squatters out of their shacks in order to take possession of the land." His face twisted into a truly ugly smile. "His tune changed after he'd squandered most of the money my daughter brought to the marriage—either giving it away to any charity with their hand out or investing in pie-in-the-sky enterprises only a nitwit would believe profitable—he came back to me, hat in hand, beggin' for my help." Symington snorted with disgust. "But the sun shines on fools as well as the virtuous, so I wasn't surprised when a wealthy bachelor uncle conveniently died and left him a great deal of property in Upstate New York. So, there he was again, steeped in money and on a mission to piss it all away. And no, in answer to your question, Stephen hadn't committed money to the railroad venture I mentioned—even though anyone with a particle of sense *would* grab the opportunity with both hands." The heated look he shot Jasper told him in which camp he placed him. "Stephen had *moral* issues about the harvesting of rubber."

Symington made possessing morals sound like having an infectious disease.

"When w-was the last time you saw M-Mr. Finch?"

"Months ago—back when my daughter was still in town." Symington's bushy white eyebrows descended. "Why?"

"Did Mr. F-Finch keep a b-business office?"

"He didn't need an office to give away all my daughter's money."

"You described him as a r-refor—"

"Reformers!" Symington spat out the word as if it were a fly he'd found in his tea. "More like destroyers! By definition, anything Stephen was involved in was a cracked idea. He was too bloody lazy to run for office or hold down a job, although he behaved as if he held a public office, the way he meddled. My son-in-law spent a good deal of his time—and my daughter's money—chasing after various causes. One week it was children in factories, the next it was corruption in the police department."

"Was he a p-proponent of the new Metropolitan P-Police Act?"

Symington gave him a look that Jasper suspected Stephen Finch had received often. "He ran his mouth about the corruption in the police department. There *is* corruption in the police department;

nobody would deny that. But why those fools thought it would be better to scrap the entire system and set up a *new one* is beyond any sensible man. And to put control of it in state, rather than city, is preposterous."

"Do you think his r–r–reformist actions earned him enemies?"

Symington made an agonized noise, as if he were beset by morons. "Of course it did! Thousands of them, I'd imagine."

"Would any of them have been angry enough to k–kill him?"

Symington's laughter sounded almost genuine as he pointed at the mayor. "Why, you're looking at one."

Wood shot to his feet, his mouth agape and face scarlet. "*Mr. Symington!* I would nev—"

Symington waved the other man's horror aside like a bothersome odor. "There were *lots* of men who hated Stephen—for a variety of reasons—but killing him would do nothing to erase the damage already done. Besides, he had very little to do with this law enforcement debacle."

"Oh? Would his d–death have eased some other p–problems?"

"No, goddammit, that was just a figure of speech," Symington said irritably, giving Jasper a look of intense dislike.

"Did your s–s–son–in–law know Sealy, Dunbarton, or Janssen?"

"Why the hell would that matter? Just because Stephen was a rich man who was murdered doesn't mean he knew every *other* murdered man in New York. *I* knew Sealy, Dunbarton, and Janssen. Surely you don't think *I* killed them?"

"D–Did you have any d–dealings with those men? Perhaps as investors in your r–r–rubber r–railroad?" Lord. He didn't want to have to say that again.

Symington's eyes narrowed. "I'm beginning to think you're rather single-minded, Lord Jasper."

"My f–father would agree with that, sir."

Symington didn't return Jasper's smile. "None of those men were involved in my current railroad venture. It's possible they purchased shares in the companies I own that are publicly traded." Symington finally managed a smile: a twisted, starved sort of thing. "I'm sure you understand *that* sort of investment takes place without my invitation or knowledge."

Jasper suspected that very little in this city took place without Mr. Symington's knowledge.

"If you're searching for some nefarious business deal gone wrong, you are barking up the wrong tree. The few business opportunities Stephen invested in over the years came through me, and I *assure* you I do not engage in nefarious conduct of any sort."

Jasper doubted that the man across from him had made all his money without at least dipping a toe into some fairly nefarious waters, but he let the matter alone. Instead, he glanced at the mayor, whose eyes had glazed and whose mind was clearly elsewhere, and asked, "Did you have any business d-dealings with any of the f-four men, Mayor Wood?"

"Huh? What?"

"He wants to know if you did business with any of the dead men," Symington barked. "Apparently, anyone who *did* is now a murder suspect." He turned to Dell. "What about you?"

Dell's eyes threatened to roll out of his head. "God, no! Didn't know any of 'em, other than from a distance."

Jasper thought that was a first for a man who claimed not just to *know* everyone but to be chums with them.

"Neither did I," Wood hastily chimed in. "Although—like the alderman—I may have seen them in public."

Jasper turned back to Symington. "So you didn't know any of them s-socially?"

"No, I did *not*." Symington shoved the words through gritted teeth. "I couldn't have met them above two or three times—if that—at various social functions." When Jasper didn't respond, Symington heaved an exaggerated sigh. "To answer the question I suspect you are *about* to ask, I do *not* know if Stephen had any business dealings with those men, although I seriously doubt it. Those three—at least from what I've *heard* about them—were too shrewd to involve them-selves with such a nitwit."

"What about s-s-socially—would Mr. F-Finch have associated with them?"

"I'm guessing they had very little contact."

"And why is that?"

Symington's lined face creased with an unpleasant smile. "I'm going to let you *detect* that particular piece of information for your-self, my lord."

Jasper had to laugh. "I appreciate you l-leaving me something, sir."

Symington's reptilian eyes flickered over Jasper's person with a look that was both dismissive and envious. It was an expression Jasper had encountered often from men who decried the aristocracy as a useless anachronism but wanted desperately to become one of their number all the same.

"I have just one more q-q-question."

"Why do I have trouble believing this will be the last? Go on," he said, before Jasper could respond. "But this is the *last* question I'll answer."

"Who do you think k-killed your son-in-law?"

"I don't know, but whoever it was deserves a medal."

The mayor gasped.

Symington glared at Wood and then Jasper. "Who do I think killed him? Are you toying with me, my lord?"

"No."

"Whores, man! Whores, for God's sake. His body was found outside a whorehouse, wasn't it? The others as well, if I recall correctly."

"But the p-prostitute arrested for the D-Dunbarton and Sealy murders committed suicide. Are you s-saying the Sixth arrested the wrong woman?"

Dell's eyes glinted avidly, and the mayor let out a horrified squawk. "No! Absolutely not. What he's—"

"I'm *saying* that *obviously* she had a partner in crime. Whoever her accomplice was, *that* person hasn't stopped robbing and killing." Symington gave Jasper a scathing look. "It's a flimflam as old as time, robbing a fornicator while his trousers are around his ankles. Surely you've seen such things in England? Whoever robbed these men got carried away."

"D-Did Mr. Finch carry a great d-deal of money on him—or something that might m-make him a t-target for thieves?"

"How the hell would I know what he kept in his pockets?" Spittle flew from Symington's mouth. "But the man was a whoremonger, so it's likely the *whores* he paid would know what he kept in his pockets."

"D-Do you know if he had d-dealings at a brothel called Horgan's?"

"Dealings?" Symington snorted. "That's prettifying it, isn't it? The man was a bloody pervert."

"Oh?"

The single syllable was enough to goad Symington into forgetting his resolution to answer no more questions. "Stephen Finch spent a good part of every night—and many days—in one whorehouse or another. If he'd approached his business interests with the same zeal he gave whoring, he'd have owned the whole damned city."

"Did you know of any other b-brothels he frequented other than Horgan's?"

"How the hell should I know?" he shouted, the veins in his temples bulging dangerously. "And what does it matter? Bastions of vice and disease, every damned one of them. Although Horgan's is a particular abomination." The old man's pale cheeks darkened.

"Oh—why is that?" Jasper asked, able to guess what Symington meant.

But Symington appeared to have lost the ability to speak.

Wood cleared his throat. The mayor was perched on the edge of his desk like a nervous pigeon, his small dark eyes flickering between Jasper and Symington.

"I'm pleased to tell you that Horgan's is closed, Mr. Symington," Dell told the older man in a placating tone.

There could be only one way Dell knew that.

Symington's nose wrinkled at the alderman's words, as if he'd just noticed something rank in the room. "Closing it won't do a damned bit of good; the vermin will just flee to the next business, like rats from a burning building." Symington shot Dell a look that said he lumped the alderman in the same category. He leaned toward Jasper, his eyes narrowed. "My son-in-law dishonored my daughter *daily*, almost from the beginning. The only sense the man ever showed was to hide his proclivities *before* he married my daughter. If I'd known what he was, he wouldn't have been allowed within a mile of her. It's a goddamned *relief* the man is dead. I thought of killing him myself on more than one occasion."

Both Dell and the mayor appeared startled by the old man's shocking pronouncement, but Symington either didn't notice or didn't care.

"It's my opinion that Stephen's carousing finally caught up with him. If a man consorts with degenerates, he should expect such an ending. In short, he lay down with dogs and came away with fleas."

Jasper wasn't sure if that proverb really applied to this situation, but he took it in the spirit it was intended.

He was out of questions, but it seemed a shame not to poke the nest a bit. "Was the l-last suspected murderer—the p-prostitute who committed suicide—from Horgan's?"

"No," Wood said. "She was from an even worse pesthole, Molly O'Reilly's."

"Is that shut d-down as well?"

Wood's eyes swiveled to Dell, who—for the first time—wore an uncomfortable expression.

"What the hell difference does that make?" Symington asked.

"None at all," Jasper admitted.

Dell and Symington frowned at him, their bemused expressions like matching bookends.

"Then why the devil did you ask it?" Symington asked.

"It is my j-job to ask questions," Jasper reminded him gently.

"Well, I'm done answering them."

"Well then," Wood said after a long, awkward moment, his anxious eyes settling on Jasper. "I'm sure you must have some questions regarding—"

"If you want to yammer at the man, do it some other time, Wood." Symington fixed his venomous gaze on Jasper. "I want this matter finished quickly. Is that understood?"

Jasper smiled. "Of course you do, Mr. Symington." He turned to the mayor. "D-Do you have a moment, s-sir?"

Wood's eyes slid to the old man, who waved him away.

"Oh, just go with him."

Outside in the corridor, Jasper asked, "I just wanted to m-make sure you never had any d-dealings with any of the victims, sir."

Wood recoiled. "What? Why would you ask? What do—" He stopped, his eyelids fluttering. And then he lifted his hand in a staying gesture. "Er, wait a moment—I now recall Dunbarton donated to my campaign fund, and I invited him to my office for a drink. But just the once. I wouldn't say I *knew* him."

"Was anyone else with you at the t-time?"

The smooth impulses of a politician kicked in. "Not that I recall."

"If you r-remember differently, p-perhaps you might let me know." Jasper handed him a card. "I'm at the Astor House."

"Yes, of course. Please don't hesitate to ask if I can assist you in any way." Wood crushed Jasper's hand and disappeared back into his lair, his door clicking decisively behind him.

Jasper stood in the hall, his mind whirling from the bizarre encounter. In the span of less than an hour, he'd been threatened, flattered, offered a business opportunity, threatened again, and lied to.

The day was off to magnificent start, and it had barely begun.

CHAPTER 21

Hy tried not to be too annoyed that he'd gone all the way up the island to talk to Haslem's mother only to learn that the woman was gone for the day. Or at least that's what her lodger had said.

Lizzy Horgan's brothel was a big building, but Hy and O'Malley were making good time searching the place, especially considering all the people wandering about and getting in their way. But at least Haslem wasn't one of them since he'd buggered off.

Hy had been tempted to go to Haslem's room immediately, but then he imagined the expression of disappointment on Lightner's face and did as he was told. After all, he owed the Englishman; the man had rescued his arse.

While he worked, he considered Lightner. Hy figured it was natural to be fascinated by a person who was so different from anyone he'd ever known.

It wasn't just that the man was the richest person he'd ever met, it was the way he acted.

Hy suspected that growing up in an orphanage was about as different from a duke's son's upbringing as possible. All his life, Hy had used his size to intimidate those around him; in the Points, a man had to plainly stake his claim or he'd end up at the bottom of the pecking order.

But all day yesterday and again today, he'd seen Lightner interact politely with people, no matter who they were: whores, crooked coppers, even the beggars he passed on the street.

Hell, even when he was beating Ryan with his cane, he'd remained civil, not hurling insults, raising his voice, or using his wealth as a weapon. He'd been as courteous to Lorie and Lizzy Horgan as he was to Hy—well, after he'd forgiven Hy for lying to him.

That's because to a man like Lightner, you're no different than a whore or a madam or a bigot like Ryan.

Hy had to accept that this was likely true; he couldn't even imagine what Lightner must make of them all. It wasn't anything he'd thought before—how outsiders saw him—and it made him uncomfortable in a way he couldn't describe.

"Detective?"

Hy turned at the sound of O'Malley's voice.

"I'm finished with the second floor. Do you need help up here?" The other man was trying to stay civil, but Hy could see he didn't appreciate being paired with a copper who'd assaulted his superior and then spent two months in the Tombs. Hy couldn't blame him; he wouldn't want to be associated with himself either.

"Did you find anythin'?" he asked.

O'Malley took a small, brand-new notebook from his pocket, and Hy hid his smile. Lightner had already inspired the boy. It wasn't a new idea, carrying notebooks—they were all supposed to do it—but Hy was ashamed to admit that none of the detectives at the Sixth, including him, had ever bothered.

But he had one today.

O'Malley flipped through pages covered with surprisingly neat handwriting. "I went through eight rooms, checked wardrobes, moved carpets to check the floor for bloodstains, stripped the beds to the mattresses, checked for panel rooms, examined walls and furniture for blood spatters that would be consistent with stabbing—" He paused, a slight flush and smile on his face as he regurgitated Lightner's description word for word.

Hy had to admit it sounded impressive.

"I talked to the girls and compared their statements with the ones you took, but there wasn't no dev—deva—"

"Deviation," Hy finished for him. "I've just got this last room, and then I'm done." He opened his own book and shared his report with O'Malley, just so the man didn't think Hy believed himself above it.

When he was done, O'Malley nodded. "Let me help with the last one."

Hy wanted to do Haslem's room alone, but then, being a loner hadn't worked out so good at the Sixth.

Well, that and thinkin' with your prick.

Hy grimaced at the thought. "Aye, gimme a hand."

Haslem might be a man, but he had just as many feminine items as any of the women. In fact, Hy thought some of the fancy perfume bottles—although he was no judge of such things—looked expensive. The only thing unusual was the absence of a jewelry box or chest, like the others all seemed to have. It wouldn't surprise Hy if Haslem had taken it with him. He couldn't blame him; most coppers would help themselves in a situation like this.

"So, that's that," O'Malley said, after moving one of the beds back to its original spot.

That had been another courteous—unusually so—thing Lightner had said: "Leave the rooms as you find them."

Hy couldn't recall another copper being so considerate of mere whores. Well, the Englishman hadn't been very thoughtful at Solange's, but even there it was only the madam's room that they'd tossed.

As Hy shoved the second bed back into place, he noticed a cigar box pushed up against the wall.

He sat on the bed and opened the box. Inside were a few letters, picture postcards, and some newspaper clippings about jobs picking apples in an orchard up in the Valley.

"Detective?"

"Hmm?"

"What do you think about him?"

Hy looked up from a packet of letters tied together with a ribbon. "Haslem?"

"No, Detective Inspector Lightner."

Hy shrugged, not wanting to confess he found the Englishman fascinating. "Why?"

"Featherstone said he couldn't be very smart, since he stutters so bad."

Hy snorted. "I wouldn't take anything Featherstone says to heart." Featherstone had started out at the Sixth not long after Hy and Ryan. The man was arrogant and thick but thought he was better than men from the Points just because his family owned a farm outside Hoboken. "Featherstone is worried about his job—and he's right to worry; he's a shit copper and a bully who couldn't find his own arsehole with both hands."

O'Malley gawked, and Hy turned back to the letter. It was written to *M.* and signed *S.* Just some general romantic foolery, but then the last sentence didn't fit:

Please don't forget the new handbills, darling. I shall think of your beautiful eyes often on your few days away. S.

The letter had no date.

"Detective?"

Hy looked up. "What?"

"You think he'll stay here and not go back to England?"

"Who are the two people in this room?"

O'Malley scowled. "How come you always answer a question with another question?"

"Noticed that, did you?"

"You just did it again," he accused.

"You'll make a fine detective."

O'Malley must have decided to take the remark as a compliment, as he looked pleased. He got out his book again and flipped through it. "Er, this room belongs to Mary Haslem, but nobody uses the second bed." He glanced around and then crouched low and whispered, "There's something *odd* about her, don't you think?"

Hy snorted. "How old are you?"

"Eighteen. Why?"

Hy shook his head, wondering if he'd ever been that naïve.

"Is that important?" O'Malley pointed at the letter Hy still had in his hand.

"I don't know." Hy put the letter in his coat pocket and closed the box before shoving it under the bed.

"You never answered my question, Detective," O'Malley reminded him.

"What question?"

"Whether Inspector Lightner will stay or go back home. Featherstone says the mayor, Davies, McElhenny, or the gangs'll drive him away. They've got a pool goin' at the station, and it's up to almost thirty dollars. You think he'll leave?"

Hy thought about the man who'd walked into the Tombs as if he owned it and sent the lazy guards scurrying to do his bidding. And then he recalled the way Lightner had disarmed Ryan and O'Connor, both of whom were big and brutish, without even turning a hair.

"Detective?" O'Malley prodded. "What do you think?"

"I think if I were you, I wouldn't bet against him."

CHAPTER 22

The Finch house sat where East Twenty-Seventh Street met Fifth Avenue. On either side of the ten-foot double doors were stone lions as high as Jasper's hips. Massive bronze lanterns flickered with gaslight, burning brightly even in the middle of the day.

The Finches' butler, Loring, almost pulled the door off the hinges in his haste to welcome Jasper into his employer's home after viewing his card. Jasper decided he'd get Paisley to print up more, as they appeared to have an almost magical quality.

"When was the l-last time you saw Mr. Finch?" Jasper asked as he handed Loring his hat and gloves.

"Last night at dinner, sir."

"What t-time was that?"

Loring helped Jasper out of his overcoat. "He dined earlier than usual—only six thirty—but received a message a little after seven and left soon after."

"Do you know who sent the m-message?"

"I'm afraid not, sir; it came by a street messenger." He hesitated and then added, "Mr. Finch came back around ten thirty and went into the library for a time before leaving again."

"D-Do you know where he went?"

"I'm afraid I don't, sir, but he did have a package with him."

"Package?"

"Yes, sir. Just before he left, he rang for paper and string to wrap a package."

"What t-time was that?"

"Around eleven."

"D–Did you know what it was he was wrapping?"

"He didn't say, sir."

"Describe the p-package."

"It looked like a slim packet of paper, sir. I offered to wrap it for him, but he declined. He left perhaps ten minutes later."

"How did he appear?"

"Appear?"

"Was he n-nervous? Happy? W–Worried?"

"Oh, I'd say he looked . . . determined."

Now there was an interesting choice of word. "Anything else?" Jasper asked.

"Nothing that I can think of, sir."

Jasper declined an offer of tea, and Loring left him to his own devices in the library. The room was dominated by a life-size portrait of Stephen and Caroline Finch. Mrs. Finch was young—certainly no older than twenty-two or twenty-three in the painting—and bore an unfortunate resemblance to her sire. The heavy jaw and beaked nose that suited Symington did not flatter his daughter.

Finch, while a good two decades older than his wife, was a golden god of a man. Jasper had known from the examination that he'd been handsome, but the artist had captured the sparkle in his eyes, and the smile on his mouth was that of a hedonist: here was a man who'd enjoyed life. And if there was a certain vapidity about his wide, doll-like blue stare, well, likely he'd had the charm to keep others from noticing.

Not Symington, though. Jasper could see from this painting that the older man and his son-in-law would have been different enough to constitute separate species.

Finch must have married for money, while his young wife would likely have been infatuated with such a handsome sophisticate. Symington, for all his bluster and dislike of his son-in-law, would have gained connections to a stratum of society that otherwise would have remained out of reach to him and his daughter.

Like any man of good breeding, Finch had a library, although the collection was rather pedestrian, with most of the books being custom-bound classics that looked as if they'd never been opened.

An ornate, carved desk with a pristine surface sat in front of a window overlooking the street. Jasper found a ledger in the top drawer.

Mr. Finch, it was immediately clear, had a dilettante's attitude toward record keeping. Some months were entirely blank, and then he must have relented, as the entries for other months were recorded down to the most minor expenditures:

Brougham wheel replaced; repair and re-varnishing of rear box: $27.13
Silk top hat: $9.50
1 case Sicilian Madeira: $3.96

And so on.

Up until about nine months ago, he'd received one sizable deposit every month. Jasper assumed that must have been from Symington, until Finch came into his inheritance. His suspicion was confirmed when he found a copy of a will tucked in a pouch at the back of the ledger. Symington hadn't exaggerated by much when he said Finch had inherited a good chunk of Upstate New York.

Based on the dearth of any sort of documentation or correspondence, Finch seemingly had done very little business. Or if he had, he was secreting proof of it elsewhere.

There were a few handbills about charitable enterprises, a thick stack of pamphlets on various social issues, four lengthy reformer tracts on poverty in New York City—none written by Finch—a handful of theatrical programs, five articles clipped from the *New-York Daily Times* about the Fugitive Slave Act, and a small stack of bills from a jeweler's on upper Broadway—an expensive establishment, judging by the cost of the items. The oldest bill was from a year and a half ago, the newest less than five days ago.

Jasper flipped through them, amazed at both the number and extravagance of his purchases. One of the older bills, for a gold ring studded in emeralds—one hundred eighty dollars—caught Jasper's eye because he'd seen a ring just like it on Mary Haslem's finger earlier that day. The most recent bill was for sapphire earbobs—costing two hundred ten dollars. Those had been delivered the very day Finch was murdered.

Jasper paused; now where had he seen sapphire earrings lately?

He shrugged, stopped chasing the elusive memory, and placed the bills on a pile along with the newspaper clippings, pamphlets, and tracts before pulling the servant cord.

Loring appeared within moments, which told him the servants were likely gathered in the kitchen discussing the man searching their master's study.

"Yes, my lord?"

"Would you happen to have some p-paper to wrap this?" He gestured to the pile on the desk.

"Of course, my lord."

"C-Could you wrap it the same way as the package Mr. F-Finch took with him?"

Loring's brow furrowed briefly at the odd request, but he nodded. "Of course, sir."

"Was that unusual—him g-going out that late?"

"Er, yes, I suppose it was. But Grew would know his habits better."

"Grew?"

"Mr. Finch's gentleman."

"I'd like to talk to him."

"He's in Mr. Finch's chambers, sir, selecting clothing for when the mortuary contacts us. Shall I have him come down?"

"Why d-don't you take me up to him?"

Jasper thanked God for American servants; an English butler would have guarded the entrance to his master's inner sanctum like a bulldog.

The journey to the master's chambers was dark; all the windows had been shrouded in crepe and the gaslights dimmed to their lowest setting, as if darkness was somehow more respectful to the dead.

They found the valet staring at a selection of coats he'd laid out across a massive bed.

"Mr. Grew?"

Grew turned as if in a trance, which is when Jasper saw that his eyes were red and puffy, the grief in them plain for even a stranger to see.

"This is Lord Jasper Lightner—the new policeman from London we read about," Loring added, when Grew continued to look mired in misery. When Grew didn't answer, the butler said, "Lord Jasper would like to ask you about Mr. Finch."

The name shook the valet out of his fugue, and he seemed to recall who he was and where he was, his shoulders straightening. "Of course, my lord."

The butler left them alone.

"What d-did Mr. Finch usually carry on his p-person?"

It seemed to take a moment for his question to penetrate. "Er, yes, sir, he wore a signet on his right hand. It was an acorn graven on a thick gold band, no stone; the inscription inside was dated

1747. The ring was his great-great-grandfather's." He walked to the tallboy dresser and unlocked the top drawer, taking out a velvet tray of watches; one spot was empty. "He would have been carrying a gold watch with a steam engine engraved on the cover. It was a gift from Mrs. Finch." Grew slid the tray back into the cabinet and relocked it.

"How much m-money did he g-generally carry?"

"Usually no more than fifty dollars in bills and coins. Every few days I would exchange any dirty or damaged money he'd accumulated with new, clean money."

Paisley did the same for Jasper.

"When w-was the last time you saw him?"

"Last night when I prepared him for dinner, sir."

"You didn't see him when he r-returned later?"

"Mr. Finch said he wasn't returning until morning, so he gave me the evening off."

"Did he ever t-talk to you about what he was w-working on?"

"Working on, my lord?"

"Business, or perhaps r-reform issues?"

Grew opened his mouth, hesitated, and then said, "No, sir."

"Anything y-you can tell me m-might help to catch his killer, Mr. G-Grew."

The valet spent a long moment in silent struggle before he finally said, "I delivered some papers for him a few times over the past two months." Again Grew agonized, and Jasper waited. "To number eighty-one Greene Street, sir." The valet radiated disapproval.

"T-To anyone in particular?"

"A man named Leonard Gamble."

"What s-sort of business?"

"I don't know, sir. There was no sign on the door, and inside there was just one room with a desk. Gamble was the only person there when I went." He frowned. "It was rather squalid."

"When was the l-last time?"

Grew's chin wobbled. "The Sunday before he died, sir."

"Was that unusual?"

"No, sir. I always delivered them on a Sunday."

"Had this b-been going on a while?"

Grew frowned in thought. "I believe since April—or perhaps late March."

"How did Mr. Finch appear r-recently—his demeanor?"

"The same as usual."

"And how w-was that?"

"Mr. Finch is—*was*—a very sunny-natured and thoughtful employer."

"How did the Finches m-manage with each other?"

Grew's face broke into a genuine smile. "Oh, they were lovely, sir. Mr. and Mrs. Finch never had a disagreement that I heard of, sir."

"N-Never?"

"No, he quite doted on her, and she held Mr. Finch in very high esteem." His mouth twisted into a tearful moue. "They were a delightful couple."

Jasper's impression was that the man was entirely sincere.

He handed the valet his notebook and pencil. "Please write d-down the address on Greene Street."

Grew quickly jotted down the address.

"Did you ever n-notice any pine sap on his shoes?"

Grew looked confused. "Pine sap?"

"Yes."

He shook his head, his gaze wary as he handed back the notebook.

"Here's my c-card. I'm staying at the Astor House for the next few d-days, if you happen to think of anything else. *Anything.*"

Grew chewed his lip as he looked down at the card. "Is it true he was killed like those last two gentlemen—the ones they arrested the prostitute for killing?"

"It is t-too early to say. Thank you, Grew. I shall see myself out."

The butler was waiting for him at the bottom of the stairs. There was a slim, brown-paper-wrapped package on the console table in the foyer.

Loring helped him into his coat, and Jasper was pulling on his gloves when somebody called his name. He turned to find Grew hurrying down the stairs.

"Yes?" Jasper asked the red-faced man, whose eyes slid to Loring and then back. "Thank you, L-Loring; Grew will see me out."

A lifetime in service kept the butler from arguing, but Jasper knew he wasn't happy at being dismissed.

"I remembered something else Mr. Finch might have had in his pocket." Jasper waited, Grew's expression growing more miserable.

"Er, I know he left with some jewelry, because it wasn't on the dressing table, where I'd left it for him."

"Jewelry?"

"Yes, my lord, a pair of filigreed silver-and-sapphire earbobs."

"D-Did you know who they were for?"

"No, sir."

Jasper suspected he was lying. "Remember where I am, if you r-recall something else."

★   ★   ★

Judging by the handbills littering the floor at the Greene Street address the valet had given him, it was an abandoned abolitionist headquarters. Jasper spoke to the building manager, who said the office had been empty when he'd come in that morning. He also admitted that Leonard Gamble was the name on the lease, and he gave Jasper Gamble's address after a bit of monetary persuasion. When it came to who owned the property, the man claimed he didn't know; he said somebody came by to collect the rent every month.

Jasper was curious to learn who owned the building; perhaps they would know why their tenant had scarpered so quickly.

But first he had to quit delaying the inevitable: talking to Captain Davies.

Jasper could see something was going on in the squat gray station house before he stepped out of the hackney. The double doors were open, and people were spilling out of the building. Patrolmen were holding the crowd at bay, and it was fortunate for Jasper that one of the policemen was Sergeant Billings, who recognized Jasper and waved him in.

Billings's grim expression gave Jasper a sinking feeling in the pit of his stomach.

"What is it?" he asked.

Billings held up the front page of the *Herald*.

"Ah, yes. I've s-seen it. I t-take it these are concerned citizens?"

Billings gave an unamused bark of laughter. "You'd think the fools would realize only wealthy men have been targeted. Davies sent a patrolman to find you. Quite a while ago."

Jasper grimaced and headed up the stairs.

Davies was seated behind his giant desk when Jasper knocked. He'd drawn the blinds to block out either the sun or swarming crowds.

"Have you seen this?" Davies held up the same headline Billings had.

"Yes—m-most pithy."

Davies's eyes bulged. "Do you find this humorous? Only three days since you swanned in here, my lord, and we have *two* murders on our hands."

"Surely you d-don't think *I'm* c-committing the murders, sir."

Davies flinched. "Don't use that tone on me."

"I've been here *less* than three days with no help other than a m-m-man who's been incarcerated these p-past eight weeks and an infant patrolman. The r-records—including postmortems—of the f-first two murders are *gone*; Captain McElhenny frothed at the m-mouth when I asked for his help; J-Janssen's body putrefied before a proper postmortem could be made; and m-my detective is dodging vigilante p-police officers from the Sixth W-Ward. Oh, and there is apparently a p-pool among your d-detectives about how long I shall p-put up with all this n-nonsense before something—or somebody—m-makes me leave. Right now I believe the b-b-best odds are on *you* precipitating my d-departure."

Davies's nostrils flared. "Let me remind you, my good *sir*, that none of this would be your concern if you'd not thrust yourself into my station house. But now that you have, you'd bloody well better earn your keep." He gestured to a pile of paper on his desk. "These are just some of the overwrought messages I've received from city luminaries wanting to know what the hell is going on. Why is this the first I'm hearing about the missing pound of flesh?"

"I'd say it was l-less than a pound. As to why you haven't heard of it, McElhenny k-kept it from the p-public in the first two cases because he feared—and I quote—'heads would r-r-roll.' "

"Jesus Christ. Tell me you have some idea—maybe a suspect?"

Jasper experienced a childish pang of pleasure at the note of hysteria in the other man's voice. "I do have one idea, but I d-d-don't think you will like it."

"*What is it?*" Davies forced the words between clenched jaws.

"It's possible these two m-murders are the w-work of different killers."

Davies closed his eyes and his lips moved; Jasper hazarded a guess that he was praying. When he opened his eyes, Jasper saw an emotion other than derision or dislike: he saw fear. "God in Heaven."

Jasper didn't think God had any part in it.

"What the hell makes you think there is more than one killer?"

"J-Janssen's and Finch's murders are v-very similar, but with a few significant dif—"

"Wait—did I hear you say the postmortems for the first two cases are *missing*?"

"*Everything* about those c-cases is missing."

Davies's face screwed into a horrified scowl. "My God—*missing* case files?"

Jasper was beginning to feel sorry for the other man.

"What did McElhenny say?"

"He believes Law destroyed them."

"Why would he do that?"

"I don't believe he d-did, sir."

Davies opened his mouth but then stared at him without speaking. Jasper could see they were both thinking the same thing: namely, that McElhenny had destroyed them to cover up a botched or corrupt investigation.

Something else occurred to the other man. "How the hell would these imitators know to cut out the flesh if even *I* didn't know about it?"

Jasper had wondered how long it would take Davies to put that together.

"Wait—" Davies held up his hand, as if Jasper had spoken. "You're *not* thinking a *copper* did this? I don't even like saying that out loud—I hope to God *you* haven't said anything?"

"No."

Davies sagged in his chair. "Do you have any suspects?"

Jasper laughed, and Davies's face darkened dangerously.

"This is *not* a laughing matter."

"I agree—the m-murders are not a subject for amusement. However, *you* expecting m-me to have a suspect—or perhaps *t-t-two* different suspects—in hand so quickly is amusing."

"Perhaps I should give this case to somebody who *would* have suspects by now?"

"I r-rather think you *should*, sir, b-because that worked out so *smashingly* the l-last time."

Jasper wished he could call the taunt back before he'd even finished saying it. It was not like him to lose his temper, but Davies's persistent hostility—coupled with his unreasonable expectations—was beyond exasperating.

Davies jumped to his feet. "I'll not tolerate insubordination from you—don't think for a second I won't send you packing!"

There it is, Jasper—an invitation to leave. Grab it and run like a thief!

"I apologize, sir. I sh-shouldn't have said that; it was d-disrespectful." Respect the rank, not the man, as they said in the army.

Davies frowned, looking like a man who'd taken a swing with a cricket bat only to find there was no ball. "You're goddamned right it was disrespectful." He flung himself into his chair. "What about the whorehouse? Brothels seem to be a common thread in both murders—hell, all *four* murders. Maybe this is a group of whores?"

Jasper was astounded at how the Murderous Nest of Whores theory kept cropping up.

"Er, there is one m-m-more thing."

"Oh God, *what?*"

"I have evidence that D-Dunbarton's body was moved to the S-Sixth."

"From?"

"About twenty f-feet from where Janssen was found—nearer Solange's."

Jasper thought the captain didn't look as surprised as he should have been. Indeed, Davies appeared to be chewing on something he didn't care for.

The captain finally shook himself, glared at Jasper, and changed tack. "Featherstone told me Peter Haslem works at Horgan's?"

Jasper frowned. "Yes, sir."

Davies brightened. "The man has a criminal record for prostitution-related offenses. We should bring him in."

"He has an alibi for the n-night Janssen was murdered." Jasper hesitated and then added, "He has an alibi for last n-night as well. We're checking it."

"Make that your first priority."

"Yes, sir."

"I need to go to City Hall *and* White Street after I'm done with you," he said, his tone accusatory, as if Jasper were responsible for the disarray in the police department. "They'll both want to hear we have some ideas—*anything*. I'm *not* telling them about your two- or three-murderer theory—not until you have proof. Until then, I'll give them Haslem and—"

"Amos B-Baker," Jasper said.

"What?"

"According to Mrs. Janssen, a man named Amos Baker told her that Janssen's l-life wouldn't b-be worth a brass f-farthing if he failed to comply with the terms of some business deal."

Davies looked just like a young boy on Christmas morning. He grabbed the paper and flipped it to the bottom of the first page. "Did you read this?"

Jasper took the newspaper and looked at the smaller headline: *Slave Ship Detained in Harbor, Captain Amos Baker in Custody.*

Good Lord. "Well, that seems rather coincidental." Jasper read through the brief article. "It d-doesn't say when he was arrested."

"It was one of the coppers from the Harbor Commission who made the arrest, so he'll probably be in the Tombs. Get your ass over there *right now* and find out where Baker was last night and Saturday."

For once, he and the Welshman were in complete agreement.

CHAPTER 23

Hy was about to hop an omnibus when somebody called his name. He turned to find Inspector Lightner sitting in an open cab.

"I'm glad I c-caught you. I'd hoped to be by earlier, b-but I miscalculated."

Hy held up a copy of the *New-York Daily Times*. "Seen this?"

Lightner snorted. "Several times."

Hy flipped the paper. "Did you see *this*?"

"C-Captain Davies showed me—he said to get our arses over to the T-Tombs. Hop in and we'll go now."

Hy's stomach pitched just hearing the word *Tombs*, but he climbed in beside the Englishman and pointed to the brown-paper-wrapped package Lightner held on his lap. "What's that?"

"Just some things I t-took from F-Finch's desk. Did you speak to Mrs. Haslem?"

"No. The woman who lodges at her place—a Mrs. Gillis—said Mrs. Haslem was gone until tomorrow. She's a seamstress who works in people's houses. Gillis is a nurse and only comes home for a few days every week or so. She said Haslem only visits his mother when Gillis ain't there."

Hy couldn't tell what the Englishman thought about that. "Oh, by the way, Lorie sent word after readin' the paper—Finch and Baker were at *her* place last night."

"Bloody hell."

Hy grinned at the man's uncharacteristic language. "They had a drink together around nine. Lorie's message said she was too busy to notice when they left."

"A known slaver having a d-drink with an abolitionist."

"Finch was an abolitionist?"

Lightner handed him a leaflet for an abolitionist meeting. "I found that at an address on G-Greene Street. F-Finch's valet said he'd delivered s-several packets of d-documents to a man named Gamble—only on Sundays. The office was rented by an abolitionist charity that suddenly c-closed up shop sometime between y-yesterday afternoon and this m-morning."

"That reminds me." Hy handed him the letter he'd tucked in his pocket. "I found it in Haslem's room. Think it's from Finch?"

Lightner read it quickly and then looked up as he refolded it. "You d-didn't ask Mary?"

"She—" Hy rolled his eyes. "*He* wasn't there when we searched. How was the visit with the mayor?"

"Not very illuminating. Although it was interesting that he had both Alderman Dell and Randolph Symington with him."

"The railroad millionaire?"

"The v-very same—he's Finch's father-in-law. He was there to tell me he d-didn't want to see the murder mentioned in the p-papers."

Hy laughed. "Too late for that."

"He also t-told me he hated his son-in-law. And then cl-claimed no acquaintance with the other three."

"I sense a *but*, sir."

Lightner's lips curved into a slight smile. "I have no evidence to b-believe he was lying—other than I t-took an immediate dislike to him."

Hy was startled to hear the man admit to such an emotion. Still, he'd bet a dollar that Lightner had been courteous to Symington all the same.

"Er, about Dell, sir—"

"He is a T-Tammany man?"

Hy nodded. "Aye, he'll be reportin' everything back to somebody. He's a wily one, sir. I wouldn't expect a word of truth from him."

Lightner was staring at the packet on his lap, his expression pensive. "F-Finch was seen leaving his house last night around eleven with a brown-paper-wrapped packet."

Hy frowned. "Finch went back to his house *after* Lorie saw him with Baker?"

"So his butler said." Lightner paused and then said, "I c-can't help feeling whatever papers he c-came back for are important."

"Do we know they're papers? You said a *package*."

"Finch's butler said it looked like this." He held up the packet.

"Why come home to fetch them at ten o'clock at night? Why not bring them out to begin with?"

"What if it was something B-Baker asked him for at O'Reilly's?"

"He's rich—why not just send a servant or messenger to fetch it?"

"P-Perhaps whatever was in the p-packet was too important? Perhaps he knew it was worth k-killing over?"

"That's a lot of guessing."

"It is," Lightner admitted. "But it's all we have right now. The last p-person to see Finch alive was his b-butler. Before that he had a drink in Five Points with Amos B-Baker—who also knew Janssen."

"Seems like knowin' Baker can be bad for your health."

"So, that's what we have: Finch, B-Baker, the packet, and then a d-dead Finch." The Englishman clucked his tongue. "I w-wish I'd known about the Finch-Baker c-connection when I talked to Symington."

"You think *Symington* had something to do with this?" Hy couldn't keep the disbelief from his voice.

"No, b-but it n-never hurts to ask."

Hy thought it might actually hurt a bit—at least when it came to their positions in the police department. "The packet might have been for somebody else. It could have been old newspapers or dirty pictures."

"I w-won't argue—we have no idea of the contents. But that doesn't mean they c-can't be useful."

"I don't follow you, sir."

Lightner lifted the packet.

"Wait—you said that was nothing."

"*We* know that."

Hy could see where he was headed, but it seemed like a bloody stretch.

"Don't think of them as p-papers, Detective."

"But you just *said* you thought it was papers."

"It's m-more than that."

Hy heaved a sigh. "What *should* I think of it as?"

"Think of it as fishing pole."

"A fishing pole," Hy repeated.

"W-We're going to see if anything is b-biting."

★　★　★

Jasper could feel the detective fidgeting beside him; he suspected Law's recent memories of the prison were weighing heavily on him.

"You d-don't need to be here, Detective."

The huge man's eyes were in constant motion around the interrogation room, where the guard had put them to wait. "Naw, I'll stay, sir."

The door opened, and the guard ushered a short, stocky, swaggering man into the room.

Unlike Law—who'd been naked, delirious, and starved—Baker looked as if he'd just been freshly shaved and dressed by his manservant; Jasper could smell his cologne from across the room.

"Thank you," Jasper said to the guard, who'd already been given a monetary incentive to leave them in private.

When the door shut behind the smirking Baker, he cocked his head at Jasper. "I read about you in the paper—the duke's son who's come to teach our coppers how to catch criminals."

"We're here to ask a few qu-questions, if you wouldn't m-mind."

Baker laughed. "Go on and ask 'em—if you're able to get the words out of yer mouth. But if it's about my cargo, I already gave my statement and I won't be changing it: I wasn't doing anything but returning property to its rightful owners. I'm only in here until my lawyer gets me out." He gave them an ugly smile. "After he springs me, I'm gonna file suit against New York City *and* the state of New York."

"We're not here to talk about your slave-tradin' activities," Law said.

"Good. Just remember I'm only talking to you because I'm *bored.* You have no authority over me. So, what the hell do you want?"

Jasper put the packet on the table, and Baker's eyes slid down to it, then back up, his expression uncertain.

"We're here to talk about Stephen Finch."

People could control their expressions and their body language, but Jasper hadn't met many who could control their pupils. And

Baker's shrank to pinpricks. He shifted the little black dots from Law to Jasper to the packet and back again. "Finch who?"

Law and Jasper laughed.

Jasper pulled a coin out of his pocket and handed it to Law. "You were r–right."

"Right about what?" Baker demanded.

"We have Finch's p–papers," Jasper said.

"Papers?" His attempt at sounding dismissive came off shrill. "What papers?"

Jasper sighed and took out another coin. "At this r–rate, I shall be skint before supper."

"I'll front you your first pint, sir," the American said with a grin.

"My c–colleague said you'd deny all of it," Jasper explained.

Baker crossed his arms, his expression no longer smug. "I don't know what the hell you're talking about."

"Are you saying you *didn't* have drinks with Stephen Finch last n–night?"

Baker scowled. "I don't know anyone named Finch."

"Are you denying you had drinks at O'Reilly's?" Law asked.

Baker opened his mouth and then closed it.

"What would you say if I t–told you we have witnesses?" Jasper asked.

"I'd tell you to get fucked."

"What about Alard Janssen?"

"Don't know that name either." His tone was dismissive, but his jaw had tightened.

"What t–time were you arrested?"

Baker blinked at the change in topic. "Why should I tell you?"

"Because a m–murder charge may be more difficult to evade than the offense you're c–currently incarcerated f–f–for."

"*Murder?*" Baker repeated. "If you think I killed Finch, you're both crazy!"

"I thought you didn't know anyone called Finch," Law said.

"I just had a drink at O'Reilly's—that's all." Baker's gaze stayed pinned to Jasper. "I left and went to Solange's. I was with Jenny."

"When?"

"I left O'Reilly's about ten."

"After your c–conversation with Finch," Jasper said.

"O'Reilly's was crowded—but I didn't know anyone. It's true," he insisted at their skeptical looks. "I was in bed with Jenny when those bastards arrested me around midnight. You can check on that if you don't believe me."

"Oh, we will," Law assured him.

"What d-did you and Mr. Finch t-t-talk about?" Jasper asked.

"Are you deaf as well as stupid? I told you, I didn't talk to him about nothin'."

Jasper hoped his own pupils didn't betray him the way Baker's had. "Are you qu-quite sure?"

"Hell yes I'm sure!"

"Did you know a m-man named Felix D-Dunbarton?"

Baker's eyes became comically round. "What?"

"What was your connection to him?" Law asked.

"Nothing! I mean I don't know him." His eyes darted between Jasper and the big detective. "What the hell are you getting at?"

"What's your c-connection to Benjamin H-Hoyle?"

"I don't *have* any connection to Hoyle!"

Jasper and Law looked at each other and then turned to Baker.

"What? Why are you looking at me like that?"

"Are you acquainted with R-Randolph Symington?"

Baker muttered something under his breath, his eyes flickering about like those of a hunted animal. "I'm done here," he said.

"We thought we'd offer you a ch-chance to cooperate."

"Cooperate?" Baker repeated, his gaze back on the brown paper package. "Do you have any idea who—" The last word was choked, as if somebody had wrapped their hands around his throat. He stood so fast the rickety wooden chair tipped over onto the stone floor. "Guard! *I want outa here right*—"

"Before you go," Law asked, "Who owns that gold-trimmed carriage that visits your friend Hoyle's house when you're there?"

Baker's entire body jolted as if he'd been struck by lightning. "*Guard!*"

The door swung open, and the guard frowned at them. "What's the racket?"

"I have nothing to say to these two. I've *said* nothing," Baker amended, a fine sheen of sweat on his brow.

"Tell us more about Hoyle and Symington and—"

"*Shut up!*" Baker yelled at Law before turning his wild eyes on the guard. "I never said anything! Did you hear me?" he demanded, staring at the guard. "I didn't say a goddamned thing to these two. Take me back to my cell."

The guard looked at Jasper.

Jasper picked up the packet and smiled. "We already g-got what we needed f-f-from Mr. Baker."

"You fucking liar!" Baker yelled, spittle flying from his mouth as he lunged at Jasper.

"Oi!" The guard grabbed Baker's upper arm and yanked him toward the hall.

"I didn't say *anything* to those bast—"

The door slammed shut with a clang, muffling the sound of Baker's yelling.

Law held out the coins Jasper had given him, grinning from ear to ear. "That was better than theater, sir."

"It's too bad he's got the b-best alibi of anyone yet."

Law grimaced. "Aye, there is that."

"He m-might not be our k-killer, but I can't help believing he knows something."

"I don't think he'll see us again after this, sir."

"No, *he* m-might not, but whoever he's afraid of m-might seek us out." Jasper smiled at the younger man. "We've baited the hook, and now we just sit b-back and see what f-fishes come up for a n-nibble."

Law laughed. "So, we're the bait now."

CHAPTER 24

Happy Lane—Leonard Gamble's residence and their next stop—wasn't far from the Tombs.

Hy was glad Lightner had brought him along to talk to Gamble; he hated to think of the Englishman wandering down one of the worst streets in the city alone, no matter how handy he was with his fists and cane.

"It's n-number twenty-one C," Lightner said, after the hackney dropped them off and he paid their driver. "What does C mean?"

"It's a cellar, sir."

Jesus, Hy hated cellars.

Two bedraggled children crouched on the bottom step of Gamble's building. "Hot corn?" one of the urchins asked without much hope.

Lightner's brow furrowed. "What are you s-selling?"

Both youngsters gawked up at the elegant stranger.

"Roasted corn, sir," Hy said. "There's children all over the streets sellin' it."

Lightner reached into his pocket, and the soft jingle of coins woke the children from their stupor. "Do you know a g-gentleman named Leonard Gamble?"

"He lives with his pa in small C," the little girl said.

"S-Small C?"

Hy explained, "It's when they divide up a room, sir. It's the cheapest."

"He left with a box," the boy volunteered, not to be outdone by his sister.

"L–Leonard?"

Both children nodded.

"When was that?"

"Last night," the two said in unison. "He was yellin' at his pa, and then he left," the girl added.

"With a box," the boy said again.

Lighter handed each child a coin. Based on the way their jaws dropped, it was a substantial amount. He turned to Hy. "Well, we're here; w-we might as w-well talk to his, er, pa."

★　★　★

Jasper wondered if his nose would ever become accustomed to the smell of poverty. It took a great deal of effort not to hold his handkerchief over his face, but that would hardly be civil to the old man lying on the filthy cot.

"Left me!" Mr. Gamble shouted, not because he was angry, but because he was as deaf as the proverbial post. "Said he needed to run! Said he was in trouble!" It took Jasper a moment to translate the heavy Irish accent. Instead of learning French and Latin at school, he should have studied Irish.

Gamble grimaced and shifted on the bed, his legs beneath the thin blanket shriveled sticks. The overflowing chamber pot under the bed lacked a cover and buzzed with flies. The room was smaller than Jasper's dressing room—half the size—and was dizzyingly hot, for all that it was a cellar. A dented pitcher of brackish water and a heel of dark bread sat on the crate that served as a nightstand.

"Did he say what he'd done?" Law yelled.

"Got a packet of money from a bloke!" He looked around the room, his rheumy eyes creased at the corners. "Paid another week here and left me," he said in a hoarse whisper.

"Good God," Law murmured, removing his hat and shoving a huge hand through his thick pelt of rust-colored hair.

Jasper crouched down beside the old man's bed. "D-Did he say the bloke's name?" he asked, using the same piercing tone he'd employed with his men in the army.

Mr. Gamble shook his head, and his chin wobbled. "Din't leave me even a penny. Used to be a good boy, but not after leavin' the army."

"Trouble?" Jasper asked.

"Aye. Caught thievin'."

"When?"

"Half a year back."

"Did he have a local?" Law asked the old man.

"A what?"

Law mimed drinking.

"The Black Cat!"

Law made an unhappy noise and said to Jasper, "It's not far from the Peck Slip Ferry dock. Not as bad as here, but close."

"Left me!" Mr. Gamble shouted, clearly not liking being left out of the conversation.

"Where did he g-g-go?" Jasper asked.

"California!"

Jasper recoiled at the blast of foul, moist air that came from the old man's nearly toothless mouth. He glanced up at Law. "Which f-ferries?"

"There's a bunch, sir: the Christopher, Barclay, Jersey City, and Hoboken, to name a few. He could be miles away by now."

"Do you have other family?" Jasper asked the old man.

"No, just Lenny."

Jasper stood. "We c-can't leave him here."

Law turned to the old man. "You need to go to the Sisters!"

The old man's eyes widened. "No! Not the nuns."

"Aye," Law argued, but without any real force. "They're the only ones who'll take you."

"Just cut me throat now!" Mr. Gamble dramatically flung back his head.

Jasper's eyebrows shot up. "Are they r-really that b-bad?"

Law snorted. "You've no idea, sir."

★   ★   ★

Hy was stunned that the Englishman wanted to accompany the old man to the mission.

"We can stop b-by the Black C-Cat when we're finished," Lightner said as they climbed into yet another hackney, this time with old Mr. Gamble, whom they'd had to carry from the cellar.

Lightner had purchased a blanket—only slightly cleaner than Mr. Gamble's—from one of the people who'd come out to watch the free show. Hy guessed the Englishman had paid at least twenty times more for the pitiful rag than its value, but the purchase had been well worth it as the old man had soiled his bedding and was covered in sores.

Hy breathed through his mouth to keep from vomiting. He didn't know how Lightner could bear the smell—or the human misery—but the other man chatted—loudly—as politely as ever, all the way to the mission.

The Sisters of Perpetual Sorrow had been one of the first to set up in Five Points. Hy experienced the same heavy sensation he felt whenever he came near the old Catholic church.

It was just his luck that the nun to answer their late-night knock was none other than Sister Mary Catherine.

"Well, if it isn't Hieronymus Law himself," she said, peering up at him through eyes as sharp as any raptor's. "Come for mass, have ye?" She exaggeratedly studied the plain watch pinned to her habit. "Are ye ten hours early, Hieronymus? Or thirteen hours late?"

Hy risked a look at Lightner, who was visibly amused to see this tiny nun raking him over the coals.

"Er, neither, Sister."

"We've g-got an old gentleman in n-n-need of your help," Lightner said, apparently deciding—correctly—that Hy was outmatched.

Sister Mary Catherine snorted. "Church of England."

Lightner bowed low, as if to royalty. "G-Guilty as charged, Sister. May we b-bring him in?"

Hy could see the old nun was tempted to have a go at the elegantly dressed—now shit- and blood-smeared—Englishman, but she must've decided he was too easy game to offer much sport.

Mr. Gamble had looked tired and ill in the cab, but he was instantly reinvigorated when he saw the good sister; the two proceeded to go at it, hammer and tongs, in Gaelic.

"What are they s-saying?" Lightner asked softly.

"Hieronymus wouldn't know, because he never applied himself to his studies," Sister Mary Catherine barked, not breaking stride in her argument with the old man.

"*Excellent hearing,*" Hy mouthed.

Lightner chuckled.

Half an hour—and an undisclosed donation, once again paid by Lightner—later, they were headed for the Black Cat.

CHAPTER 25

The Black Cat was a pub so vile that it would have been better called *The Rathole*, as that creature, and not a cat, was one of the first things they saw upon bellying up to the bar.

"I wouldn't drink anything here," Law said under his breath as they watched a grossly obese rat amble over one of the beer kegs behind the bar.

As slow as the rat was, it was still moving faster than the barkeep.

Jasper noticed two identical-looking men sidling out of the bar just as two other men came in.

"The Lowery brothers are the two who just oozed out the door," Law said, following Jasper's gaze. "They're snitches."

"Do you want to st-stop them?"

"Nah, you'll never meet a bigger pair of liars. We'd get better information out of that rat." He squinted at the two men who'd just entered.

"Do you r-recognize them?"

"The one with the brown hat used to be a copper. The other one, I don't know."

"What do you two want?" the barkeep said, his beady gaze on the brown-wrapped packet sitting on the bar.

Jasper slid a coin across the pitted wood. "Information about a m-man said to d-drink here."

"I don't sell information about my customers." He spoke loudly, halfheartedly rubbing the sticky bar with a truly filthy rag. "All I sell here is drink." He leaned close, as if studying a stubborn stain, and whispered, "Meet me in the alley." He stood up and in a louder voice said, "So either order or get the hell out."

"Think we should report them to the New York City Board of Health?" Law asked as they entered the alley, which looked cleaner than the pub.

"J-Judging by the size of that r-r-rat, I was thinking we should report them for keeping unauthorized c-cattle."

Law chuckled. "What do you reckon the chances are that he'll come out here?"

Jasper spun his stick in a lazy circle. "I'm expecting the t-two gentlemen who came in when the brothers left—they never t-t-took their eyes off us."

"Aye," Law agreed. "And they looked far too clean to be drinkin' in a dump like—"

"Oi!" The two men from the bar came around the corner, another three trailing behind them.

"G-Good evening," Jasper said pleasantly.

"Not for you, it ain't," one of the two leaders said, making the others laugh.

"The one on the right has a knife in his boot," Law whispered.

"Ah, then I'll t-take the one on the r-right," Jasper said, not bothering to lower his voice.

"The hell you will," the knife bearer—apparently the spokesman—said.

"Have you c-come to give us information?"

"Naw, we come to take *that* offa ya."

"This?" Jasper held up the package, which was beginning to look a little rough around the edges.

"Yeah, that's right."

"Is that all?" Jasper asked.

"Naw, it ain't *all*. You need to m-m-mind yer own f-f-feckin' business." Again his cronies roared.

Beside him Law said, "Oh no."

Jasper had to laugh. "How w-w-well you know me already, Detective."

"Can't say as I blame you, sir," Law said. To the five men, he said, "We're coppers; you might want to rethink things."

"Coppers, aye? So where's your badges?" one of the men behind called out, emboldened by their leader.

Law reached inside his long sack coat and pulled out the truncheon he kept in a holder at his belt. "Here's my badge." He lifted the distinctive stick that was assigned to every New York City policeman.

"Give us the package," the nearest thug said. "And quit pokin' about."

"P-Poking in what?" Jasper asked.

The knifeman stepped closer. "If you know what's—"

Jasper was holding the cane in his left hand, so he executed a *latéral croisé*. The thin stick made the air whistle as he swung it in a one-hundred-eighty-degree arc, striking the man's knife arm in the elbow.

He shrieked, grasping his elbow.

Jasper tossed the stick to his right hand and swung the cane point in a *latéral extérieur a bas*, which hit the second man in the side of the knee, causing him to leap up and yowl, holding his damaged knee.

While he was busy hopping about, Jasper finished off the first man with a *coup de pied bas*, a low, direct kick to the shin with the heel of his boot.

The three men in the back turned and ran.

Law glared at him, his expression one of profound annoyance. "Maybe next time I could have a bit of warning, sir."

Jasper grinned, his elevated heart rate invigorating. "It seemed a b-better idea than a p-p-protracted exchange of insults and b-boasts."

Law crouched and pulled the knife from the dazed man's boot.

The hopper was still leaning against the wall, his expression a mix of pain and rage. "You've made a big mistake."

"Who sent you?" Jasper asked, spinning his cane.

The man turned to Law. "He don't know any better, but *you* should."

Law threw the knife down the alley, and the blade skittered along cobbles into the darkness. "Do I know you?" he asked.

"You know who I work for."

"And who would that be?"

The other man's mouth tightened.

Law turned to Jasper. "Would you like to beat a name out of them, sir?"

Jasper smiled and took a step forward.

"Bill Finnegan!" the man yelled, staggering backward, tripping, and sprawling on his arse.

"Do you know him, D-Detective?"

"Another low-level thug," Law said. "Finnegan don't know shit, but he works for Devlin McCarty."

"McCarty will skin you alive, Law."

"What are we supposed to quit pokin' in?" Law asked, seemingly unbothered by the threat.

"He didn't tell us," the man said in a sulky tone more suited to a two-year-old than a thug-for-hire.

Law turned to Jasper. "You wanna arrest these two for assaulting a police officer, sir?"

"They didn't d-do much assaulting. What's your opinion?"

"Naw, they're little fish." He gave the leader an insulting smile.

"You've both just made the biggest mistakes of your lives!" the man yelled as they walked away. "It's too bad you won't live long enough to regret it."

"Let's head toward Water Street," Law said once they'd left the alley, his voice distracted.

"I c-can only assume Devlin McCarty is what you c-call a ward boss?"

"Aye."

"Do you know him?"

"Aye." Law sounded profoundly unhappy.

"What's your opinion?"

"I don't suppose you'd consider quittin' the case?"

Jasper smiled.

"How about runnin'?"

"You mean we're in d–danger."

"I'm pretty sure it'll mean trouble if we keep on this."

They trudged in silence, the noise from the street ahead drifting toward them.

Law jerked a thumb over his shoulder. "You think those two were following us since we left the Tombs?"

"It's possible."

"What do you reckon about Gamble?"

"I have a b–bad f-feeling about Mr. Gamble."

"Those men wanted that packet."

It wasn't a question, but Jasper nodded.

"You figure Finch was killed for the papers?"

"Yes."

"And now they—whoever *they* are—think *you* have the papers?"

"Yes."

Law looked at the packet Jasper still held in his hands. "It doesn't really matter *what's* in there, does it?"

"No."

"Jaysus. What do you think, sir?"

Jasper laughed. "I think this is what a w-worm f-feels like on a hook."

CHAPTER 26

Pale early-morning light filtered through the only window in Mrs. Haslem's tiny parlor. "Do you r-realize how much t-trouble Peter could be in?" Jasper asked Louise Haslem, feeling like a bully when the small woman cringed.

Mrs. Haslem was as slight and fragile looking as a bird. Like Peter, she was pretty, but her fine-boned face was nothing like her son's more striking features. Jasper suspected her frail appearance was deceptive; she'd reacted fiercely enough when he made the mistake of calling her son *Mary*.

"His name is *Peter*. I gave birth to a *son*," she told him, eyes blazing. But now she'd lost her fire.

"Where is P-Peter?" Jasper repeated.

"If I knew, I'd tell you."

"Did he ever m-mention a man named Stephen F-Finch?"

"No, sir."

"He was a customer of P-Peter's—he never mentioned any c-customers?"

"He knew I didn't like what he did; he never dressed like *that* here. And he never mentioned no men's names." Mrs. Haslem's skin was too dark for Jasper to see a blush, but he could certainly hear the woman's shame.

"When w-was the l-last time he visited?"

"Last Wednesday."

So, not the night of Finch's death, as Mary had claimed. Jasper could feel the weight of Law's stare. "How d-did he seem?"

"Happy. He's always been happy." She hesitated, then said, "Peter ain't done nothin' *bad*, has he?"

"Not that w-we know of," he temporized, "but evading police questioning is a c-crime in itself."

She nodded jerkily, her tears welling over.

Well done, Jasper.

Jasper wished he could sink through the plank floor of her humble parlor. "You needn't c-c-cry." He cut a glance at Law, who just shrugged and backed away. The big coward.

"Please, take this." He handed her a handkerchief.

"Thank you." Unlike the rest of her, Mrs. Haslem's hands were not delicate. She had the swollen joints and thick fingers of a woman who'd spent her entire life working—*hard*.

"I can't, Peter," she whispered to herself, then looked up at Jasper, the words spilling out of her like water from a cracked jug. "I know what we been doin' was dangerous, but we couldn't just do *nothin'*!" She squeezed her eyes shut and sobbed into the handkerchief, her slender shoulders shaking.

Jasper and Law stared at each other. Law shrugged and jerked his chin toward the woman—as if Jasper somehow had a better way with her.

He narrowed his eyes at the detective but said, "Er, *what* have you been d-doing, Mrs. Haslem?"

She went to the small kitchen and riffled around in a cupboard. When she came back, she held a handful of paper.

The New York Freemen's Society for the Abolition of Slavery was printed across the top, the rest of the page taken up with news items and, Jasper saw, a notice for employment.

"Who g-gave you these?"

"Peter wouldn't tell me—some gentleman where he worked paid him good to give them out—and it was helpin' people, so—" She shrugged. "They needed to be changed all the time, since it wasn't safe to have the same meetin' places."

"Y-You mean because people would d-disrupt the speakers?"

"Speakers?"

"Yes—aren't these for abolitionist meetings?"

She glanced at Law and then back to Jasper and then seemed to make a decision. "It's a way to help people get to Canada now that it ain't safe here." Her voice became stronger. "It ain't safe here for *any* of our kind—escaped or free. They've been grabbin' people off the street—not carin' if a body has legal papers tucked away at home. I wanted Peter to go with me, but he never would." Her eyes, which had become fierce again, clouded with worry. "But now I *have* to get out. They tole us we've only a month before we gotta leave."

"Leave where?"

"Seneca Village. All of it's gettin' torn down."

Jasper looked at Law, who nodded. "They're buildin' the new park here—it starts at Fifty-Ninth. The city took all this land some-time back usin' some law or other."

"They've been burnin' houses, so we gotta move." She gave Jas-per an imploring look. "I should've made him go to Canada. What if something happened to him?"

Jasper took a card from his case and handed it to her. "If you l-learn anything about P-Peter's whereabouts, you c-come see me at the Astor House—no m-matter the time of day or night."

"I will, sir. I promise. I—" She hesitated.

"Yes?" Jasper prodded.

"You're coppers—are you gonna—?"

"No, ma'am. We'll not turn you in," Law said, looking sheepish at the anger in his voice.

★ ★ ★

Neither of them spoke as they walked back toward Seneca Village's main street. Jasper noticed what he'd failed to see on the predawn carriage ride to Mrs. Haslem's: a good three-quarters of the houses were empty, most of them stripped of doors, windows, and anything of value. He couldn't help wondering where all the people who'd once lived there had gone.

"So," Law said after they settled into a hackney. "Finch was run-nin' escaped slaves to Canada and usin' Haslem to do it."

"It c-certainly looks that way."

"Why would somebody kill him for that?"

"Why was he t-talking to Baker?"

Law heaved a sigh. "Yeah, I don't know. There just seems to be more every time we talk to anyone."

Jasper met the detective's eyes. "I think it's t-time for you to tell me what h-happened with Miss Grady—and how you ended up in the T-Tombs." Jasper could see the muscles flexing like steel beneath the bruised skin of the other man's jaw.

After a long moment, Law sighed and nodded. "I knew Caitlyn from the orphanage; we grew up at St. Pat's. We stayed until we were thirteen, and then the sisters found us jobs. Caitlyn was pretty—real pretty—so she got a job uptown, workin' in one of the big houses as a maid." He cut Jasper a quick look. "And no, it wasn't in Dunbarton or Sealy's houses—just some other rich arsehole. Anyhow, the husband got Caitlyn pregnant and then gave her the sack. She tried to get rid of the babe herself and almost died. The sisters wouldn't have no part of her because of the abortion. So she ended up at O'Reilly's."

He grimaced. "This next part I learned from reading her confession—after she was dead. She claimed that she was with both men more than once and they shorted her money. She said when she went to get the money back from Sealy, he tried to touch her, and they scuffled. She hit him and he fell, and she took the chance to kill him. Said Dunbarton accused her of Sealy's murder, so she killed him too."

Jasper gave a snort of disbelief. "And all th-this happened in M-Murderer's Alley—*twice?*"

Law nodded. "I know. Her confession was so full of holes it made a sieve look watertight. Everyone I talked to, all the other whores, said the two men were terrified of disease; they were well known for paying top dollar for *girls*, not twenty-four-year-old prostitutes. And nobody seemed to care that Caitlyn wasn't even five feet tall and that one of Dunbarton's legs weighed more than her. His postmortem showed he'd been drinkin', so McElhenny claimed he was probably as drunk as a lor—" Law stopped. "Er, beggin' your pardon, sir."

Jasper chuckled. "N-No begging necessary. D-Did she happen to mention why she g-garroted and stabbed and cut out his flesh?"

"Her confession didn't say a damned thing about the missing flesh." He moved his jaw side to side, as if he was chewing over words, but then shrugged. "That's when things really went sideways between me an' McElhenny."

"Go back a bit. Why d-did McElhenny arrest her in the f-first place?"

Law scowled. "It was the damned dress."

"Dress?"

"Aye, one of Caitlyn's, with blood all over it. Once McElhenny got his hands on that—"

"T-Tell me about this dress."

Law chewed his lip hard enough to reopen the split. "I found it in her room."

"*You* f-found it?"

"I'd been fuckin' her, a'right?" Law squeezed his eyes shut. When he opened them, they were filled with shame. "I'd started seein' her a few weeks after Sealy's death. The trail was goin' cold. Hell, it *had* been cold from the beginnin'. The mayor was ridin' McElhenny, who'd been ridin' me and Donahue. You know how it is: arrest somebody. *Anybody.* McElhenny finally hauled in an old drunk, beat the hell outa him, and charged him for Sealy's murder." His mouth twisted with disgust. "It was bloody embarrassing. Anyhow, me and Donahue went into O'Reilly's to have a few. We had *more* than a few. Donahue went up with a girl, but I was still drinkin'. Suddenly Caitlyn was there, takin' my hand and leadin' me up to her room." He gave a bitter laugh. "I was a fool."

Jasper waited.

"Two days later, Dunbarton's body was found. The mayor tore a strip off McElhenny's hide, so he was twice as crazed as before. We tossed everyone out of the buildings in Murderer's Alley: women, children, sick people, old people—he was determined that *one* of them was the killer." Law snorted. "But one of the things about packin' twenty bodies to a room—other than death and disease—was that each of 'em had at least ten witnesses. Things were bad; the mayor was on a rampage, and McElhenny was like a man possessed. I went to Caitlyn that night; I got drunk and stayed with her. I was dressin' for work the next morning and looked in her dresser." He scrubbed a hand over his bruised jaw. "Christ. I just wanted a towel to dry my face, and there was this wadded-up dress, which seemed odd, 'cause Caitlyn was tidy-like. There were reddish-brown stains all over it. When I asked her about it, she said it was a female issue and that it had happened a while ago. She said the laundry woman couldn't get the stains out." He cocked his head at Jasper. "I ain't no fool—even though I'd been actin' like one—an' I thought there musta been a mighty lot of blood. She had an answer for that too. Said she'd tried to soak out the stain but just made it worse. I asked her about Sealy and Dunbarton—what she was doin' those nights. She said she'd been out with her monthly curse when Sealy was killed and had no alibi, but she'd been with a salesman the night Dunbarton was killed. She didn't know his name, just that he was from Tannersville and came to the city to sell dye."

Law stopped, his eyes distant, as if he was having some sort of inner struggle. After a long moment, he shrugged and said, "She wanted me to get rid of the dress, but—" He shook his head. "I couldn't. She begged me to find the man she'd been with, said if McElhenny found out about the dress, they'd have her in the Tombs in a heartbeat. I knew she was right." He gave a disbelieving snort. "If Dunbarton had been killed on Saturday night, she'd have had *me* for an alibi, but—"

"I'm s-sorry," Jasper said, arrested. "What did you say?"

"Saturday night is when she was with me. Sunday night—the night Dunbarton was murdered—she claimed to be with the dye salesman."

"What day was D-Dunbarton's body found?"

Law squinted in thought. "The morning of April fourth."

"So April third was the night of the M-Morissey-McDaniel fight?"

Law looked surprised by the question. He paused, as if searching his memory, and then shook his head. "No, the fight was on a Friday—I remember because I went to O'Reilly's after and—" His cheeks darkened, and he shrugged. "Why do you ask?"

"Jemmy Hart claimed he found D-Dunbarton's body the night of that f-fight."

"*What?*" Law appeared dazed. "Was Jemmy sure?"

"He was c-confused about the actual date, b-but he claimed it was the n-night of the fight."

"Jaysus. That would've changed *everything*." A myriad emotions flickered across the big man's face, none of them pleasant. "I want to talk to Jemmy about this."

"M-Me too," Jasper said. "But I want to hear the r-rest of your story."

Law sucked in a deep breath and let it out slowly. "So here's where I did a stupid thing—*no*, another stupid thing. I told her to do *nothin'* while I went to find this dye salesman. I knew it might take some time—but I had no idea. Good God! Every third house or farm seemed to be makin' dye. I'd been away almost six bloody days—it took three days just to get there—and was startin' to lose hope when I found the man." Law shoved his hand through his hair, leaving it in rows like red corn. "'Course he was married and denied it." He gave Jasper a mulish look. "I ain't proud, but I beat the bastard, tied him up, and brought him along. I was halfway back when Ryan and two patrolmen showed up to arrest me. The dye salesman said I'd coerced him, so they let him go."

Law was an excellent liar, but people always gave themselves away, and with Law it was his direct stare—or rather the lack of it when he wasn't telling the truth. Something in the last part of his story was a lie.

"How did McElhenny l-learn about the dress?" Jasper asked.

"Well—and this is all secondhand, because I wasn't there— but *somebody* mentioned seein' Caitlyn and Dunbarton arguing at O'Reilly's not long before he died."

"Who?"

"I don't know." Law looked pained. "The thing is, that's not exactly hard to believe. Caitlyn was—well, she had a temper and could be argumentative. Anyhow, once the first person mentioned the argument, then all these *witnesses* came out of the woodwork. Some of them said they'd heard her threaten him for money or she'd kill him."

"D-Do you believe that?"

"I don't, but once that started goin' around, they started pokin' around and learned that I'd asked the laundress about a bloodstained dress, which of course looked bad—for Caitlyn *and* me. I'd left the dress at my place for safekeeping. I know, I know," he said at Jasper's snort of amazement. "After finding it, McElhenny moved fast—detaining Cait-lyn on suspicion. I'm sure she tried to tell them about me goin' to find the dye salesman, but after a few days in jail, she gave them whatever they wanted." Law gave a bitter laugh. "McElhenny had been *lookin'* for a reason to gimme the sack after—" He stopped, chewed his lip, and then shook his head. "Well, that don't matter. I know it was him who made up those lies about her givin' me money to keep quiet." He cut Jasper a rebellious look. "I never took a dime from her. But I couldn't blame her for sayin' whatever they wanted her to say. That fuckin' McElhenny was—" A muscle ticced in his jaw, and he gave another harsh, mirthless laugh. "Anyhow, by the time Ryan brought me back, Caitlyn had already hanged herself. So, that was that."

The lies and truth were too tangled for Jasper to separate, but one thing stood out. "Their only evidence was a bloody d-dress? I'd imagine b-bloody garments abound in a br-brothel."

Law sighed. "They also found Dunbarton's watch when they searched her room."

Jasper couldn't have heard him correctly. "I'm sorry?"

"Caitlyn had his watch in her room—Dunbarton's—with blood all over it."

Jasper stared.

"Is somethin' the matter, sir?"

"Jemmy Hart claims he *prigged* D-Dunbarton's watch the night he f-found him."

Law's jaw sagged.

"How d-did they know it w-was Dunbarton's watch?" Jasper asked.

"I wasn't there, but I think Mrs. Dunbarton identified it."

"Mrs. D-Dunbarton identified it," Jasper repeated, because he couldn't think of anything else to say.

"If that's true, then how the hell did it end up in Caitlyn's room?" Law asked.

"Hart said he s-sold the watch."

Law's forehead creased. "You think somebody bought it and planted it in Caitlyn's room?"

"It d-does sound far-fetched, but I g-got the impression Ryan doesn't like you; do you think—"

"I think he'd frame *me* in a heartbeat. But Caitlyn? Why? And how would he get the watch to begin with?"

"These are all g-good questions. We n-need to find out where Hart sold the watch and see who *they* s-sold it to."

A rap on the window made them both jump.

It was O'Malley; they'd been so intent that neither of them had noticed they'd arrived at the station house.

"Sorry to interrupt, sir, but Leonard Gamble's body was found this morning, floating near the New Orleans Pier."

CHAPTER 27

O'Reilly's saloon was doing a booming business, and it took Jasper several minutes to part the crowd and reach the bar. He recognized the barkeep as the man who'd served him the last time.

"What can I get you?"

"I'm l-looking for Jemmy Hart."

"Why? Is he in trouble?"

"No, I just want to t-talk to him."

"I ain't seen him for a few days."

"Is that unusual?"

"Sometimes I don't see him for a week."

"Any idea wh-where I might find him?"

"He bunks up with a bunch of others over in the Old Brewery."

"He l-lives in a brewery?"

"Nah, that's just the old name for it."

"Wh-where is that?"

He looked Jasper up and down. "Are you thinkin' to go *alone*?"

"Be still my heart, it's His Lordship!"

Jasper had hoped to ask Hart what he needed to ask and then get out. He should have known better. He turned to find Lorena Paxton grinning at him.

"Come to pay your bill, my lord? Or were you hopin' to slip in and out unnoticed?"

Something about her question made his face heat.

"He's wantin' to go look for Jemmy."

The madam grimaced. "A more pestilence-ridden hole than the Old Brewery you've never seen. It's dangerous even in broad daylight—especially those tunnels. Don't go alone; wait and take Law with you." Before Jasper could respond, she turned to the barkeep. "Two Kilbeggans." She winked at Jasper. "Since you've no longer got plans to go muckin' about in places you don't belong, you can entertain me." She elbowed a man off the nearest barstool and took it for herself.

The barkeep put two brimming shot glasses on the sticky bar top. The madam handed Jasper a glass and lifted the other. "Here's to new friendships, my delicious lord." She threw back her head, the ivory column of her throat taut as she swallowed, smacking her lips in a way that was raw and suggestive.

When in Rome, Jasper.

Jasper sighed before tossing his own drink back, not his method of choice when it came to spirits. "Thank you," he said hoarsely, pushing the glass to the bartender.

"How about another?"

"Why do I f-feel as if you wish to get me d-drunk, Mrs. Paxton?"

She gave him a hard look.

"Lorie," he amended.

"Pour His Lordship a pint, Jimmy." She smiled at Jasper. "You can have a little fun."

"Fun," Jasper repeated.

"You sound like you've never heard the word."

He hadn't—at least not the way she'd used it. "T-Tell me how you know Detective L-Law," he said, although he already knew.

She shook her head. "Always workin', you. I know Hy from St. Pat's Ass." Jasper almost choked on his beer, and the madam grinned. "There, that's more like it. Saint Patrick's Asylum for Orphans is over on Duane and Chatham. Hy's younger than me—not that you'd know it." She gave him a saucy, suggestive look. "I didn't know him well until he came here. He was just a babe—fifteen or sixteen. Nothin' like he is now, just all elbows and knees. I gave him his first ride."

"I think you are t-trying to p-put me to the b-blush."

"You bet I am." The amusement drained from her face. "You want to ask me about Caitlyn but worry I might slap your face like I did Hy."

Jasper couldn't deny that was a concern.

She sighed. "It was the usual story—a randy employer got Caitlyn pregnant, and those old crones over at St. Pat's wouldn't help her."

"So she c-came to work for you?"

"Not right away. She was young enough to pass for a virgin, so she went to Solange's, where somethin' bad happened, so then she came here."

"What h-happened?"

"Caitlyn never said, and I never asked, sugar. We *all* have stories we don't wanna tell."

He couldn't argue with that.

"Whorin' was never a good job for Caitlyn, and she sure as hell didn't want it for her sister."

"S-Sister?"

"Amy, Caitlyn's little sister. More like a daughter—almost ten years younger than Caitlyn. It was a good thing Amy was gone by the time Caitlyn was arrested." She shook her head. "She worshiped Caitlyn."

"Gone?"

"Caitlyn got her onto the Orphan Train—or she got Hy to do it."

Jasper wasn't sure where to start. "Orphan T-Train?"

"It ain't a *real* train. It's run by the Children's Aid Society; they find homes for orphans away from the city."

"When was this?"

"I'm not sure, exactly, but it couldn't have been long before Caitlyn got arrested. Just ask Hy."

Oh, Jasper planned to ask him.

"What d-did you think about Miss Grady and Detective Law?"

Lorie snorted. "First—men are dumb."

Jasper laughed.

"I ain't jokin'. I told Caitlyn to leave Law alone, but she wanted to know what was goin' on with the case." Lorie shook her head. "I can't deny Caitlyn had a fierce hatred for Dunbarton, and I do remember her sayin' that whoever killed him should get a reward."

"Where d-did this hatred come from?"

"He'd treated her badly back when she worked at Solange's." She shook her head. "I was right fond of Caitlyn, but the girl had the brains of a squirrel."

"And S-Sealy? Did she know him?"

"I never heard her say a thing about him."

"B-But she confessed to killing him."

"Her confession mentioned *a lot* of horseshit that made no sense," she said darkly.

"Do you b-believe what McElhenney claimed—that Caitlyn gave Detective L-Law money?"

"You need to ask' *him* about that, my lord. All I'm sayin' is that Hy Law was properly named; the man is as law-abidin' as they come. He loves his job and wouldn't have put it at risk for a jaunt down cock lane." Her eyes flickered to Jasper's ears—now hot—and her grin returned. "You have beautiful skin, my lord, but it likes to give you away, don't it?"

"You're a m-menace, Lorie."

"Thank you, kind sir," she said with an exaggerated Irish accent.

Jasper slid a coin across the bar before pulling on his gloves.

"You leavin' already? Why don't you come upstairs with me— you're lookin' a bit Mondayish."

He was feeling a bit Mondayish. "I'd not be much sp-sport, I'm afraid."

"If you're tired, it just so happens I've got a bed."

"I s-suspect that very little s-sleeping would go on in it."

She grinned. "A girl's gotta keep tryin'."

"Thank you for the d-drinks."

"If Law comes lookin' for you, I'm tellin' him I warned you."

As Jasper turned to go, she caught his arm. "One more thing, my lord." Her expression was pensive. "If you repeat this, I'll say you're lyin'. Watch out for Terrance Ryan—you humiliated him, and he don't like you one bit. Caitlyn humiliated him, and look what happened to her."

"How?"

"She wouldn't fuck him. Told him he was too mean and ugly—in front of half my bar."

"When was this?"

"Ages ago—but I don't think he forgot. Caitlyn made an enemy of Ryan and ended up dead. Be careful, my lord."

★   ★   ★

Park and Baxter connected to Worth Street, which was the fifth spoke of Five Points, one of the most infamous intersections in the English-speaking world. Jasper knew it wasn't his imagination that hundreds of eyes watched him as he walked down Baxter; he felt like a scrap of fresh meat tossed into a dogfighting pit.

He'd thought there was no reek worse than Mr. Gamble's rooms; he'd been wrong. A choking, unmoving funk hovered over Five Points, blocking out the sun. It was as if the cobbles themselves exuded a mephitic stench the earth could no longer contain.

While his eyes and nose watered, some reptilian part of his brain triggered the small hairs on his body: *Danger!*

His left hand acted on its own volition, his fingers closing around the delicate wrist just leaving his overcoat pocket.

"Ow!"

He looked down at what he'd caught: human, dressed like a male, anywhere from nine to fifteen, depending on nutrition.

"Lemme go—I wasn't d-doon nothin'!" He fluttered in Jasper's grasp like a moth battering itself against a window. All around them, people went about their business.

"I'm l-looking for somebody," Jasper said, deciding the boy might as well be of use, now that he had him.

Yank, yank, yank.

"His name is J-J-Jemmy Hart."

The boy stopped jerking, light-gray eyes blinking up out of a face that hadn't seen a washcloth in weeks, if ever. "You've g-got a stammer."

At first Jasper thought the boy was mocking him, but then he saw he wasn't laughing.

"What's your n-name?"

The lad's jaw dropped lower, but then something—hope?—flashed in his eyes. Jasper released his wrist; the boy didn't bolt.

"J-J-J-J—" He scowled and spun on his heel. Before he could get away, Jasper caught his upper arm and turned him back.

"N-Never let it win; never let it t-take your words from you," he said with more force than he'd intended.

His captive's nostrils flared dangerously, and he wrenched his arm away. "*John!*"

"It's b-better when you shout?"

John gave an abrupt nod.

Jasper had noticed that too. It served its purpose in the military, but one could hardly go about yelling in drawing rooms, at dinner tables, and in widows' bedchambers.

He reached into his pocket and took out his card case. Paisley had put his cards in his most modest holder today. Even so, the unembellished gold drew every eye around them—or so it felt—when he took out a card and handed it to the boy, who snatched it.

"C-Can you read?"

"Aye," John said scornfully, giving the card a cursory look before tucking it into his rags. "Ain't s-s-s-s-s*tyoopid*."

"I'm looking for Jemmy Hart. "

"Rag-and-bone man," John said, his lips curving in a self-congratulatory smile when he got the words out clean and quick. Jasper knew the feeling.

John rubbed his fingers together in the international symbol for money.

"When you've t-taken me t-to him."

John set off down the street and Jasper followed, aware he was likely following the boy into a trap.

They walked less than a block before John stopped in front a grayish clapboard monstrosity with pale splotches of yellow paint here and there, like a building afflicted with jaundice. Down both sides ran narrow alleys, one surely no wider than three feet.

The boy jabbed a finger to the southside corridor. "M-M-M-*Murderer's* Alley." He shot said alley a murderous look and then pointed to the other side. "Den of Th-Th-Th-Th—" He threw his hands up and stomped toward an old woman sitting on a stump at the corner of the house.

She was selling torches, among other things, so Jasper bought two, and the woman shook out a phosphorus match—what they called lucifers in England—and lit both torches.

John headed for the front doorway, which had no door in it.

Inside, the crush of bodies and odor of unwashed skin was oppressive. But worse than the smell was the heat generated by so many people.

John headed for a black hole that seemed to have opened up in the floor.

You're a fool, Jasper.

But his feet followed the boy down the stairs.

John didn't stop on the first level but continued down and down. It was cooler, but the air was fetid and humid.

There was yet another set of stairs, but John turned right, leading Jasper down a corridor so narrow he had to turn sideways. The rooms off to the side were more like slots in a file cabinet; faint light glimmered in a few. Jasper glanced at his flickering torch; if a fire started in this building, none of them would escape.

John stopped midway down the corridor and pointed into a dark slot.

"Mr. Hart?" Jasper asked, holding up his already guttering torch. Inside he saw three human forms. "M–Mr. Hart?"

One of the shapes emerged from a filthy nest of newspapers. "He ain't here."

Jasper couldn't tell if the speaker was male or female.

Beside him, John's torch flickered out, and the boy cursed. Jasper reached into his pocket and handed him the silver tube of lucifers he always kept on his person.

"D–Do you know where he is?"

"Eh?" the voice grunted querulously, shuffling under the paper.

"*Where. Is. He?*" Jasper enunciated clearly and loudly.

Eyes glinted in the dim light, and two other figures stirred.

"Who're you?"

"A p–police officer."

"That's who took 'im," another voice chimed in.

"Which p–policeman?"

Two pairs of eyes now glinted back at him.

Jasper reached into his trouser pocket and took out two coins of unknown denomination. He flipped one to each person.

"Ryan and another copper."

It wasn't the name he'd been expecting.

"When was this?"

"The day he met you."

"How—"

"He told us about you—said you'd paid him to talk about Dunbarton. He ain' come back."

Jasper felt sick. "D–Do you know if he uses a p–particular pawnshop?"

"Matt Kelly's."

"Where's—"

"On the corner, across from Chang's."

Jasper reached into his pocket for two more coins, sending them spinning through the gloom. His torch began to flicker, and he turned. "John? I need—" He blinked into the empty space around him. Why, the little bastard! He'd buggered off. And he'd taken Jasper's lucifers with him.

CHAPTER 28

It was after three o'clock when Jasper returned to the Astor House.

"D-Did Detective Law come looking for me?" he asked as Paisley helped him out of his coat.

"No, sir."

Apparently Law had enjoyed no more success with his errands than Jasper had.

"I n-need a bath—and a massage." The muscles in his neck, shoulders, and back were so tight he could barely move.

"Very good, sir."

The visit to the pawnbroker had been an utter waste of time. The man who owned the shop—Mr. Kelly—could teach clams a few things. Their increasingly hostile back-and-forth—Jasper asking various questions about Hart, the watch, and how Mr. Kelly felt about spending some time in the Tombs—had been interspersed with people drifting in and out, most of them clearly involved in criminal pursuits.

No amount of bribing, begging, or threatening could make the older man recall the watch or Hart.

Jasper dropped into a chair and listlessly pulled off his tie while Paisley removed his ankle boots and stockings.

He flexed his liberated toes while he unbuttoned his shirt. Paisley's hand appeared in front of him, and he dropped the cuff links into the offered palm before heaving himself to his feet and shedding shirt, trousers, and drawers in a trail behind him while he headed for the madak cigars.

He lit one, inhaled deeply, and then flopped onto his bed on his back, closing his eyes while the cigar worked its magic.

By the time he climbed out of the steaming tub an hour later, he was feeling almost human. The ache in his head had gone from a full-blown bugle blast to a muffled pounding.

Jasper had fallen asleep under Paisley's magical hands when the bell in the foyer jolted him awake. Paisley covered him with a towel from the warmer before leaving the room.

"My lord?"

He must have dozed again, because he woke with a start. "Yes?"

"There's a Mr. Grew to see you."

Grew? Comprehension slowly shoved its way into his foggy brain. "Ah, yes, I'll see him. Go f-fetch some clothing."

Ten minutes later he entered the small study to find one very nervous gentleman's gentleman.

He suspected it was Paisley and not him who terrified the man.

"Welcome, Mr. Grew. Please have a seat. Can I get you a d-drink?" he asked the valet, who clearly had no intention of being seated in Jasper's presence.

"Oh. Well. I should hate to—"

"How about some b-bourbon? I'm new to it but find it delightful. I'd like to know your opinion of it."

Grew looked visibly pleased. "Thank you, my lord."

"Please, have a s-seat," Jasper said again as he handed over the glass.

Grew perched his bum on the very edge of the chair, prepared to flee at any moment.

Jasper lifted his glass and gave Grew a questioning look.

"Oh." Grew hastily took a gulping drink, coughed, and then said, red faced and hoarse, "Excellent, sir."

"Ah, good. So, how m-may I help you?"

Grew put the glass on the side table with a shaky hand and reached into his breast pocket. He extracted a small bundle tied with a piece of twine and handed it to Jasper.

"I never would have said anything if he'd not been murdered, but if these can help you in any way, I just—please, sir, don't let Mrs. Finch see them. She's such an innocent lady, and Mr. Finch cared for her, even though he—well, even though he might have strayed."

Jasper counted seven letters. He pulled out the top one. It was brief, barely a quarter of a page, the writing loopy—almost childish—and riddled with misspellings.

My darling,

I no you didn't want me to rite again, but I wont use names. Nobody will no. If I cant at leest rite to you wen I'm feelin low, I will die.

I need to see you. I am in constant agony thinking about you—nowing you might be somewere else, in the arms of an other. I'm sory I fussed at you the last time we were together—you no how I get jellus.

I put up the notises you wanted.

Yore lover forever—M

"There is no d-direction or postmark?"

"They came by messenger."

"D-Did Mr. Finch respond?"

"Yes; those I delivered myself."

"To?"

"Er, Mr. Finch's tailor, he'd used the place often for exchanging messages with, er—"

"Certain friends?"

Grew nodded with relief. "Yes, exactly. I brought the letters or—"

"Or?"

"Well, sometimes he sent little presents that way, er, if the *friend-ship* was over."

"When did the last of these c-c-come?"

"A week before Mr. Finch died."

"When d-did he last send something?"

"That same evening."

"N-Nothing since?"

"Well, not through me."

"D-Did he ever use anyone else?"

Grew shook his head. "But I know he occasionally went himself."

Jasper went to the secretary desk and took out a piece of paper and a pencil.

He handed both to Grew. "Please write d-down the address."

When Grew handed him the address, the valet said, "About the letters, sir—"

"I sh-shall see they are destroyed if they are of n-no use."

"Thank you, sir. Keeping this to myself was a burden."

Jasper was relieved he had no such letters for Paisley to find. At least he didn't think he did.

After the valet left, he read the rest of the letters, which were much like the first, containing protestations of love mixed with apologies for jealousy.

The door opened, and Jasper looked up from the last letter.

"You have another visitor, sir."

"Well, who is it?" he asked when Paisley just stared.

"A female, my lord." He said the word *female* like another man might say *the apocalypse*. "She calls herself Mrs. Felix Dunbarton."

"G-Good Lord. I hope you didn't leave *her* st-standing in the foyer."

Paisley sniffed. "I put her in the sitting room. Shall I bring her in?"

"No, I'll go to her."

Mrs. Dunbarton was staring out the window in the direction of City Hall when he entered.

"I'm t-t-terribly sorry to have kept you waiting, Mrs. D-Dunbarton."

She turned from the window, her yards of black crepe rustling.

"You appear to have engaged a member of the royal family as your manservant," she observed.

Jasper laughed. "Paisley will be p-pleased to hear himself d-described that way." He gestured to a chair. "Please, won't you have a s-seat?"

"I cannot stay. I've found somebody for Agota."

"Ah. That's excellent," Jasper said.

Mrs. Dunbarton stared up at him, her expression expectant.

Jasper was at a loss. "Er, thank you," he added.

"I thought you might wish to see her off."

"Oh. Yes, of course. I'm so p-pleased you r-recalled my interest." And he was, too, although the suddenness of it all was rather strange.

"I'm sorry I didn't give you more notice," she said, with her usual aptitude for mind reading. "It was a last-minute arrangement, a private orphanage on Rivington run by a Baptist couple. They've got a family who are soon to be headed to Wisconsin, where they've purchased a farm."

"W–Wisconsin," Jasper repeated, unable to place the name.

"A newer state—only ten years old."

"Ah, I see. Let me fetch my hat, coat, and cane, and we can be off."

Moments later he was escorting Mrs. Dunbarton—so completely veiled that her own parent wouldn't have recognized her—toward an ancient heavy-bodied carriage driven by none other than her butler, Cates, who was dressed in the garb of a coachman, a groom sitting beside him.

Jasper handed Mrs. Dunbarton inside, where a very happy Agota was waiting to greet him. She flung her arms around him, squeezed the breath out of him, and babbled a tearful stream of unintelligible words.

"Oh, h–here now, d–d–don't cry," Jasper murmured, patting her shoulder, mortified to his very bone marrow.

Mrs. Dunbarton smirked. "It seems you have a quite an effect on females of all ages, my lord."

Once Agota had her fill of hugging him, she sat back in the seat beside him, staring up at him with an embarrassingly worshipful gaze.

Jasper smiled and handed over his cane. He'd brought along another silver-handled walking stick, this one with ornate Celtic carving and a large sapphire set in the top of the handle.

"I see your butler does double d–duty as your coachman," he said, as Agota studied the glittering stone.

"Cates is exceptional. He worked for my parents after leaving the army and came with me when I married. He's clever and discreet."

"You r–require discretion often?"

"Often enough."

"How . . . mysterious."

"Not really, my lord. But it *is* more difficult to move about freely when one is female. It's comforting to have a servant who won't sell the private details of my life to a newspaperman."

Jasper had to agree; Paisley would go to the rack before he'd speak about Jasper or his affairs.

"From the army to b–butlering. Qu–Quite a change of careers for him."

"Perhaps in England that is unusual, but this is America. We are a country that rejected the divine right of kings and embraced the equality of man."

"A c-commendable philosophy."

"However?"

Jasper gave her a quizzical look.

"It's a commendable philosophy, but . . . what?"

"I'm a guest in your c-country, ma'am; it's not for me to c-comment."

She gave an unladylike snort. "Oh, pooh."

Jasper laughed.

"You get away with that quite a bit, don't you?"

"What's that?" he asked, and then wished he hadn't—because she would tell him.

"You chuckle or flash your charming smile or wield those romantic eyes like weapons when you don't wish to answer a question or when you consider a subject vulgar. I must sound envious of your beauty and charm." She gave a bitter laugh. "I *am* envious. But that's how you get on, isn't it? On charm and beauty? And nobody ever holds you to account. Quite the opposite—they all but fling themselves at your feet."

Jasper's face heated at her hostile accusation.

"What?" she demanded, looking livelier and younger than he'd ever seen her. "Don't be a coward—tell me what you were thinking. Speak your mind, for a change."

"I'm *thinking* that you just called me a cowardly dandiprat."

She gaped, as if he'd yelled the words rather than delivered them in a cool, level tone. "You didn't stammer when you said that."

Jasper turned away and looked out the window, annoyed that he'd snapped at her. He didn't stammer when he was angry, but as he was so rarely angry—usually only his father could bring it out in him, and now, it appeared, Mrs. Dunbarton—it hardly mattered.

"I'm sorry."

Jasper turned at the sound of her voice, but she was looking down. "Mrs. Dunbarton?"

She glanced up, her cheeks a fiery red. "I'm sorry for being so awful to you."

Jasper gave an embarrassed laugh. "Please, think n-n-nothing of it, Mrs. Dunbarton. I know you were only t-teasing me."

"I *wasn't* teasing; I was being spiteful. I wanted to hurt you."

Jasper's confusion was now complete. "Why? Have I off-offended you in s-s-some way? If so—"

"Of *course* you haven't offended me. I doubt you would even know *how*. Your manners are delightful. *You* are delightful. You're just so—so—*perfect* it brings out the shrew in me."

Jasper felt the headache he'd banished earlier returning with a vengeance. "I'm sorry I—"

An ear-splitting *bang* shook the coach.

Jasper grabbed the girl and pulled her to the floor as pulverized chips of carriage rained down on their heads. He yanked Mrs. Dunbarton down beside Agota and covered both their small bodies with his.

The second shot took out a window and showered his back and hatless head with glass.

Shouts and the sound of numerous feet moving came through the broken window. The panel slid open, and Cates's face appeared.

"Get us the hell out of here, C-Cates," Jasper ordered.

Blood was trickling down the other man's temple. "I need you outside, my lord. *Now.*"

Beneath him, Mrs. Dunbarton squirmed and reached for her reticule—a large ugly thing, he'd noticed earlier.

She pulled out a miniature pistol. "Here," she said, a fierce light in her eyes. "You might need this."

CHAPTER 29

Hy had questioned almost every tenant at the Greene Street address, which had taken nearly two hours, but it had been worth it. He could hardly wait to tell Lightner what he'd learned.

Unfortunately, he had to wait for O'Malley, who he'd sent off to get them something to eat a half hour ago, as the man was about to drive him mad with his incessant yattering. Hy hadn't wanted him along, but Lightner had insisted.

"He'll never l-learn if we don't t-teach him."

Hy agreed, but that didn't mean *he* wanted to do the teaching.

A scuffing sound behind him made him turn. "It's about time you got back—"

"Hello, boyo. Fancy seein' you here." Ryan was grinning from ear to ear, his eyes glinting with malice.

"What do you want?"

Ryan peered around the empty office. "Where's your protector and his cane?"

"Why? Did you want another thrashin'?" Hy took a step toward the smaller man, and the two patrolmen who flanked Ryan puffed out their chests and moved closer. "I see you've brought *your* protectors. This ain't the Sixth, though, is it? You're a bit out of your territory. What are you doing here?"

"What I'm doin' is your bloody job, out lookin' for Peter Haslem, 'cause you and yon l-l-l-lordling let him scarper."

"Why are you *here*? Think I'm hidin' Haslem in my pocket?"

"I heard over at Horgan's that Haslem had some connection with this place."

"I can't imagine Lizzy Horgan allowing the likes of you into her business."

Ryan sneered. "Well, a right unimaginative git you are, then. Turns out you don't know everything. Anyone with an ounce of sense can see Haslem was fuckin' the two of 'em—Finch and Janssen, the sick twists—in Haslem's little panel crib and things got outa hand."

"Horgan's doesn't have panel cribs, Ryan." Panel cribs—secret rooms where a pimp or another whore might hide, waiting for a convenient time to pop out and rob a customer—were places you often found in the poorer brothels. "Only an idiot would accuse Lizzy Horgan of underhanded dealing. Besides, we already searched Horgan's."

"I'm guessin' you an' O'Malley couldn't find yer own pricks, so I'll have to go into Horgan's and do a bit o' searchin' myself."

"Is that what you reckon?"

Ryan took a step toward him, not stopping until Hy could smell his unwashed body. "You oughta be thankin' me instead of givin' me lip. I reckon we've solved your bloody case for youse."

"Go tell McElhenny—I'm sure he'll be thrilled to arrest whoever you want—with or without any evidence. Hell, you can always beat a confession out of somebody—at least out of women half your size."

Raw hatred glinted in Ryan's eyes. "I'm just here to deliver a message."

"Consider your message delivered. Now piss off."

"I ain't done yet. McCarty wants you."

The name sent a shiver down Hy's spine.

Ryan laughed with spiteful glee. "Even a squarehead like yourself knows not to shrug off *his* invitation."

Hy found it amusing that Ryan used terms like *squarehead*, as if calling someone out for being half German was an insult. "So, you're delivering messages for thugs now."

"Right enough I am. If you don't think you'll be doin' the same, you're a bloody fool."

"I'll go when I'm finished here."

"Nah, you'd best come *now*, boyo." Ryan pressed the knuckles of one fist—which Hy saw were wrapped in heavy brass—against his open palm.

"Don't make me shove your knuckles up your arse."

Ryan grinned. "McCarty didn't say what condition you needed to be in."

The other two men took a step closer, and Hy knew he couldn't take them as quickly as Lightner had. He lacked a cane and fancy skills, and they were ready for him.

"I need to leave a message for somebody before I go."

"Nah, boyo, that won't be necessary." Once again Ryan's baton moved too quickly for Hy to dodge, and this time Lightner wasn't there to stop the blow.

The last thing he heard as he dropped into darkness was ugly laughter.

CHAPTER 30

Jasper and Cates stood back to back between the coach and the mob spilling out of the saloon. Jasper had tucked Mrs. Dunbarton's pistol into his overcoat pocket, hoping to keep firearms out of the situation.

A man wearing what looked to be a freshly slaughtered animal carcass tied around his shoulders swaggered up to them.

"Walked into a war, ye have," he said in an almost unintelligible accent. His pupils flared when his eyes landed on Jasper's ruby signet ring.

"Let the carriage pass, and you can have my wallet, money, and watch." For once there was no stuttering.

But his adversary laughed at him, even without the stammer. He turned to his crowd of twenty or thirty men, who seemed to be springing up from the cobbles around him.

"Ja hair that, fellahs? Man says oi can *have* what's already moine."

His appreciative audience roared.

Jasper's antagonist took a step forward, and Cates's hand moved in a blur, a pistol aimed at the other man's head. At this range, Cates couldn't miss. "I have only two bullets," the soldier-cum-butler said in his precise English accent. "But all I need to kill you is one."

"Moi men'll rip yeh ta poices—and however's in that coach as well." He leered. "Woimen, I'll wayger. I—"

A blood-curdling scream came from down the street, cutting off whatever he was about to say. It wasn't the scream of one person but hundreds. And they were all charging toward them.

Men who'd been spectating and laughing only seconds before turned and surged like a single organism to meet the threat.

Jasper took advantage of his antagonist's inattention to deliver a punch to the man's throat, sending him to the ground gasping and writhing.

"Go!" Jasper yelled at the wild-eyed groom still seated on the box.

The groom snapped the reins. *"Haw!"* The coach's heavy frame gave a loud screech of protest at such abuse but sprang forward.

A few of the gang members had lingered rather than engage in the brawling. One grabbed Cates's arms from behind and held him while his mate commenced to deliver a pounding.

Jasper strode toward them, spinning his stick and seizing it in the middle before swinging. The weighted handle cracked against the base of the man's skull, and he grunted, releasing Cates and staggering around to face Jasper.

"You bloody bastard!" He stumbled drunkenly, clutching the back of his head with one hand.

Now liberated, Cates threw an uppercut that connected solidly beneath his aggressor's chin, the punch snapping his head back so hard Jasper was surprised it didn't fly off his neck. As it was, blood—and perhaps a piece of tongue—spewed from his mouth as he fell back into two spectators. All three tangled and collapsed into a writhing pile of arms and legs.

Jasper's opponent had regained his footing but was weaving and blinking. The man was a member of the "charge your opponent head on, no matter what the circumstances" school of thought and came at Jasper with a guttural roar.

It was too easy.

Jasper executed a low kick to the shin with the instep of his boot. While his aggressor was howling and hopping on one leg, Jasper brought his stick around in a *latéral croisé* and caught him beneath the ear with the heavy silver handle, putting him down.

He turned to the butler. "Come on!"

Cates didn't appear to hear him; he stared at the mob of men clashing only feet away, blood lust in his eyes.

"Cates!"

But Cates ran straight at the two warring gangs.

"Good God," Jasper murmured, as Cates was swallowed up by the throng of bloody, flailing, knife-wielding men.

Jasper turned and headed toward the street the carriage had disappeared down.

Behind him, somebody noticed his retreat. "Stop, you!"

"Not bloody likely," he muttered, running down an eerily empty street, vaguely aware of eyes watching from darkened windows that stared like lifeless eye sockets on both sides of the street. The citizenry must have been warned, because gone were the usual corner gatherings, stray children, and impromptu stalls selling anything from boot repairs to live hens.

There were streetlamps, but only one in every four or five worked. The cobbles beneath his feet rolled and pitched, as if they'd been the victim of a thousand frost heaves.

Behind him, the boots kept pace.

An odd triangular-shaped building up ahead caught his attention—he *knew* this place; the building wasn't far from Horgan's, so the street ahead must be Bowery.

Jasper's lungs were on fire and he sounded like an overheating locomotive when he slid around the corner, the heels of his boots slipping on something slimy. He caught hold of the nearest— unlighted—lamppost to stop himself, staring at the Boschian image that met his eyes: hundreds of men fighting against the flickering, hellish background of a building on fire.

Voices shouted behind him, drawn by the violence like hounds to blood.

Jasper sprinted across Bowery and toward the narrow alley, not stopping until he reached the door with the number fourteen scratched into the age-blackened wood: Horgan's. Without much hope, he pounded on it.

"He went this way!" a man yelled from the street.

Nowhere to hide, Jasper turned and waved them closer with his stick. "Come on, then—b-both of you."

The first man dropped into a crouch, the ax in his hand flicking as nervously as a cat's tail.

The second man—small and wiry—hung back.

The ax wielder stopped a few feet away. "If ye give it up nice and—"

Jasper executed a *figure fouetté*—aiming low so that he didn't injure himself or fall on his arse—and the roundhouse kick caught his opponent by surprise. A sickening crack filled the air as Jasper's boot connected with man's bent knee; he fell to the filthy cobbles, screaming. Jasper took a step toward the second thug, who turned tail and ran. A noise came from his left, and he turned just as Horgan's door flew open, whacking him hard on the shoulder.

"Bloody hell!" He staggered and caught himself on the rough brick wall to keep from falling.

A pair of hands grabbed one of his arms and yanked him into the darkness.

CHAPTER 31

Hy awoke with a gasp and a yell, an incompatible action that turned into coughing as cold water ran down his head.

"Best get up," Ryan's voice ordered. "He's waitin'."

McCarty.

Hy wiped the fetid water from his face with his coat sleeve before lurching to his feet.

"You look as pretty as a picture, Law." Ryan opened the door and shoved Hy inside.

Hy stumbled but caught himself, looking up into the small, mean eyes of Devlin McCarty.

The last time he'd seen McCarty was four years ago, back when Hy was a new detective and McCarty was just another henchman working for the last boss—a man who'd not kept a close enough eye on his underlings and had paid with his life for his mistake.

McCarty grinned, as if they were long-lost mates rather than two men who'd once vied for the same woman's affection. A woman who'd chosen McCarty.

"You're a bit ragged looking, even for a po-leese detective. I guess the pay is shite." McCarty chuckled and gestured to the chair in front of his desk, which currently held his booted feet, a large crystal ashtray, a bottle, and two glasses. "Drink?" He picked up the bottle of Kilbeggan.

"Aye, why not." Hy wondered if it would be his last.

"You can go, Ryan," McCarty said, not sparing a glance for the other man as he leaned forward with Hy's glass.

Ryan scowled at Hy with open hate; Hy winked and lifted his glass in a toast.

"You've an enemy there, Hy," McCarty said when the door slammed shut.

Hy sipped his drink.

"Taste of home, eh?" McCarty asked, even though neither of them had ever come within a thousand miles of the Emerald Isle. "How's it like, workin' with an English lord?" he asked, sounding genuinely curious.

"He's a good detective."

"But rides a high horse, eh?"

"Not really."

McCarty's face tightened at Hy's too-abrupt answers. "Enjoy your wee vacation in the Tombs? I came to see you, you know—but you were beyond noticin' by the time I got there." He barked a laugh. "McElhenny told tales of you down at t'pub—how he enjoyed makin' you grateful for his piss."

If McCarty was hoping to rile him up, he was barking up the wrong tree. After staring death in the face for eight weeks—which had felt like eight hundred—a bit of ribbing about how he'd drunk piss was nothing.

"Ryan said you wanted to see me."

McCarty's eyes narrowed, and Hy knew the other man didn't like having the subject changed unless he was doing the changing.

"I saw Niamh not long ago."

Hy hated the way his heart stuttered at the sound of her name.

"She don't look so good these days—not as pretty anymore." McCarty's thick lips curled into a smile, his eyes sly. "Workin' off South Street by the Hansen Pier, if you've a wish to visit her. She offered herself for free—just for old time's sake." His expression of disgust said what his reply had been.

Hy supposed he should feel vengeful satisfaction to know the girl had paid for choosing McCarty over him, but all he felt was sickened.

"Ryan said you wanted to see me," Hy said again, aware he was courting danger but unable to stop himself. Not an unusual occurrence.

But McCarty—as changeable as a weathercock—just laughed. "Aye, that's true enough. I brought you here to tell you that youse two—you and Lord Lummy—need to put your attention to findin' Haslem. He's yer killer."

That's what Hy believed too, but—stubborn contrarian bastard that he was—he'd be damned if he admitted that to McCarty.

Instead he said, "What makes you think Lightner takes orders from me?" Hy figured Lightner was the sort to dig in like a wood tick if anyone interfered with his investigation. Hy had a feeling the Englishman didn't like being told what to do; he could appreciate that.

"I reckon you could be convincin' if you had a reason. Can you come up with a reason yourself, Hy? Or do you need me to give you one?" McCarty swirled the expensive liquid in his glass, and something Hy wasn't expecting—indecision—flickered in his eyes. "It's time somebody told the duke's son that neither White Street nor Park Row calls the shots in the Points."

"All right, I'll warn him off," he lied. "Is that it?"

"I think you know it's the least of it, boyo. I'll be needin' those papers."

Hy stilled. "What papers?"

"Do you think I'm stupid, Hy?"

Hy wanted to say *yes* so badly that his tongue bled from biting it. "I ain't lyin'; I don't know anything about any papers." That was true. Sort of.

The faint flicker of McCarty's eyes told Hy the other man didn't know what papers he'd been ordered to collect, and that fact—being excluded—was making him furious.

"Mack! Jake!" he yelled.

The two bruisers must have been waiting outside the door.

"Now," McCarty said, swinging his feet off the desk and dropping them to the wooden floor with a loud thump. "Let's see if I can help you remember which papers."

★ ★ ★

Elizabeth Horgan's hands fumbled with the three hasps.

"Let me," Jasper said, after she'd dropped the padlock the second time.

Jasper closed and locked all three locks. They were in a big kitchen, with dirty crockery piled next to a washbasin and flies buzzing around an overflowing slop bucket.

Elizabeth Horgan looked nothing like the woman he'd seen only yesterday. Her hair was unbound and unbrushed, a wild inky-black corona around her pale face. Her eyes had tiny specks for pupils, and her eyelids were heavy. A fresh-looking bruise darkened her right cheek, and her breath—her very pores—exuded the sickly sweet smell of heaven.

"What happened?" he asked, his heart pumping more furiously than when he'd been running.

She wore only a midnight-blue dressing gown, loosely tied. The silken flaps parted with her every movement, exposing a pale strip of skin that ran from the valley between her breasts and over a smooth expanse of stomach to the black curls covering her sex.

Jasper wrenched his gaze up.

"They've broken the front windows and are looting," she said, her voice utterly lacking inflection. "But I have a place." She caught his hand with a clumsy swipe and yanked him along with surprising strength.

Only now did Jasper realize the sound of smashing and yelling was not coming from the alley but from the brothel's saloon. She pulled him to a corridor that led in two directions. To the right was the sound of breaking glass and raised male voices; she turned left. Dead ahead was a section of wood paneling, open just a crack, a dull red light emanating from within.

"We're safe here," she said, releasing him and pushing the make-shift door wider. Voices came from the direction they'd just come. "Quick!" She pulled him inside.

Jasper put out a hand to stop her from slamming the panel shut, instead pulling it closed softly. It was a heavy slab of wood, like the door to the alley.

He made short work of three more padlocks. "The lamp," he whispered as the sound of boots and voices drew closer. "Put out the light." He pointed to the gap beneath the door, and she stumbled to the single lamp and turned the key, plunging the room into darkness, but not before Jasper saw the low mattress, the lacquered, inlaid tray, the opium lamp, and the pipe.

The wave of hunger that hit him almost drove him to his knees. Even when the light was off, the image was still branded into his mind's eye.

A slender hand fumbled against his chest, the fingers curling around the lapels of his coat and pulling him closer. She laid her head against his shoulder. "Your heart is pounding," she whispered.

It was; Jasper could hear it thundering in his ears. He didn't know if it was the danger of the last few minutes or the danger in this room.

"What's happening?" he asked.

"White Street had a warrant for the mayor's arrest. But when Captain Walling from the Met went to serve it, a riot broke out right on the steps of City Hall. Somebody said Tallmadge called on the Seventh Regiment to put down the fighting. But the gangs—" She shivered. "Once they started . . ."

Yes, Jasper knew: blood lust.

A shout came from beyond the door. "There's a door here—I know it." Somebody began banging the wall, first with fists and next with their bodies, flinging themselves at it with the single-mindedness of grunion assaulting a beach.

"Open up, or I'll set the bloody door on fire! You'll roast in there like crabs in your shells."

"That's the door to Mamble's—that empty furniture place next door," a new voice yelled. "Ain't nobody answerin' 'cause there ain't nobody there, ya pillock. Come on—they're drinkin' all the best stuff. There ain't gonna be nothin' left."

The door shook with more pounding.

"I'm leavin'," the second voice declared.

"Oi, wait up, you sot! McCarty said to bring the top shelf back to 'im. I'll not be the one havin' to tell—" The voices disappeared into the distant hum. Elizabeth Horgan's body went limp, and she sagged against him.

Jasper held her with one arm, slid his free arm beneath her thighs, and lifted her, holding her cradled against his chest. She weighed nothing.

"Miss Horgan," he whispered into her fragrant hair, which was inches from his face, a few long tendrils tickling his nose. "Miss *Horgan*."

She groaned and shifted in his arms, her breasts pressing against his chest as she snuggled against him.

Jasper ignored his body's predictable response; the last thing a person wanted after smoking opium was sexual congress. Miss Horgan was more interested in using him *as* a mattress than bedding him just now.

Her soft, even breathing told him she'd fallen into a stupor. Jasper took a step in the direction of the pallet he'd seen on the floor, hoping like hell there was nothing left on that bloody tray.

★ ★ ★

Jasper knew the moment she was no longer sleeping. He also knew she didn't *want* him to know she was awake, because she kept silent, her breathing measured. Her euphoria would have begun to wear off, and she'd know the sorts of questions he would ask.

"Where is M-Mary?"

She shifted on the thin mattress. "What time is it?"

"I don't think it's b-been more than a c-couple hours."

"Are they still out there?"

"I heard singing the last time I p-put my ear to the door. When did they b-break in?"

"Just before I let you in. It was the sound of shattering glass that brought me out of the room." She paused and then said, "I suppose you're curious as to what I was doing in here."

Jasper's lips twisted into a bitter, hungry smile he was grateful she couldn't see. "No, I'm n-not curious. Are you the only one here?"

"I sent all the others away as soon as things began to go bad. Ryan was here earlier, looking for Mary—to arrest her. Mary didn't kill Finch."

"But she knows who d-did," Jasper guessed.

"Yes."

"Do *you* know who killed him?"

She hesitated. "Yes."

Jasper waited.

"It was Ryan—Mary saw him."

He struggled to absorb her answer, not wanting to think what it meant for Jemmy Hart—last seen in the violent copper's company. "Why d-didn't you tell me?"

She gave a laugh of disbelief. "Do you know who *Ryan* works for?"

"Who?"

"I don't mean a specific name; I mean the organization."

"You th-think T-Tammany had Finch killed?"

"*Somebody* sent Ryan; who else can use the police department like their private army? Stay out of this—you can't protect us. You can't protect yourself."

Sadly, Jasper suspected she was correct.

"Does Mary know what h-happened to the papers Finch had that n-night?"

"How do *you* know about that?"

"Where are the p-papers, M-Miss Horgan?"

"Mary said she was going to get them, but she never came back." Jasper heard the fear in her voice. "Ryan ripped Mary's room apart looking for them. The only thing good about his visit is that it told me they hadn't caught her. Yet."

"Is he the one who h-hit you?"

"Yes, but I didn't say anything. I knew if I told him *anything*, I'd end up like Finch. That made taking a few slaps and punches easy."

"T-Tell me what happened."

"Mary and Finch—"

"Were helping escaped s-slaves get to C-Canada."

"You knew that?" she asked.

"D-Do you know what's in the p-papers?"

"How did you find out about those?"

"*Miss Horgan.*"

He heard her teeth chattering and pulled her close. She resisted only a second and then grabbed him as fervently as she'd done earlier.

"It's Finch's signed confession, along with documents that will prove certain men were selling arms to rebels in the South." She hesitated. "It also describes a plan for a rebellion in the North—a fake rebellion—they're going to make it look like a bunch of freed-men did it."

"*What?*"

"You were right about Finch and Mary believing they were help-ing slaves escape to Canada. You can't have public meetings any lon-ger, because the slave-takers show up. So there was a sort of code: Mary would post notices for jobs, but it was really to get people out. At least that was the idea.

"But this last Monday Mary heard a story from a young boy. The boy was one of a group of escaped slaves who'd gone to meet the people who were supposed to take them to Canada. Instead, the men who met them worked for Amos Baker and took them to a sort of prison. They divided people into two groups: those who'd be taken south and sold and a few that were kept behind because they wouldn't fetch enough money to bother.

"The boy was one of those kept behind because of his clubfoot. The men threw him into a cellar with a few others, some who'd been there for weeks. Their captors would get drunk and taunt them, telling them how they were more valuable as corpses—how they were going to kill them and make use of their bodies for their fake slave rebellion in Albany. They'd make it look like freed slaves had tried to overthrow the government of New York. Baker's men would end up looking like heroes because they'd shot the rebels and foiled the rebellion."

Jasper shook his head in disbelief. "B-But that's—"

"Outlandish, stupid, foolish, and dangerous? Yes, it's all those things. But you've seen the way things are here. Every day there's more grumbling about the freedmen taking jobs away from whites. The democrats blame the abolitionists for worsening relations between the states. There are plenty of people in the Points *and* uptown who believe slavery is not New York's concern. Most people don't care unless it matters to *them*. This rebellion—no matter how stupid— would turn the tide against freedmen."

"Tell me what happened with F-Finch."

"After Mary heard the escaped boy's story, she sent Finch a message; he came almost immediately and listened to the story himself." She paused, then said, "I always thought Finch was just another rich man playing at being an abolitionist, but his fury over what he'd helped them do—"

"Them? Them *who?*"

"He said Symington came up with the plan to get more freed slaves to Canada and brought Finch in to help him."

Jasper couldn't help it; he laughed.

"I know, I know," Miss Horgan said. "It's hard to believe Finch could be so stupid. He said there were others helping, but everyone's identities were kept secret because of potential punishment under the Fugitive Act. I'll be honest, I don't really understand it all because *Finch* didn't understand it all. I'm guessing Symington kept him ignorant because they were using him."

That was a fair guess.

"After talking to the boy, Finch went straight to Symington."

Jasper could just imagine the old man's reaction.

"Symington told him he was being a fool—to forget about the slaves being sold because that was just the law. He told him about the guns and how he'd put them both in a position to make millions. He said Baker made some deal with people down South: guns and slaves for money. While everyone was focused on the rebellion in Albany, the real one would take place in the South."

"Why would Symington *t-tell* him all this?"

"Symington told him his neck was in a noose too, because nobody would believe he could have been that stupid and naïve."

That *did* sound like Symington. "Are you sure Finch d-didn't know? I simply c-can't—"

"If it's any consolation, Finch *did* realize what a fool he'd been. And he was livid. He wasn't a smart man, but I think he really loved Mary and did this because he wanted to help."

"Why d-didn't he simply c-come forward? Why compile this-this *dossier*?"

"He didn't think he'd live to tell the story. Symington must have guessed what was on Finch's mind, because he threatened him—he told Finch that Dunbarton and Janssen had angered his other partners and look what happened to them."

"S-Symington *said* he had those men killed?"

"Finch said Symington never came right out and admitted it." She hesitated and then said, "I can't help thinking Symington planned all along to kill Finch—after this s-so-called rebellion."

Jasper agreed. "He would have made an excellent sc-scapegoat—if he were d-dead and linked to an abolitionist society."

"It all sounds so far-fetched that I wouldn't have believed it if Finch hadn't been murdered exactly the same way as those others. These people—Symington and the others—they'll obviously kill whoever gets in their way."

Jasper didn't comment on the killings. Instead he asked, "What d-did Mary see?"

"She was supposed to meet Finch late Monday night; don't ask, I don't know where. She was about to get out of the hackney when she saw a police wagon roll up beside Finch. Ryan jumped out and hit him on the head. The next time she saw him, Finch was in the alley, dead."

"D-Did Mary say anything about the p-papers?"

"She said it happened too fast to see if Finch had anything with him. But Ryan wouldn't be tearing everything apart if they had them, would he?"

"I wouldn't have thought so."

"Finch said he wanted to write the truth down for Mary. He said it would be her insurance if anything happened to him." She paused, then added in a choked whisper, "I think those bloody papers might be the death of her."

Jasper feared she was correct.

★   ★   ★

Jasper woke in complete darkness and found a soft, sleep-heavy body draped over his. The evening came back to him in rush: he knew the truth but didn't have a scrap of evidence—other than the testimony of an ex-convict prostitute who dressed in women's clothing, had no alibi, and had last been seen arguing with the deceased.

Whoever had sent Ryan to kill Finch—whether it was Symington or someone else—would not hesitate to kill two whores, a disgraced New York copper, and a foreign policeman to protect themselves from charges of treason and God knew what else. In the current chaos, it would be so simple for four people to disappear.

Jasper needed Finch's papers.

Elizabeth Horgan shifted, and her leg jostled the one part of his body that was eager to face the new day. Jasper sucked in a breath and was about to carefully move her leg off his erection when her hand slid between his vest and shirt. For a moment, it just rested there. And then it began to slide down his abdomen, over the waistband of his trousers, stopping on his placket.

Jasper gritted his teeth and laid a stilling hand on top of hers. "I d-don't need payment to help you and Mary. It's my j-job, Miss Horgan."

"You not only talk like an honorable man, you behave like one too."

Jasper didn't think it was honor that was thrusting against his drawers just now.

He felt hot breath on his neck and ear. "I don't *need* to do it, my lord; I *want* to. Besides," she added, her voice heavy with amusement. "Lorena Paxton has a pool going as to which of us would have you first."

Jasper seemed to inspire pools. "How m–much?"

"It's up over fifty dollars."

He chuckled. "So r–really it would be *me* d–doing *you* a favor?"

"Let's just agree this can be mutually beneficial."

The irony of his situation was not lost on him; he was surrounded by his greatest temptations.

To his left was a tray that likely contained enough opium to solve today's problems—at least for a few hours.

To his right lay an entirely new set of problems.

Of course there was a *third* option: get up and leave like a smart man.

Her leg slid around him, the heel of her foot hooking beneath his hip and pulling him closer.

Jasper gave up struggling. And then he turned to the right.

CHAPTER 32

Jasper returned to the hotel just before daybreak to find Paisley climbing the walls.

He'd been too exhausted to chronicle his evening and had fallen face-first into his bed and slept like the dead, waking around nine. It still wasn't as much sleep as his aching head needed, but today wasn't a day to sleep.

He took a sip of strong, black coffee and worked his way through a third newspaper, which had a slightly different version of the events of the previous night than the other two. But they all agreed on one thing: the mayor had been arrested but then released from police custody less than an hour later.

Jasper heard the bell ring, and a moment later Paisley entered the room. "Patrolman O'Malley to see you, my lord."

Jasper smiled at the sight of the terrified young man, who was visibly cringing away from Paisley. He gestured to the empty chair across from him. "Have a s-seat, O'Malley. Thank you f-for responding so quickly to my m-message. Another pot of c-coffee, Paisley," he said, not turning away from the boy, who was still gawking. "Sit," he repeated, as O'Malley hovered on the brink of fleeing.

"Where is Detective Law?" he asked, once O'Malley was seated.

"I dunno, sir. We were at the place on Greene, and the detective sent me out to get somethin' to eat. But when I got back, he was gone."

"He left you n-no message?"

"No sir, nothin'. I waited two hours."

"D–Did he say—"

The doorbell rang again. "Ah," Jasper said. "That must be him now."

But the person who flung open the door was *not* Law.

Jasper and O'Malley stood as Elizabeth Horgan stormed into the room, Paisley several steps behind her.

"Ah, Miss H–Horgan," Jasper said, looking from her frantic, tear-stained face to his servant.

Paisley's eyebrows rose one hundredth of an inch—a shrug from him.

Her red-rimmed eyes flickered from Jasper to O'Malley. "The Sixth Precinct has Mary—they're charging her with the murders of Alard Janssen and Stephen Finch." She swallowed noisily. "And they say they have a witness."

★   ★   ★

After much arguing—with Paisley—Jasper went, alone, to the tailor shop Grew mentioned.

It was too easy. He walked in, said he was collecting something Finch had left, and walked out less than a minute later with a brown-paper-wrapped packet of documents. He perused the documents during the brief cab ride back to the hotel: Finch's confession bore out everything—and more—that Miss Horgan had said last night.

Three-quarters of an hour after returning to the hotel, Jasper was in another hackney, this time with O'Malley, headed to the Sixth Precinct.

"You will stay in the c-carriage and wait outside the station," Jasper repeated for the third time.

O'Malley nodded. "Yes, sir, I will stay in the carriage."

"And if I don't c-c-come out of the s-station in an hour?"

"I will find a boy to run word to your servant, er, Mr. Paisley. I will not leave my post or stop watching."

"And if you see *me* l-l-leaving the station?"

"I'm to follow you and then send a message to Mr. Paisley from wherever you end up." He said Paisley's name with a great deal of reverence.

"Good." Jasper absently smoothed the fingers of his gloves, his gaze drifting over his cane, the same one he'd carried yesterday.

"I've been lookin' into the things Detective Law told me to investigate," O'Malley said, clearly uncomfortable with silence.

"What s-sort of things?"

"Er, about the pine sap."

"Ah, of course." Jasper had forgotten about that bizarre detail.

"I went to furniture manufacturers, railroad car manufacturers, boatyards, and even some theaters around Solange's."

"Theaters?" Jasper said, momentarily distracted by the odd information.

O'Malley nodded, his eager expression reminding Jasper of a hunting spaniel when it brought back a game bird. "I was talking to an old man who makes fine furniture, and he said back in olden days, people used it for glue to make wigs and beards and such."

"How interesting." Jasper's thoughts drifted back to the scene in the hotel room he'd just left.

He'd been grateful that Miss Horgan had brought him news of Haslem's arrest, but it meant she'd disobeyed him and stayed at the brothel rather than finding someplace to hide for a few days.

Oh come, Jasper, calling her Miss Horgan after last night? And then again early this morning?

Jasper regretfully pushed thoughts of this morning—and late last night—away. He'd left Miss Horgan—*fine*, Elizabeth—in Paisley's capable hands. This time she'd not argued about staying away from the brothel.

Perhaps you should have Paisley act as intermediary with all your lovers?

Jasper sighed. It was going to be one of *those* days: a day when his sly mental companion occupied the forefront of his scrambled brain and hurled abuse.

"What are you going to do?" Elizabeth had demanded after promising him not to return to Horgan's.

"Yes, my lord, I should like to know the answer to that as well," a second voice had chimed in.

Jasper had turned to find Paisley standing in the doorway, unabashed about his eavesdropping.

"I'm going to leave shortly. First, I'll give the concierge a message to deliver. Then I am going to the Sixth P-Precinct to m-make sure McElhenny doesn't do anything r-rash to Mary."

"I will accompany you, my lord," Paisley said.

"N-No, you will not."

Paisley got *that* look on his face.

"I have another t-task for you."

"Task, my lord?"

"Is the house on Union S-Square ready for occupation?"

"It is *furnished*, if that is what you are asking. But ready for *you*, my lord? I still need—"

"P-Pack a bag for yourself—and for me, as well," he added, since Paisley's face had hardened into a stubborn mask. "You will g-go with him, Miss Horgan. Do *not* go back to your b-business for anything. Paisley will purchase whatever you need."

And then Jasper gave Paisley a brown-paper-wrapped packet of papers. "Take them to Rutledge's Bank."

Paisley had the key to the lockbox, as he'd been the one who'd taken all Jasper's valuables to the bank when they'd arrived.

"If I d-don't return—or if you get word from O'Malley—you can please me by keeping Miss Horgan safe and having this delivered." He gave Paisley a fat envelope with a London address. It was a desperate measure, and whoever was watching Jasper—and he knew somebody would be—would likely do anything to get their hands on it.

Paisley had looked thunderous, and ten minutes of argument had ensued. But, in the end, he'd grudgingly agreed to obey. Whether he would do so was anyone's guess.

"—sixty-seven theaters in the city," O'Malley said, his eyes wide and wondrous. "And that's not counting the ones that aren't *real* theaters, like schools, even some churches—our St. Mary's has a small stage for the Nativity. I played Joseph one year. You wouldn't—"

The streets were less trafficked after yesterday, and the wheels brought Jasper closer and closer to the decision he'd made.

Where the hell was Law? The man hadn't met him as planned or sent a message. *Had* he scarpered? The pang of disappointment he experienced at the thought was surprising. But he wouldn't blame him if he had; Law had told him after the Black Cat just who they were up against.

What if something bad happened to Law thanks to your prying? Have you considered that, Jasper?

As a matter of fact, he *had* considered it. And then he'd shoved it to the back of his brain. As possibilities went, it wasn't an encouraging one. If somebody *had* taken him—and if he were still alive—Jasper would have about as much chance of finding Law in New York City as he would in the middle of the ocean. Jasper worried his lower lip, hoping like hell that Law was currently relaxing on a train or boat headed anywhere else.

"—have you ever heard of that, sir?"

"I'm sorry?" Jasper said.

"Copal, sir—have you heard of it?"

"Er, used for adhesion?"

O'Malley's forehead furrowed.

"G-Glue."

"Yes, sir, that's it. Well, it seems there are two sorts. Both are used in—"

You should never have come to this country, Jasper.

What the devil is the point of such a comment?

Jasper immediately regretted asking that. He knew that hearing voices in one's head wasn't normal—arguing with them was likely even worse.

Tell the driver to turn around. The divisions in the police are symptoms of a greater, more lethal sickness. This country is on the verge of violence. None of these problems are yours.

That might be true too, but Haslem—and perhaps Elizabeth and Law—would suffer and maybe even die if he ran.

"Why not go to Superintendent Tallmadge?" Paisley had pleaded. "Everything I've read says he is an honest man fighting the corruption of City Hall."

Jasper had read the same stories.

But Finch had been a well-intentioned reformer too, and look what he'd been tangled up in.

As for the mayor? Yesterday's antics—resisting arrest, inciting Municipal policemen to riot against Captain Walling when the legal head of the Metropolitan Police was serving a warrant—demonstrated that he had no respect for the law. Wood could have lied about his connection to Dunbarton—after all, Jasper knew the mayor owned several ships of his own—and he was clearly a crony of Symington's; maybe he was shipping guns and slaves and *he'd* been the one to call in Ryan to kill Finch?

The men involved in this plan—no matter how ridiculous parts of it appeared—had been actively engaged in treason. The punishment for treason was death.

If two prostitutes and a lone interfering Englishman happened to get killed while the conspirators protected themselves, who would complain or care? And if somebody demanded an investigation—highly unlikely—Jasper knew better than anyone how little investigating would get done in this environment of corruption and chaos.

He'd learned a great deal about what was going on, but he still had no real evidence—other than Finch's rambling and rather deranged confession—and didn't know nearly enough.

The only thing Jasper knew for sure was that this conspiracy was worth murdering for.

Chapter 33

Jasper glanced at the clock that hung on the captain's wall, wondering if the things he was about to say next would have McElhenny throwing him into an interrogation room beside Haslem. Wondering if he'd taken a chance on a hunch and made a dreadful mistake in coming here.

Wondering if McElhenny would ever get tired of the sound of his own voice.

"If you're here to thank me for doin' your job, you shouldn't have bothered," McElhenny said, grinning like the cat who caught the canary.

"I'm here to t-tell you that your witness—the young p-prostitute named V-Velma—could not p-possibly have seen what she claimed to see. Haslem is not the k-killer, Captain McElhenny, and you are making a d-dreadful mistake—yet again—if you're t-trying to force a confession out of him."

The other man's mouth tightened. Unlike Davies, who was a smart man, McElhenny was the sort who'd been promoted up the ranks as a reward for his unquestioning obedience to authority and a willingness to dirty his hands.

"I tell you what, *my lord*, we've been runnin' our city just fine until you got here."

"Other than Velma's useless st-statement, what's y-your evidence?"

McElhenny frowned. "Evidence?"

"Yes, Captain—evidence. You might have h-heard it referred to by a sh-shorter word—*proof*? What *proof* do you have to arrest P-Peter Haslem for the murder of Stephen Finch?"

McElhenny's face purpled, and he jumped to his feet.

"In this police department, there is a chain of command, *Detective*; perhaps you've heard it called by another word—" He faltered, a look of confusion crossing his dull features and ruining what had begun as a very clever riposte. "Orders!" he shouted, when he failed to find the word he wanted. "What you are, sir, is *in-sub-ordinate*." He smirked in triumph at having spit out such a mouthful.

Jasper felt like applauding. Instead, he asked, "D-Do you know where Detective Law is?"

McElhenny's confusion looked too genuine to be feigned.

"First, he *ain't* no detective. Second, if you want to find him, ask your own damned captain, since he's workin' at the Eighth. Now, as for *proof*, we have the—"

Somebody rapped on the door.

McElhenny scowled at whoever it was but waved them in. "What?"

Jasper turned to find a nervous-looking patrolman.

"Er, I'm s'posed to give this to you, sir." He held an envelope toward the furious captain.

McElhenny snatched it and ripped it open, taking out a single sheet. His eyes moved rapidly over the contents, his face overtaken by a mass of twitches as he made his way down the page.

His hands were shaking by the time he finished. He fixed Jasper with such a look of hatred that—for a moment—Jasper thought he'd pull out a gun and shoot him.

But a lifetime of bowing to his masters was too much to overcome.

He wadded up the paper and flung it to the floor before turning away, as if he couldn't stand to look at Jasper a moment longer. "Get him the hell out of here!"

★ ★ ★

The carriage that had been waiting for him outside the Sixth Precinct dropped Jasper off on a street that looked familiar. But Jasper was beginning to realize that a lot of Five Points looked familiar—at least when it came to the unremitting grimness and poverty.

He walked up cracked and stained stone steps to a house that must have once been an imposing mansion. Two men stood on either side of the door; they had just as much humanity in their cold, pitiless eyes as the stone lions they were leaning on.

Without speaking, they opened the door and led him into a foyer stripped of everything of value except a battered but magnificent marquetry floor depicting a sixteenth-century map of the known world. *Here there be monsters.*

Accurate indeed.

"Liftyeams," one of the brutes said.

"I beg your p-pardon?"

The two men looked at each other and laughed.

The one who hadn't spoken jerked a thumb at his partner. "He said to lift your arms." They both laughed at what Jasper supposed was their idea of an English toff's accent. "We need to check you for guns," the other one added.

Jasper had always found the lilting cadence of an Irish accent charming. It struck him as considerably less charming as the big man patted him with what felt like excessive force. He paused to look at Jasper's watch. "Noiyce watch."

"Thank you."

The man gave it a lingering look, then tucked it back in Jasper's vest pocket.

Once he'd been sufficiently searched, Jasper picked up his cane, which he'd leaned against the wall.

"Ah, naow." The second man held out his hand. "We heared about how you beat Ryan just loik a girl."

They both laughed, and Jasper handed the cane over.

The staircase was missing planking, so they stepped carefully. On the second floor they turned down a corridor. At first Jasper believed the way was strewn with rubbish, but when one lump moved, he realized it was bodies—crouching, sitting, lying bodies. Young boys, by the look of it. Foot soldiers in training, he supposed.

The men ushered him into a room that had once been the library. The only things that hadn't been stolen were a great number of books. The room smelled of damp, rotting paper and mold.

A desk sat dead center in the room, three carved spindle legs and a stack of books holding up the fourth corner. There was a man behind it, his feet propped up on the surface.

"Ah, my lord, come in, come in." His host gestured graciously to the ragged wingback chair in front of the desk. Jasper's two companions took up positions on either side of the library door.

Their leader was smiling, but there was barely suppressed fury in his eyes.

Ah, so somebody else *has received unpopular orders.*

"Drink?" The man waved to a bottle.

"N–No thank you."

He barked a laugh. "It's true then—you've got a st–st–stammer."

Jasper smiled, and the men behind him chuckled.

"I hear yer pa's a duke, aye?"

For some reason, Jasper felt like the man across from him was deliberately pouring on the blarney.

"Yes."

"What's that make you?"

Jasper raised a brow. "A duke's son."

The men again chuckled. But this time their employer cut them a filthy look that shut them up. Violence crackled in the air; Jasper wouldn't have been surprised if the other man took a pistol from his desk drawer and shot all three of them.

"My da was a fighter." He grimaced and then added, "Well, he was before he killed a man durin' a bout—then he was a murderer. Died in jail. So I'm a murderin' boxer's son." He shrugged. "But in America, nobody cares about what my da did or who he was. I'm judged on me own merits." He pulled his feet off the desk and let them fall with a deliberate *thump* that sent up puffs of dirt. "What I *am* around these parts is in charge—the boss, you could say."

"Understood," Jasper said, although they both knew perfectly well that the man across from him might be *a* boss, but he was not *the* boss.

"I reckon you bein' new here, you didn't know about me and how things work."

"I b–beg your pardon, but I'm afraid I d–don't know your name."

One of the men snorted and then attempted to conceal it with a cough.

"You shut your holes." The "boss" glared at his henchmen before turning his anger on Jasper. "I'm Devlin McCarty—the man who says what is what around here." McCarty drew out the silence. "The papers, where are they?"

"They're s–safe."

"I want them."

"You c-can have them as soon as my c-conditions are met."

"Papers first."

Jasper tried to suppress a twinge of irritation and failed. "P-Perhaps you should speak to the m-man who is brokering this deal, Mr. McCarty."

McCarty leapt to his feet. "I ain't s'posed to kill you if you hand over the papers. So here's your last chance, *your highness*: Where. Are. The. Papers?"

"You've h-heard what I have to say."

McCarty looked pleased, rather than angered, by his words. "Jake—give the man his stick." He grinned at Jasper. "I heard about the beatin' you gave Ryan and those two fools Bill Finnegan sent to the Black Cat. Get up. I want to see it. Go on."

Jasper turned just in time to catch his cane.

McCarty jerked his head at one of the men. "You can go first, Mac."

Mac didn't hesitate before lunging at him. The man wasn't sluggish—but he was too big to stop quickly.

Jasper pivoted on one foot, spun the cane end over end, and twisted his wrist at the last minute to bring the heavy silver handle down hard on Mac's skull as the big man's feet slid on the grit-covered floor.

Mac grunted and dropped to his knees like a huge sack of stones. Jake, who'd paused to watch his mate, didn't commit the same error. Instead he moved with the light, dancing step of a boxer, holding his fists up in a confident, relaxed guard.

Jasper stepped back and bumped into the chair he'd just vacated. Keeping his eyes on Jake, he shoved the chair toward him and then lunged, using it like a shield. While Jake reached out to stop the chair, Jasper brought his stick around in a horizontal arc.

But Jake was too fast and grabbed the cane in the middle.

Jasper's right hand shot forward with no direction from his brain. The heel would have hit Jake's throat hard enough to knock him breathless, but at the last moment Jake yanked on the cane and jerked Jasper toward him.

It happened too quickly to pull back, and his hand delivered a lethal punch to the fragile architecture of Jake's throat.

Jake's eyes flew open, and a strangled noise came from his gaping mouth. His hand tightened convulsively on the cane, and he dropped to his knees, gasping for air. The bigger man would have taken Jasper down with him if Jasper hadn't pushed the button in the cane's handle that released the sword from its wooden sheath. He spun around, short sword at the ready.

"That's bloody brilliant," McCarty said, grinning broadly as he aimed a pistol at Jasper's head. "You're fast with that stick, milord, but you can't outrun a bullet. Toss it onto the floor."

Jasper complied.

McCarty gave Jake's faintly shuddering body a quick, dismissive look. "A real shame, that. Jake was a good man. Now turn around and open the door."

Once he'd done so, McCarty shoved him into the hall.

Dozens of eyes peered at him through the gloom.

"Go on." The tip of the gun jabbed into his shoulder. "Down the stairs. All the way down."

They trudged downstairs.

"You got till we reach the bottom to do this the easy way."

Jasper could tell by his tone that McCarty was hoping he would choose some other way.

They passed through a massive kitchen and a series of still rooms and finally arrived at another door, which was flanked by two more men.

"Give 'im the lantern," McCarty ordered.

Jasper took the lantern, and McCarty gestured with his pistol to the pitch-black opening beyond the doorway.

This set of stairs led down into cool, clammy darkness. The cellar was composed of several rooms: cold storage, a locker that had probably once held cured meat, and a heavy wooden door with a lock blackened by age.

The pistol gestured to a large iron key that hung off a nail. "Unlock it and open it."

Jasper did as he was ordered. When he opened the door, he lifted the lantern high. There, sitting against the far wall, was Hieronymus Law, shielding his eyes with a big hand, squinting up at him.

Jasper couldn't help smiling. "Ah, Detective Law. We really m-must stop m-meeting this way."

CHAPTER 34

Hy woke with a start; it took him a few seconds to recall that he was somewhere in McCarty's shitty house behind Bowery. He had no idea of how long he'd slept. His jaw ached, the back of his skull was sore to the touch, and it hurt like hell when he breathed.

Big Jake Jessop and Gordon "Mac" Mackenzie had held him between them while McCarty gave him a proper dusting. And then they'd thrown him in here. Wherever they were keeping him was every bit as dark as the Tombs.

He wondered whether Lightner had noticed his absence yet. If he had, he'd likely think that Hy had done a runner. Hy *should* have done a bloody runner; he'd been a fool to stay here after Lightner sprang him.

He heard the murmur of voices outside the door and scrambled upright as the key grated in the lock; light stabbed his eyes, and he raised his arm to shield them.

"Ah, Detective Law," a dry, amused voice said. "We m-must stop m-meeting this way."

McCarty snorted. "You two can have a cuddle and then pull your heads out of your arses. You've got until midnight to *give* me what I want—if you've not made up your minds by then, I'll just *take* what I want." He shoved Lightner inside and slammed the door, throwing the room back into utter darkness.

There was a moment of silence before the Englishman spoke. "I m-must say, I'm glad you're here—although I d-daresay you'd rather be elsewhere." His voice was as calm and courteous as ever; did nothing rile the man?

Hy heard the scuffing of shoes, and then air moved around him, bringing the same cologne smell he recalled from the Tombs. He felt Lightner lower himself beside him.

"Sorry I couldn't warn you, sir. Where'd they catch you?"

"Oh, I went to *them*, Detective."

Hy shouldn't have been surprised; he'd seen that glint in the Englishman's eyes—the glint that said Lightner enjoyed danger.

"They want the papers, sir."

"S-So I surmise."

"They think you *have* them."

"I do."

Hy heard the smile in the other man's voice. "Jaysus. How?"

"That's n-not important. What *is* important is that we c-caught a fish, Detective. You should feel p-proud of yourself."

"Hard to feel proud if you're dead, sir."

"Yes, there is that," Lightner admitted with a chuckle. "T-Tell me how you g-got here."

"Ryan and his goons came for me when I was at Greene Street."

"P-Patrolman O'Malley said you'd disappeared."

"I'm glad he wasn't there. Oh," he added, "you'll never believe who owns that building."

"Randolph Symington."

"How the hell did—?"

"It's a l-lucky guess." Lightner hesitated, then said, "Let me t-tell you what I learned last night."

Ten minutes later, Hy was sitting in stunned silence.

"Do you believe it all?" he finally asked.

"That Finch was so s-stupid? Yes."

"You think it would work—I mean, to divide the country?" Even as he asked the question, Hy knew it would. "Never mind," he said. "I reckon people's emotions would run too hot to think straight. Jesus," he said, shaking his head, "what if nobody stops this thing? Do you think it could start a war between the states? North and South?" The idea was unthinkable.

"I don't know," Lightner admitted.

"What about the killings? Do you think Symington ordered all of them murdered—like Finch thought?"

"Well, we have a connection between Hoyle, D-Dunbarton, Symington, and Baker, and then we've got M-M-Mrs. Janssen's story tying her husband to Baker—but we don't know if the deal Baker was threatening Janssen about was the same one. I don't understand the m-motivation to kill Dunbarton and Janssen, unless they threatened to expose the p-plot—as Finch seemed prepared to do. And then there's S-Sealy. How does he f-fit into any of it?"

"What did Mrs. Janssen say Baker threatened that day? That Janssen had better pay?"

"That was p-part of it, although I d-don't recall the exact words just now. She also s-said something along the lines that B-Baker couldn't be responsible if *they* didn't d-deliver the goods."

"So maybe that's what happened. They—whoever *they* are—didn't pay, and Baker couldn't deliver the goods—the guns?—and so . . ." Hy trailed off.

"Perhaps," Lightner said, after a long pause.

"You don't sound like you agree, sir."

"Something just d-doesn't *fit*."

Personally, Hy thought a lot of it didn't fit.

Hy stretched his legs out and then winced at the pain in his back. "How long have I been here?"

"Almost t-twenty-four hours."

"Er, I know you said that you went to them—er, who is *them*, exactly?"

"I sent a m-message to Dell, telling him I had the p-papers and wished to speak to whoever was l-looking for them. I also m-m-mentioned that I would be at the Sixth and that Haslem's safety and the f-future of the papers were closely linked. And then I was b-brought here."

"Jaysus." Hy shook his head in admiration. "How did you know?"

"As m-much as everyone seems to loathe Dell, they t-tolerate him. I deduced he represented p-powerful interests."

"So then, you getting' thrown in here was all part of the plan?"

Lightner laughed.

Hy wished he'd never started this conversation; the man had to be crazy. He kept that unhelpful thought to himself. "*Do* you have a plan for getting us out of here, sir?"

"G-Getting nervous, Detective?"

"A bit. And also hungry."

"I have to admit I hadn't expected to end up l-locked in a cellar."

That wasn't the answer Hy had been hoping for.

"T-Tell me about Caitlyn Grady—what r-really happened."

Hy opened his mouth to ask what he meant, but the thought of lying left him feeling heavy and tired. He sighed. "How could you tell?"

"You're a v-very direct man. And then, suddenly, you weren't. Also, I c-consulted a map, and it shouldn't have t-taken you three days to get from here to Tannersville."

"Caitlyn wanted me to take her little sister to Philly, to a woman who'd agreed to help her."

"Is this p-part of the Orphan T-Train?"

The question surprised him. "Caitlyn mentioned the Orphan Train people once or twice, so I assumed it was them."

"That's who the m-money was for—Caitlyn's sister."

"Yeah. I don't know who saw Caitlyn giving it to me—hell, maybe she told somebody—but McElhenny latched on to that like a shore crab to a rock."

"The girl was p-pregnant?"

"How did you know?"

"It was a guess."

Hy couldn't tell from his tone what he was thinking, but he could make a few guesses. "It was Dunbarton's—the kid." When Lightner remained silent, he said, "Sir?"

"I'm listening."

"Caitlyn knew—after Dunbarton ended up dead—that things would look bad." He sighed. "Go on, you can say it, sir."

"Things l-look bad, D-Detective."

"I know, sir, but I thought of that—that Amy might have killed him, even though she's barely fourteen—and I looked into her alibi. The girl had a damned good one—she was workin' at some mansion on Long Island the night he was killed." He sighed. "Of course now—thanks to Jemmy—we don't know *what* night that was. Anyhow, even though Amy had an alibi, there was still Caitlyn—people would say she took revenge for her baby sister. Caitlyn was madder'na wet hen at Amy for sellin' herself at Solange's, and the poor girl was glad to get away from her—complained all the way to Philly about how Caitlyn wouldn't let up on her. By Amy's way of thinkin', she was just sellin' something that would likely be taken from her if she kept workin' in service. This way, she said, at least she got paid for it. 'Course she never expected to get pregnant. I think the real reason

Caitlyn got mad is that Amy waited too long to get rid of the baby. By the time she went to Philly, she was a good five months along."

"You know where she is?"

"The woman who took her said gettin' people away from their pasts was the only way to give 'em a new start. She said Amy could write in a year or two, once she'd had some time. Anyhow, that's why it took so long to get to Tannersville. I should have taken care of Caitlyn's business first, but I never thought she'd be arrested." He shoved both hands into his hair and pulled hard enough to hurt. "Jaysus, but I fucked up handlin' all that—I know it. I still can't believe that Caitlyn would kill herself. She was one of the few kids from the orphanage who still went to church. Caitlyn was Catholic. Even after what the nuns did to her, she was still Catholic."

★　★　★

As amazing at it seemed, Jasper dozed. He woke with a startled gasp, taking a moment to recall his predicament.

"You awake, sir?"

Jasper yawned. "Yes. D–Did I sleep long?"

"Not long. Still, I'm impressed you can sleep at all."

"A skill I p–picked up during the war."

"What's it like, sir? Bein' in a war." When Jasper didn't immediately respond, Law said, "Sorry, I'm not meanin' to pry; it's just—"

"Boring and uncomfortable."

Law gave a choked laugh. "No. Really, sir?"

"I'm only p–partly jesting. It is days of tedium p–punctuated by moments of t–terror. Nothing in life afterwards is ever as v–vivid." He thought that sounded rather sad when spoken aloud.

"That sounds kinda like the last thirty-six hours. Think they'll kill us?"

"I don't know," Jasper admitted truthfully. "But I do know that if anything h–happens to me, Paisley will make them s–sorry they were b–b–born."

"Aye, that's true enough, I reckon. Wouldn't want to get on his bad side myself."

Jasper heard the amusement in the other man's voice.

"That must be strange, sir."

"I beg your pardon?"

"Havin' servants—especially one like that?"

Jasper gave a startled chuckle.

"You probably think that's a dumb thing to say."

Jasper heard the embarrassment in the younger man's voice.

"I only l-laughed because I'm afraid I don't know what it's like *not* to have servants. P-Paisley has been with me since I was fifteen."

"Even when you went to *war*?"

"Lord, I c-can't imagine telling P-Paisley to stay behind when I purchased my commission—he d-didn't want to stay behind *today*." Indeed, Jasper half expected the man to come smashing through their cell door at any moment. "In truth, servants m-make one's life easier in some regards, but they also c-complicate your life. I've had f-friends who often f-feel the need to get away—to b-be alone." Jasper didn't have such needs. Well, unless one counted going off alone to procure a bowl of opium.

"I didn't think about that," Law said.

Now it is your turn, Jasper.

Surely the man doesn't wish to speak about an *orphanage*?

You are a snob.

Jasper sighed. "What's it l-like to g-grow up in an orphanage?"

"I guess it's the same in one way—in that you're never alone. I wasn't always there; my folks died of cholera when I was five or so, and then I lived with my German grandmother until I was seven. After she died, I lived in the streets before the sisters took me in. They were strict, but they were fair. Mostly, although—" He broke off, and Jasper heard the sound of keys rattling.

Jasper pushed to his feet as the door opened, but the lamp was too bright for him to see who held it.

"Come with us, Yer Lordship."

Law stepped forward with him.

"Not you, Hy. You stay here." Several dark shapes invaded the room, and the sound of scuffling came from beside Jasper as two sets of strong hands dragged him out of the cell.

CHAPTER 35

McCarty slammed Jasper against the wall, his hands fisting Jasper's lapels in a way that would surely annoy Paisley. "It's ten minutes to midnight, *milord*. Thought I'd give you another chance before I take old Hy out of the hole and put my pistol to his head. You ready to get my papers?"

Jasper saw two of the man, and his head was ringing so loudly he could barely hear. "I b-beg your par—"

Fortunately, McCarty's fist struck him in the stomach this time, because Jasper wasn't sure he'd stay conscious after one more blow to the head. As it was, he vomited the contents of his stomach onto McCarty's heavy boots.

"God*dammit*!"

McCarty hit him again; this time there was nothing left to come up but bile.

Jasper knew, by the way the other man was beating him, that giving up the papers wouldn't save him—nor would it save Law— and it would most certainly condemn Paisley to a painful death, because his headstrong valet would march to his grave before uttering a peep.

McCarty shook him until his teeth rattled. "I'm tellin' you, this ain't—"

The door to the library opened, and McCarty's head whipped toward it. "What in the name of—" He stopped, his expression of shock almost comical, and his hands loosened on Jasper's coat.

Jasper began to slide to the floor, but McCarty caught him beneath the arms.

The man who stood in the doorway was dressed in a suit that might have come off Savile Row. And he was scowling. "Help him to that chair," he ordered in a clipped, annoyed tone.

"Aye, sir. Er, I didn't know you were—"

"*Now*, Mr. McCarty."

McCarty shoved his shoulder under Jasper's arm and dragged him toward three chairs. Or perhaps it was only one. He released Jasper unexpectedly, and he dropped onto his tailbone, biting his tongue. The new pain and taste of blood took his mind off the agonizing ache in his skull.

"Lord Jasper?" The newcomer leaned down and extended his gloved hand. "I'm Daniel Anderson."

Jasper opened his mouth, but the only sound that came out was "Urgh."

Anderson's smile dimmed, and he turned to McCarty. "Bring me a glass of whiskey and see yourself out," he snapped.

Even in pain, Jasper could enjoy watching McCarty's face turn a dangerous beet red. The man hesitated a long moment before obeying, handing the glass to Anderson, and then stomping toward the door, which he slammed hard enough to shake the entire house.

"Take a drink, my lord."

It probably wasn't what he needed, but it was certainly what he wanted. Jasper drank half the glass, gasped, and then threw back the rest.

It could have been one minute or ten that passed, the alcohol doing its part to ease the aches in his body, if not in his head.

When he opened his eyes, it was to find Anderson leaning against the desk, his brow furrowed with concern.

"I'm sorry I wasn't here sooner. And I'm sorry if McCarty manhandled you. Men like him are useful to us, but not for the subtler transactions."

"Who is *us*?" Jasper croaked.

"Oh come, my lord—I'm sure you know who I represent. I believe the first job you did for Her Majesty was of the covert sort."

Jasper's mouth opened, but he had nothing to say. How had *this* man learned what he'd done in France at the behest of the Home Office?

"It was clever of you to guess Dell was the best way to send a message," Anderson said. "But you needn't have bothered—I've had somebody following you from the moment you left Baker at the Tombs. I know your valet deposited something at Rutledge's today. If you don't give me the papers, I shall get them out of him."

The man's bored tone was more chilling than McCarty's fists.

"What will you d-do with them?"

"That's none of your concern." His eyes were utterly opaque and expressionless, out of place in his handsome, pleasant face.

"You're p-protecting them—Baker, Symington, Hoyle. Who else is involved?"

Anderson lips flexed into a facsimile of a smile, but his eyes remained fixed and hard.

"Why?" Jasper persisted.

Anderson took off his hat, tossed it on the desk, and poured two fingers of whiskey into the remaining glass. He lifted the bottle toward Jasper.

Why not?

Once they were both in possession of whiskey, Anderson spoke. "Have you ever heard of the so-called Conspiracy of 1741?"

"No."

"It was a group of slaves accused of fomenting rebellion against the New York Colony. Men and women were hanged and burned at the stake, all on the word of a young bar wench who enjoyed attention. Relying on her word alone, over one hundred slaves and powerless whites were hauled in, threatened, and promised freedom if they could implicate others in a conspiracy that didn't exist. For months new suspects were incarcerated. Once the last of the conspirators was executed, people began to look at their neighbors. Soon the only way to be safe was to implicate others. Who knows where the witch hunt might have led? To Rome, some people thought, if the young woman naming names hadn't finally leveled an accusation at somebody who could defend themselves. My point? No matter how asinine this plot sounds, there are plenty who will grasp it with both hands, especially in the current political environment.

"Can you imagine the public outcry if people learned that Southern agitators were purchasing arms and planning a rebellion against the government of New York in order to start a war—*with the assistance of Northern millionaires*?" He laughed, and it sounded genuine. "The last time rebels thought they could leave the Union, the president was strong enough to crush their revolt. But the situation now is . . . well, let's just say it's unlikely the U.S. Army could waltz into a Southern state and then waltz back out again. Not without cost."

"H-How long have you known about all this?"

"Long enough. We'd just begun to move when you and Mr. Law began poking around."

"I suppose you'll offer the conspirators a b-better deal—use their connections against their Southern c-collaborators?"

"Surely you d-don't expect me to answer that question?" His pleasant expression chilled. "As if the current political tensions aren't bad enough, there's an economic storm of unprecedented proportions on the horizon. Men like Symington and Dunbarton didn't involve themselves in such a stupid—not to mention dangerous—plot because they *wanted* to. Dunbarton's reckless investments and *embezzlement* at Ohio Life and Trust are about to become public knowledge. Symington's overreliance on credit—and his inability to pay even the interest—will destroy him and take dozens of other wealthy men with him. As for the poor? Those barely surviving now?" Anderson shook his head. "This might be catastrophic. And you, my lord, would like to make it even worse by doing what? Publishing Finch's confession and possibly starting a war?"

"I'd l-like to do my job."

"Yes, well—so would I. I'm afraid I need those papers, my lord. There's no point in saying you won't do it; you're not the sort of man to sacrifice the lives of—" He paused and ticked the fingers of his hand. "Well, that would be five lives, including your own." He cocked his head. "Or are you?"

Jasper had believed that life with the duke had inured him to feelings of powerless fury. He would have been wrong.

"You won't be losing anything by handing them over—you can reassure yourself of that. Any thoughts you have of releasing them to newspapermen?" He shook his head. "We wouldn't let that happen. And if you *did* manage to convince someone to print them, you can rest assured there would be no witnesses left alive to confirm such wild, lunatic tales." Anderson cocked his head. "I can see by your expression you don't agree with me. But I think you know there is no other option. I'm sorry you've come to our country and this is the first case you were handed. It does not reflect well on our leadership." He shrugged. "But these are unsettled times and call for drastic measures."

"Like m-murder," Jasper said flatly.

Anderson shrugged again and took a sip of whiskey.

"So a m-murderer will go free?"

"On the contrary; Detective Terrance Ryan is already in custody."

Jasper hadn't been expecting that. "What about whoever ordered Sealy, Dunbarton, and J-Janssen's deaths—because I'm assuming they were part of this? Who had them killed? Symington, B-Baker, and Hoyle?"

Anderson smiled. "Mr. Ryan claims he acted alone—I'm sure he'll let us all know his reasons in his confession. The only connection we really have between Stephen Finch and the ridiculous plot is Mr. Symington—and he will suffer a fatal heart attack—" Anderson took out his watch. "Correction, he *has* suffered a fatal attack, five minutes ago. God rest his soul."

Jasper's jaw sagged at his ruthless callousness. "What about Amos B-Baker?"

"Mr. Baker was released from the Tombs earlier today. His ship is out of impound, and he will continue his work—work that is legal under federal law, by the way."

"Slaving."

"Tsk, tsk. It is the law, and you are a lawman—as am I. It's not our place to legislate, my lord. We are but the instrument of justice."

"I suppose B-Baker will now be w-working for you?"

Again, Anderson just smiled.

"And Hoyle?"

"Mr. Hoyle is the recent beneficiary of a lucrative contract with the United States Army. He'll be too busy making us side arms and rifles to fill any outside orders."

"And who is r-responsible for the murder of G-Gamble?"

"I'm afraid I don't know who you mean." Anderson sounded bored.

"And what about J-Jemmy Hart—did Ryan kill him too? Or haven't you heard of him either?"

This time Anderson's expression really was blank. "I've never heard of a Jemmy Hart."

Jasper felt a surge of optimism; perhaps the old man was still alive.

"So, I g-give you the papers, you charge Ryan with Finch's murder, and you release Haslem."

"Ryan is already in custody for the murder of Janssen and Finch."

Jasper laughed. "J-Janssen?"

This time Anderson's smile was not an expression of amusement. "Yes, J-Janssen. That investigation is *closed*, Detective Inspector."

"B-But *why* would Ryan imitate the m-method of the earlier k-killings?"

Anderson shrugged, his expression one of annoyance. "I don't know—nor do I care. What matters is whether we have an agreement."

"What about all the p-people on Baker's ship?"

Anderson frowned. "Who? The escaped slaves?"

"Yes, those p-people."

"They'll go with Baker. He has the authority—indeed the duty—to return them to their owners."

"I w-want them released."

Anderson's nostrils flared. "You are in no position to demand such a thing."

"Oh, I believe I am."

"I could kill you right now—then get the papers from your bank." He smiled unpleasantly. "I don't need to make you such a generous offer; I could tie up *all* the loose ends, *my lord.*"

Jasper crossed his arms and smiled with a confidence he was far from feeling. "You can kill me and take whatever papers my v-valet deposited." Jasper smiled at Anderson's sudden comprehension. "But the f-first place y-you'll find the real documents will be on the front p-page of a newspaper. If no N-New York paper will take them—d-doubtful, since there are over th-three hundred—then they'll make their w-way to the London *Times*, which is owned b-by a friend of m-mine. You r-really don't think I came here without t-taking precautions? All the witnesses m-might be dead, but I've written a c-compelling statement of my own to go along with F-Finch's. I am a d-decorated officer—my word will c-c-carry some weight. As to *why* you should r-release those people? How about the fact that you are not only allowing men to g-go free who are guilty of conspir-acy, murderer, and treason; you're actually r-r-rewarding them with lucrative employment? No. You'll have your p-papers after those p-people on Staten Island have been released."

Anderson's eyes bored through Jasper, and Jasper experienced real fear—an emotion he'd believed he was no longer capable of feeling since Balaclava. After some of the longest moments in Jasper's recent memory, Anderson tossed back the rest of his drink and stood.

"I'll give you twenty-four hours to have a boat at Staten Island—a boat that had better disappear five minutes after the last passenger boards. Haslem will be free within the next few hours. There is a carriage out front waiting to take you and Detective Law wherever you'd like to go. I shall expect the papers by the end of the day tomorrow. *All* of them." He put on his hat and picked up his cane. When he got to the door, he turned around. "I can see you are a man accustomed to getting his way, my lord, and that you'll be tempted to dig around in these murders even though a woman was arrested for the first two and Ryan has confessed to Finch and Janssen. But leave it alone; let go of your need for justice this once." His mouth pulled up into a twisted smile. "Instead of thinking about what you haven't managed to achieve, be grateful for what you have."

"And what is that, M–Mr. Anderson?"

He smiled wryly. "You mean other than freeing an innocent man, putting a confessed killer in jail, liberating fifty-some fugitives, and helping to conceal a treasonous conspiracy that might have driven my nation to war? I think we both know the deaths of Sealy, Dunbarton, and Janssen were likely a mercy for many, many young girls. Forget about justice and be satisfied with that, my lord. Be satisfied with mercy."

CHAPTER 36

What became known as the Great Police Riot was the only matter on most people's minds in the days following the chaos of June sixteenth.

The Sixth Precinct's arrest of one of its own for the murders of two wealthy businessmen didn't sell as many papers as the pitched battle on the steps of City Hall. As a result of the larger story—and probably with a little assistance from the mysterious Daniel Anderson—Terrence Ryan barely occupied more than a few columns on the front page of the major newspapers, quickly drifting into the hinterlands once he'd signed a full confession for both murders.

The Sixth Precinct claimed that the arrest of one of its own was evidence that corruption in the Municipal-controlled police department was nowhere as bad as the reformers had claimed.

White Street claimed it was evidence of Municipal incompetence.

Symington's death—a peaceful passing in his sleep—made only a corner of the financial section.

The dismissal of all charges against Amos Baker never made it into any of the papers Jasper read. Nor was there any mention of the disappearance of fifty-three freedmen and women from the quarantine facility on Staten Island.

Haslem was freed and, wisely, took his mother to Canada.

Jemmy Hart was still missing, but no body had been found. Jasper paid another visit to the Old Brewery, but Hart's associates were also gone. Jasper hoped it was the transient way of life, rather than anything nefarious, that accounted for Hart's unknown whereabouts, but he wasn't optimistic.

Jasper and Law had finally been given an office of their own—the roomy one across from Davies's. No decision had yet been made about bringing in more detective trainees, but Jasper believed an actual office was a step in the right direction.

As for domestic matters, Jasper had moved into the house on Union Square the same day he'd been released from McCarty's basement.

The first week in the new house had been hectic, but Paisley was a miracle worker, and now, after ten days, life had settled into a pleasant routine.

Jasper had just finished his breakfast and was reading through the shipping news when Paisley entered the room.

"This just came for you, my lord." He handed Jasper a cream envelope; on the back flap, the initials *HMD* were embossed. Jasper recognized the envelope because it was the fourth of its kind he'd received from Mrs. Dunbarton since moving into his house, and the second in two days. Yesterday's envelope had contained an invitation to a play to be put on by the young ladies of Mrs. Dunbarton's school.

"You can take this." Jasper motioned to his almost empty plate. "Please pass along my compliments to Mrs. Freeman."

Paisley looked torn. The new cook was turning out to be a strong-willed individual who wasn't tolerating Paisley's attempts to maintain dominance over the kitchen. His valet was accustomed to ruling the roost with an iron fist and didn't like ceding power. However, he *did* like how much more Jasper had been eating since Mrs. Freeman joined their staff.

Jasper opened Mrs. Dunbarton's latest envelope; it contained an invitation for dinner that night. He was rather surprised at both the invitation and the short notice, as he'd just had dinner at her house a few days earlier. She'd made it her mission to introduce him to every individual involved in charitable enterprises in the city. Her dinners included the sort of people who valued her good works over her scandalous disregard for mourning.

Jasper had decided he quite liked the clever, sharp-tongued little woman. While her wit—when it came to him—was as barbed as ever, he found her company oddly . . . stimulating.

Perhaps that's because you speak to her rather than just take her to bed.

Jasper had to admit that was a fair observation. In the past, an invitation to a widow's house had generally meant an invitation to her bedchamber, but Mrs. Dunbarton appeared genuinely interested in his acquaintance rather than his person.

That knowledge left him vaguely uneasy.

You needn't fret; once she gets to know you, she'll learn you're just a cracked, empty vessel and quickly move on.

Jasper was not in a mood to be drawn.

In addition to dinners, she'd given him guided tours of her boys' school, girls' school, and both the libraries, as well as a small farm across the river in New Jersey. With each visit, more ice had melted, until he'd been able to see the person who lived behind the facade. Her devotion to the poor and downtrodden was not mere posturing; she was one of the most selfless people he'd ever met.

Jasper penned an acceptance to her invitation and rang for a foot-man to run the message next door.

He finished reading the last of the morning papers and then headed to his chambers. As he made his way up the stairs, he realized he was smiling. It took him a moment to pinpoint the source of his pleasure: it was the invitation to dinner tonight. For the first time in as long as he could recall, Jasper was actually looking forward to the evening ahead.

★ ★ ★

Cates answered the door when Jasper rang the bell at eight o'clock that evening.

"Good evening, my lord."

The older man behaved as if their night brawling with members of the Dead Rabbits, Roach Guards, and Bowery Boys had never taken place; perhaps Jasper had imagined it all.

"Good evening, Cates." He handed over his hat and cane and examined the man's face as he slowly stripped off his gloves. Cates kept his eyes properly downcast—as a good English butler would—his person as immobile as a statue under Jasper's inspection. "Mrs. D-Dunbarton tells me you were a s-soldier in the Queen's Army?"

There was only the slightest of hesitations. "Yes, sir, many years ago."

Jasper looked in the big foyer mirror, watching as Cates lifted his coat from his shoulders. "Where did you serve?"

"I was in India for seven years. I left in '48."

"I shouldn't want to be there now," Jasper said.

"No, sir."

Jasper glanced around the foyer. "Am I d–dreadfully early or hor-ribly l-late?"

"You are my only guest, Lord Jasper." Mrs. Dunbarton was descending the curved marble stairs. "I hope you don't mind we are dining à deux."

Jasper smiled up at her. "Since I've already d–destroyed your rep-utation by d–dining alone with you once b–before, we m–might as well take advantage of the situation."

She gestured toward the hall rather than the stairs. "I thought we'd dine on the terrace. At this time of the evening, it is actually quite pleasant."

Jasper opened the door at the end of the hallway and followed her into a delightful room with two French doors open to the back garden.

"This is my breakfast room, but I find it infinitely more comfort-able than the dining room in the summer. Whiskey?"

"Thank y-you."

She poured two glasses. "I imagine things have slowed down now that you have the killer in custody."

Jasper studied the landscape that hung over the large buffet. "Ah, w-well, crime n-never sleeps."

"Did you just coin that phrase?" She handed him a glass.

"W-Would it impress you if I said I h–had?"

"You are quite impressive enough already."

Jasper gave her an only half-mocking look of surprise. "Why, Mrs. D-Dunbarton—was that an actual c-compliment?"

Her gaze dropped to her glass. "I wonder—"

"Yes?" he prodded curiously.

She glanced up at him through her eyelashes; he'd have thought the action coquettish in any other woman. "Won't you call me Hetty?"

This time his surprise was genuine; did the prickly widow *like* him?

"I'm sorry—that was dreadfully forward—and American—of me." She turned away, and Jasper committed a far larger faux pas by catching her by the upper arm and stopping her. She didn't try to pull away, but she didn't turn toward him either.

The black crepe was warm beneath his fingers. "Why are you r-running away?" he asked softly.

"You must have women flinging themselves at you incessantly."

Jasper smiled at the mental image.

"I'd like to think I'm different because I appreciate you for more than your appearance, but—"

"But?"

"I'm no better."

Jasper turned her gently toward him. When she would not look up, he took her chin in his fingers and tilted her face. He smiled when he saw she'd squeezed her eyes shut.

"Look at m-me, Hetty."

Her mouth twisted willfully, but she opened her eyes. "Yes, *Jasper*?"

He grinned at her spark of defiance. "D-Did you invite me to d-dinner to seduce m-me?" he teased.

Rather than making her smile, as he'd hoped, his comment elicited a grimace. "I'm such a foo—"

Jasper lowered his mouth over hers. She was tiny, and he had to bend almost in half.

Her body stiffened, but she didn't move away. Her lips were unspeakably soft, and she tasted of whiskey. She was breathing in sharp, shallow gasps, and it took only a moment to discern she'd never been kissed—at least not properly. The knowledge helped restrain the surprisingly strong urges rampaging through his body, and he softened his kisses.

Her hands alighted on his hips, her fingers clutching him. Jasper drew her closer, and her lips parted.

It had been years—if ever—since he'd spent so much time kissing a woman. His last lover had been as carnal and jaded as Jasper, and they'd sated their passions in almost violent physical couplings. This was innocent yet satisfying.

It was Mrs. Dunbarton—*Hetty*—who broke away first.

He thought she might shy back, mortified by her behavior, but instead she laid her cheek against his chest and exhaled a long, shaky sigh, her slender arms tightening around his torso as she nuzzled him—like a small animal burrowing for safety.

They stood that way for several long but not uncomfortable moments.

Again, it was she who moved, releasing him and stepping back.

Her cheeks were a fiery red, her eyes a dark navy. "You feel as lovely as you look." She swallowed. "But if you'd like to go—"

Jasper knew she wasn't talking about dinner. "I'd l-like to stay, Hetty."

★   ★   ★

Hy rolled onto his back and closed his eyes, breathing like a winded horse.

Cool, strong fingers slid over his sweat-slicked chest and pinched one nipple—*hard*.

Hy yelped. "Christ, Lorie! What the hell's wrong with you?"

He turned his head to find Lorie staring at him. "You're lathered like a winded nag and breathin' like an old man."

"I didn't hear you complainin' a minute ago."

She snorted. "A minute is right."

Hy swore under his breath.

Her hand slid down his body and she grabbed his limp prick, making him gasp. "I guess I should count myself lucky that this thing works at all." She gave him an almost painful squeeze before releasing him and pushing off the bed.

They were in her room—an honor she'd not afforded Hy before. Honestly, he wasn't sure why she'd afforded it to him tonight, and he was beginning to wonder if it was worth all the post-fucking abuse.

He'd been minding his own business, drinking with his cousin Ian, when she'd picked him out of the crowd and beckoned him up the stairs to what was certainly paradise. Now that he was doing his thinking above the waist, he wondered what she wanted.

He couldn't say he knew Lorena Paxton well—he doubted anyone did—but he knew her well enough to understand that she was a businesswoman who didn't give out free fucks.

She returned to the bed, naked but for black stockings, garters, and two glasses of whiskey. Good God, the woman was magnificent.

Wordlessly, she handed him a glass.

He paused—drinking in her tall, shapely body as she threw back her liquor—before emptying his own glass.

He groaned with pleasure as the fine whiskey burned its way down his throat. "The good stuff," he said by way of thanks when she returned to the bed. She ignored his gratitude, instead crawl-ing across the mattress on all fours, resembling a dangerous cat. She settled her naked bottom on his hips and stared down at him.

"I need to ask you somethin'."

Here it comes. "Yeah?"

"You know how Caitlyn sent Amy off on one of those orphan trains?"

"She told you that?"

Lorie rolled her eyes. "Obviously."

"What about it?"

"I have some of her money—Caitlyn's. It was tied up when she took the rest of her money, and now I wanted to send it to Amy."

He shrugged. "Why are you tellin' me?"

Her hand moved like a striking snake, and she twisted his nipple again—the other one this time.

"Goddammit!" he yelled. "Why'd you do that?" He held a pro-tective hand over each nipple.

"Would I be askin' you a favor if I knew where to send the damned money?"

"Oh."

"Yes, oh. I went to that place—the charity—but they won't give out information. I thought maybe since you're a copper, they'd tell you."

He glared at her. "You didn't have to fuck me for that—you know I'll do what I can."

Her lips twisted in amusement. "Maybe I *wanted* to get you between my legs, Hieronymus Aloysius Law."

"That *ain't* my middle name." God, did he hate that stupid name, which had stuck to him like glue at St. Pat's after some wise arse hung it on him.

She gave him a smacking kiss while sliding her hand between their hips and waking the dead. "So you'll ask?"

Hy groaned—this time with pleasure. "Aye, whatever you want."

CHAPTER 37

Jasper was halfway through his morning routine—which he'd started later than usual, thanks to his late night—when Paisley entered the room.

He'd been working the small bag but stilled it with one hand while pushing his sweat-damp hair off his forehead with the other. "I n-need a damned haircut," he said, while the matter was fresh in his mind.

Predictably, Paisley ignored him. "Mr. Law is here, my lord."

Jasper had thought they were taking the day off. Had he gotten the date wrong?

"He said it was urgent."

"Bring him in."

Jasper picked up his towel and wiped off his face and torso before pulling on his shirt. He liked his new exercise room, which was light and airy and had once been his breakfast room.

Thinking of breakfast rooms reminded him of last night; he'd stayed at Hetty's until almost four o'clock that morning.

You're a fool, Jasper; she's not a casual sort of woman.

Perhaps I don't want *a casual sort of woman.*

Jasper enjoyed a moment of triumph at having shocked his inner critic into silence.

The door opened and Law entered, his eyes flickering around the room before settling on Jasper. "I didn't know you boxed."

"Only with a b-bag. Would you care for coffee or tea, D-Detective?"

"No thank you, sir."

Jasper nodded his dismissal at Paisley.

"Sorry to disturb you on your day off," Law said when the door closed. "But I needed to ask you somethin'."

"What's on your m-mind, Detective?"

"Remember how I told you about Amy—Caitlyn's younger sister?"

"The girl you took to Philadelphia. You said it was arranged b-by some society?"

"They call it the Orphan Train. The thing is, they *didn't* arrange it."

"What do you m-mean?"

"Lorie asked me to get Amy's address, since she had some of Caitlyn's money to send her. I went to the Orphaned Children Mission on Mulberry—the place Caitlyn said Amy had been living. But they had no idea what I was talkin' about."

"Y-You mean she'd never been there?"

"She'd been there, but they never set Amy up with a family because they couldn't place a pregnant girl. The man I talked to there said they sent anyone they couldn't help to one of the other charities they worked with." Law shook his head in wonder. "You ain't gonna believe this, sir, but it was one of Mrs. Dunbarton's charities that took Amy in, some girls' school."

Jasper frowned. "Explain."

"I thought at first that maybe Mrs. Dunbarton did it after she went to see Caitlyn. You know? When Caitlyn asked to see her? I figured maybe Caitlyn mentioned her orphaned sister and Mrs. Dunbarton took pity on the girl—somethin' like that."

It sounded exactly like something Hetty would do. But why wouldn't she have mentioned such a thing?

"But here's the thing, sir—Mrs. Dunbarton didn't take Amy *after* she talked to Caitlyn; she took Amy outa there a month *before* her husband was murdered."

★   ★   ★

Jasper felt like he was under a compulsion or spell; he didn't want to be here, yet here he was.

Turn around and do what Anderson said—forget about it, his mental companion pled.

"Sir?"

Jasper forced his attention back to the waiting guard. "I'm ready."

When the cell door opened, there was Ryan, leaning back in his wooden chair, balancing on two legs and smirking up at Jasper. "Well, well, l-l-look who's come calling."

Jasper waited until the door closed behind him for answering. "I appreciate you agreeing to t-talk to me, Mr. Ryan."

"I ain't got nothing else to do. But that doesn't mean talking to me won't cost you."

Jasper reached for his wallet.

"No. Don't give *me* the money. I want you to send it to some-body."

"Your w-wife and children?" Jasper recalled reading something about Ryan's family in the newspaper.

"Naw, she's been taken care of all right and tight." He glanced around the four stone walls, as if somebody might hear, and leaned forward. "I want something for my ma, back home. Moira Ryan in Clifden, Galway. I'll want two hundred dollars—and I don't want her to know who it came from; she's got enough on her plate without knowin' about me swingin'."

It was an exorbitant sum, and they both knew it. "What d-do I get for that amount of m-money?"

"You get what you've come lookin' for—you want answers, about a couple o' things, but mainly you're wondering about the watch. I thought I'd get me neck stretched with nobody the wiser." He didn't exhibit any shame about his admission.

"Tell me where you b-bought D-Dunbarton's watch," Jasper said.

"That's what old Hart told ye, aye?"

"Where is Mr. Hart?"

"Hell if I know."

Jasper heard the truth in his voice. Besides, why not admit to another murder if he'd done it? They could only hang him once.

"You thought it was me who done the old bastard, eh?" Ryan shook his head, his expression marveling. "I have to admit I was sur-prised as hell to hear he'd confessed to robbin' a corpse—and a rich one, at that. You must have a bit of magic to ya. But you're not as clever as you think." He held up a hand. "But wait, I'm gettin' ahead o' myself. When we moved Dunbarton—"

"Who is w-we?"

Ryan chewed his cheek. "Why not?" he asked, more of himself. "Me and Featherstone and a patrolman named Kennedy." He laughed at whatever he saw on Jasper's face. "Give over on that one, mate—it's too good a money maker. And it don't go through Davies, if that's what you're thinking, but he and everyone else knows about it—even holier-than-thou Hy Law."

Jasper had no intention of believing anything *this* man said about Hieronymus Law. "Why d-did you keep Dunbarton's body another d-day?"

"Because we fucked up. Featherstone thought to shake more money out of that French whore. Turns out the woman has brass balls. By the time he pulled his head out of his arse, it was broad daylight and we were stuck with a feckin' corpse. It was lucky it wasn't hot. We kept 'im in the wagon until the next night and then dumped 'im."

"Did you move S-Sealy?"

"Aye, that's why Featherstone wanted more money—*two* rich men killed in spittin' distance of her place? The price shoulda gone up; we shoulda gotten triple." He shrugged. "Anyhow, unlike Sealy, who'd not been robbed when we found him, I saw Dunbarton had no watch, wallet, or even coat, so's I knew somebody had already gone over him. I figgered it was old Hart—he an' Fast Eddie been fightin' about that stretch for years."

"So y-you went to the p-p-pawnbroker he was known to use and bought the w-watch."

Ryan grinned at Jasper. "You still don't get it, do you? I didn't *buy* Dunbarton's watch, you poor dumb bastard; the one I planted on that Grady bitch was just a watch I *liberated* from a rich drunk we arrested one night."

Everything Ryan said had to go through translation at least once or twice. This, however, Jasper understood immediately.

An odd sensation rocked him, like the sudden, violent shifting of the deck of a ship.

Don't jump to conclusions, Jasper, the voice cautioned, not mocking for once.

Jasper realized Ryan had been talking and he'd missed it. "What d-did you say?"

"*I said* that I got the idea when things started to go south for the whore—the dress, the people talkin' about her argument with Dunbarton. All I had to do was smear a bit o' blood on it and stick it in a drawer when we came to search her room." He laughed and stared at the far wall, shaking his head wonderingly. "It was so *easy*; nobody gives a damn about a whore. McElhenny was so bloody desperate that I probably could've told him what I'd done and he'd have been fine with it."

"Why?"

Ryan's homely face twisted with rage. "*Why*? That little bitch *deserved* what she got. She was a *whore*, and yet she was too good for *me*?" His fury flared. "It wasn't enough to reject me; she had to do it in front of a crowd. And then she let that bastard *Hy* up 'er skirt, but not me? Well." He snorted, his expression smug. "She played her games; I played mine."

He glared at Jasper, but his anger slowly gave way to amazement. "I'll be honest, I never thought she'd swing for it. I thought they'd just hold her until somebody got around to askin' the widow to look at the watch. But McElhenny didn't give a shit, and Donahue—who'd been workin' the case with Hy—had fucked off back to Ireland, and Hy was off doin' whatever he was doin'." He shook his head. "And then the stupid bitch actually *confessed*." Ryan gave a bark of grating laughter. "I couldn't believe it! Still, I figured there'd be problems when the captain gave the watch back to the widow, but I *saw* Mrs. Dunbarton's signature on the form identifyin' it. And this wasn't the sort of watch you'd mistake—it had a fancy ship on the cover." His gaze turned inward. "I still don't know why she lied. Maybe she just wanted it to be over with? Maybe she was glad somebody killed the bent bastard?"

Jasper pushed his racing thoughts aside and focused on the man across from him. "Why d-did you confess to Janssen's m-murder?"

Ryan's laugher was genuine this time. "Oh, you're somethin', my lord. Let's just put it this way: I've got a wife and five brats. I might not like any of 'em too much, but it's still my job to protect my family. Anyhow, I fucked up a simple job, and there ain't no way I won't hang for Finch. The money was to sign off on both, so I figured I might as well be hanged for a sheep as a lamb." He narrowed his eyes. "You say I said *any* of that an' I'll call you a liar."

"Who ordered you to k-kill Finch?"

Ryan laughed.

"I'll pay you whatever they're p-paying you—j-just to tell the truth. About all of it—who is p-paying you, who ordered you to k-kill Finch."

Ryan shook his head. "And how will that protect my family? Besides, no matter what, I'll still swing for Finch." He gave Jasper a look of deep loathing. "Anyhow, I don't care if you offered me every bloody penny in the Bank of England—I still wouldn't do what you want. I was so damned happy when McCarty said he was gonna kill you. And he could have, too. But no, that would've been too easy—too smart. Instead he had to fuck about and play his little games, so somebody jerked *his* chain and reminded him that he's nothing but a dog. So here you sit." He grinned. "And here I sit—with something you *want*. For once in your life, my fine lord, you ain't getting' what you want—no matter if you offered me ten times what they paid. Has that ever happened to you before?" He didn't wait for Jasper's answer. "Your sort has been crushing people like me for centuries. You think I left Ireland because I *wanted* to?" He laughed harshly. "I had fourteen sisters and brothers—and *nine* of 'em starved when the man who owned the land we farmed kicked us off. Nine. My mother had to sell herself—sell her own children—to make ends meet." Ryan's jaw worked. "So, no—you *can't* buy everything you want." He shoved his chair back hard enough to hit the wall. "You can go fuck yourself." He pounded on the door with the heel of his hand, and keys jingled in the lock so quickly that Jasper knew the guard had been listening.

The door opened, and Ryan stepped out into the corridor. "Don't forget your promise. Two hundred; you gave your word," he called over his shoulder as the guard led him away.

★ ★ ★

Jasper knew where he'd find her at this time of day.

The ten-minute walk from the Tombs to the girls' school felt like twenty years.

Go home, Jasper. Forget what Ryan said—the man's a murderer and a thief. He framed an innocent woman for murder and is proud *of it.*

Jasper knew the voice was right.

How can you know he's telling the truth?

He couldn't know.

If you go digging around, Anderson will find out. You know that he'll make good on his threat if you renege on your deal.

He knew all that.

But still he couldn't turn back. He had to ask her; he had to know.

A woman was locking the door to the New Beginnings School for Young Ladies, and she smiled when she saw him, obviously recognizing him. "Lord Jasper, how nice to see you again! You must be looking for Mrs. Dunbarton."

Jasper had no idea who this woman was.

Her keys rattled as she unlocked the door. "She's in the costume room. It's just before you get to the girls' quarters. She's making a few last-minute repairs for our final rehearsal."

"R-Rehearsal?"

"Yes—tonight is the first performance of the play."

"Ah," Jasper said, because he couldn't think of anything else.

She smiled, her thin cheeks flushing. "I wrote it, you know."

"Oh?" Jasper had no idea what she was talking about.

"The play—I wrote it. I wanted to call it *Independence*, but the girls were wild about *The Fifty-Five Founding Fathers*, even though there will only be seventeen of them on stage." Jasper felt like he was in a play himself—a farce, where he was going through the motions while inside he was flying apart.

She opened the door. "Please remind Mrs. Dunbarton to bring a bit of extra glue. Patty's wig keeps—"

Jasper shut the door on her last words, his rude behavior giving him a brief qualm.

The school was silent but for the sound of his bootheels on the floor—nothing like the last time, when it had been filled with girlish chatter. He followed the hallway to a room he'd not visited because it had been occupied with girls working on some project.

Today the door was open. There were a half dozen large tables, all cluttered with fabric, pots of paint, tufts of what looked to be hair or fur, and other theatrical detritus. At the far end of the room he saw an open doorway.

Hetty was inside, plying her needle on a garment, sitting on a worn velvet sofa. On the end table beside her were bits of fabric and a spirit lamp with a small pot.

She must have heard his footsteps. "Oh, Miss Daniels, I'm glad you've not left. I've got this for—" She looked up and froze.

The flash of fear was gone so fast that Jasper wouldn't have seen it if he'd not been looking so closely. Had she always looked at him this way and he'd missed it?

Her cheeks darkened, and he knew she was remembering last night, when he'd laid her out in her monastic cell of a bedroom and explored every inch of her body.

"What a lovely surprise, Jasper. I didn't expect to see you until—"

Jasper's shoe had become stuck on something, and he tried to tug it loose, almost pulling it off in the process. His blood pounded in his ears as he leaned against the wall to look at the sole.

"Oh, those girls and their glue. I'm so sorry, but I have something that will take it off. I'm afraid they got it everywhere."

Jasper touched the sticky, clear blob and lifted his finger to his nose, knowing what he'd smell before he smelled it.

"It's made from pine tar."

He could hear relief in her voice; no doubt she was pleased to be discussing such a mundane matter.

Jasper was reminded of that day at Balaclava; there was no screaming and no loud explosions or smoke, but he had the same sick sense of inevitability in his gut.

He looked up slowly.

Her eyes flickered nervously. "Last year one of the girls read something about Elizabethan actors making their own glue for wigs, beards, and such, and they weren't happy until they tried it. So now we use it in all our productions. I'm afraid it makes a dreadful mess." She gave a breathless laugh, her eyes dropping to her hands, her cheeks flushed as she babbled. "My poor maid has been driven half-mad cleaning my shoes—"

"Stop. Just . . . stop."

He thought she might keep lying, but all the energy seemed to drain out of her.

"It was the watch, wasn't it?"

Jasper sagged back against the wall. "Good Lord, Hetty. *Why?*"

Her head whipped up, and the fire that defined her burned in her eyes. And something else, too—*dislike*, or was it derision?—for *him*?

"*Why?* Wouldn't a better question be *why* a man like Felix was not only allowed to destroy, but to do so with the knowledge—if not the outright approval—of the men who run our city? *Our country?*"

"It is *m-murder*, Hetty."

She laughed, the sound wild. "It was *vengeance*, and *not nearly enough* for the untold girls whose lives he destroyed—including mine. Can you imagine what I felt when I learned I'd married a *monster?*"

"Surely there was another way?"

"*What* other way? Why did you bring Agota to me, Jasper? Why were you so insistent that she get out of the city? Wasn't *that* breaking the law? After all, I'm sure Madame Solange paid for the girl and she was twelve, more than old enough by the laws of this city; laws made by the very same men they benefited. How many lives did Felix, Wilbur, and Alard ruin? How many more should they have been allowed to ruin? It wasn't just vengeance, Jasper—it was justice, and it was *mercy*."

"You speak of m-mercy, yet an innocent woman died for your murders."

He saw something—pain? Regret? Shame? But whatever it was, she quickly tucked it beneath her mask. "Caitlyn Grady's death was . . . unfortunate."

"Unfortunate."

Her eyes flashed at his flat, sick tone. "What? You think I was *pleased* with what happened?"

"You c-could have saved her."

"Yes, I could have." She flung the words at him. "But at what cost? It was a sacrifice of the one for the many."

"The end justifies the m-means?"

"In this situation it does, Jasper. And if you cannot *see* that—" She paused and shook her head, as if she were engaged in an internal argument. After a long moment of silence, she said, "I want you to know that Miss Grady was not an innocent victim."

"Are you saying that she *did* k-kill your husband?"

"I'm saying she knew what she was doing."

"She was with a m-man that night. She couldn't have—"

"You have nothing—no evidence, no proof—and you *know* nothing. If you accuse me of murder, I will deny it to my dying breath. Besides, I have an unassailable alibi; I wasn't even in the city when Felix was murdered."

The truth struck him like the proverbial lightning bolt, and he laughed. "I c-can't believe I've been so *stupid*."

She frowned. "What?"

"You said any w-w-woman might be angry enough to k-kill her own husband, but why would she kill another's?" He shook his head in wonder. "You all but handed me the truth, d-didn't you? You d-didn't kill your own h-husbands, you killed *each other's*."

She looked away, but not before he saw the truth.

"It's *b-brilliant*, and so very simple."

Small details suddenly stood out, and Jasper scrambled to put them in the correct order.

"It w-was Emma Sealy who killed Janssen. The doctor said she'd been ill for a while. That's why there was a gap: she was too ill to do her p-part a few months ago, wasn't she? Emma is left-handed—as was the p-person who killed Alard Janssen—I noticed that when she served me t-t-tea." He snorted softly. "Her h-hands were bleeding through her g-gloves; she m-must be in pain."

Fury burned in Hetty's icy blue eyes as she glared up at him.

"Mrs. Sealy t-talked about her dead husband as if she still *loved* him. Why did she agree to s-such a thing? Was she regretting it when it came her t-turn? Did you and Mrs. J-Janssen have to threaten her to do her part? Did you r-remind her that you'd done yours? Because I know you would have gone f-first, Hetty." A muscle in Hetty's jaw ticced. "You couldn't just allow her to shoot J-Janssen. Any old murder wouldn't do—it w-was all to send a message. Three wealthy men, mutilated and m-murdered the same way, all outside a n-notorious virgin peddler's whorehouse. B-But your message got muddled." Jasper shook his head as one piece after another fell into place. "You m-must have been *furious* when the bodies were moved from S-Solange's. I d-don't understand about the p-pine sap. Did you lure them *here* to k-kill them?"

"You have nothing," she said.

He cocked his head as he studied her. "You d-don't feel any guilt—but what of the others? It's not the syphilis that has d-driven Emma Sealy to l-lock herself away in that place, is it? She's sick with guilt at what she agreed to do—what she's d-done."

Hetty flung aside the garment she'd been clutching. "Emma is a *fool*. She's dying from syphilis because Wilbur gave it to her. He as good as *murdered* her, and yet she still loved him!"

"And Mrs. Janssen—"

"Alard was the worst kind of hypocrite—a reformer who raped little girls. As for me? Well, I have the best reason of all. I promised the girls I brought here a *better* life—a safe place to live. And do you know what I did to them? Can you guess? I delivered them *right* to the very men I'd tried to protect them from. Oh yes," she said, reading the revulsion in his eyes. "Felix and his sick friends bribed the guard I hired to protect these *defenseless* young girls—don't bother looking for *him*, by the way—to act as their own personal procurer, bringing them virgins in this very *room*. They scheduled their rapes for Saturday nights and took turns—all so very civilized. I don't know how long it went on before I realized the horror of what I'd done—" Her laugh was tinged with hysteria. "I'd provided them with the very commodity they'd once had to go *searching* for. Hesperis Dunbarton, the great humanitarian, was even worse than despicable Solange Dupuy." Her voice dripped with self-loathing. "You're absolutely right I went first. When Wilbur Sealy came for his Saturday perversion, he found *me* instead of a harmless, drugged little girl." She stared through him as if seeing somebody else. "It was a bad decision to do it here. I never expected so much blood." Her gaze sharpened and settled on Jasper. "Death was too easy an escape for those three—I just wish they'd suffered more."

"You m-mutilated them while they were still alive—they would have suffered p-plenty as you hacked out your pound of flesh."

"They *deserved* it, and I'd do it all over again." She gave a mirthless snort and shook her head. "It was all so *perfect*. Except for the watch—that damned watch. Was it that policeman? I thought, with the case files gone—"

Jasper gaped. "That was *you*?" he asked stupidly.

He deserved her derisive laugh. "Finding a bent copper willing to destroy a few files is easier than getting a table at Delmonico's—and costs considerably less. How did you find out about the watch?" she persisted.

"Detective Ryan t-told me."

She nodded, looking unsurprised. "I regretted lying the moment the words slipped out of my mouth—especially since Caitlyn had already stupidly confessed. But once I'd spoken, it was too late to take them back." Her expression shifted to one of regret. "I wish you'd never figured any of it out, but I can't say I'm surprised." Her voice softened. "You have no proof, Jasper, only the word of a corrupt policeman. It would be my word against his, and who will people believe? You can allow justice to be done without feeling as if you've failed in your duty. We are untouchable, my lord. You have nothing."

She was right: he had nothing.

When you are left with nothing, Jasper—then you must use that. The voice belonged to Eugene Vidocq.

Jasper recalled just what had started him on this wretched journey this morning: Law's visit.

"We know about Amy G-Grady, Hetty."

She stared, her eyes blinking rapidly. He began to think his bluff was just that: a bluff.

But then she laughed—a forced, brittle sound—and that's when Jasper knew he had her; Hetty knew it too.

"I have no idea what you're talking about."

"Detective Law—the p-policeman Caitlyn entrusted to take Amy to Philadelphia—just received a l-letter from Amy. She's g-guilt ridden about what happened to her sister. Detective Law has gone to c-collect the girl and b-b-bring her back." Jasper hesitated, then said, "Tell me how it st-started, Hetty. Did she b-blackmail you? Was that it?"

For a moment, he thought she'd tell him to go to hell. But then her brilliant blue eyes shuttered and her shoulders slumped.

"No, Caitlyn didn't blackmail me—she didn't want money. She brought Amy to me because she wanted me to know what kind of man my husband was." Her lips twisted bitterly. "As if I didn't already."

Her gaze sharpened and focused on Jasper. "Do you know what Caitlyn said when I went to visit her in that horrid cell?" Jasper opened his mouth, but she wasn't interested in his answer. "She said that Felix never even recognized Amy that night." She shook her head, wondrous. "I was stunned. I couldn't understand how that was possible." Her jaw hardened. "And then I realized—those countless girls weren't even *people* to him, just objects for his pleasure."

Her breathing had become harsh and shallow, and her eyes blazed at him. "The idea for everything was *mine*, but all of us agreed to it—even Emma. She still loved Wilbur, but she knew that he'd keep spreading disease and death to more girls and that she'd be an accessory if she did nothing to stop him."

A long, charged moment of silence hung between them, and then Hetty cocked her head, her expression curious. "Amy is a fourteen-year-old girl—thirteen when she was made pregnant by a man no better than a rapist. Tell me, Jasper—will you really punish her?"

"I don't mete out punishment, Hetty."

She gave a bitter laugh. "No, because that would require you to take a stand. It would require you to *be* something more than just form. It would require substance. The reason you can be so placid and calm is because there is nothing inside you to disturb." Suddenly, her face crumpled, her composure dissolving with shocking rapidity. "I'd hoped you were coming to care for me. How could you do this?" She brushed her cheek with the back of one hand, sniffed loudly, and then reached for the ugly, oversized reticule that sat on the settee beside her.

Her reticule.

Jasper's body acted before the thought was fully formed.

But she was faster and swung around and caught him two long strides away.

"Stop." She leveled the gun he'd returned to her only days before at his chest. At this range, she could hardly miss. It was a small-caliber gun, but it could kill.

"Step back," she ordered. "Another." When he complied, she said, "I didn't mean what I just said about you lacking substance." She smiled, her eyes dry. "I just needed to distract you. You're caring and kind, Jasper. It's the horror of war that has left you detached. I understand that. I know it was naïve and foolish of me, but after last night, I'd hoped—"

"It's not as grim as it appears, Hetty. There were extenuating c-circumstances—"

"*Don't,* Jasper; don't lie to me. I'm not stupid; I always knew there was a chance somebody would say something—let something slip." She smiled wryly. "What's the saying? Three can keep a secret if two of them are dead? I've written a letter confessing to all of it, and it's in the safe. Cates knows the combination, and he knows what to do with the letter. I confess, Jasper. It was me—I killed all of them. Don't go after the girl—don't ruin her life."

"Hetty, I'll—"

"No. Whatever you're going to say doesn't matter. You see, everything will change soon. *Everything.* I was so foolish. I thought—" She muttered something Jasper couldn't hear, then said, "Felix was embezzling from Ohio Life and Trust. Men came to talk to me a few days ago." She gave a laugh of disbelief. "He's been stealing from them for *years*—since before we were married, even. They only discovered it after he died, and they're still untangling it all. They said he'd begun to replace some of the money just before he died, but not nearly enough. They'll take me to court for whatever they can get—which is everything. I shall be destitute and will have to move back in with my father—I'll be a child all over again."

Jasper knew, then, why she'd invited him into her bed. "I c-can help you. I'm a w-wealthy man, Hetty. We can—"

"You're a good man, Jasper—the sort of kind, handsome knight a homely young girl like me always dreamed would rescue her. But you were too late."

"Put d-down the gun. I give you my *w-word* that I'll help you."

"I believe you would—even after what I've done." Her hands wavered slightly, and then she said, "If I put down the gun, will you still arrest me—us?"

He hesitated less than a second, but it was enough.

The gun steadied and she smiled sadly. "Close your eyes, my lord."

"No!" He took a step toward her, but his boot stuck and he staggered. "Hetty—"

"Good-bye, Jasper."

Jasper launched himself at her, but the bullet went through her brain before his feet left the floor.

Epilogue

Jasper personally delivered Hetty's body to her house.

Cates seemed to have aged twenty years, and looking into his guilt-ravaged eyes, Jasper saw the truth. The butler might not have wielded the knife—indeed, he doubted Hetty would have allowed it. But Jasper suspected he would find a katara—a ceremonial Indian dagger, with its signature H-shaped guard—somewhere in the older man's quarters.

And the knotted rope, a classic weapon of the Thuggee—a group bent on vengeance—was apt for three women seeking their pound of flesh.

He told Cates to destroy the letter and left the older man to his guilt and grief and went to White Street.

Jasper didn't know whether Tallmadge believed the story he'd told him—that Mrs. Dunbarton, distraught to learn she was soon to be penniless, had taken her own life—or not.

He *did* know the man didn't want the truth; who would? Jasper wished with every particle of his being that he'd not gone to Ryan. He wished he'd not hesitated when she asked if he'd arrest her. He wished—

He wished he could relive the last few hours and do things differently.

He wished that instead of holding a dead, cold body in his arms that evening, he'd just finished watching young, well-cared-for girls perform a play celebrating the founders, men who'd done a less-than-exemplary job of protecting them.

Perhaps after he returned home from the play, he might have slipped next door, using the side entrance to the house—the way he'd come in from Hetty's that morning. If he had been fortunate, he might have been in her bed even now, making love to a woman who deserved to be loved.

Instead, he was headed down Baxter Street at midnight.

Why?

Why not? Where else did he have to go?

The men and women he passed on the street looked like they were up to nothing good. Either was Jasper, or at least he soon hoped to be.

He passed one of the many grim alleys that this side of the island possessed. A bawd and her customer were leaned up against the brick wall, too involved in each other to notice Jasper.

He'd briefly considered going to Horgan's tonight; the city had mysteriously dismissed its violation, and she was back in business. Jasper knew he could find some measure of comfort with Elizabeth Horgan. After all, she was a woman who understood vice—especially his.

But he didn't want to be with another woman. Not tonight.

What he wanted was to get his brain to stop turning things over and over, like a farmer working arid soil.

Wrong or right, he'd already decided that he would let the matter die with Hetty. Emma Sealy, Zuza Janssen, and Amy Grady could live with what they'd done.

But making that decision didn't mean he could stop his thoughts from churning. He needed something to help him forget. How was that for irony?

He paused at a street crossing and looked up to find O'Reilly's. The saloon was so full of humanity it was bursting at the seams. The off-key music, sounds of revelry, and bright lights repelled him.

He kept walking.

There were children selling corn next to women selling their bodies. Two shirtless men fought on the side of the street while a handful of others cheered them on and wagered. A boy hawked a penny paper that promised to guide its readers to the best brothels with the cheapest, youngest girls.

Where Park intersected Baxter, a shadow detached itself from the wall and headed in Jasper's direction.

Jasper knew who it was before the slight figure passed under the nearest lamppost. "J-John, how are you this evening?"

It was impossible to see beneath the dirt to tell if the boy was blushing, but his expression of remorse told him it was a possibility. He held out his hand, and Jasper saw his silver canister of lucifers in the boy's grubby palm.

"S-S-S-S—*fuckin' hell*! Sorry I pinched it," he blurted loudly.

Jasper slipped the canister into his pocket. "Thank you." He resumed walking.

"Where ya g-g-g-goin'?" John asked, taking two steps to Jasper's one.

"Isn't it a b-bit late for you to be out?"

John scowled up at him.

Jasper took that to mean he had no home. He stopped, reached into his pocket, scooped out all the change, and held the money toward the boy. "Here."

John stuck out a hand.

"Both."

When he complied, Jasper dumped all the money into his cupped palms. "Go find somewhere safe for the night—f-fill your b-belly."

Once again, John tagged along beside him, his trousers—held up by sheer ingenuity—now jingling with each step. "You shouldn't b-b-b-be d-d-down here."

Jasper glanced left and right before crossing the street; there wasn't much other than foot traffic at this time of night. Even the omnibuses had stopped running.

John crossed with him. "Ain't safe," he muttered.

No, it certainly wasn't—but Jasper wasn't in danger from the things John was warning him about.

Down the block from the Old Brewery across from Matt Kelly's pawnshop was a business with a shop front that had Chinese characters painted on the glass.

The interior was dark, but a candle burned in the corner of the window, which displayed pots of herbs, some books, a few bolts of fabric, and other sundries.

Jasper pushed the door opened, the soft tinkling of a bell announcing his entrance. Before he stepped inside, he turned to the boy.

John was staring up at him, his brow furrowed with concern, his eyes flickering between Jasper and the shop beyond.

"Go on," Jasper said. "I'll be fine." He closed the door in the boy's face, not wanting a witness to his weakness, even if it was only a street urchin.

A French door behind the counter opened, and a young man stood in the doorway. He didn't seem surprised to see a well-dressed man standing in his darkened shop at midnight.

He dropped a perfunctory bow.

Jasper inhaled the familiar scents that filled the air and held them in his lungs before slowly exhaling: it felt like coming home, but without all the bothersome rituals.

The other man was a stranger, but he knew what Jasper wanted without needing to ask. He stepped back and gestured for Jasper to follow.

Jasper walked through the doorway and closed the door behind him.

AUTHOR'S NOTES

Writing a work of historical fiction is always an exercise in walking a fine line: how much history and how much fiction.

As an historian writing fiction, I often find the decision of what to cut and what to keep a painful one. If it were up to me, this book would be eight hundred pages long. (Not including endnotes.) Fortunately for readers, my wonderful editor—Faith Black Ross—was on hand to curb my excesses.

One of the areas I had to condense most brutally was the Byzantine politics of the period. For example, at first glance it appears New York City is easily divisible into two camps in 1857: nativist versus immigrants and their supporters. But this easy and clear division is not supported after you delve more deeply, and personal interest often superseded politics or group affiliation.

If you want to read about New York City, I *enthusiastically* recommend getting your hands on a copy of Pulitzer Prize winning *Gotham: A History of New York City to 1898*, by Edwin G. Burrows & Mike Wallace. This book is amazing. *Gotham* isn't just one of the best history books I've ever read, it's one of the best books I've read, period.

In addition to reducing much of the history to more easily comestible "bites," I've also taken liberties with a few dates, police procedure, and historical figures.

For example, I've conflated the events of May–mid-June 1857. I also make reference to Coulthard's—or the Old Brewery—when it had actually been demolished in 1852. The first change I made to streamline the story. The second change I made because I'm fascinated by the Old Brewery and wanted to give it a small—if erroneous—part in Jasper and Hy's tale.

Of course, the most obvious fabrication I engaged in is Jasper's position with the NYPD, which is entirely a product of my imagination.

However, it's worth pointing out that the Detective Department of the London Metropolitan Police—often colloquially referred to as the "Detective Branch,"—really did participate in at least two detective training programs with other countries. See Rachael Griffin's "Detective Policing and the State in Nineteenth-century England: The Detective Department of the London Metropolitan Police, 1842–1878" (2015).

Lastly, one of the unavoidable results of writing anything historical—fact or fiction—is the danger of imposing modern thoughts/attitudes/behaviors on the past.

Although I've engaged in as little anachronistic meddling as possible, I've softened speech patterns, limited jargon, and avoided potentially offensive terminology whenever I felt it would add to reader enjoyment.

Interestingly, the one area where it might appear I engaged in the greatest anachronism—1857 tolerance toward homosexuality—is actually a matter of historical record. For example, Mary/Peter's character was (loosely) inspired by Peter Sewally, a fairly well-known transgender prostitute during the era.

Unlike Britain, where sodomy was punishable by death until 1861, homosexuality wasn't criminalized in New York until the end of the nineteenth century. That's not to say homosexuals escaped abuse, but extant literature tends to support the contention that the degree of tolerance in the 1850s was greater than that in the 1950s.

S.M. Goodwin
June 10, 2020

ACKNOWLEDGMENTS

Huge thanks to Pam Hopkins, who reads everything I send her and is always supportive and enthusiastic about my work; she really is the world's best agent!

I'd also like to thank Faith Black Ross and the wonderful staff of Crooked Lane Press who welcomed me with open arms right from the get-go and have made working with them a true pleasure.

Thanks to my fantastic beta readers: Shirley & Brantly, who listened patiently as I killed off people in a variety of ways. I'd especially like to thank George, who read this manuscript more than once and whose thirty plus years' experience as a criminal prosecutor have proven endlessly helpful.

Thank you to the New York Public library and the Smithsonian, both of whom have responded to bizarre requests and emails about 1850s maps of NYC. I'm especially grateful for the NYPL's digitization of the New York City Directories. Those are an amazing treasure trove that make me proud to admit I love reading the 1850s version of the phone book.

I owe a massive debt of gratitude to those authors and reviewers who've generously donated their time by offering to read an advance copy of ABSENCE OF MERCY: Dianne Freeman, Tessa Harris, Darynda Jones, & Edwin Hill, to name the early reviewers. It's an honor to have your names associated with my work.

Last, but not least, thanks to my family—especially my mother and my spouse, both of whom put up with more whining than any human beings should have to endure!

31901065887889